Cat in a Kiwi Con

By Carole Nelson Douglas from Tom Doherty Associates

MYSTERY

MIDNIGHT LOUIE MYSTERIES:
Catnap
Pussyfoot
Cat on a Blue Monday
Cat in a Crimson Haze
Cat in a Diamond Dazzle
Cat with an Emerald Eye
Cat in a Flamingo Fedora
Cat in a Golden Garland
Cat on a Hyacinth Hunt
Cat in an Indigo Mood
Cat in a Kiwi Con

Midnight Louie's Pet Detectives (editor of anthology)

IRENE ADLER ADVENTURES:
Good Night, Mr. Holmes
Good Morning, Irene
Irene at Large
Irene's Last Waltz

Marilyn: Shades of Blonde (editor of anthology)

HISTORICAL ROMANCE
*Amberleigh**
*Lady Rogue**
Fair Wind, Fiery Star

SCIENCE FICTION
*Probe**
*Counterprobe**

FANTASY

TALISWOMAN
Cup of Clay
Seed upon the Wind

SWORD AND CIRCLET
Keepers of Edanvant
Heir of Rengarth
Seven of Swords

*also mystery

Cat in a Kiwi Con

A MIDNIGHT LOUIE MYSTERY

Carole Nelson Douglas

A Tom Doherty Associates Book
New York

CAT IN A KIWI CON

Copyright © 2000 by Carole Nelson Douglas

This book is printed on acid-free paper.

A Forge Book
Published by Tom Doherty Associates, LLC
175 Fifth Avenue
New York, NY 10010

www.tor.com

Forge® is a registered trademark of Tom Doherty Associates, LLC.

ISBN 0-312-86955-X

First Edition: May 2000

Printed in the United States of America

0   9   8   7   6   5   4   3   2   1

For Scott Merritt,
with thanks for unflagging, sometimes nagging
devotion to Midnight Louie and all his works.
Live long and prospurr!

And for Kim Innes,
with thanks for the aid of her many computer and design skills.
May the digital Force always be with you!

Contents

Give Me a Coffee Break . . . !

There she sits, sipping that loathsome beverage called coffee.

For my charming roommate, Miss Temple Barr, it is just an ordinary morning here at the Circle Ritz apartments and condominiums, with attached wedding chapel out front.

Come to think of it, it is never an ordinary morning in Las Vegas in general, and at the round, residential fifties-vintage Circle Ritz in particular.

But we live here, and there is nothing we can do about it.

I am in my accustomed spot atop the morning paper, absorbing the day's news and preparing to begin my own A.M. ritual, which fortunately does not involve imbibing a brew of bitter beans. (Or picking pecks of pickled peppers, either.) In a moment, my Miss Temple will focus enough to realize that I am reclining on her accustomed reading material. She will grab a thick corner and tug.

My muscular twenty pounds will not move. The *Las Vegas Review-Journal* and I will slide together over the glass table-top like partnered Olympic skaters, but only a smidge. Miss Temple will sigh and lean forward.

She will tug harder.

By then her baby blue-grays will be a tad more open. A petite pair of parallel tracks will appear between her eyebrows.

She has *such* an adorable expression when she wants something. Who could say no to those big appealing eyes, that fluffy fox-red hair, the annoyance-wrinkled little pink nose? It is no wonder that we fully furred dudes cannot resist these furless little dolls. And my Miss Temple is a particularly attractive example of the breed, if I do say so myself.

Since we all have our dark sides (and since mine is built-in, as I am clothed in jet-black from nose to toe to tip of the tailbone), I must admit to a triumphal thrill to see those lacquered hot-pink nails clawing at my morning paper so ineffectively. They do not even retract. How pitiful . . . so I subtly shift my weight and allow her to extract the quarter-inch-thick pad of fresh newsprint from beneath my torso.

And then I hold my breath.

I am not clamping down on the distribution of the morning newspaper just because I like to curl up on mattress pads made of newsprint and reeking of fresh ink. I am, as always, thinking of my Miss Temple. I have seen a bad omen in the morning paper, without even looking inside to read my horoscope. (I am an October 31–born Scorpio, naturally, the do-not-cross-me sign of the zodiac.)

But Miss Temple scans the front-page headlines as she makes her first go-through, skipping right past the feature photo on the lower left front.

It is an arresting photograph, featuring some of her species in particularly *outré* garb, but then I consider all garb *outré*.

No, it is not the more bizarre manifestations of her

species that sets the hair on my hackles on edge: It is the single and singular presence of a creature of my kind.

For I recognize that long, narrow, masked face and lean predator's body even though it is accoutered with enough leather and chains to ride a Harley. The feral, feline, and ferocious Hyacinth is out of deep cover and making public appearances again. My Miss Temple has not given me time enough to peruse the photo's cutline, but I skim the text when she has retreated behind the opened paper to cruise the news inside.

I would recognize that incarnation of hot blood and cold heart anywhere, even when the owner is going by the alias of "Phsst, psychic Kir-khat of the Kohl Kompendium."

Right. And I am "Tony the Tiger."

Well, sometimes I am, in fact. I squint tigerishly at the small, sans-serif type in which they always set cutlines so no one can read them but the photo-subjects' mothers, with magnifying glasses. I theorize, ignoring Miss Temple's gasp as she moves on to open yesterday morning's mail today.

Hmmm. I receive an absent-minded pat on the pate. (I cannot help that my cogitating little nothings sound like a purr.) If the exotic Siamese Hyacinth is back in town, so might be her evil mistress, the disappearing magician Shangri-la. The last time Miss Temple and I saw them both, we ended up abducted and confined to coffins.

I will have to hie over to (what humongous hostelry does the tiny type feature this time?) the New Millennium Hotel and Casino and find out what is going on among the alien set apparently taking over the joint.

It looks like it is going to be a pulp-fiction kind of day for Midnight Louie. Maybe even a week.

Chapter 1

Wake-up Calls

Carmen Molina brushed her heavy dark hair as if she were beating it, heaved a sigh at herself in the mirror, then slammed the brush down on the toilet tank top.

The swamp cooler in the hall made the old house's air dank and faintly chill, and turned her usually straight thick hair into a fright-wig frizz. She scowled at her ungovernable mirror image. All the better to scare you with, you crooks! Who cared that a homicide lieutenant had split ends? Not she.

Still, smearing a streak of Nearly Natural Rose lipstick over her mouth, which acted more as balm than cosmetic, she couldn't help noticing that her recent work schedule showed. Her half-Latina, light-olive skin always looked jaundiced when she was tired or sick. Her brilliant blue eyes only highlighted the tendency.

"Thanks for the off-the-wall genes, Dad," she muttered to the mirror, fighting the tiny twist-off cap from a pot of the cream blush she used to simulate health. Then she dabbed some stuff the Penney's sales clerk had called concealer under her eyes. The fatigue smudges still leaked through, but less bruisingly. There. Reasonably presentable for another twelve-hour day.

"Mariah!" she yelled into the house's other rooms. "Are you eating breakfast? We've got to get going this morning."

"Yeah!" came the return yell. "Cereal and skim milk."

"Good!" Carmen sighed again. Her resolve to lower the tone of domestic life by only talking when in the same room was not working out lately. "Be right in."

"The cats want the cereal."

"Let them get their own Special K!"

Carmen rushed through the bedroom, grabbing essentials to stuff into blazer pockets: car keys, ID, wallet, change, file (a ragged nail would nag at her all day), pausing only to unlock the gun safe and move the .38 to her ankle holster. Some detectives-turned-desk-jockeys didn't carry, but she'd patrolled the streets of south L.A. for too long not to prepare for sudden violence anywhere, anytime.

Tabitha and Catarina, the two half-grown tiger-striped cats, were indeed nosing the bowls of milk-drenched cold cereal on the kitchen table. Carmen swept into the room, swept the cats to the floor, and sat herself down.

Mariah leaned against the countertop, slurping soggy cereal into the nooks and crannies of her braces. Off in another year, hallelujah!

"You gonna be late again tonight?" her daughter managed between munches.

"Probably. Why? Got a hot date?"

"Fun-nee." Mariah made a revolted face that could have been inspired by either the cold breakfast or the maternal crack.

Carmen started mashing her own cud, not too guilty about cold cereal as long as it was fortified with vitamins and fiber. Mariah was in that same mushy stage of development, her body amorphous with baby fat that might melt off (or might not), her glossy dark hair cut in a less-childish bob lately, her green-white-and-navy-plaid school-uniform jumper as loose and unrevealing as the sloppy T-shirts and baggy shorts the public school kids wore as their own uniform. At twelve-wanting-to-go-on-twenty, she was both intrigued and scared green by the boy-girl dance already rearing its preacne head in the sixth grade.

"What about the weekend?" Mariah asked.

"My, I'm in sudden demand around here. What about the weekend?"

"Moth-er. You promised. Will you be off?"

"I don't know yet. What promise?"

"You know."

"Not any more." Carmen chewed amiably, intercepting Catarina as she lofted onto the table top again, and placing the young cat firmly on her lap for a forcible petting.

Mariah sighed, a much bigger and better public production than her mother's smothered private exhalations. "I don't see why I can't go alone."

"Because you're not old enough," Carmen answered automatically, running her eyes over the front page. No new murders. Yet. "Go where?"

"How can you forget? The big con."

"Con?" Carmen frowned. The word meant "scam" to her.

"Convention. You know. At the new hotel. The biggest science fiction convention ever. Everyone will be there, Xena and Hercules and Buffy and those *X-Files* people you watch and a bunch of kids and actors and writers and artists. 'TitaniCon. The King of Cons.' "

"*King* of cons? Oh, don't remind me. . . ." Carmen shook her head. At least *he* was out of her life. She'd avoided getting drawn into that wacko Elvis case, although she'd heard about it.

"The biggest ever." Mariah was still young enough to believe that bigness alone was a convincing recommendation. A true child of Las Vegas.

Carmen shoved aside the empty cereal bowl and crinkled newspaper, then pulled the coffee mug she'd microwaved before dashing into the bedroom, front and center. The contents were still steaming. Ah.

"I'm sorry, honey. You did tell me something about this 'con' thing. What is it again?"

Now that she had the floor, words seemed to fail Mariah. "It's . . . everybody goes and some of them dress up, and it's for all the science fiction books and comics and TV shows and movies. You know."

"Kids go?"

"Sure. Who do you think reads and watches this stuff?"

"Will there be adults present?"

"Who do you think writes and acts in this stuff?"

"But it's not supervised?"

"Well, the hotel is supervising it, I guess."

"That's not good enough. I'm not going to let a twelve-year-old wander alone through some kind of weird exhibition."

"It's not weird, it's fun! And it's only this whole weekend. Ever. It's to open the New Millennium."

Carmen shook her head, watching frustration evolve into loss on her daughter's face. "This weekend."

"Starting Thursday. Through Monday. But Saturday and Sunday's the best time to go."

"Mariah, I just can't promise anything in the next few days. You know how my work runs in frantic streaks. This is one of them."

"Please!"

And how many times had Carmen wailed that word into the impassive refusal of her mother's face? The two eternal one-word pleas of powerless childhood. ¿Por qué? Why? And por favor. Please. She supposed that she even looked like her mother by now. Actually, those two words were as significant for adults, too.

"Maybe," she said, wanting to bite her tongue already. "Maybe I can manage something. I'll see today what I can do."

"But today's Tuesday!"

Carmen stood, dislodging the purring cat. If only kids purred and asked for things with the silent meow. "We have until Thursday, right? Besides, you can't take off from school."

"It's open in the evening."

"And you're going to go over there in the evening? Solo? Not you, *niña*. Now. Did you do the cat box?"

"Oh . . . right away." She turned and raced off to handle the chore, sure to be a model kid until she got what she wanted.

Carmen Molina smiled. If only she had this TitaniCon to motivate her child every weekend.

Matt Devine yawned and checked his watch, then glanced at the phone.

He really should act on the small item in the morning paper. For some eerie reason, while checking out the "Lifestyles" section, his eye had snagged on a small-type name he knew. And that had reminded him of his "homework" assignment.

Not really homework, but part of his journey of personal growth, he pointed out to himself, tongue-in-cheek. *Personal growth.* Matt winced at the expression. His mouth felt as if he had gargled cod liver oil.

He yawned again. Just a nervous gesture. A delaying tactic.

Swallow your medicine, he told himself. *And do it fast, before you taste it.*

He picked up the tiny notepad that held the few business and personal phone numbers in the brave new universe of a thirty-something ex-priest-turned radio shrink who was wrestling with making a living, making friends, and making time for a social life, maybe even a sexual one.

He paused to consider the bizarre array of phone numbers, another delaying tactic, but it provided a certain self-insight: his fellow-tenant Temple's number, number one. His landlady Electra's. ConTact, the hotline counseling service he had worked for full-time until recently. (Now he only needed to sub occasionally as an unpaid volunteer. He missed the gang, but he was part of another, smaller one.) Next the number for the radio station that paid him so handsomely he felt guilty, WCOO. Also the home phone number of Leticia Brown, his producer and the on-air personality known as Ambrosia. Tony Fortunato, his agent's number. *Agent!*

Homicide lieutenant C. R. Molina's work number. His mother's number in Chicago. Frank's number at the FBI. The ex-priests' group contact number. The 1-800 number of the Amanda talk show.

By their phone books ye shall know them.

He laughed to and at himself. This freebie notepad advertising a local pharmacy felt too confining and informal for such a heavy load of whos and wheres and wherefores. *Get thee to a stationery store and buy some slick address book.*

Or did single men not do that sort of organizing thing? Little black books, that's what bachelors had. Did men of the world keep track of business and pleasure separately: Rolodexes for work and the infamous little black book for play?

Matt looked at the last number listed in his meager litany of friends and acquaintances made in the last year. The offbeat "business" number he was hesitating to punch in had been there for just two weeks.

Might as well get it over with. Maybe no one would answer. Ten A.M. He was just rising after his midnight stint on the radio advice show, but most people would be out and about at this hour.

So . . . chances were pretty good that he wouldn't connect this time.

Nothing to do but try, no matter how half-heartedly. This would be good for him.

He pressed the numerical sequence, realizing his throat had gone dry and his palms damp. On the third ring, someone answered.

After the opening "hello" and "hi," he got to the nitty-gritty without preamble. An aftertaste of psychic cod liver oil hovered like halitosis over the mouthpiece.

"I thought," Matt said, finally coming right out with it, "that we should get together."

Max Kinsella contemplated the noble fir tree.

Lots of noble fir trees.

The University of Nevada at Las Vegas campus was infected with them. They cozied up to the bunkerlike architecture the desert climate inspired like arthritic great-aunts and great-uncles braced by the picnic tables at a family reunion. Their roof-high, time-twisted limbs and leaning trunks both depended on and buttressed the buildings. Like most people, they were part clinging vine and part stalwart support.

Max loped along the endless walks between the scattered buildings, nimbly dodging the press of students ambling between classes, feeling the exhilaration of running an informal obstacle course. He didn't get out among crowds often but had always liked them, sensed them as a kinetic flow, himself as a random element avoiding collision and detection, almost as if he could remain invisible by avoiding the accidental contact, as he used to imagine when he had been a child. . . . as he had faithfully practiced both personally and professionally since he had so suddenly become a man in northern Ireland, ages and instants ago.

He always walked like a man in a hurry, unless he wanted to give a different impression; then, he seemed to move so slowly some people mistook him for indolent.

Today he was eager to get where he was going; once there, he would power down into slow motion. A man six-feet-four always needed to make less of himself, especially in his profession.

Although no longer a practicing magician, his biological clock was on performance-schedule time still. After years of late-night gigs, it seemed indecent to be out and about before eleven A.M.

It was too easy to wander into academic buildings. Max found easy entry disappointing. It made him feel he was alone in the world, and the building did seem strangely deserted. He took the stairs two at a time, his rubber-soled shoes hardly making a sound in the echoing space.

Arriving unannounced had become a habit.

Chapter 2

Syn Thesis

Max followed the numbered doors down the empty hall until he arrived at the one he sought.

He entered without knocking, not knowing if the room would be occupied or not. It didn't matter. Either way, he would come away with the information he sought. The only unknown was whether it would be given to him, or if he would take it.

As quiet as the grave.

Like any good break-in artist, Max first looked for another way out, and found it: a closed door leading to an adjoining room. Next he looked for signs of recent occupation: a cooling coffee mug, car keys splayed on the paperwork, an open briefcase, an uncapped pen or unretracted ballpoint.

Despite a desktop buried beneath an arrangement of papers in the shape of an Aztec step-pyramid, the room seemed decently deserted.

Max riffled through a few steps of the pyramid and scanned the bookshelves. All he found were student papers and dusty Ph.D. theses. The topics were intriguing, from Mayan magicians to shamans in Siberia and Tibet.

But he wasn't interested in ancient magic.

He turned the brushed chrome knob on the exit door as delicately as if it led to a safe.

He sensed a much larger room beyond before he had opened the door a few inches. Maybe it was a hint of chill air. He stepped through into the cool even light of overhead fluorescent lamps.

The space was classic institutional twentieth century. Mottled-beige vinyl tiles turned the floor into a monotone chessboard. A larger-scale chessboard of plastic light grids and acoustical tile stretched above. Distant windows set in aluminum-silver frames let in daylight so transparent it hardly cast a shadow.

But besides more bookshelves and cabinets and files, all in shades of the same bland putty-blond that covered monitors and computer towers and printers these days, the large room offered a man-made forest in its center. Aluminum-framed pegboard uprights held framed posters, forming an oversized book of magic acts of all times and places to page through.

In the lukewarm light, too dim for an exhibition and too bright for any dramatic effects, Houdini's eyes glared like an animal's from his chain-bound form.

Other eyes from this impressive convocation, a magician's Hall of Fame, watched Max from their hand-tinted or printed posters.

What he was looking for was here among the hinged panels. Max edged toward the dead and living magicians as silently as they regarded him. He moved down the line, flipping the huge panels from side to side, never sure whose hypnotic glance would confront him next.

Meeting Gandolph the Great, for instance, only two flips past a section on Blackstone was a shock.

Max stared at a poster image of his now-dead mentor looking as he had before Max had been born. He hadn't recognized him for an instant. The young Gandolph could have played a slight, mischievous Puck pulling back the curtain on a slumbering

Bottom. He was not the sedate, heavy-set middle-aged man Max had known.

Then Max focused on the figure he had really been searching for: the girl in the background, smiling like a model in an Ipana ad, and as much ancient history as Gandolph and that vintage brand of toothpaste were. Max couldn't smile back at Gandolph and his long-ago assistant, Gloria Fuentes, both grinning in youthful glory, and both grinning corpses now. Both dead in mysterious, possibly murderous circumstances. Both filed away in unsolved case files.

Max contemplated the gaudy poster and the almost cartoon-quality poses of the figures. When this was made, Gandolph's retreat to Europe was unthinkable, and the pretty girl with the pertly posed bare legs was dreaming of fame and fortune. They had been employer-employee, but also friends. Max remembered Gandolph grinning to recollect his heyday when he worked with the "Girl of Many Parts," especially in the severed lady illusion. Gloria would wave her graceful, perfectly manicured fingers and wiggle her lively, perfectly painted toes from various apertures. She would fold that perfect 36-24-36 body in hiding places behind and under and between, always unseen while in "plain sight."

She would have had to have been agile and quick. It made Max wonder how someone had been able to slip up behind her with a garotte many years later. Tricking others made you a harder target to catch off-guard.

He flipped the panel, looking for more posters featuring his dead friend and the more recently dead assistant. One flick of the wrist revealed something unexpected behind the pegboard: a bald, youngish man in thick, black-framed glasses standing on the other side, who produced a grin as wide as Gandolph's upon seeing him.

"I thought I heard someone in here," the gnome noted.

Max was startled. He refused to show it, but Max was shocked speechless. Adrenaline charged through his synapses. He was used to causing these effects, not suffering them.

"The Mystifying Max, I presume." The man's impish grin never subsided. "What a surprise. Your posters are on the other side of the row, if that's what you're looking for."

"I'm not."

"This isn't a vanity call?" the man asked. "You aren't aching to see where you fit in my informal Hall of Fame?"

"Obviously," Max said, vanishing behind the panel containing Gandolph, "I fit here."

The man quickly pulled the panel away again, but by then Max was no longer there. The man laughed with delight, then ducked under the panels to the other side.

"So few credit the magician's truly awesome physical abilities," he said, looking around.

Of course he saw nothing.

He sighed. "I always admire a good illusion, but I'm afraid it's my delusion that I'd really like to talk to you. If you came here, I can only hope you'd like to talk to me."

A clap of hands echoed sharply in the exhibition rooms. The man turned, to find Max behind him. He lifted an eyebrow.

"You're right," Max said. "Mere acrobatics. But I'm a bit rusty."

The man nodded, sympathetically. "Almost a year, isn't it?" He put out a small, neat hand. "Jefferson Mangel, professor."

"Mystifying Max, retired."

"A shame. I won't ask why. It's enough that I should benefit from a . . . visitation. Look, here's your section."

"Section?"

"Oh, yes. I'm quite an admirer. I like them all, even the hopelessly hokey, but the truly elegant are a vanishing breed."

Max bowed, watching the years of his career flash by under the professor's riffling fingers. "Heidelberg?" he interrupted. "You have Heidelberg? I was an apprentice then still."

Max's control wavered again. He had looked impossibly young in that poster so far in his past. He had never kept scrapbooks; it was too dangerous. Unsettling that this man had scrounged together more shards of his life in magic than he had.

"You were always interesting," Mangel said. "Most American magicians don't start in Europe. Old World audiences are very demanding."

"A good place to start then."

"I guess. Say, would you like a cup of tea? Or there might be some German beer in the fridge."

"Most professors don't have German beer in the fridge."

"I'm an unconventional professor. Tolerated, but considered a bit manic on my favorite subject. The only reason I survive in academe is that I stress the metaphysical aspect of magic."

"The theory that magic is a metaphor."

"You've heard of my class?"

"I've heard of the theory." Max followed the professor to a small room off the exhibition area, where kitchen counters surrounded a table and four chairs.

"Tea or beer?" Mangel asked.

"British or German? I'll take the beer, Professor."

He nodded. "Call me . . . I was about to say 'Jefferson,' but lately I've been reminded how stuffy that is." He smiled in remembrance of some incident. "Call me Jeff."

"Jeff." Max sat, looked around, felt oddly at home.

Jeff threw him a happy, nervous glance as he decapitated the metal tops off two tall brown bottles. "I can't tell you how pleased I am to meet you. I've seen your various acts a few times. I'm not surprised that you quit the circuit, but I sure am sorry."

"Why aren't you surprised? I was."

"Well." Jeff sat across from him, grinning like a twelve-year-old. "Every top-drawer magician ends up in Vegas with a shot at a big-money hotel contract. You were one, you were here, and I always felt you were, simply put, too good for Vegas."

"But you just said Vegas is the pinnacle."

"For a certain kind of magic. Larger-than-life magic. Inflated magic, I guess, like the stock market. The kind that can crash from its own bloated overweight. Your magic was always . . . imperially slim."

"And thus prone to self-destruct. I've read the poem, too."

"Ah, but to look at it in passing . . . the envy of all. Why have you come here?"

"Not to look at myself in passing. I'm an admirer of Gandolph."

"An interesting magician. He turned his back on the art and became obsessed with uncloaking psychic frauds. Too bad."

"You prefer that psychic frauds remain cloaked?"

"No. I prefer that good magicians practice their art. But they generally grow old, exhaust themselves, and develop a conscience."

"Is that what you think I've done?" Max took a long swallow of the excellent lager.

"You? No. You had years of performing left in you, perhaps a lifetime. Gandolph, though . . ."

"You disapprove of his crusade to unmask psychic tricks?"

"I have no right to disapprove of anything. People who fool needy hearts into believing the impossible are uncommon crooks and should do time. I just hate to see good illusionists devote their old age to stripping away illusions."

"You, and the Synth."

Jeff choked on his beer. When he could speak again, he asked, "The . . . what?"

"You heard me. And you've heard of the Synth. Why does it frighten you?"

Jeff's hand ran over his bald head, as if in search of hair that used to be there to run his fingers through. "The Synth. I've never discussed it with anyone. Just read about it, here and there between the lines, in my magic books." His bright glance darted away like a minnow. "It's . . . been mentioned for an impossibly long time. I'm talking Medieval times. Syntheology."

Max smiled at the coined term. "It was a system? Like alchemy and alchemists?"

"Not like alchemists. People were fascinated by them and what they purported to do. People feared the Synth."

"It can't have been connected to magic then," Max suggested.

"Magic is connected to the mysteries of religion and ritual, and both of those were dominant forces then," Jeff said. "And both inspire fear."

"Gandolph died last fall," Max said abruptly. "Did you know that he died in disguise?"

"No. Why would he be in disguise?"

Max shrugged. The mysteries of Gandolph were not his to reveal. "Gloria Fuentes is dead, too," he added casually, watching.

"Gloria? I didn't hear anything about it."

"The police don't want you to."

"Police? Then her death was suspicious, too?"

"Her death was murder, plain and simple."

Jeff's fingers now riffled into the sides of his nonexistent hair, and ended up cradling his face. "Gandolph. And now Gloria . . ."

"You know something about her?"

Jeff shook his head over the bottle of beer. "Only that she'd come in a couple of times lately. Come to think of it, she was asking about Gandolph, wondered if I'd acquired any 'artifacts' from his estate. She seemed more than simply saddened. . . . I'd say 'distressed' by his death."

"She should have been. It was suspicious."

"How do you know?"

"I'm a magician. Suspicious circumstances are my stock in trade. Both detecting them, and using them."

"Gloria dead. I can't believe it. Her coming here just a few days ago. And now you." Jeff looked up, shock turning into suspicion. "And that, that charming PR woman who was so interested in Gloria. Don't tell me she's dead, too."

"Better not be," Max said, almost growled, surprised by the thought into anxiety. "What information do you have on the Synth?"

"A few old books and vague references, that's all. You think that—?"

"I think that I'd better see all you've got."

"How are you involved in this?"

"I'm a retired magician," Max said. "What else do I have to do but meddle?"

They left their beer bottles half full and withdrew to the professor's office, where he said the oldest books were kept. After they entered, Jeff Mangel turned to lock the door to the exhibition rooms.

"Good idea. Even the display panels may have ears." Max sat on the small side chair meant for students, feeling like a Swiss army knife confined to a pincushion. He guessed that Jeff's sudden smile was a compact man's reaction to Max's long, angular form overlapping the chair.

The professor turned his back to conceal that smile, then pulled down one narrow-bound title after another from the shelves. "I wish I had a suitably impressive volume for the subject matter."

"Such as . . . ?"

"Oh, some gigantic tome bound in sharkskin with a water-buffalo-horn clasp studded with Russian cherry amber like drops of blood. All I have are a selection of bound theses."

Max eyed the half dozen slim volumes. "Not too impressive. Yet they mention the Synth? I'd never heard of it until Gandolph's death last fall."

"I hadn't heard of it until a couple of years ago. That's when I started hunting down references. Not a single contemporary history of magic mentions the Synth. But the ancient texts do, and these obscure papers started doing so about fifty years ago."

"Really. Then the . . . movement, or whatever it is, . . . is a revival."

"Possibly." Jeff was paging through the soft-bound books.

Max glimpsed typescript. These booklets weren't even printed, but were merely bound versions of typed academic papers. "Who wrote these?"

"Mostly communications majors with stage experience. Our proximity to the Strip encourages taking magic as a performance art more seriously than it is elsewhere."

"Hence your exhibition."

"No, my exhibition is a personal enthusiasm. My collection was outgrowing my home, so I 'donated' it to the university."

"What do you have on Gandolph and Gloria Fuentes?"

Professor Mangel turned to a computer at right angles to his desk. "More than I have on the Synth. And on you. Your background was always appropriately mysterious. Let's see. . . . Gandolph is extensively documented, from "Local Boy Waves Wand" in his hometown paper to "Ex-magician Pries into the Paranormal" just a few weeks before his death. Gloria was pretty much a background figure in the posters and photos, and stayed that way after Gandolph retired."

"Can you print out that list of articles on Gandolph?"

"Sure." He tapped the appropriate keys. A printer was soon spitting out pages.

Jeff turned back to Max. "Can you enlighten me about your disappearance after the Goliath engagement?"

"Personal business."

"Somehow I suspect that you're going to tell me the Synth is personal business, too."

"It is. In fact, I'd appreciate you keeping my . . . reappearance quiet."

Jeff shook his head. "This is maddening for a scholar of magic like myself."

Max relaxed into a smile. "Lend me that pile of Ph.D. papers, and I'll tell you about some of my special effects."

"But nothing on the Synth."

"No."

"Nothing on Gandolph's death."

"No."

"Nothing on Gloria Fuente's death, either."

"No."

"Consistency is the hobgoblin of little minds," the professor charged in frustration.

"A 'foolish' consistency," Max corrected. "A wise consistency is the mark of good magic acts, and a few other things." Max leaned forward to take the thin volumes, and printout, in one hand.

Professor Mangel stood, too, though the effect was less majestic. His next words, however, had the sound of a formal incantation.

" 'The Magician has characteristics in common with those of

the criminal, of the actor, and of the priest.' I wonder in which role you are acting so mysteriously now."

" 'Wonder.' That's the name of all their games, isn't it? You know you'd hate it if it were too easy. Walk me out and we'll talk."

They were silent as they left the building, until they were on the now-deserted walks. Class was in session all over campus, and here, perhaps, too.

"Your finale," the professor began. "A mélange of Cirque du Soleil, Houdini, modern dance, and shell game. An extraordinarily busy ending for a one-man show. How did you manage it?"

Max laughed. "A high price for the rental of a few obscure books, professor. Are you sure you want to ruin the illusion?"

He shrugged. "A dark stage, a strobe light flashing. You illuminated at every flash: high in the air, walking on air. Here, there, everywhere, like the 'demmed illusive Pimpernel' from the classic swashbuckler. And with every revelation, white cockatoos seeming to perch on your shoulders, until the strobe light finally stopped, and the stage lights came on. You stood alone, in black, against a black curtain, against a tiered living curtain of hundreds of cockatoos on perches of various heights, making a kind of feathered fountain. It was spectacular."

"Since working solo in Vegas is considered a sign of stinginess, my only choice was to multiply myself." Max hesitated. "I find myself almost unable to reveal my secrets."

"Perhaps I can help you."

The two men paused in the absolute open, no building, no tree, no human being near them.

Jeff Mangel smacked his lips, a gesture of considered thought with him.

"I mentioned Houdini. He was a master of the staged event and the meticulously practiced and engineered illusion. Most people think magic is ninety percent tricks. But, like inspiration, with Houdini it was ninety percent perspiration. He was strong beyond belief and acrobatically adept in a way his muscle-mishapen body gave the lie to. I suspect sheer acrobatic mastery accounts for you appearing at such different points on the stage during the split-second flash of a strobe light, and meticulous timing, of course. One missed beat, and you would have been caught in the act of moving, instead of being showcased as *having* moved at inhuman speed. Every image was a bow of sorts. Did you conceive it all yourself?"

"I work alone," Max said firmly.

"No man is an island," Professor Mangel said as firmly. At Max's expression, he grimaced, then gestured to a bench under a towering pine tree. "Sit down. Let me interview you. I have a feeling this is my first, and last, chance."

"You're not carrying a tape recorder?"

"What a notion! I'm a professor, not a spy. The only tape recorder is here." He tapped his hairless temple.

"Bad enough," Max grumbled, but he followed the man to the bench in question. He'd gotten what he wanted; time to give a little. A very little.

Sitting outside was pleasant at this time of year. The granite bench was still a bit chilly, but warmed quickly to the flesh resting on it. The sun was warm, but not blistering. Pansies laid a purple and yellow carpet over a distant hummock of landscaping.

"So," Jeff began. "You started practicing magic in school? Grade school? High school?"

"Grade school."

"Were you more curious, or shy? Most magicians were one or the other as boys. Or both."

"I never was an overtly shy kid. I just discovered young the magic of being a magician: 'Amaze your friends,' like the hokey magician sets advertised. If I ever was self-conscious, I forgot to be that way fast."

Revealing himself, in any way, to anyone, violated almost twenty year's discipline. But Max found himself remembering as well as revealing. The role of class prestidigitator had fit him like a magician's white glove. Of course he had been drafted for basketball in high school. All the tall, gangly guys were. And the sport had suited him. What was it but quick moves and feints, dodge and deceive, conceal and then reveal when ready, when everyone else was looking in another direction and you were suddenly under the net, leaping, rebounding the ball off the backboard into a perfect drop through the hoop, as if you'd always been there, in an alternate time zone, while they'd been rushing around chasing your shadow on the mirror-polished wooden floor the color of melted caramel.

They'd joked that he should try out for the Harlem Globe Trotters, who were as much a magic act as an exhibition team. He'd globe-trotted, all right, solo.

Max forgot about the man beside him and surveyed the landscaped campus. It was flat land, offering vistas as formal and remote as a chateau garden. Precious groves of shade dappled a concrete grid seared by almost-year-round sunlight. He stretched his long legs so the light warmed them while his torso remained cool in shadow.

The meeting with Professor Mangel left him feeling oddly discontented. The man's admiration, genuine as it was, felt like a valedictory. "The Mystifying Max" was part of the history books now. His forced disappearance a year ago had given his act a perfect ending. To resume it now would be anticlimactical, the kiss of death for a magician.

Students ambled or scurried by, laden with backpacks and the earnestly distracted expressions of so many late white rabbits.

Here he was, in his mid-thirties, a man without a visible profession, a family, a country even. He didn't even have a college degree, although he could produce a convincing one in several subjects on cue. His haphazard European education was worth as much or more than any formal degree, he knew, but he would always have to manufacture a history and identity to deal with the real world.

For a moment he envied the feckless education and chemistry and communications majors passing before him, pinned like garden-variety butterflies to predictable pursuits and potential professions. They could stop and give name, rank, and serial number at any instant. He, instead, was always in a state of remanufacturing himself to fit the place, the time, and the person.

Right now that person was Professor Jeff Mangel. Max turned

on the charm, answered questions without saying anything. Mangel listened as if their roles were reversed: he student, Max teacher. Finally, satisfied and even a bit flattered, the man rose to say good-bye. He was probably about Max's age, and from another world.

Max balanced the paper-bound books on one knee after Mangel's figure had faded into the between-class crowd, and thought.

He had played one consistent role since high school, since his cousin Sean's death in northern Ireland: guardian angel to the world. Of the two Irish Midwestern cousins holidaying on the "auld sod," one had died in an IRA pub bombing; one had died inside with a terminal case of survivor's guilt. In the U.S., seventeen-year-olds were still boys. In a land savaged by religious and civil strife for five centuries, they were men, able to die a man's death. And so young Max had felt a man's obligation to avenge Sean's death, thereby losing his assumed course of college, his family, and his country.

First he found and fingered the pub bombers; then another secret group found him: a shadowy global antiterrorist organization that trained Max as a magician . . . and as an undercover agent with an agenda to detect and destroy attempts at international violence. He performed magic tricks through Europe and beyond, his real work unsung and anonymous: these potential bomb victims saved here, those possible kidnap victims protected there.

When he had begun to play the U.S. as both magician and undercover operative, he had met and fallen in love with Temple, drawing her with him from Minneapolis to Las Vegas. Now, in a city that had become his own backyard for too long to be as safe as it should be, his guardian angel duties had become specific and personal: to protect Temple from the dangers of loving him. Temple had no idea of his secret past until his enemies' pursuit forced him to desert her without warning. When he ventured back, an IRA associate from the bombing days surfaced, expanding Max's halo of protection to cover Temple's endangered circle of acquaintances, including his rival for her affections in his absence, Matt

Devine. Max's undercover history had finally accrued enough bad Karma to make him a sort of Typhoid Mary, contaminating everyone he touched.

The Irish had seen themselves as exiles for centuries. He was of Irish ancestry, but as American as apple pie with Häagen-Dazs ice cream on it, and yet he had managed to turn himself into a pariah in less than twenty years.

Call it the easiest, and hardest trick of his career.

Chapter 3

Cat on a Hot Neon Sphere

I have seen some multibillion-dollar, godzillion-room hotels go up in this town, but the New Millennium is the first I have ever eyeballed that resembled a whole solar system.

A dude would need a space ship to get into the place.

You may have heard of Planet Hollywood. Well, this is Planet Pizza Palace. You enter a huge Saturn. Its rings form a King-Kong-size water slide that angles from ground zero to the height of the new Paris Hotel's Eiffel Tower mockup.

Even gazing at the galaxial splendor from across the street I can hear the screams of happy humans eager to combine a fatal fall with drowning. When the street in question is Las Vegas Boulevard, aka "the Strip," that is a long way for screams of any kind—delight or dismay—to carry.

The whole place is made up of bubble domes in various colors: blue-and-white for Mother Earth, green for Father Uranus, red for Uncle Mars, yellow for Aunt Venus, silver for

Cousin Mercury, orange for Brother Jupiter, and pewter for Sister Pluto. I am guessing at the planetary identities here, and I have to guess even harder at the astrological signs etched on them in reflective glass outlined in neon for nighttime viewing, but many of them are of the animal kingdom: the crab, the scorpion, the goat, the ram, the fish and, of course, Leo the lion. You would think the Hollywood cat would be content with lording it over the entrance to the MGM Grand down the Strip, wearing enough gilt to costar in a remake of Mr. Bond's *Goldfinger*, but, no, the gloryhog has to disport on the silver curves of Mercury like he was an imprimatur of something.

Naturally I need a closer look so I can sneer at Leo's self-aggrandizement from near enough to hiss and spit my disapproval.

Crossing the Strip is always a challenge for one of my short stature. My pins do not cover enough territory to make it through on one green light. Luckily, the powers that be in Las Vegas have recognized that not even tourists wish to wear their toes to stubbier nubs than usual, and they have installed walkways over the Strip as well as monorails between some of the behemoth hotels along it.

Thus it is that I shortly am wafted on a moving sidewalk over the Strip. I glide along, unable to see any sights except the footwear of my fellow travelers. Two colored streams of water move counter to my own motion. Although they are perfumed and colorful, they lack snacks of the finned variety. From the canopy above that shelters us against the sunlight comes a recorded voice welcoming us to the New Millennium, 3001. Talk about rushing things; 2001 hasn't even hit yet. But that is Las Vegas, always ahead of the rest of the planet. What would you expect of a location that boasts eleven of the twelve biggest hotels in the world?

While I meditate, I am attracting attention. It is always thus.

"Look, Lester," a middle-aged lady cries. (It is always a

middle-aged lady. They are a tender-hearted sort, but do not know that I am an independent, noir kind of guy who needs good intentions directed toward himself like a hole in the cannoli.) "That cat acts like it knows where it is going. Is that not cute?"

Lester apparently has no opinion.

"Maybe it is lost. Maybe we should take it to the shelter."

Lester apparently has no opinion on that either, but I certainly do.

"Oh, look! It is getting away, poor thing! Kitty. Here, Kitty. . . ."

That lady had better watch out, or Leo just may come leaping down off his heavenly body at her.

Now I am at the "Spaceport" entry beneath the looming (and shrieking) rings of Saturn. It looks like a flying saucer, the fifties riveted silver-metal variety. Call me Gort. The bad news is that this debarkation ramp is the only entrance into the place. It is pretty wide to accommodate crowds of people, but there is no door, just a whoosh of air that makes the tourists squeal.

A whoosh of air will make my hair stand up, but even worse, this entry system will make me stand out like a big black hairball on a cue ball. I prefer doors that force people into tight lines and allow me to ankle my way in beside them, looking like somebody's footwear. Well, Eskimos wear mukluks, and I might resemble a mukluk if you looked at me real quick out of the corner of your eye while sneezing.

The robot types guarding the thin air that serves as an invisible door do not look like the kind prone to admit local vermin. Or even the occasional mukluk.

I look around for my usual means of illegal entry: climbing something to the second story. But I spot no handy palm tree. No trees at all, in fact. The only lofty structure is the water slide hitherto noted.

Water is wet. Slides are slippery. This is not my kind of fire escape, even when I am going up, not down.

At least the people queuing up for a ride on this thing are in a nice, messy clump.

Our chariot awaits. This is a yellow PVC raft ripe for the puncture of one of my shivs. I must remember to keep my weapons sheathed like the little gentleman while hitching a ride on this contraption.

I curl myself behind a man in black jeans until he looks like he is wearing bell bottoms, and edge forward as if his legs and I were one. As he enters the yellow banana boat to the stars, I leap in and hunker down.

I hear the ominous sound of safety harnesses clicking shut all around me. No parachute for Midnight Louie. I will have to make like Batcat and leap from the life raft into the wild blue yonder of infinite space. I will have to boldly go wherever my shivs can cling.

Our raft jerks into line, then begins climbing.

And humans consider this "fun."

I stare up at the glitzy surface of Saturn, hotel-room windows dotting its swollen surface like stars in the firmament. I do not want to exit into some tourist's plate-glass window.

I spot a rash of neon, the "ill" in the New Millennium sign. Some might take this for an ill omen, but the raft is rushing past it, and I know that where there is neon, there is a service hatch to fix it through.

I bound up to the black bejeaned knee; I rebound out . . . into outer space.

"It is a bird!" a passenger shouts at the instant of my catapult.

"It is a plain black wrapper," another misdiagnoses.

"It is superfluous," cries another. "It is gone, and so are wheeeeeee."

They rocket off, a yellow flash, while I paddle all my limbs until they touch something solid, then snick out my pitons and curl everything that can cling to whatever I have within my grasp.

It is the six-foot-high "e" in "Millenium."

I drop down to the crossbar, then to the base. A platform runs behind the whole shebang and I run along it. Pretty soon I encounter the anticipated exit: a porthole sort of flap the size of a human torso. If it is not locked; I am in like Flynn.

If it is locked, I am stranded like a fly dropping on a pyramid.

Chapter 4

Lawful Encounters

"Have you seen Louie?"

"Why, no, Temple dear," Electra's voice responded over the phone. "Is that scamp AWOL again?"

"Probably. I thought he might have slipped up to Matt's place, like he's been doing lately, but Matt's out."

"Six o'clock. That's odd. Matt's usually here about now. I'll come right down."

"Electra, you don't think we've got two scamps out and about?"

"You never know," she answered ominously.

"Anyway, I want to show you a letter I got today. Well, actually yesterday, but I didn't open it until this morning."

"Something interesting?"

"Something . . . interesting."

On that note Electra hung up. Temple could almost hear her hustling her muumuu down from the penthouse apartment to Temple's place. Electra Lark viewed her landlady duties far more broadly than most, and Temple was glad of it. It made the Circle Ritz feel more like a dorm than an apartment building, and that suited the place's fifties ambiance and Las Vegas's burgeoning influx of population. The nearby bedroom community of Henderson was the fastest-growing community in the U.S.

Temple's doorbell rang, just like in some fifties sitcom, and she admitted Electra, who could have played the ditsy neighbor in a fifties sitcom. If Temple sometimes felt she got into Lucy Ricardo–type situations involving crime and comedy, Electra was a born Ethel Mertz, warm, nosy and game for just about anything.

Today she was game for gambling, apparently, to judge by the pattern of scattered cards that covered her muumuu, and the red and black tiny-heart barrette that nestled in her silver—literally silver curls. Now in the Centrum Silver age bracket, Electra had decided to use her age-whitened hair as a canvas to express her agelessly youthful spirit.

"What's up, kid?" she asked. "Something involving law and order, I hope. Or has Elvis called again?"

"Elvis is in a quiet phase," Temple said, leading Electra to her living room loveseat where two tall glasses of ice tea awaited on the coffee table.

"I've seen Matt's new car in the parking lot. Did Elvis really give it to him?"

"The donor was anonymous, so who's to say?"

"It's cute. I always liked Volkswagen bugs. Takes me back to my salad days, when we thought love was free, and pigs could not only fly on the proper illegal substances but also wore badges."

"I have no special affection for the car model, although it is cute, I guess, but I don't have much affection for cute, either. It's what men call me when they want to ignore my work. The only 'Bugs' I saw around when I was growing up were rambling wrecks driven by equally rambling old hippies."

"There are no old hippies! Hippies don't age, dear, not really; they just look that way. The redesigned 'Bug' is a perfect symbol of the generation."

"If you say so. What do you say about this?" Temple held out a letter.

Electra lifted the clear-plastic reading glasses hung on a chain around her neck, which always vanished against the wild patterns she wore, and installed them low on her nose. "I wish they'd set those word processors in bigger type! What kind of lawyer would use a letterhead of a cartoon-character gavel saying, 'Here comes de judge'?

"And are you suing her, or is she suing you? I wish they'd speak English instead of legalese. What's going on here?"

"The Great American Forum, the people's court."

"The people's court. You mean small claims court. This isn't one of those televised shows where people call each other names?"

Temple nodded while Electra continued. "And you're going to be one of those flakes who goes on it for the entertainment of all the other flakes on the other side of the camera? Do you have the time for that sort of thing?"

"Thanks to getting a fat annual retainer from the Crystal Phoenix, I have time nowadays for all sorts of flaky pursuits, including murder. Besides, this court date isn't until next month. And what's wrong with flaky pursuits?"

"Nothing, for me. But you're a freelance public relations specialist. It might be bad for business if you were viewed as a flake."

"Actually, it might be good for business. PR specialists are supposed to attract attention."

"But negative attention?"

"No attention is negative in this town. And everything a PR person experiences adds to her expertise. I can't lose. Besides, who knows who might want to hire me after seeing the show? Everybody says they don't watch those shows, but they do. Don't tell me you've never watched a talk show, or a court show, or a world's most crash-prone cops chase show? Or the Cloaked-Conjuror-revealing-the-secrets-of-the-swamis show?"

"I might have whooshed past when looking for something else."

"Well, 'whoosh' no more. I'm going to be on the Judge Geraldine Jones show. She's an ex-marine, and former Clark County family court judge."

"Why?"

"Over Louie. That Ashleigh woman kidnapped him, then had him surgically altered, knowing he was my cat. I want compensation."

"But, dear, he's better off fixed."

"That doesn't matter. I would have fixed him in a more traditional way had Savannah Ashleigh not laid her fade-creamed hands on him."

"She did save you the cost of a neutering."

"What about the pain and suffering? To have Louie missing, and then turn up dumped on my doorstep in a bloody satin pillow?"

"They almost never award anything for pain and suffering."

"I thought you didn't watch those shows."

Electra shrugged disarmingly. "I do have to pass by them to change channels, and I do have to change channels a lot, given the selection of what gets on TV these days."

"It doesn't matter what I get. I want to expose that bubble-brained, so-called 'actress' to the larger population. After everyone hears what she did to Louie, she'll never eat sushi in this town again!"

Chapter 5

Once Is Not Enough

Until now, Matt had always arrived here with the motorcycle and parked in the mesquite-shaded driveway. Pulling up to the front curb with a car felt odd.

Driving a car felt odd. Much as he had disliked the Hesketh Vampire and its borrowed, speed-silvered metal profile, the friendly streamlined bulk of a redesigned Volkswagen beetle felt, well, weird.

But then, when you knew the man supposedly behind your driving the car, it should have.

Walking up the front sidewalk instead of the driveway felt dangerously formal. The fading sun warmed Matt's back, making his shirt seem to melt like heated honey. Even March could be warm in Las Vegas.

Ringing the doorbell, he felt he should have a bouquet or corsage clutched in one sweaty palm.

This is an assignment, he told himself. *You've always asked, advised, other people to loosen up and take chances. Go forth and do likewise.*

"Hi." She answered the door, smiling, and swept it wide. "Come on in."

Matt did. The usually empty great room was now accoutered with two tow-headed kids raptly glued to the TV, which was airing something loud, full of swooping, changing images, and almost dialog-free.

"The sitter's popping corn in the kitchen," Janice said. She turned to the great room. "Kids. Mr. Devine is here. Want to say hello?"

They turned in tandem, unformed, uncommitted faces surveying him with a disconcerting lack of judgment or interest. "Hi." "Hi."

They turned back to the enthralling screen.

Janice shrugged an apology for preteen manners. "At least you know they're not hostile."

Matt smiled. "I know I'm not interesting. That's a relief, actually."

"For me, too. Oh. Here." She handed him some small rectangles of paper. When his glance queried her, she shrugged another apology. "Coupons. Got 'em at the fast-food place. Discount on our destination."

"But . . . I asked. I'm paying."

"I know. But I'm a soccer mom. I can't resist a discount. So shoot me."

"I don't think so." Matt pocketed the chits from Long John Silver's. *Appropriate,* he thought: *they were indeed going on a voyage.* He opened the screen door, then waited while she locked the door.

"Nice night." Janice paused as if about to enter a new element and needing a moment.

He wondered why they were there himself, about to embark on something as vague as a "date," with expectations as probably separate as two people could have. He sensed that she was as bewildered as he was by unsaid implications. She wore her usual interesting but unintimidating clothing: a hand-embroidered top, ankle-brushing skirt, swinging handmade earrings.

"A car," she said, stopping halfway down the walk. "Is it yours? I mean, the motorcycle—"

"I guess it's mine. A gift from an . . . admirer."

"A gift?"

"Read the license plate."

She moved forward to do so in the waning light. "Two hundred and eighty-one Rock?"

Matt sighed. "Elvis gave away an estimated two hundred and eighty cars in his lifetime."

"Elvis?"

"We've been in touch. On my radio show."

"Elvis."

"Or . . . suitable substitute. This car was left outside the station with my name on the keys."

"Well, it's neat. A Volkswagen?"

"Elvis is in retirement. He's sixty-five. He's slowed down a little."

Matt opened the passenger door, and Janice ducked in.

"Thank you." She grinned. "Thank you very much."

Matt went around to the driver's side, reminded of his prom—his "prom" date with Temple only a few months ago. No. That was the point. Temple was to be forgotten. Max Kinsella was back in town, Temple Barr was taken (again), and Matt was lucky to have met Janice Flanders, a talented artist and attractive single mom, to practice his sorry social skills on.

The car felt awfully cramped as he started it, although it had plenty of head and leg room. He wasn't used to a ceiling any more. He'd never been used to someone sitting beside him. He missed the Vampire, of all things.

But the Beetle made this possible, this formal "date" of a night out, with dinner and attraction planned and agreed upon, with discount coupons in his sports-coat pocket.

Get me outa here, some inner voice screamed. And then another voice said, *It's just Janice, and you like her, even if you don't really know her.* And both facts were totally true.

She was shaking her head beside him. "Do you know how long

it's been since I went out and did something on my own in this town? I mean, with another adult?"

"I know kids tie you down."

"Kids consume you. Mr. Flanders now, he's got his every other weekends, but they don't do doctors' and dentists' appointments on weekends, or dance classes. He does do movies, I guess."

"Maybe this is something the kids would have liked."

"No. This is for me. Mama. I may not have been a Trekkie as a kid, but I know there have been four, count 'em, incarnations of *Star Trek* for me to to learn about. I suppose this is alien to you, too."

"No."

"No?"

"It was a good idea to keep up with what kids were seeing. I was the youngest priest in the parish and expected to 'relate' to kids."

"Really? Did you get along with kids?"

"Pretty well. It wasn't anything serious, Janice. I wasn't responsible for them. I just had to 'interact.' I suppose I treated them like little adults, and they liked that."

"They would. But you didn't have to get them to bed on time, or to do their homework, or to eat properly."

"No. I just had to encourage them. Easy, good-guy job. Kind of like being a divorced father, I suppose."

She grinned at him. "You got it. Well, *we're* the kids here tonight. I am ready to forget all my cares and woe."

Matt smiled back. It was a good start. "So am I."

The Las Vegas Hilton was well off the Strip. An elder statesman among Vegas hotels, its rectilineal bulk flaunted none of the theme-park façades that lined the Strip nowadays, but it was already in its second incarnation. Its first had been as the International Hotel. Elvis had broken Las Vegas performance records at the hotel under both its names, but now it was home base for another out-of-this-world attraction: *Star Trek:* the Experience.

Matt wondered what Elvis would make of that. He'd still been around for the TV series but was probably more in thrall to inner than outer space by then.

"I'm so glad we can check this out." Janice leaned forward to peer through the windshield at the looming buildings. "Go around to the back. It's easier to enter there."

A long circle brought them to a smaller parking lot.

"Did Elvis really give you this?" Janice asked on exiting the Volkswagen. "What happened to Stutz Bearcats?"

"I don't think he ever gave those away. He wasn't nuts, just generous. And, no, I don't think he did 'donate' this car. I'm afraid it was some deluded Elvis fanatic. Now I don't know what to do with it. Maybe donate to some worthy cause in turn."

"I wouldn't be so sure this isn't a genuine Elvismobile. He might be on his uppers if he's still alive and out there. You can't expect the estate to bankroll a ghost. So he might have to watch his pennies, like all retirees these days." She looked back at the car as they walked away. "Nice redesign. Like a mercury teardrop on wheels. It almost smiles."

Matt shrugged.

"You don't like it?"

"It seems . . . closed in."

"You're just used to the wind and the sand in your hair."

"Helmet."

"Helmet. And that doesn't feel closed in?"

"A matter of perspective, I guess."

"Most things are."

They entered the shadowy, cool interior, glimpsing a row of distant, elevated, giant television screens featuring races and games in progress. Meanwhile, there were the usual aisles of slot machines to weave through.

"I appreciate your indulging my maternal needs," Janice commented.

"Who's indulging who? I asked what you'd like to do."

She sighed. "I don't know any more what I'd 'like' to do. I just know what I *need* to do next."

"Lucky for me that your need-tos involve recreational sites. Besides, I haven't been on my own long enough to discover what my druthers are."

"Isn't it the pits? No matter your role in life, you end up either not knowing what you want, or, if you do, not being allowed to get it."

But Matt had stopped walking to gawk. A massive chamber lit by red and blue neon opened up ahead of them, like the strutted interior of a vast spaceship's cargo hold.

" 'Cool,' as Jenny would say," Janice quoted her daughter.

"Impressive," Matt agreed, gazing up at a model of the starship *Enterprise* suspended against the lofty rafters as if stranded in inner space instead of outer space. "The famous Frisbee with a fin," he said, admiring the lights that defined the rim and upthrust tail. His glance moved back to Earth, and ground level, where it was business as usual despite the exotic shell surrounding them. "I suppose we can take these rows of slot machines for a race of androids."

"Slot machines ye have always with you," Janice agreed. "Oh, look! What are those lights?"

Matt studied the protuberances at the side of the slot machine. He waved a hand through the space between. "I guess you operate them by interrupting the beam. Want to lose money at the wave of your hand?"

Janice shook her head. "Listen, do you mind getting in the ticket line? I have to visit the—" She waggled her fingers toward the bar across the room.

Matt followed the trickle of people boldly going through the vast interior to clot into a line before a kiosk. That was the future for you: travel at unthinkable speed to arrive at the same old traffic jam. He had only shuffled ten feet forward when Janice rejoined him.

"Wild," she said. "The bathroom is all stainless steel, and the mirror frames light up when you run your hands under the automatic faucets. The mirrors have animated holographic images that show up while you're washing your hands. They're ads for these far-out products and services. Guess that'll be the future, more ads everywhere."

They inched their way to the ticket booth, where Janice's coupons got them discounted tickets to *Star Trek* the museum and the simulated-motion ride. Beyond that, the shops awaited.

Surrounded by fans more avid than they, Matt and Janice snaked up a ramp bordered on one side by a lit timeline illustrated with film stills of the *Star Trek* universe before and after classic *Trek*. On the other side, glass cases displayed costumes and props from all four television series based on the concept.

"You want to read all this?" Janice asked, peering down at the endless illuminated history of a future that never was.

"No, I don't need chapter and verse of a history lesson. What I liked about *Star Trek* was its visionary approach and Utopian mission, and the messages only got more subtle in the later series."

"Oh, my kids would love that." Matt raised his eyebrows. "An adult who actually approves of what they watch." Janice's eyes widened and looked past him. "Just beam me up. Do we have to go *past* that?"

Matt turned.

A gigantic man with long curly dark hair wearing clothes from a heavy-metal band guarded the bend in the line they would soon pass by.

"It's a Klingon warrior, but just think of him as the Cowardly Lion," Matt said, "and look at his feet. He's wearing at least six inches of platform built into his boots to make him loom like that."

In an instant, a big-headed, bat-eared, bald gnome in purple velvet and gold lamé joined the giant at the intersection.

"And that little guy beside Jumbo the friendly lion?" Janice asked.

"A Ferengi. A peaceful race, unlike the Klingons. Merchants. But I'd watch him more than the warrior."

"Rumplestiltskin? Why?"

"They're very sexist."

She just nodded. "Obviously, I haven't been watching enough TV with my kids."

"Is that why you wanted to visit this attraction?"

"No, I don't need to know a Klingon from a Cling-free strip, but I do want to make sure the ride is tame enough for them. I've been promising them a visit. You don't mind being a guinea pig, do you? Single mothers don't date unless something about it is useful for the kiddos."

Matt nodded, surprised by how shocking the word "date" sounded when mentioned so casually. He never had "dated," and was relieved that so far it wasn't an uneasy proposition at all.

For that he credited Janice's laid-back manner. She radiated the hard-won serenity of someone who had to put her own maturity ahead of anything else for a long time. Nuns had that quality, he realized. And mothers.

But Janice was a stranger in alternate-reality land. Without thinking, he put his hand on her elbow as they neared the glowering Klingon and smirking Ferengi.

The Klingon was chatting with a couple who had paused to take his photograph. He had the deep, rumbling tones of any actor who'd ever played the various Klingon characters on the various *Star Trek* shows, from Worf to assorted guest stars.

Janice regarded him with a little wariness. "Isn't that a Wookie?" she whispered.

"Wrong universe. *Star Wars.* Wookies are tall but hair-covered. Think Abominable Snowman. You've probably heard of the lead Klingon, Worf."

"I've probably heard a lot that didn't exactly sink in," she agreed.

As they passed, the Ferengi suddenly reached out to stroke Janice's sleeve. "Nice material. I'd give you a latinum bar for sixty bolts of Umahn fabric."

Janice stopped and stared. "I'd rather have a chance to sketch your portrait. Might make my kids with braces feel a lot better."

The Ferengi grinned through his overcrowded mouth of sharp teeth. "Umahn woman always finds Ferengi irresistible." He glanced at Matt. "I am sorry you are so ugly, Umahn man. So I will resist your woman, as you are a guest here."

Janice burst out laughing as they moved on. "A greedy *and* self-important race. Imagine that wombat-face calling *you* ugly. But that mask is something. Did you see how naturally it met the eyes and the lips? Must be hot to wear all day."

"I don't know how they do it, except that they're obviously actors who enjoy getting into character. I am struck, seeing these guys in person, by how much the science fiction series borrow from Greek tragedy."

"How?"

"Masks and buskins. The ancient amphitheaters were so huge that actors wore oversized masks that completely covered their faces, and stood on high platform shoes called buskins."

"Greek tragedy." Janice regarded him with mock awe. "Keep that to yourself, or my kids, when I object to their watching some stupid futuristic movie, can say, 'But, Mom, it's Greek tragedy.' "

They were still laughing when they exited the museum passage into a foyer where they were counted and assembled with twenty-some people into a group.

A uniformed female crew member, as brisk and military as a recent Citadel graduate, instructed them to "board."

"Now this I recognize," Janice said as their group was urged to step onto certain floor marks as they moved deeper into the starship. "Disneyland. If we want to stay together, stand behind me, not beside me. That's the way we'll be funneled onto the ride."

Matt followed her advice as they were escorted onto the bridge of the *Enterprise,* and a scenario that blended their presence with the *Star Trek* world was laid out.

"This is amusing," he told Janice. "We're like extras in a film-set crowd scene. It really feels like you're in a show."

She was studying the skeletal young women barking commands in their unforgivingly taut uniforms. "A young woman's job, no question. They're so serious. What do they do in the interim between groups?"

"Wait. I do feel like a sheep, though," he added as they were moved out of the bridge and lined up before a set of elevator doors, which whooshed open to reveal a small chamber with several rows of seats.

Exactly as Janice had said, they marched into the aisle in front of them and sat like robots in the seats that matched their places in line.

These theater seats had safety belts, though.

"Let's see." Janice repeated the warnings given them before entering the ride chamber. "I'm not pregnant. Don't know about back or neck problems; everybody's had something wrong there sometime. Think it's safe?"

Matt shrugged. Kids loved plunging into the unknown. He was old enough to feel a wiggleworm of anxiety in his stomach.

"If that old lady can do it," (Janice nodded at a curled silver head that looked like Barbara Bush's two rows ahead of them) "I can." She eyed Matt encouragingly. "We can do it."

Thanks, Mom, he commented to himself.

Everyone searched for room on the floor to place any loose items, but before they could think about it, the blank screen in front of them flared alive, pulling their "ship" into place for release from the *Enterprise* into space. They dove into a vast, black sea. Their agile vehicle swooped, paused, shot high, then low, soared, plunged, seats bucking to match the motion before their eyes.

What a helicopter-roller coaster ride, only Matt had tried neither one. For breathless minutes, the passengers were visually and physically swooped into starry space, chased by enemy vessels, dodging blasts, firing back, and finally slingshot back down to Earth and a safe landing.

Sight and sound and motion vanished as abruptly as they had begun. The space riders sat still for a few seconds, survivors happy to still be here.

A young voice lifted from the front seats. "Do we get a discount on the next rides?"

Beside Matt, Janice groaned softly. "Mine will be the same way. Why is once never enough for the under-fourteen set?"

Chapter 6

Lost in Space

This much I know is true: It is always easier to get *out* of where you are not wanted than to get *in* where you are not wanted. Subterfuge will get you in nice and quiet, but curses, kicks, and hullabaloo generally do the high-decibel job when it comes to getting escorted out.

But now I confront the opposite problem. It was no great trick finagling my way to the anticipated trapdoor near the New Millennium's larger-than-life-size logo, given that I am the Houdini of housecats. Now that I find the door is locked, getting back to where I began my assault on a sign has become a challenge on the scale of climbing Mount Everest.

I hunker down in the scant shade of the crossbar on the "e" in "New." At least it is only March and long, hot summer is not here yet. Otherwise, with my ebony-hued duds, I would be sun-tea in about an hour and a half.

Although my acrobatic feat in getting me to this prominence, so to speak, was hard enough, a similar leap back to the water slide would be impossible. To get here, I leaped from a moving vehicle to a stable surface. To get back, I would have to time my bound to coincide with the split-second passage of a speeding raft. If I missed my car, I would land on a fast-moving slick of H^2O, probably just in time to get rammed from here to Kingdome come by the next yellow PVC raft.

Luckily, I arrived here in the late afternoon. The burning sun is declining behind the western mountains.

Because of the shade, I am virtually invisible. For now, this suits me. Later, it could be fatal. But I will worry about later . . . later.

At all-too-regular intervals, the train of ragtop rafts goes hurtling past, regaling me with screams and distant drops from splashes. At least I will not want for water. It is, however, chlorinated. And fishless. So I will have to wait for total darkness for an opportunity to put my plan into action, without the extra brain food of a fish in passing.

Chapter 7

Quarks of Nature

What a perfect place for a rendezvous: A restaurant and bar where the lighting is dim, the air cool enough to encourage hunkering close over the tabletop candles. The menu was original, to say the least, and some of the spiritous specialties of the house came in two-gallon-size containers with glass straws built-in.

Matt watched a massive globe of red-orange liquid conveyed to a party of six, including two children.

The waitress noticed his gaze. "Ten ounces of liquor," she said. "They're having the virgin version, of course."

Matt wished he hadn't asked. "Virgin" was not a word he wanted to hear in this context.

Janice, he was relieved to see, was ignoring the chitchat in favor of scrutinizing the menu. "If Kyle and Jenny were here, they'd definitely have the 'Cheese Borgers,' but I'm leaning to something more adventurous."

That was Matt's cue to read his menu. Something on the "Prelaunch Sequence" caught his wandering eye: the Holy Rings of Betazed. Translating the description, Matt arrived at batter-fried onion rings offered with an appropriate trinity of dressings: spicy remoulade, ketchup, and ranch dressing.

Under "Command Decisions," the Talaxian Turkey Wrap, he discovered, was not a dance, but a "Delta Quadrant" version of a club sandwich.

"I'm leaning toward an 'Offspring,' " Janice said after a thoughtful silence. "That ground-mustard-caper remoulade sauce sounds worth the trek."

"Very exotic," Matt agreed. "I'll try the Flaming Ribs of Targ. Szechuan barbeque sauce and cilantro peanut pesto sauce should definitely be out of this quadrant."

"Everything all right, folks?"

A gnarled hand accessorized with glittery-gold nail polish brushed Janice's shoulder. "Nice fabric."

Janice craned her neck to regard another Ferengi face, and smiled. "Just fine. And what you're wearing isn't too tacky either. Love that lamé."

The Ferengi polished his painted nails on a broad embroidered lapel. "I like a Umahn with good taste in attire."

"I like your taste in faces. Is that one hot to wear?"

Despite the elaborate appliance that turned his teeth into fangs and covered every other feature but his eyes, the Ferengi's expression managed to convey shock, then rapid thinking.

"Is the Umahn female trying to flirt with this poor Ferengi serving boy? She thinks that I must resort to false faces to make my looks attractive? No, I am unadorned. Not one enhancement has been made to the face my moogie bore. I am glad you like it."

"You don't understand," Janice said. "I'm an artist. I also do sketches for the police, and might even get into postmortem reconstruction of faces. I know you're role-playing here, but, between us two, I'm just so curious about how extensive that mask construction is. I would think it'd contain a lot of rubberized material and be very hot to wear."

The Ferengi laughed. "The Umahn female is too flattering. I

grant you that the Umahn face is not much to speak of, like that one there." He pointed at Matt. "A pity he is so ugly. I can see why you are interested in my handsome Ferengi features, but I assure you that they are completely natural. We Ferengi do not have so much vanity that we must enhance our inborn good looks. Now you will excuse me. The management would frown on me bedazzling one lady guest longer than another. *Bon appetit.*"

"I've never heard a Ferengi speak French before," Matt commented as the creature moved on.

"At least you know what a Ferengi is. I wouldn't have known one from a Ferrari before tonight. That's what I get for painting while the kiddos are watching TV. But why wouldn't he answer a few simple questions about his getup?"

"It would probably break his contract, or the spell. I bet it's a kick for the fans to think they're in the real unreal world, and he meant it when he said the management would get on him for discussing makeup and costuming. This is 'Star Trek: The Experience,' and that requires that the fantasy not be broken, for anything." The waitress was back to take their dinner orders. "What about one of these exotic drinks?"

Janice eyed the family bending over the glass straws protruding like satellite prongs from their witches brew, then gazed at Matt. "Let the fantasy be unbroken. I'll take a miniversion of that."

After Matt had ordered and the waitress had gone, she added, "That family cauldron with straws reminds me of Norman Rockwell's famous painting of a soda fountain, as done by Gahan Wilson! Wouldn't you know it would take a futuristic theme to bring back a glass version of the humble straw?"

"So. What's your verdict?"

"On what?"

"The ride. Safe enough for the kids?"

"It was *just* safe enough for me. I'm not used to being jerked around as a form of recreation." She leaned away while minigoblets of exotic color were placed before them. "And I'd sure hate to have a migraine on that thing. But, yeah, they can go on. Even better, I now know I can face going on with them. Mother as a wimp does not fly these days."

"Do you do everything with the kids in mind?"

"Everything? No . . . well, sometimes not everything. But a lot. Why, getting on your nerves?"

"No. I'm just impressed."

A tower of golden onion rings stacked on an upright stick made a one-point landing in their midst. The dressing pod's three-point landing occurred soon after.

"I'm surprised these aren't called Mr. Spockrings," Matt observed.

"Him I know. The logic machine with pointy ears and black bangs. But why name onion rings after him? Does he make people cry?"

"No, but upright on a rod is a very space-conserving and logical way to serve these, uh, Earthling staples," Matt said, helping himself to the top ring.

"The kids would love this," Janice agreed, munching. "Sorry. I keep grading everything on a kid-factor scale. I'm not used to being in adult company."

"Is that why you like doing police sketches? A radical change of pace?"

"I like doing art, any kind of art, because I'm good at it, and the only way to get better is to keep trying something new. But I can't keep up the art forever."

Matt, caught in serious munching, managed to look inquisitive enough to keep her talking.

Janice turned the funky goblet on the table, watching it, not him. "This is a community-property state. We could have split the assets and argued over them, but I wanted to keep the house for the kids' sake. The child support's been enough to allow me to stay home with them and dabble in earning some bread with art money, but my five-year grace period will be up soon, and I'll need a steady income."

"I guess I was lucky to get two mug sketches out of you at bargain basement prices. You should have charged more."

"You didn't look like you could afford it."

"How could you tell? That borrowed motorcycle I rode looked pricey."

"But *you* didn't."

"Well, I can afford it now. You accept retropayments?"

She shook her head, smiling, her beaded earrings shimmying a "no" with her pantomiming lips. "Working with you was payment enough. Face of a choir boy and first you have me sketch this elderly sleaze-guy, then you come back, and it's a black-Irish Madonna you want a mug sketch of."

"You thought she looked like a madonna?" The notion shocked Matt to his bones.

"No, *the* Madonna. You know, super-bitch in a bustier. MTV. Why do you looked relieved? Oh, I guess your 'Madonna' is an icon, not a rock idol. Naturally I wondered what a straight-arrow like you had to do with these out-of-character types. And that was before I knew you were an ex-priest."

"Maybe you should get a job screenwriting," he joked, deflecting her away from his past and back to her own future plans, as he had hoped.

"No writing! Art's always been my long suit. So . . . I've been taking interior design classes at UNLV. Got to get some kind of accreditation. At least in that field, work experience counts, too. *If* I can get a job. Selling furniture is the entry-level position. I could join a design firm if I put together a portfolio."

"Sounds good. You never know what'll turn up. I'm living proof."

"On live radio. When you told me what you were doing now— interviewing Elvis."

Janet shook her head as their food arrived, her chicken sandwich cut into an "off-world" triangle, his ribs garnished with exotic unknowns.

"Life is unpredictable," Matt said, laughing. "As you can see, I've discovered that clichés get you through a lot of talk radio."

"Speaking of clichés, I never expected to end up a single mother of two."

"How'd it happen?" Matt asked, wondering if he should.

Before, when they had been together for less time, Janice had seemed more self-assured. That's why he'd asked her out. If he had to go through these hoops, and apparently he did, he'd prefer to do it with someone confident about the course.

But her edgy, slightly provocative attitude toward him had softened. He felt he was out with an old friend he suddenly didn't know. But maybe that was what dating was about: becoming friends. Maybe intimations of possible intimacy were easier between strangers.

"The classic story," Janice finally answered. "We got married after college, the art major and the business major. We worked, got a house. He worked his way up; I got pregnant, stopped working. Two kids. Bigger house. Bigger salary for him, longer hours. Then his own firm. Enough money so that my working seemed redundant. I got into kids; he got into toys. Some of them wore bras. Training bras, I think," she added sardonically.

Matt felt his expression slowly sour in empathy at the slow-growing pain of those years, at the inevitable dissolution.

Janice shook her head as if avoiding unseen gnats. "I can't really blame him, or me, or the kids. We all did what we were supposed to. We just didn't keep it all together."

"What's he doing now?"

"Same things. Making money. Buying toys. Bigger house, younger woman, no more kids. Yet. That's the trouble with younger women. If I'd managed to give him sixty percent of my attention *and* give the kids sixty percent, maybe it would have worked."

"But what about some time for you?"

"Exactly. I really am an artist. I need to do it. So I can't say I'm unhappy about the split. I manage to give the kids maybe fifty percent of my time and get some of the rest for myself."

They both had managed to eat most of their meals during this recitation. The onion rings had dwindled on their alien spindle to three cold survivors. Their Easter-egg-colored drinks, fruits and rum, were ice-cube diluted puddles in the bottom of their glasses.

Matt got out his credit card, thinking maybe he ought to have more than one. Share the riches.

Janice laughed softly at nothing, maybe herself. "Anything ever come of my sketch? The hot-looking lady with ice-cold eyes?"

"Oh. Her. No. I had a friend in the FBI check her out. No trace."

"A woman like that is constitutionally incapable of leaving no trace . . . unless she wants it that way."

"True."

"Who was she anyway?"

After Janice's frankness, Matt felt obligated to confess something personal. He had so little of that nature to reveal.

"A stranger who was apparently trying to get to someone I know, just barely. A brutally bitter person. So she cut me."

"My God!"

"A superficial razor slash actually. That's all. Nothing life-threatening. Seems she hates priests, even ex-priests."

"Razor? That's the kind of freak who'll throw acid."

"Oh, great. Something else to worry about."

"Sorry." She was silent as the waitress returned with the credit slips. Matt signed and pocketed the receipt. The act seemed to stamp the "date" with "official."

They ambled out of Quark's and through the space-ship casino, Janice ducking into the rest room again and advising Matt not to miss checking out the men's version.

He smiled as he headed in that direction. Rest rooms as must-see tourist spots. Only in Las Vegas.

The men's was the same sterile, stainless-steel model that Janice had described. There were no holographic mirrors over the urinals. At least he didn't think so.

He waited among the slot machines, beginning to realize that women would always take longer in these things. He was afraid to ask why.

Las Vegas's raucous slot machines were evolving into modern, muted mechanisms. Many didn't take and spit out coins nowadays. *Ka-ching, ka-ching.* They took bills and toted the win/loss rate via on-screen computer-game-style animations. Hands in pockets, he watched a video poker screen while a pair of mobile white gloves dealt the cards. The gloves moved like disembodied servant hands in a French fairy tale, elegant and fascinating, but they repelled him, too.

Perhaps they reminded him of the vanishing magician, the Mystifying Max, who had managed to resume his interrupted relationship with Temple and remain invisible at the same time. Matt found it galling to lose out to a man who was only half there, but he had to admire Temple's loyalty to her one-time live-in lover. "Constancy" maybe said it better. Her relationship with Kinsella didn't have the benefit of formal vows, but she had remained truer to him than Matt had to his vocation, although for a much shorter period of time, and although Matt had never betrayed any of his priestly promises of poverty, chastity, and obedience.

"Waiting for the white rabbit?" Janice's voice asked behind him.

"It is a wonderland, isn't it?" He turned with a smile. Janice's height always surprised him. He wondered if she carried a lunch bag of leftover adolescent angst about being a fairly tall woman, the way Temple regretted being so petite.

Probably not. She was not nearly as tall as Molina and seemed like someone who'd always been confident. A realist. Temple would be amazed to know that he found Janice much less sexually threatening. Temple's unconscious ultrafemininity attracted him like a never-doused signal beacon; Janice seemed to turn her sexuality on and off at will, taking the pressure off someone skittish like himself.

Skittish. Yeah, that described his approach to the opposite sex, or lack of approach. What did ex-father Nick really expect him to do when he dated? Get to know women as pals? Pick one to sleep with for the first time? Find a life partner?

"Do you like Las Vegas?" she was asking.

"I don't know if you 'like' a place like this or just learn to live with it. What keeps you here?"

She took his arm as they walked out, a sign of postdinner relaxation, nothing else. Janice made a deprecatory face. "*He* lives here. I want the kids to know their father. He's not a bad father, as fathers go."

"You don't think much of fathers."

"I think they're too great an invention to be semiretired at an early age. I don't know where it goes. You look at your first baby, and there's this overwhelming feeling of wonder and mutual amazement and pride and fear and gratitude for each other. It's like an or . . ." She glanced at him, then swiftly away. "Then before you know it, the have-tos eat all that up. Eat you both up, and you've lost it. What's between you. So you get angry, with yourself and each other. You must have seen this scenario in parish work."

"Divorce is still pretty forbidden; Catholics go for annulments rather than dissolution. Or stay together, grimly. It was always the hardest thing to counsel for. The chasms were uncrossable, and priests, of course, can't know what happens between the euphoric couple who took wedding vows and the distant partners who can't seem to discuss the weather without bickering. Maybe that's another reason I'm leery of having kids."

"You don't like them?"

"I don't know any well enough to *not* like them. No, I seemed to get along with them, was even a popular priest with 'em. But it's easy for me. I've never had to be around kids all the time, or lay down the law more than occasionally. I think they're pretty lucky to have mothers rather than me."

Leaving the Hilton was a shock. The day had turned to dusk, and the air went from air-conditioned frigid to a lukewarm that felt like swimming in Jell-O.

They paused at the top of the shallow stairs to inhale the evening. Natural scents were dampened by all the buildings, but the air was a perfect match to body temperature.

"Nice." Janice studied the bruising eastern horizon that reflected the sunset unseen behind them. "No stars yet."

"What do you call that?" Matt pointed to the west where the top of the Luxor flashed its powerful beam that was visible to satellites.

"Nothing any wise man would follow," Janice dismissed it.

The Strip's new skyline was silhouetted against blushing blue sky. Matt did a roof count: the Paris's blue mansard; the hotels built like steel and concrete tidal waves frozen in time, the Monte Carlo and Bellagio being the newest; the tri-winged Mirage, the current format in favor, its three-spoke design offering windows with views on six sides, belying the buildings' huge bulk. Ersatz landmarks were also lighting up the oncoming night: the top of New York, New York's Empire State building, the Paris's Eiffel Tower, even giant cranes rearing up almost as high as the soaring roofs.

"I have a confession to make," Janice said. "I've always wanted to do a velvet painting of this. Awful idea, isn't it?"

"Where would Elvis be?"

"A small figure in the front, next to a Volkswagen?"

"It'd never sell."

"No. Elvis would have to be a constellation in the sky above the Strip. Now there's a guiding star for you."

"Please." Matt looked around cautiously. "Don't give any developers ideas. Say, what's that?" He pointed to a new blaze of neon glory just firing up tube by tube near the Belladonna and Kingdome. "Has somebody up there heard you?"

"I hope not! It's not the Titanic. I don't think that's off the ground yet."

"I thought the problem for the *Titanic* was getting back on the ground."

Janice was frowning into the fading daylight and the brightening neon. "I heard something, or the kids told me something. . . . I know! The, um, New Millennium. Speaking of constellations. Look. It's a solar system."

"When planets collide." Matt watched the rings of Saturn fill in with pink and orange strips of light as if an invisible hand, possibly white-gloved, was sweeping colored chalk over the Stripscape of Las Vegas.

As he watched, a newly lit section suddenly was quenched. "Did you see that?"

"Something went nova. Now it's a black hole."

"So 'new' it's already on the fritz."

"Multibillion-dollar buildings these days . . ." Janice shook her head and let her glance lower to the parking lot.

It was jammed now, though it had been reasonably empty when they had arrived, but "the Bug's" sleek silver, twenty-first-century form stood out almost as seriously as the mercurial sculpture of a Hesketh Vampire.

Something, or somebody, was always keeping Matt in the lime-light despite himself.

Chapter 8

Black Hole

I do hate to pull the plug, so to speak, on a brand-new light show, but my personal shine-ability will be seriously dimmed come dawn's early light if I do not get off the face of this planet.

My day-to-day experience with neon is nil. I have always worshiped the Great God Gas from afar, like the tourists. I do know that the gases come in two colors: argon, which is as blue as Hyacinth the Siamese cat's eyes, and neon, which has an orange-red color like Hyacinth's eyes when they glow dangerous crimson in the dark. Pour the two bright gases into variously colored and/or coated glass tubes and stew until they become electrically excited by current. Presto! You get forty-some flavors of the Rainbow—the colors that make all these giant glowworm signs around Las Vegas look like the aurora borealis on LSD. So I do understand the process.

I also understand that it is up to me to get someone up to me.

My mama did not rear any light-socket-sucking kits that lived, so I hunt around for a handy implement. Surely a careless workman has left something behind to cause accidents and make insurance companies very unhappy. I prowl along the level passage behind the sign's thick Lego-style structure. If I had a hammer . . .

But I don't, so a full Dr Pepper can a workman left behind will have to do.

Poor Dr Pepper, so misunderstood. I play kick the can until it is in the proper position. Until the lie is just right, and the wind is not a factor. Then I boot it right at a narrow neck of glass that connects the backboard to the hot, pulsing signage. I have pressed "Enter" by remote control, so to speak.

The sign snaps and hisses its fury as the glass shatters, gas pours out the broken tube, and air enters. In the wink of a firefly's eye, a long strip of Day-Glo orange goes dead gray.

Now, I am gambling here. Ordinarily one bum light bulb on a Christmas tree the size of Rhode Island is not about to be noticed, no matter how much the hoi polloi are urged to let "this little light of mine shine."

So anyone seeing a missing strip on the bottom crossbar of the "e" in the "New" in New Millennium is like expecting someone to notice an eyelash on a page of hyphens.

But.

The New Millennium lives up to its name pretty well right now. It is indeed new. I am sure these lightworks are under scrutiny. No town knows the importance of putting your name up in lights like Vegas. Actually, I would like to see *my* name up in lights someday. Nothing too overbearing. Neon against a tasteful black-marble plaque: Midnight Louie, PI.

But first, I must kiss this billiard ball of a building good-bye.

So I wait, facing into the western mountains as the sky

above them darkens to provide the perfect camouflage. By now I am as anonymous a background as the night, although the highlights on my satin cuffs and lapels reflect violent hues of orange, red, and blue neon.

I have arranged myself to the left of the trapdoor. Doors generally open to the right, and I will be afforded some obscurity behind it.

If it opens.

If it does not, I will be forced to attempt unmanned flight back to the water raft, which even now rushes past me, its passengers' shrieking, laughing faces painted a rainbow of neon colors. Had one not had an ancient philosophical bent and the ability to think deeply on other things in such a situation, one very well could go bonkers. Or color-blind.

While I am successfully ignoring my situation and its dangers (Midnight Louie does not yowl and carry on like a treed kitten), I am surprised to be suddenly hurled back against Saturn's smooth stucco surface, still warm from the day's sunlight.

The trapdoor has opened, and then some.

"This door is jamming on something," a voice complains.

This door pulls inward, then whacks outward again with full force.

Luckily, I have edged along the ledge to avoid being squashed like a coal-black cotton ball.

Soon two burly workmen are marooned up here with me, except that all I have to do is tippy-toe over an engineer boot or two and I am on to new adventures beneath the planet of these apes, and they are up here pressing shattered glass into their palms.

While they are yelping and cursing like a pack of dogs, I leap the size-thirteen boots (which are probably a couple points higher than their combined IQs) and plummet into a dark, confined space.

Immediately, I am punished for my cavalier attitude toward lesser beings Who Cannot Help It. I am on an interior slide, with no water to slick the surface. My flailing feet scrape painted metal, but resistance is futile. I am corkscrewing down the darkness to who-knows-where.

It is all I can do to restrain myself from shouting "Wheeee" like the happy idiots on the external slide. At least they have light and water as well as insane speed.

Oops! I make three tight turns and am spit out into bright light. Flailing again, I manage to curl my limbs around some parallel bars that I am plummeting past. I always had an acrobatic streak. It is a family trait.

So there I end up. Limbs curled fore and aft on what turns out to be a metal ladder. Below me unfolds a vast and complex space filled with wonders and some pretty weird-looking creatures creeping around. It is like looking into a giant artificial peony crawling with ants.

I do not like ants. They tend to clog the sinuses.

However, they are so far below me that I don't have to worry about them. I have to worry about me getting down, so I can then worry about ants. I evaluate my situation. I can see well now but still lack food and water, and my stomach is growling.

Far below me, bizarre spaceships cruise like alien spiders on some invisible web. It would have to be spiders. I hate spiders. If I slept too long near the Crystal Phoenix koi pond, they would start weaving webs in my whiskers.

I am at the top of an intricate maze of black metal pipes and meshes. I have a narrow, pierced-metal ledge to cling to, but my shivs keep slipping through the holes. The ledge extends left and right as far as I can see.

In a burst of irony, I realize what my only firm support is while I plot my next move. It is something that people call a catwalk.

Chapter 9

Invisible Man

"That was fun," Janice said on the way home. "I hope you don't feel too used."

"Me?" Matt had been brooding about how unfair it was to use her as a set of training wheels for the sociosexually challenged.

"The dry run for the kids." She smiled apologetically in the faint light of the dashboard. "The demands of single parenthood call for piling on. Every action must serve two purposes, at least."

"Don't feel guilty. I've got a corner on that commodity."

"You? Why?"

"This is a dry run for me, too."

"Oh." Her purse was a flat, beaded-suede rectangle with dangling fringe, which she occupied herself in detangling.

"Do you want to stop somewhere for a drink? Talk?"

"You mean, do something adult?"

"So they say."

She checked her watch. Always. "What a radical idea. Yeah, sure."

"We're near your neighborhood. Any idea where——?"

"No. Let me think. There's a place in a strip mall. Can't guarantee the ambiance."

"I've had it up to here with ambiance."

"Then turn left at the next corner."

He followed her directions to the one-story shopping center with a checkerboard of business signs still lit. Most flamboyantly lit was the corner sign reading The Lucky Lounge.

"Ooooh." Janice frowned and bit her lip. "I didn't remember the sign."

He had already parked and come around to liberate her, or, in this case, to lock the door after she had liberated herself.

They walked into the usual dimness lit by pockets of lights here and there: over the bar, the jukebox, on the perimeter, the glassed-in candles on each table.

They edged into the space together, looking for the one right place to sit that wasn't too near smokers, too far from the bar, too close to an overhead speaker piping in medium-hard rock music, too intimate, or too public.

By the time they settled on a table all the unspoken criteria had been modestly met.

While Matt's eyes hunted for a waitress, if there was one, Janice hung her purse cord over the back of her wooden captain's chair and pulled it close to the small round table with a two-inch-thick varnished wood top.

The scattering of people sitting at the bar, the video poker games built into the bar surface reflecting off their pasty faces, looked like *Twilight Zone* escapees.

"From Quark to Quaaludes," Janice quipped, picking up the small Plexiglass display that advertised featured drinks, all exotic, all dangerously dosed with multiple liquors, all colored oddly.

"The great tranquillizers of modern life," Matt commented, "media and medications."

Janice nodded seriously. "You nailed it. If there are two things I fear most that my kids could get tangled up in, it's some nutsy violent rock star, computer game, TV/movie/record cult. Or drugs. Or both."

"Anyone looking for an easy escape will push himself onto dangerous ground."

"Like your friend Elvis."

"Please. I was dealing with manifestations of the Elvis cult, not Elvis in person."

"You think."

"I'm getting the impression that parenthood is as scary a role as I thought it was."

"No, it's rewarding, really. If you like whitewater rafting."

A waitress appeared as if conjured to take their orders. Matt supposed she'd been busy behind the scenes. He ordered a beer, Janice a wine spritzer.

The sumptuously illustrated display of exotic drinks was shoved to the side.

"So." Janice said, sitting back. "Tell me about your new job."

He did, in the middle of which their drinks arrived.

"You were on the *Amanda Show*?" Janice asked when he finished. "I paint to it sometimes."

"You paint to television?"

"I like to keep up with the unreal world." She spun the foot of her wine glass, then looked up at him. "Matt, this has been great, but I'm wondering what brought it on."

"Does something have to bring it on?"

"With you, yes. You're not hunting your stepfather anymore. So is your next quest . . . ?"

"Next quest." He sipped. "That makes me sound like a robot."

"No. Like a knight. Are you looking for maidens to rescue? Because my earth shoes are too solid on the ground to let me get swept off my feet."

"I'm looking for people to know. I haven't had that luxury, not really. I know this sounds corny, but I was too busy trying to know God, and myself."

"Well, you can't know other people without knowing yourself."

"Exactly. With me, I'm doing two things at once."

She nodded soberly. "I realize we're not coming from the same place. My parents were California agnostics; absolutely inclusive of all races and lifestyles, except religion. I like stability. I try to give it to my kids, but I'm not looking for a new daddy for them, or a new husband for me. Been there, done that. Kinda like things the way they are now."

"What *are* you looking for?"

She laughed, to herself, putting her dominant left hand to her neck and ducking her head. Janice had so few trademark gestures that Matt felt transfixed. A left-handed female artist was unique enough that he expected her to surprise him.

"I'm not sure you'd approve or even understand. In fact, I *know* you wouldn't do either."

"Am I that . . . rigid?"

"No. Not at all. But you'd have had to have been through a lot of life that you haven't." She sipped her wine, looked up at him from over the rim, bit her lip, and spoke again. "What I'm looking for is an Invisible Man."

"Invisible man?"

"Yup. Someone who's there, and not there." Janice's eyes lifted to lighting fixtures cloaked in heavy stained glass, as if searching the dimmed lamps for constellations of meaning. "Someone I can take home to meet the kids, but who won't stay overnight. Someone with his own place and his own life. Someone who's there when I need him, and out of my hair when I don't. Someone intelligent, interesting, presentable, attractive to me, but who has his own life, as I have mine, and they don't have to overlap, just coexist. Of course, to you, the whole idea is immoral. To me, it's a very pleasant fantasy."

"A relationship without muss and fuss. You really think that's possible?"

"Why not? Look. I don't want a meal ticket. I might be able to use one, but I don't want it. That's part of what ruined my marriage. My kids come first until they're out of the house, by then . . .

whoa, I don't even want to think how old I'll be. The women's magazines say that it's never too late, but those hormones get awfully hinky as time goes by. I need an Invisible Man. Someone whose own life is full enough that he doesn't need to intertwine it with mine. That's all."

"It sounds pretty cold."

She lifted an eyebrow. He'd never seen her so animated. Maybe it was the wine. Maybe it was the liberation of expressing what she really felt.

"You're not damning me to hell."

Matt opened his hands. "Who am I to judge? You said it: I haven't lived enough life to understand."

He thought about the inadvertent triangle he had formed one leg of: Temple, Max Kinsella, himself a lame third. He still fought strong feelings for Temple, but he was out of the picture, except in his own mind. Except that your own mind is eighty percent of the picture.

"What you say is interesting," he finally admitted. "You strike me as a very centered person. I can't argue with your conclusion. In fact, I would almost say that what you describe is what I need: to be involved and yet somehow free. Maybe it's a universal fantasy."

"Why did you ask me out, Matt? Other than the fact that I'd indicated I was interested?"

"Because I like you. I'm intrigued by your life in art, in crime sketches, in being a mother. And, I need to learn the exotic species 'woman.' I've been infatuated with a woman who's not available, it turns out. I'm on the rebound, I guess they say, not only from a vocation, but from a relationship that never was."

"And she isn't the gorgeous creature in my sketch?"

"No! I know enough not to touch that woman with a switch-blade."

Janice smiled. "Glad to hear it. Maybe we can do business."

She lifted her wine glass, the rim tilted toward him.

Matt felt that the only response her gesture demanded was to lift his tall beer glass and chime its rim with hers.

He was amazed that an invisible man could make such a racket.

* * *

Despite their frank talk at the bar—or maybe because of it—Matt found himself dreading the end-of-the-date ritual of escorting Janice to her front door.

At least her kids were somewhere behind that barrier, forming their own kind of barrier, even if only asleep.

"This has been fun," Janice said as they walked slowly up to her entryway.

Out here, in the suburbs, the night was quiet, and the stars at the darkest top of the sky glittered with aloof glamour.

"Yeah," Matt said. "I never would have had a *Star Trek* experience without you."

"That's an advantage of having kids. They pull you back into what you thought you outgrew." Janice plumbed the depths of her soft purse for the door key.

Although she was anything but a frivolous woman, Matt reflected, her clothes and accessories all had a soft, unconstructed feel. She'd hate the comparison, but she was a walking velvet painting.

Matt realized that except for the drive to the Hilton, this was the first time tonight they had been really, truly alone, with nothing to do.

Janet made an impatient sound and sat on a wooden bench in the small landscaped area beside the door where the muted exterior light was brighter.

"Key," she explained, still digging for it. She finally pulled the key out, but remained sitting.

"You know, Matt, I'm just realizing that I set up this whole evening to hit you over the head with everything that's confining about my life, with my parental obligations."

"It *has* been an eye-opener. Do you know why you did that?"

She hesitated. "I think I'm afraid of taking advantage of you."

"I thought that was the guy role. I've been feeling the same way."

"That's what boy-girl stuff is about." She laughed uneasily. "Now I'm sitting here kicking myself."

"I'll join you." He sat beside her.

They were silent for a moment, listening to the night, which wasn't making much noise at all.

"What would you do," Matt finally asked, "if you didn't have all those responsibilities."

"If. Probably scoot you right in. Sleep with you."

"Sleep?"

"It's a euphemism, I know. But that's really the best part, after all the bells and whistles. Having someone you trust enough to sleep with and wake up with. That's what my marriage was until my ex-husband betrayed that part. It wasn't the extracurricular sex, really. It was the trust."

"Hopin' to be honest and tryin' to be true."

"Yeah? That sounds like a quote."

"It is." Matt didn't explain. Quoting "St. Temple" to a woman he hoped would help him forget her didn't seem kosher. And Temple had so far been his only patron saint in the path to sexual experience, if you could regard that as a spiritual journey, and Matt was beginning to think that you had to.

"I'm so damned tired of being an adult," Janice said. "Thinking through every move, worrying about money and social problems that might ruin my kids' lives. Policing them, policing me."

"A Mr. Invisible would help that?"

"Yes! Didn't you feel anything, that first time you came over to my house?"

"Scared?"

She laughed, as he had intended. "That's what makes you so damn take-advantage-of-able. I sensed it then, the sudden high of maybe being in control of us going out of control. I guess men feel that much more than women. Men who've been around."

"Men who've been around, *that is*," he finished her sentence. "Not me, that's for sure."

"That's why you're so attractive to women, you know."

"Yeah, I finally do know that I am. I've finally accepted that it's my looks. Can't help that."

"Looks never hurt, but it's really your innocence. I'm beginning to get why some men get hooked on virgins."

The word, especially applied to him, was profoundly embarrassing for some reason he couldn't explain. What was a matter of integrity inside the priesthood felt like a source of shame and ignorance outside it. Maybe it just made him feel less adult, the very state Janice longed for.

"My kids are hooked on *Buffy, the Vampire Slayer*," she said thoughtfully, "without quite realizing what they're seeing. Which is maybe the way it should be. Here's this high-school chick with superhuman strength who slays demons, but when she offers herself body and soul for the first time, to the guy she loves, a reformed vampire, an old curse kicks in and he turns on her. Calls her a stupid slut for loving him and showing it. That's the classic female dilemma: the guy wants sex with you more than anything; if you do it he's satisfied and you're now worthless, to him and everybody else, who he'll be sure to tell all about it. What's worse, being innocent and ignorant and having no self-esteem? Or being experienced and betrayed and having no self-esteem?"

"That's what I wonder."

"At least with guys having sex is a positive. Manhood achieved. Girl conquered."

"Not for me."

"That's the attraction. For once I feel less vulnerable than the guy. It's a big responsibility, which might be why I sabotaged myself tonight. And why you're such a prize."

"Not proven," Matt said.

"Worrying about AIDS is another big pain," she went on, "another overdose of being adult all the time. There goes spontaneity." He felt her glance slide sideways to him, felt the speculation. "Of course you're still shrink-wrapped. You're a regular time machine. You'd be safe."

"*If* I'm telling the truth that I never violated my promise of chastity."

"And *if* I'm telling the truth when I say I've got a clean bill of health despite Mr. Flander's bedroom shenanigans elsewhere. At least I have the papers to prove it. You probably haven't bothered to get them. See? Here we are *talking* about it. *Papers*. Might as well be adopting a puppy. Why bother?"

"I'm afraid I don't know yet."

"And, oh God, I'd like to be the one to take care of that."

She had spoken in an intense almost-whisper, like a prayer. She had also taken him right back to his first visit to her house, to that startling, confusing, exciting moment outside her bedroom door, when he'd become aware that they could be within inches of crossing that threshold, the kids away at computer camp, the house quiet and shaded from the daylight, a clock ticking audibly somewhere like a regulating heartbeat when their own cardiac rhythms were suddenly erratic. Erotic.

"You remember," she said. "That was a magic moment."

"Are there many like that?" he wondered.

"No. It's when it first occurs to strangers that they could be more-than. You can't predict it. You can't plan for it." She sighed. "And you can't always act on it. Usually don't."

"Then it wasn't just my hesitation?"

She shook her head. "No, dammit. But you did feel it?"

"I felt . . . tempted."

"I'm flattered."

"You should be. You're a very centered, serene woman. I can't exactly define it. That's somehow fascinating to me."

"Even after a one-night, remedial course in Single Parenting one-oh-one?"

He laughed at her self-deprecating description of their first date. First? Did that imply a second? "What do you do after the magic moment has passed?"

"That's what we're here to find out, I guess. Try for another? Damn, there are the kids, and the baby-sitter. I guess we could have gone back to *your* place, but then the initiative would have been up to you. Here, on my turf, it's up to me and it's not possible. Not the way it was that day."

"Which is maybe why that was a magic moment."

"After the forbidden, the suddenly grasped opportunity is the next great turn-on."

"I don't know if I can do any of this."

"You can try."

Matt tried not to hold his breath. "You know that I'm getting over someone?"

"Who isn't?"

"Even though we didn't do much of anything."

"You don't have to tell me that."

"I have to tell me that." They were silent. "You're right. You can talk it to death."

She put a hand on his arm. On his shirt sleeve. He felt the warmth of her fingers seeping through.

And then he suddenly knew he was going to do it. He was going to kiss Janice. Maybe it was because he liked her, maybe because she was being honest and he appreciated that, maybe because the situation seemed to demand something, maybe because he was feeling a reprise of the magic moment the first time he'd met her. . . .

It was probably not going to go well. He felt stupid and awkward and wasn't even sure he'd like it, and he felt guilty about Temple and a little angry with himself for feeling slightly unfaithful, to something or someone. By the time their lips met, and somehow they did, he felt something else; he felt his hands on the velvet-painting of her jacket, felt hushed and excited at the same time, as her house had felt around them in the hallway outside her bedroom, felt possibilities and fears, felt desire.

"Hey," she said.

The kiss had ended as mysteriously as it had begun, but they were collaborators now, past some invisible barrier. More intimate.

"I wish you *were* invisible," she said softly. "Then you could 'come in and see me sometime.' I guess you could slip over the wall into my bedroom. I've got a French door to the side patio."

"The Don Juan fantasy."

"Yeah. You know, think of the service he provided to all those ladies sold into arranged marriages in those days. Nowadays women are more liberated. We've got *un*arranged marriages. I guess my marriage doesn't count, since it wasn't Catholic, right?"

"I think all marriages 'count.' The consequences sure do."

"The only consequence I'm thinking about now is you."

"That's good, I guess. You deserve some time off from thinking about consequences." He found his lips fondly brushing her hair as they pulled away. The moment, magic or not, was over.

"Thanks for a great evening." She stood up, put a hand on his shoulder. "And stay right there. If you see me to the door, I might drag you into my cave."

For a few moments after she disappeared into the mellow rectangle of light beyond her front door he remained on the wooden bench, feeling the evening chill sucking the warmth out of him.

But he had to move on. Eleven o'clock, and the baby-sitter would be coming out soon. He couldn't be caught mooning on the stoop.

But he wasn't mooning; he was just trying to make sense of it all.

So he returned to the Beetle's shiny silver shell and drove home, aware of invisible people moving through the rote of their lives all around him, feeling pretty invisible himself.

Chapter 10

Imagine Seeing You Here

After a while of staring into the abyss, which resembles the seven levels of Hell, from all I have heard, I realize that the busy spaceships below are robots. They are programmed on tracks in the ceiling above me and suspended from matte black rods, far too thin and slick for me to use as a fire pole.

Besides, what would I do once I was astride what resembled a cross between a mechanical condor and a grappling hook? I also suspect that once I am down on their level I would discover that they were far larger than I thought they were from up here.

So I sit back and think. Obviously, if workmen got up, there must be a ladder down, likely a completely vertical one anchored to a wall. If I must deal with a ladder, I greatly prefer the two-sided models that open to a gentle angle and sport wide, flat wooden struts instead of metal rods. There is no way I am going to descend fifty feet on what amounts to an oversized zipper track.

Meanwhile, my stomach is not getting any quieter.

I look along the catwalk to either side, finally discerning an interesting dark hump at the far left end. Compared to the mechanical monsters battling below, it actually looks organic.

I am ready for organic matter, so I totter along the metal mesh, careful to keep my shivs from snagging in any holes. It takes a while, but as I approach my discovery I realize that it is bigger than I thought, and even more organic than I suspected.

All species like partners in misfortune, but my new-found friend has outdone me in the help-needing department. He, or It, is beyond help. I pace along its length—not easy when my discovery almost covers the mesh's entire width. Its length is not insignificant either. By carefully keeping my steps regular, I calculate it is fourteen four-feet long. A four-feet is the length it takes for me to move each of my limbs in turn, times repetitions of same movement while going from head to toe of the prone figure.

Fourteen four-feet. I sit back to do a mental sum. Where is Miss Temple's touch-tone purse calculator that she is always mislaying just when I need it?

Whew. This fellow is almost seven feet tall. Can that be right?

I bend to take a good look at what I presume to be the head. Yes, this critter could be as long as it wanted to be, for I have never seen its like before.

The face and head are covered by large irregular spots, like one of those padded and clawed big boys in my own family tree, the leopard. I sniff the hide and get an odd odor of glue.

There are eyes on this beast, but they are closed.

I surmise it is time for my examination to move into serious waters. I lean my mug closer for the whisker test, moving my vibrissae above the fallen face and waiting for a breath of air to stir them.

Nothing. Either this is not an air-breathing species, or it is one dead dodo from someplace long ago and far away.

I leap upon what would be the chest were it human or nearly so. The surface lies still beneath my feet. It is possible that I could attempt a crude form of CPR (Cat Pounding Resuscitation) by jumping up and down until I had raised a heartbeat, but I see that such measures will be too little too late.

My toes curl in automatic horror. Whatever this is I am standing on, it is dead, and it is human under the skin, however bizarre. It may even have been murdered.

I am not hungry any more. For now.

My main problem is to draw attention to this death in the wings.

I study the lie of the corpse on the catwalk. Two of its four limbs are dangling over the edge. It will take some patience and strain, but I may be able to use tooth and nail to tug and push the body until the dead weight will tip the scales of balance and send it plummeting to the floor far below.

Such a plummet will not do the state of the deceased any good, and may well confuse the cause of death, but I see no alternative except a stink to high heaven.

As for my own means of descent, my only option will be a plunge to the top of the suspended good ship *Enterprise,* or a hope that someone will have the sense to investigate where dead body has fallen from, and come up to find me lost in space.

I opt for staying put until I am found, but helping the dead guy fall to earth so they know where to look for me.

I sink my teeth into some metallic and faux-leather fabric and start tugging. Once again, everything is coming up corpses just in time for my Miss Temple to enter the scene.

Chapter 11

Party Line

When the phone rang, the portable was buried under the news-
papers on Temple's coffee table.

She shucked several sections aside to reveal it, then clamped
the receiver to her ear. "Yes?"

"You sound busy."

Max's vibrant baritone could mesmerize the tone-deaf long distance. Temple smiled and settled back into the sofa cushions.
They hadn't connected for a few days. "Up early for a nighttime
guy, aren't you?"

"I'm reforming. And I'm betting you're reading the morning
paper right now."

"Where are you calling from?" Temple peered toward her balcony patio. Max was always showing up where—and when—he
wasn't expected. This time he seemed to be simply calling. "Reading the paper? Of course. An ex-newsie can't resist cold type and
hot stories."

"Have you got to the death yet?"

"I make a point of not reading the obituary pages. It's an irreversible sign of aging, like crow's feet."

"I'm not talking obits. I'm talking a news story."

"Let's see." She rattled newsprint importantly so he could hear it. "Car crash on ninety-five . . . a light pole fell on a tourist. Oooh."

"Violent death," Max corrected her tersely.

"Violent death!" She rattled the papers seriously now, knowing he'd never tell her exactly where to look. Magicians, even nonpracticing magicians, were like that.

"Oh." Shock kept her from saying anything else for a moment. "This is terrible. I knew him."

A pause. "Well, I suppose I did, too, through his work. But not personally, really, though you tend to think you know someone like that when you don't."

"Who do we really know?" she asked philosophically, including Max Kinsella in the question. A sudden and violent death always brought on the clichés. "That's true. Maybe I just liked him."

"You did?" Max sounded surprised, even a little shocked.

"What was not to like?"

"Well, he was a pretty thoroughgoing villain."

"Really? Do you know something about him I didn't know?"

"Temple, are we talking about the same show?"

"Show? He was killed doing a show? A . . . magic show? The paper doesn't say anything about that. What are they hiding?"

"He was killed here in Las Vegas, yesterday."

"Yeah, but I meant a show in Las Vegas. Whenever."

"You mean that you really knew this guy? Personally? How would you?"

"Nothing personal, if you're worried. I just interviewed him."

"When?"

"A couple times. In the recent past."

"You're sounding awfully vague. Is there something that you think I shouldn't know?"

"No! Well, all right. Yes. I confess."

"Temple, don't get miffed. What do you confess? That you killed him?"

"No, silly. I asked him about the Synth. I'd decided to do some scouting on my own."

"Now that I don't like. But why would you ask a Khatlord of Kohl and Suzerain of the planet Khrahud about the Synth?"

"Gosh, is that some secret society title from the Synth?"

Max was beginning to sound annoyed, which he did very well. It helped a lot in getting cars fixed. "It's a title from the Kohlian Suzerain on the planet Khrahud. You ever hear of *Space Trooper Bazaar*, the television show? The guy was an actor."

"Professor Mangel moonlighted as an actor? He didn't seem the type."

"Mangel? Your source on the psychics at Gandolph's last stand? He's not dead."

"Yes, he is, and I feel really awful about it, Max. In fact, if you wouldn't keep confusing me, I could settle down for a serious sniffle. I just saw him a couple weeks ago."

"I just saw him yesterday, and I'm not about to sniffle, but I am seriously disturbed if you're telling me he's dead, too."

"Max, what page of the paper are you reading, dagnabbit?"

"What you taught me was called the 'second front.' "

"I'm on page B-twelve inside the second front, and the news story ain't a vitamin shot to the psyche, I'll tell you that."

This time *she* heard ostentatiously rattling pages.

Meanwhile, she checked the second front, skimming the story to the end.

"Max, you didn't finish the story. It was not an *actor* who played a Khatlord Suzerain on *Space Trooper Bazaar* who died from a fall at the New Millenium, but an unidentified fan of the show dressed up as a Khatlord. Apparently a major exhibition of "Let's Pretend" called TitaniCon is opening soon. Did you find the inside story on the professor?"

"My God." Max gave Professor Mangel several long moments

of silence. "You're not kidding about crying. He was a young guy, not even forty."

"Your age." Temple had recently learned that once you hit thirty every post-thirty death diminishes you as the ever-adolescent twenties soul withers in the blast of reported early death. "Not much information in the story."

"Nothing about time, place, weapon. I smell coverup."

"Who's *your* dead guy, and why are you telling me about him? I watch some of the science fiction shows but not *Space Trooper Bazaar*. It sounded too military." She rustled her way back to the second front. The below-the-fold story featured a photograph of a fifty-something man with a leopard-spotted, dramatically bony face. Temple skimmed the type. "No wonder we're confused! They ran a picture of the actor who turned out *not* to be dead, not the deceased fan, which is logical, since he's unidentified. Not much about the circumstances in this case, either."

"Why did I call about the space opera guy? Never mind. It just caught my eye. What I really don't like, Temple, is Mangel dying so soon after seeing me, and seeing you."

"Were you asking him about the Synth?"

"Yes."

"I thought you were too busy following up on that snarl Molina suckered you into, the dead stripper, to investigate the Synth. That's why I went to see the professor. He'd always been very nice to me, and he was really enthusiastic about his work."

Max's voice tautened. "I know. He was enthusiastic about mine, too. Acted as if he were receiving a heavenly visitation, at the very least. He can't have been killed too much later. I've got to find out more."

"Why were you calling me about the dead actor who's really a nobody?"

"Oh. I almost forgot. It says at the very end of the story that a stray black cat loose in the New Millennium Hotel-Casino drew attention to the body."

"A cat?"

"It's ten A.M. Do you know where Midnight Louie is?"

"Uh . . . I'd better look into that. I'll call you back."

"Never mind. I'm coming over."

"To comfort me?"

"No. To figure out how to make things very uncomfortable for one Lieutenant C. R. Molina."

Chapter 12

Prime Directive

Stone walls do not a prison make, nor iron bars a cage. . . .

Oops . . . let me rephrase those immortal words, which like a lot of immortal words are fine to declaim but not always accurate when applied to the stresses of modern life.

I can tell you right now that bars of any stripe make a pretty effective cage, especially when you are on the inside looking out.

Here I sit, on the morning after finding the New Millennium as hard to crack into as a dinosaur egg, in a space large enough to contain a lion or a tiger. Little me.

You can bet that I will not patronize any zoos except the kind with natural environments after this experience. I am minded to think rather more kindly of a dude I met on my last case. Perhaps Chatter was so obnoxious because of caged living conditions. Then again, the obnoxiousness might have been native to his limb of the family tree.

There is nothing in this rectangular space except one painted back wall, three walls with a view—the bars and a cold, hard surface to sit on. It is cold enough to freeze the cotton balls off the Easter Bunny. He sure would not be hippity-hopping down the rabbit trail after icing his end on black Plexiglas for several hours as I have been since hotel security found me on the catwalk. And okay, my iron bars are not iron but clear Plexiglas. They are just as inflexible though.

What really bothers me is the *Titanic*-anchor-weight chain coiled in the corner, attached to an empty, studded leather collar big enough to encircle a giant-size pizza.

Makes me wonder what sort of cellmates may come lumbering along any minute.

Naturally, I have attracted a crowd.

I am not pleased to notice among them a man and woman who are peering in as if they know me. I certainly do not know them.

"It is a black cat," brilliantly observes the woman, who is almost as petite as my dear little roommate doll, Miss Temple Barr.

The man, who has that unfortunate human facial adornment known as a mustache, squints and frowns. "I wonder if we could do a DNA match with the cat hairs we collected from the Blue Dahlia case."

While I am thinking of what lawyer I can get to make sure that my hairs—in custody or out of it—remain my personal private property, a third party bends a head to study my incarcerated state.

This one is young and shaggy and male, but not very intimidating, despite being in a state of agitation.

"Say," he says, "I am going to need that cage for the Uthrellian Lionx. You will have to move your pussycat."

The man and women reverse their admiring bends and stiffen.

"This is not our cat," the woman says huffily.

"We are the police," the genial man adds. "We just

needed to corral the cat while the body is being moved."

The petite, dark-haired woman, who is blessed with eyes of an appealing shape and slant, frowns. "What is a Uthrellian Lionx?"

The blue-jeaned man turns to point at a creature that has escaped everyone's notice while their attention was directed to my svelte form, or perhaps to the large body zipped into a black-green bag and about to leave the premises.

The beast is about eight feet high, covered with either crusts or scales and possibly some wiry orange hairs. This, I discern instantly, is the warty fifty-inch neck for which the giant dog collar in my cage was designed.

Hey, this dude is welcome to my accommodations. If I can eel out this three-inch space between the Lucite rods, I am history. I go so far as to propel myself forward to rub against the bars. Hint, hint.

But no one is watching me now that the Lionx has appeared on the scene. I have to admit the upstager is impressive.

"Is it a Wookie?" the petite brunette babe asks.

"Is it a Great Ape?" the mustachioed man inquires.

Is it a Yeti, I myself am wondering. Or the bastard son of King Kong?

The huge shaggy head nods and bobs at our interrogation, but Blue Jean Man answers, after pulling out a cigarette and lighting it.

A cloud of nasty smoke emits from his mouth like visible halitosis, surrounds his head, and drifts up to the nostrils of the monster itself.

"It is an animatronic puppet," Blue Jean Man explains. "I need that cage to park it when it is inactive. We don't want anyone messing with it."

Well, *pardonnez moi!* And here I thought I was taking somebody else's parking space.

Never mind. I rub the clear plastic bars until they are

buffed to a crystal-clear shine. Let me out of this puppet buffet!

"You got room for a cat at home?" Mustache asks the Babe-ette.

"No way, Morey."

"This death looks like an accidental fall, or maybe suicide. These fan types in costume are hard to figure. Either way, I guess we'll have to let this little dude walk."

She shrugs. "You want to tell the lieutenant about his presence on the scene?"

"I thought we were partners."

"Not in suicide, pal."

Morey the Mustache nods.

He reaches toward some hidden mechanism.

A snick-snack, and one section of the bars spring ajar.

I am through like midnight ectoplasm.

"Will the hotel want us to release him outdoors?" China Doll asks.

It is a good question. It is such a good question that I take the opportunity to streak away for parts unknown before anyone can come up with an answer.

I must pull this vanishing act in the full glare of publicity, but who will be watching me when an eight-foot Lionx is picking his nose?

In moments I am light years away and lost among the stars—the stars of TV, film, computer animations, and such, of course.

"Excuse me, Mr. Spock," I mutter under my breath, dodging a dude with a set of ears that would do a vampire bat proud. Anyone ever notice Mr. Nimoy's in-character resemblance to Nosferatu? Nobody but the dames, who have always gone for us dark, dangerous, aloof dudes with big ears (Mr. Spock) and noses (Sherlock Holmes) and sharp teeth (me and Dracula). Kind of a composite of Little Miss Riding Hood's wolf, come to think of it.

But a wolf is a canine, and I do not like to think much about canines, unless the canines in question are my very own teeth and about to sink themselves into something succulent in the protein family. Like À La Cat's Salmon Succotash with Oysters Rockefeller. (Well, one Rockefeller *was* eaten by cannibals.) I believe the same thing happened to an ancestor of mine vis-à-vis a saber-toothed tiger, but you never hear of Oysters Louie.

There is a lot of undercover opportunity at this joint, I discover. In addition to the massive domed Saturnalia room in which we all cavort at the moment, there are several spacey-looking chambers leading off from it through doors shaped in every configuration but the same old, same old rectangle.

And everywhere there are people, and nonpeople, all lugging boxes and pulling dolleys loaded with boxes and generally moving outer space inside the New Millennium.

I pass a portly fellow who I am sure is William Shatner. I pass a bald fellow who I am sure is Patrick Stewart. I pass them again. And again. I begin to realize that I am passing the characters they play, Captains Kirk and Picard, respectively. I pass a dame in a skin-tight catsuit who could be any number of imaginary characters. I pass a lot of Blue Jeans and his brothers, all grunting to import and install the portable elements that are changing this part of the hotel interior into an alien bazaar.

I am so eager to take in this nonterraforming process that I overstep my bounds (when have I not?) and actually find myself in the "normal" part of the hotel, near the entry area, the first infestations of slot machines, and the hotel registration desk.

Here mill around people who do not have misshapen tubers growing on the bridges of their noses, just sunglasses. What a shock! Already they look hideously abnormal to my alien-oriented eyes. The only odd-colored skin I spot is dabbed with white sun screen. Although there is a magnificent starry, starry sky rotating in the rotunda above us, featuring every constellation known to earth, it seems a piddling display compared to the giant-size photomurals of alien cities going up inside the Saturnalia dome.

I pause only to examine the sky for signs of any new constellations in the form of Elvis, and failing, decide to retreat back to the scene of the crime.

I am halfway there, thankful for the black marble floor that makes me into my own shadow, when I stop dead. I have just seen a familiar face, and it is far more personal than any I watched on a TV screen.

It is the face of the dead guy whose fall to earth I have so charitably overseen not three hours ago.

He, too, is larger than life, but that may be because he is depicted on an oversized photoposter that is lit from behind to resemble life. Words hover over his spot-faced head and at his booted feet: THE MAN IN THE IRON MASK. THE CLOAKED CONJUROR WILL MYSTIFY AND ENLIGHTEN YOU AS HE REVEALS THE ENIGMAS OF THE MASTER MAGICIANS. The Andromeda Amphitheater under the stars. Shows at 7 and 10 P.M.

I pussywillow my way on velvet pads to the base of the display. This critter is dressed in what looks like a spandex tux with black shirt, tie, and gloves. Although his head-covering mask is fastened on by a Acme Safe–quality chain and padlock, it looks less like iron and more like black-velvet-and-bronze spandex in a spotted pattern eerily similar to the strange face of the dude who was hung out to dry in the upper reaches of the Saturnalia dome earlier today.

Here, I think, is where and when worlds collide. However *outré* this fellow's garb and mask, he is obviously just another magic act, only he debunks the illusion to reveal the mechanics beneath. The dude from the other planet, however, is supposed to represent some sort of alien being.

It strikes me how close this far-out science fiction stuff treads to real life, if you can consider anything that goes on in a Las Vegas hotel real life.

I wonder how Mr. Mystifying Max would feel about a dude

plying the same trade as his by spilling all the trade secrets. On the other hand, MMM is semiretired now, from all I can tell, and plying another trade entirely that is equally shrouded in secrets.

I indulge myself with a long pout on the behalf of my Miss Temple, who deserves better than a Cheshire cat of a significant other. Of course, I must admit that I myself come and go at arbitrary intervals, as suits my purposes, grinning all the while, but that is different.

Speaking of different, I must not forget my prime directive in coming to the New Millennium. There is a minx of a sleek and sensual nature hiding out somewhere here, and it is up to me to find her among all these alien life forms, the females of which seem invariably to be alien minxes of a sleek and sensual nature, inhuman variety.

I can hardly wait to discover what my own species' *feline fatale* is up to this time.

Chapter 13

Quicker than the Eye

"Well?" Max stood with folded arms in Temple's open front door, looking right and left. "Is the feline Temple guard dog in residence?"

"I'm afraid Louie's out. And about."

"I wish he'd been out and about at the University of Las Vegas campus instead of on the Strip."

Max walked in and sat, unchallenged for once, on the sofa. He picked a few telltale black hairs off the beige arm, and from Temple's aqua knit top when she sat beside him. "Messy fellow, isn't he?"

"Cats shed. What can I say? You really think it was Louie at the New Millennium?"

"He does have a thing for hotels. The Crystal Phoenix, for instance."

"Poor little guy, it was the only home he had before I found him and took him in."

"I think, Temple, that he took *you* in. At least I wear a lot of black," Max stretched his long left arm along the back of the sofa, indifferent to any cat hairs it might collect.

Temple leaned her neck into his elbow crook to stare at the apartment's arched ceiling and its undulating waves of reflected daylight. It was like watching sand ripple under the hushing pull of a wave. It helped her think.

"I just know," she said, "that you've been naughty and hacked into the police computer again. I am so . . . sad about Jeff Mangel. Such a neat guy. Like a little boy under that professorial pomp. I wonder if my going to see him—"

"Play that game—Russian roulette with the gun of guilt—and you make me the triggerman. It happened only hours after I left him."

Temple raised her head. "Did you like him?"

"I only met him once."

"You only met Cher once, too."

He maintained his bland expression, with visible effort. "That's me, the Typhoid Michael of the current generation."

Max had never referred to himself by his actual given name before. It didn't suit him as well as the acronym of all his given names—Michael Aloysius Xavier. Temple tensed, full of contrition, and curiosity. "Maybe we're always coming along a little too late, instead of instigatingly early."

"Either way it's disturbing." He smiled at her sober face, which she knew was looking earnest and troubled, and kissed her nose.

Max, the eternal entertainer, always crushing his own needs and feelings to lighten other people's. The cost to him was high, but ever since his cousin's death in Ireland he had felt obliged to pay it. If people knew his painful history, they'd better understand his loyalty. On the other hand, it was tough always coming in second to a ghost.

"What did you find out?" Temple asked.

"Not much. That worries me. The police are keeping this case under wraps. They've involved their cult unit, and they haven't released the crime scene yet."

"Which is . . . ?"

He stroked his fingers through her hair, then pulled her close. "The magic exhibit at the university."

"Oh, God, where I saw poor Jeff Mangel last."

"And I first, and last."

"That's right. Will the police know?"

"Do they have your fingerprints on file?"

"No. Yours?"

He took her hand in his warm, comforting custody. "Not any more."

"Max, you must be leaving a cyber trail."

"I hope not. Besides, Molina would think she was losing her marbles if she went into my file and *didn't* find something different."

"But they could get your prints again?"

"Maybe not."

Temple shook her head. He shook her hand, admonishingly.

"I wish you hadn't decided to visit Mangel again, Temple. The Synth is international. All you can do is draw unwanted notice."

"I'm sorry."

"Not so sorry that you couldn't go back there, though?"

She looked up, disbelieving. "You want me to go back? With you?"

"We each visited Mangel recently, asking about the Synth. Something got him killed. I want to see that unreleased death scene. Maybe if we jogged both our memories, we might figure our why Mangel was killed."

"What if it's because of us?"

"Then we live with it and look for the people who did it."

"People, plural?"

"This is a conspiracy, Temple. There has to be more than one player."

"Creepy. Do you think Professor Mangel was involved?"

"I think he *wasn't* involved, and that's what got him killed. Now." Max pulled some slim, blue-bound volumes from the bag at his feet. "I'm going to skim these books—I happened to borrow the whole of Mangel's reference library on the Synth before I left him yesterday—while you dress up like a UNLV coed as only you can."

"We're going over there now? In broad daylight?"

"Narrow daylight never did a thing for anybody, as far as I know. You will be the front woman, and I will be the inside man, and we'll all be in Scotland afore anyone else with ideas."

"I can't believe you're inviting me along on an . . . operation."

Max laughed. "I haven't got a surgeon's license, love. It's just minor surgery, but I could use a good anesthetist. You don't mind?"

"It's a little scary, but I'd rather be a little scared than left out of your life. Will there ever be an end, Max? You said in New York that maybe you could get clear of your undercover past. Go back to working as a magician. Settle down and marry the magician's assistant. You gave me a ring—"

"Which was promptly taken from you."

"I wish we knew where that nasty magician Shangri-la went to."

"Taking your ring, on stage in plain and public sight, was a threat, a message to me that I wasn't going to be allowed out of the game. Even if my allies wanted to help me, my enemies wouldn't forget. The only way my family has been preserved from retaliation is because I cut off all communication with them years ago. I should have never gotten involved with you."

"But I was irresistible." She tried to joke away the grim reality.

"Yes," he said soberly. "You were. Are. So. I can't do anything but what I've always done: keep on keeping at them. If you can help, maybe we can neutralize them. You're at risk anyway."

"From the IRA?"

"From the extreme wing of the IRA, which never forgets or forgives, like most terrorist organizations, and like Kathleen O'Connor."

"Kitty the Cutter. Why'd she go after Matt when it's you she knew and loathed from northern Ireland?"

"Because she couldn't find me—yet. Because attacking innocent victims is a favorite torment of hers. Because she wanted

me to know no one even remotely connected with me is safe."
He frowned. "Because something about him infuriates her, as I
did."

"And you still can't tell me everything, not even about what
Molina asked you to do, that you feel got an innocent, bystanding
stripper killed."

"There are innocent strippers, you know."

"I know. But there aren't any innocent secret-keepers. That's
why I'm so happy you're letting me help you investigate these webs
of conspiracy. Keeping me safe and stupid isn't going to help our
relationship in the long run."

"I'm glad you foresee a long run. At least I can share everything
I know about this Synth, which I seem to have irritated without
knowing why."

"But you know so little about it," Temple said, exasperated.

"Then we've got a lot of progress to look forward to."

Temple was very glad that she had bought some gunboat-style tennis shoes for surreptitious work. With white anklets and her curly
red hair, she thought she looked like a clown, but she should easily pass for a college undergraduate on any campus around. For
once, looking younger than her age would be an advantage. She
managed to dig out a pair of blue jeans she had once invested in
when she thought she would take up riding. (The horses were too
high and wide for her legs, and ponies were not an option.) She
found the baggiest top she could and a slightly too-chic backpack-
style purse, into which she dumped her trade paperback collection
of computer program how-to books, which were big and thick
enough to simulate textbooks.

"What are you going to go as?" she asked Max when she
emerged from her bedroom as Carrie Coed.

"Aren't you cute enough to take to the corner soda fountain? I
don't have to dress up. I'm most effective when I'm not seen, or
heard."

"I wish I knew where Louie was," Temple commented on the way out to the parking lot.

"Watch out for getting what you wish. Or wishing for what you get. What car shall we take?"

Temple scanned the lot to guess what Max was driving today. She couldn't resist a teensy dig.

"Too bad we can't take Matt's Elvis offering."

Max scanned past Electra's ageing pink Probe and Temple's aqua Storm, even more decrepit, a few Civics and minivans, and finally focused on the sleek silver Bug.

"No. Elvis hasn't gone environmental! Say it ain't so."

"It does have blue suede upholstery," Temple said.

"Devine's not giving up the Vampire for *this*, blue suede interior or not?"

"The Vampire was never his to give up."

Max's eyes, their pleasant natural blue color today, which struck a happy medium between her wimpy blue-gray and Molina's arresting azure, sparkled like something emerald-cut and very expensive. "I hope that applies to other things."

Temple wasn't going to answer that one. If Max *hadn't* returned . . . but alternate realities belonged in science fiction books, and the present never benefitted from trying to second-guess the past. She squinted at the unfamiliar dark gray sedan sitting by itself.

"So. The Nissan Maxima's yours? Somebody up there has a sense of humor."

"Down here, too, I hope?" Max bent to look her in the face. "This will be hard. Mangel loved illusion," he added softly. "He would like the fact that we are penetrating the illusion someone has probably wrapped around his death. He was my greatest fan, because he understood what I did more than anyone. We're not violating his privacy. We're redeeming his life. Yes?"

Temple nodded, too shaky to speak. Death had a face and a voice this time, not just a name. Jeff Mangel was, in a way, her mentor in magic as much as Garry Randolph, the Great Gandolph, had been Max's. Jeff had tutored her out of sheer love of his subject. She regarded Max as he opened the Maxima door for her with as much panache as if it led into a limo.

Actor. Priest. Criminal. The magician was an amalgam of all of these, according to Edmund Wilson as quoted by the late and doubly lamented Professor Jefferson Mangel. Which role controlled Max's dominant hand? Or was there a fourth hand, a fourth role? A good magician always had more hands than seemed possible. And a bad magician . . . ?

Chapter 14

A Date with an Angel

Matt sat on his handsome red couch shuffling tri-folded speaking invitations like oversized playing cards.

Tony Fortunato's motto was: Free TV equals paid live performances, and plenty of both: pay and performance dates. Matt's one brief, not-so-shining hour on the *Amanda Show* had returned tenfold in speech gigs, all of them offering what Matt considered obscenely high honoraria.

They were scattered all over the country and the calendar, a cornucopia of worthy causes that he should be donating to, not taking from.

On the other hand, parishioners had always praised his sermons, and *they* passed the plate, didn't they? But not for him personally.

Matt laughed at himself, then sobered.

Juggling speaking dates was a way of distracting himself from a more troubling date. Last night with Janice.

Matt threw down the letters on his K-Mart cube table. Like

WCOO's phone-in Elvis, he didn't know who to call anymore, and dialing his own show was out.

Thanks to Janice's frankness, Matt had concluded that there was no point in him playing the dating game. He wouldn't learn how to live and love in the millennial world; he'd just discovered that he wasn't up to either.

The lame triangle he endured with Temple and Max was nothing compared to the complications of seeing a divorced-woman-cum-single-parent. Children to consider, not just a big black alley cat, every baby step of the way. And what had happened to the cliché that women were crazy to grab some hapless guy and get married? He had read the statistics that fewer and fewer people under thirty were marrying these days and had tsked absently at what that implied about living together without the bonds of holy matrimony. Bonds! How many centuries had that phrase survived unchallenged? Apparently, today's woman was taking the phrase all too literally and bolting from the fold.

And, Matt thought ruefully, he could see Today's Woman's point.

If "sin" was a word that had been used too long and too often as a lash instead of a guideline, "responsibility" was a word that was all too often lacking from the male vocabulary. Countless well-meaning women like Janice had marched down the aisle and into the burdens of being a primary parent for twenty-years-to-life. Was it any wonder that they were content to let the kids come first? And should it be any other way?

He supposed it was a perfect solution for a lot of unattached guys in their thirties, a relationship without financial or emotional responsibility.

Problem was, like he'd told Temple once, he was sixteen going on thirty-something. He felt he had to do all the things everybody else had tried and got so wrong: find the right woman, marry, and then . . . well, he wasn't ready to confront having kids yet, was he? Not with his abusive past. Would marrying a woman with kids excuse him from the obligation? Not unless he was applying wiggle-worm dogma to the dilemma.

But if you weren't going to put "sin" in the equation, what about "safety"? The survival instinct. Unanchored sexual relationships picked up perils in every port, from STDs to a skewed emotional compass.

Matt was ready to throw up his hands and join a monastery, except they wouldn't have him in this state of indecision.

How did anybody manage a sane life? Maybe no one did.

The phone caroled for attention, and he welcomed the interruption. He had more possible callers nowadays: the radio station, Fortunato, assorted strangers wanting things. He suddenly realized that Temple wasn't the axis of his world, or his worries, anymore.

"It's Molina," the phone said.

And Molina.

"Glad I caught you in," she went on. "I've . . ." A very unMolinalike hesitation occupied empty air waves.

"Anything I can help you with?" he asked.

"As a matter of fact . . . a little thing, and also a big thing."

"Oh?"

"Oh. Listen, I don't have a lot of time, that's why I'm calling."

Matt could tell from the slight distortion in her voice that she was pinching the phone receiver against her shoulder while she talked and shuffled papers with her free hands. Hotline work plus hosting a talk radio show had made him sensitive to every nuance to be wrung out of a phone call.

"I hate to ask you this," she continued. "Ouch! Paper cut." He smiled to have his mental image confirmed so graphically. "This is a lot to ask, Matt, and, believe me, I wouldn't be bothering you if I had any alternative."

He waited.

"Do you, um, . . . what do you know about television?"

"I watch it now and again, but most often I just complain about how little good programming is on."

"Not exactly a minority opinion. I suppose you've never heard of *Babylon Five*, or *Xena*, or *Buffy the Vampire Slayer.*"

"I've seen them. A quick way to keep up with the parish kids, and I prefer unreal programming to so-called reality programming."

"Really?" Molina's voice lifted into a more enthusiastic vocal range. "You like that stuff?"

"As much as anything on TV. But—"

"This is personal," she said quickly. "Purely personal." Her voice lowered, as if making a confession. "I promised Mariah I'd take her to this damn TitaniCon they're holding at the New Millennium. And I'm up to my ID in murder-ones. If you could baby-sit, chaperone, take the kid to this insanity, I'd be so grateful I might even say thank you."

"When?"

"It wouldn't eat into your radio sked. The thing opens Thursday at five P.M. and, of course, she's just gotta be there, then the whole weekend, Friday night on. I don't want her out later than ten P.M. School's on Monday, thank God. I know it's a lot to ask, Matt. I don't even know how much of Mariah you can stand. She's a decent kid, and it'd be good for her to have some adult-male company I can trust. I know it's nuts to ask you, but—"

"Consider it done."

"What?"

"I said, fine. Just tell me where and when to pick her up."

"You can start Thursday afternoon at four, at my place. Dolores will be there. I should be home by ten, then again . . ."

"Crime takes no holiday?"

"Not for my unit lately. Listen, are you sure what this means? From what I hear about this TitaniCon, it will be crawling with weirdos in weirder outfits."

"I used to a wear a pretty weird outfit myself."

"Fun-nee. Oops, I sound like Mariah. I didn't know early adolescence was catching. Well. Thanks. I don't know what you'll hold me up for, for doing this."

He maintained radio silence. He knew that would worry her more than anything else, a suspect who won't talk.

"Do you know how to find my house?"

"I remember."

"Good. I'll leave some money with Dolores. It costs to get in, I understand, and then there's the junky trinkets kids have to buy.

Mariah gets an allowance, so let her spend it, but if she has to, absolutely has to go over, you could spring for it from the kitty."

"Let her have fun, but don't let her overdo it."

"Right." Molina was beginning to sound like she was having second thoughts. "Are you sure you know what spending a weekend with a twelve-year-old is like?"

"No. It should be a growth experience for us both," he said piously.

"You're sounding way too laid-back about this."

"Carmen, calm down. You needed somebody to take Mariah to this con. You've got him. Don't second-guess your luck."

"I must say you're the answer to a mother's prayers. What's up?"

"Would it help if I told you I could use a change of scene, and age group, at the moment?"

"Yeah. Maybe."

"Consider it done."

"All right. I don't have time to argue with your lemming tendencies. Smart of me to ask somebody who had virtually no experience with preteenagers."

Matt hung up, smiling. He understood that a lot of people would run screaming from escorting a kid to a theme park.

Molina couldn't understand what a relief a date with a twelve-year-old would be after what he'd been trying to go through.

Chapter 15

Dance with the Devil

A few trees rimmed the huge campus parking lot, cars claiming all the shady parking slots underneath them.

"Another black car," Temple complained. "Don't your shadow suppliers know that black soaks up rays in this climate?"

"Apparently not." Max parked the Nissan in its place in the sun and turned off the engine, staring out the windshield at the peaceful university scene.

"I can't believe someone killed him on campus," Temple said softly.

"I don't think they had much time." Max got out and scanned the deserted lot.

"Everybody's at class."

"Somebody wasn't yesterday."

Temple nodded. "It's hard to think—"

"Think the unthinkable anyway, and you'll be keeping up with our opponents."

"Our? Opponents?"

"They've probably seen you here. Our."

Temple nodded again, knowing she looked ridiculous in her Courtney Coed gear, like Buffy the Vampire Slayer, or something.

"You know the way to the building," Max said. "Just go up to Mangel's office. I'll get there my way. Don't worry if the door's locked. It won't be for long."

She nodded.

"Operations" required a lot of nodding, she was beginning to see.

She turned, hefted the dangling book bag, and headed for the gently rolling sidewalks that led to formal campus walks and gardens, all lit from above by a relentlessly shining sun.

People were walking toward her, away from her, alongside her.

Not Max. He had vanished the minute she had headed off solo. She knew that, although she knew better than to turn back to verify the notion.

Occasional glances slid over her, and away. They were accepting, dismissing. A couple of guys looked momentarily interested; most didn't.

Older woman, she mentally warned these twenty-something window shoppers. *Don't believe everything you see.*

But this was the automatic, careless attention and ignoring that went on in crowded public places all the time. No one looked suspicious.

She went unchallenged to the communications/performing-arts building and got all the way to the third floor before she slowed down and considered her next course.

A flash of yellow, like the ribbons they put around trees to commemorate victims of sudden crime, caught her eye down the hall.

She guessed it blocked the entrance to Professor Mangel's office and the much larger exhibition area beyond.

CRIME   SCENE   DO   NOT   PASS   CRIME SCENE   DO NOT PASS

Temple read the familiar black type on yellow banding. Yellow journalism.

CRIME   SCENE   DO   NOT   PASS   CRIME

SCENE   DO NOT PASS GO   CRIME SCENE
GO DIRECTLY TO JAIL   CRIME SCENE   CRIME
SEEN   GO DIRECTLY TO JAIL. . . .

Temple took a deep breath. This wasn't just a crime scene. This was Professor Mangel's workplace.

The door behind the tape cracked open a foot. Max stood in the opening. "Duck under."

She slipped through the door, sighed relief when it shut.

"Temple." Max's eyes searched hers, held them. "This is a staged crime scene. A play. A set. Remember that."

"Like at . . . the Guthrie?"

He nodded. "Only you know the absent actor. Don't let them cast him in the wrong play."

His warning disturbed her more than anything about this expedition.

She hardly noticed when he produced a pair of latex gloves to match his own.

"Our prints are probably all over this place," she pointed out.

"But no new ones. Prints don't have expiration dates."

The office they stood in was dark. Max led her through it quickly, circling her wrist in his cool, antiseptic grasp as if taking her pulse.

Unlit, even by daylight, the exhibition area was a shadowland. She glimpsed magicians in the revealed posters. In the dimness, their smiles of prestidigitational triumph morphed into evil grins.

Something was wrong. The display units no longer stood in rectilineal ranks. They curved away, like objects in a concave mirror.

But wasn't it convex mirrors that you put up to catch thieves in the act?

Max took her hand, squeezed tight.

And then she saw that all the straight rows of posters in their aluminum frames had bowed away, like warped wood, into a semicircle.

And in the center of the void their distension had caused lay a vacant circle of vinyl tile.

Only . . . not . . . quite . . . vacant.

Temple couldn't tell if she had suddenly inhaled, or if Max had squeezed her hand so tightly that she couldn't breathe.

Symbols overlay the tile grid, as if superimposed on transparent paper. Vague, alien symbols—part higher math, part primitive brain. Ideographs by an idiot savant. Like some untranslated language. Like cosmic shorthand. Like an obscene scrawl in an inarticulate tongue.

Accent marks touched the glyphs. Accent marks in maroon.

She glanced at Max. "Blood?"

He nodded.

"Not . . . Jeff's?"

He shrugged. "I haven't found anything in the police lab reports yet."

Temple looked up at the surrounding displays, once so innocuous.

The master magicians were all leering at the empty symbols in their midst, demonic gleams in their painted eyes.

"What about the posters?" she asked.

Max nodded. "What about the posters? Do you remember what was there?"

"What . . . *was?*"

"This scene has been staged. I suspect the posters have been manipulated, too, but I don't know how. You're the only one who saw them before I did."

She moved toward them, skirting the ugly marks on the floor. She could understand why the police hadn't released this scene yet. The photographs had to be studied before permission was given to purge the floor.

"I . . . was interested in the Gandolph/Gloria sequence," she remembered, heading for where those had been. "And yours on the other side. Jeff had to show me them, too."

"Well, I'm history," Max said sardonically.

Temple ducked under the displays, one small step for her, one giant lunge for Maxkind.

She should have been paging through a riot of Mystifying Max posters.

There were none.

"A demented fan, no doubt," he commented, unsurprised. "And where do you remember the Gandolph/Gloria sequence being?"

Temple ducked back under.

The poster frames were full, but not a one of Gandolph remained.

"Gandolph's posters aren't anywhere else?" Temple asked.

"I'll look again." Max disappeared down the endless hall of poster doors.

Temple felt herself pulled back to the tattooed floor as if it tilted like a drain into the crude central design drawn in blood-red. The image resembled the outline of a house drawn by a kindergartner: peaked roof, slightly flared sides, slightly bowed bottom. An odd tail of line angled away from the bottom left corner.

She sensed Max coming up behind her and thought out loud. "Five sides: floor, each upright side, and the two lines that meet to make the roof. It's a pentagram!"

"Or a kite on a string," he answered wryly. "This scene's been set up to freak us out. Don't take the props too seriously."

"This one means something. It's too weird not to."

"Impeccable logic, my dear Holmes."

In turning to answer Max, she stumbled against something and backed up, appalled at the idea of disturbing a crime scene.

Then she was even more appalled. The low bench she'd bumped into held a metal bowl and an exotically designed dagger. A pair of entwined thigh-high, black leather, high-heeled boots sagged beside it like a pair of drunken boa constrictors. Black strings from an industrial-strength corset trailed on the floor like dried gouts of blood. A riding crop, a black metal collar and mask . . .

"Props," Max said behind her. "Remember what I said about a staged scene."

"This is S&M paraphernalia."

"Remind me to ask how you know."

"Is it meant to look like a ritual sex murder—?"

"Interesting question. Do you think the police are smart enough to ask it?"

"No. Max, not Mangel. Never Mangel. He was innocent as a boy with a new magic set, and at the same time a very wise man. Do you know . . . how he died?"

"It wasn't pleasant."

"All for a staged scene."

"These are not amateurs. Amateurs would have enjoyed their depravity more. More scattered blood stains. More props. This is just enough. It's disturbing that the posters have been removed. I was afraid of that."

"*That's* disturbing? I would say murdering Professor Mangel, wrecking his reputation is a lot more disturbing."

"That, however horrific, doesn't involve us. The posters do."

"Us?"

"Us."

"Then maybe there's a message there for us. If only we could get copies of Molina's crime-scene pix."

She heard a tsk. Looked. Max brandished a black something the size of a mascara wand. It clicked again, so softly that it sounded like a tsk.

"Smile," he said, focusing on her surprised face. "You're on Candid Crime-Scene Camera."

Chapter 16

Close Encounters

It helps to think of Las Vegas as one big block party and costume party combined.

There is a hotel-casino for every theme, scheme, and dream on this planet.

As a dude-about-town, I am used to seeing parking valets in kilts, croupiers in togas, and glamorous little dolls in all sorts of getups, ranging from little to nothing. I was on hand for the Elvis impersonators, the strippers, and the romance-novel cover hunks, after all.

But I have never seen the likes of the wardrobe and makeup for this gig.

Some of it is pretty familiar—familiar to anyone who has ever cruised the multichannel reaches of a television remote-control device.

I wander unnoticed in this hullabaloo of human and inhuman species and all their works. Most of those works are in the process of being set up for the weekend show.

So it is that I am able to weave among beings both once and future, from ancient heroes like Hercules and his friends the satyrs, nymphs, and gods to cyborg conglomerations of man, woman, and machine. You notice they almost never try to mind-meld we furred Earth mammals with all those metal and microchip enhancements.

Obviously, we are the superior species. We are not always trying to tamper with our genes. It would be amusing to imagine Commander Data of *Star Trek: The Next Generation* as the puny-sized pet and his cat, Spot, as a giant, computer-enhanced master.

See Data run. See Spot run. See Spot licking his circuitry. See Data run out of data.

I fear this environment encourages flights of fancy, and I am surprised at myself for indulging in such pursuits.

I am still trying to figure out how the vagrant Khatlord lookalike ended up out of his element and high enough to take a fatal blow of some kind. While work crews bustle high above and deep beneath this temporary space-station-cum-time-machine, most of the costumed players keep their feet, or pods, or tentacles pretty tightly on terra firma.

I must admit that my crime-fighting instincts have been lulled by the aura of familiarity surrounding most of the people and props that are being assembled here for the weekend TitaniCon.

It is amusing to rub shins with some of the most feared beings of the farthest reaches of outer space. The Borg, for instance, are olefactorily irresistible to my sensitive sniffer. Those leather leg braces are more chewable than Tums for the tummy. Not to say that Hercules and his brethren and cistern with their sandals leather-laced to the knee are less addictive.

There is something about the smell of natural hide that brings out my most primitive hunting instincts. These are not the higher-level intuitions that serve me in my investigative capacity. These are raw, racial memories. My kind have always been closet leather-and-feather freaks.

Feathers, however, are not in high supply here. Not as revered as they are at the Rio Hotel-Casino, which has a Mardi Gras bent.

So imagine my surprise to stumble across another cage, this one of a much smaller variety than the great Uthrellian Llonx's accommodations, sitting ignored on the floor near a pile of rich fabrics and alien hand devices. (See what I mean about past and future meeting?)

There are, in fact, several cages clustered together, each half-filled with greenery.

This is the first evidence I have seen of anything vegetable, so I draw near and try to figure out why anyone would keep plants in cages, unless these are carnivorous Venus fly-trap plants, which these are not.

There are other breeds of carnivorous plants, I have heard tell, but these before me look an innocuous sort. I go so far as to thrust my whiskered mug between the wires to sniff out what's odd about this arrangement.

Imagine what I think when the plants sniff back. In fact, they snuffle, which is much louder than a sniff, and far less refined.

I hunker down. I am not leaving this vicinity until I know what is what here. At least the light is dim, and the noise. In fact, there is a tarpaulin stretched over the entire cage assembly.

My rear member twitches with interest, which it is seldom wont to do in the presence of mere plant life. I sit as motionless as rock. I wait.

Soon I am rewarded.

A creature comes strolling out from the vegetation.

Like all things great and small on this scene, it is one weird bird.

Picture a fuzzy Nerf ball on a tripod. Color it green. Then

set two of the tripod legs walking and the third stabbing. There you have it. Tribbles on stilts, except these don't chirp. They snuffle. And I do mean "they," for in the adjoining cages, others of like ilk have come stuttering out from the foliage on their stick legs. I recall the Tribbles from the classic *Trek* script, fuzzballs without locomotion. These have plenty of locomotion, thanks to those toothpick gams.

They are supremely indifferent to my presence. Their needlelike noses begin to dig about in the box of loose soil that makes up the unforested half of the cages.

Some are the size of your average chicken, before Colonel Sanders. Some are smaller. I look for any telltale mechanisms, unable to decide if their outer covering is hair, bristle, or feather. Perhaps a coconut was alien-abducted to the Kohl Kompendium and forced to propagate with a radiator brush.

One of these strange birds brushes against the cage grille. My whiskers contact its outer tendrils. Gross! I have just crossed vibrissae with feathers so fine that each one resembles a hair more than a quill.

This close encounter stirs the natives. The brushee freezes in place, then lets loose an eerie wail: *"keewee kee-wee keewee."*

Well, *wee* on your own time, buddy. Or buddette. Telling the gender of these walking fungus-coated cheese balls would be a job for a team of NASA scientists.

Another cry goes up: *"Khat-khat khat-khat."*

Guess they have heard of me. The littlest ones vanish into the underbrush. The bigger ones shrink away from the cage sides but stay put.

A larger bird with a particularly punk spiked haircut swaggers over to me.

"Get outa here, mate," it cheeps in a falsetto so I can't tell if it is a him or a her.

Either way, I am not its mate, and I say so.

There is a general mocking squalling. Apparently I have

amused Team Tennis ball. (I am thinking of the Day-glo yellow-green kind, which is a pretty close color match to these babies.)

"You are khat," the gutsy critter spits out. "Enemy."

"That may be so where you come from, but I am retired from the predatory life here. I have a keeper who feeds me. I do not need to eat rug fuzz."

They mull this over. Perhaps the caged life has eased their ethnic hatred, for the head bird bobs over and extends its long beak through the grille to thrust it into my chest hair.

I hold utterly still. It is necessary to allow ignorant natives their primitive get-acquainted rituals. But it is hard to keep quiet when I realize that their obnoxious sniffing organs are at the end of their beaks instead of up against their faces where all civilized critters keep them.

Snuffle, snuffle, in the rich ruff of my neck fur. The cost of knowledge is high. I will never watch another *National Geographic* special without a shiver of distaste.

My contact withdraws its probe and impales its blade in the filthy soil inside the cage, satisfied that I am not imminently dangerous.

"What are you doing here?" I ask.

"We are visiting stars."

Un huh.

"From what solar system?" I inquire politely. You and your Aunt Mercedes.

Their beady little eyes blink in concert. "We are from the same planet as you, unfortunately," says the spokesthing. I would not be so bold as to guess gender, if any.

"You are a warlike breed," it goes on with a superior sniff, "and too immature to advance very far beyond your own paltry planet, thank Tane Mahuta."

Right. I have heard this party line before. Carnivores are too violent to deserve to live. It is a sentiment usually uttered by herbivores.

Except that I spot a Tribble-lodite gobbling something

long and wiggling that its nose has sucked up from the soil. This is the same old story: Our prey is okay; your prey is no way.

"Are you Irish?" I ask, nodding at the mossy color of their whatever.

A species-wide sigh.

"The costume department deemed our brown garb too dull to photograph well. We have been dyed."

Oh, now I get it. These are a bunch of Easter chicklets. Well, they are not any worse than a pink poodle.

"Quite a bilious green," I comment sympathetically. "I prefer primary colors myself. Like black."

There is a general stabbing of noses into the ground.

"We know," grinds out a critter from a distant cage. "It is the price of stardom."

"Stardom! Why did you not say so in the first place? You are not stars, literally. You are *guest* stars."

"That is right," the chief Tribblestick says.

"And where do you guest from?"

They exchange nary a glance. That is when I tumble to the fact that they are pretty much blind. Then they all chirp at once.

"A land of mountains and valleys."

"A land of water and desert."

"A land of smoke and cloud."

"A land of safety and danger."

"New Jersey?" I hazard.

"New Zealand," my main source screams.

The rest duck back into the greenery at its boldness.

"There is a round, brown, fuzzy product of New Zealand," I ruminate.

"Kiwifruit," it says.

"Right. Green inside, like you guys are green outside, but artificially so. Are you intelligent fruit? That is a new wrinkle in alien species. I must say that I am impressed, and you have nothing to fear from me. I never eat fruit."

"We are not fruit! We are kiwi bird. We are mascots of an entire nation. That is more than khat can say."

So, rub it in! Now at least I have confirmed from their own lips . . . beaks that these are birds. I sit up to study them. No tail, no wings. Just fuzz, feet, and nose. These guys could give Ugly Ducklings a bad name.

But I must admit that I admire their spunk. I admire it even more when their leader tells me that, aside from colonies of thirty-five thousand North Island Brown Kiwi and ten thousand Great Spotted Kiwi, there are only a few hundred of the other three family lines surviving on this remote moonscape called New Zealand. Apparently, this Tane Mahuta, who must be the kiwi version of my kind's big kahuna, Bastet, has not been doing a good job of preserving the chosen species.

Since my particular color of cat lost millions to chromatic cleansing a few centuries back and is endangered to this day, I can sympathize with these odd ducks, once I get past their chronic sinus condition.

"So. What kind of roles do you get in these science fiction epics? Is there any future in it?"

"We are mostly walk-ons," a North Island Brown pipes up from a far cage. "Some of us wear these chorus-girl head-dresses."

"We get a hot-pink marabou boa around our necks," my main kiwi grumbles.

"Tell me about it," I retort. "Wait until they make you wear a flamingo fedora."

They groan, and snuffle, in chorus. I think I have won my audience.

"So who do you see of a suspicious nature wandering about?"

"Besides you?"

"Present company excepted, of course."

They pick at their plates, i.e., stab their noses into the worm-rich dirt, then my source answers. "There is one of your kind, but very unkind."

I am not sure if this strange khat is not very catlike, or if it is just plain mean. So I wait. Silence encourages information dumps.

"Keewee, keewee, keewee," the others agree in chorus.

My ears hurt, but I manage not to flatten them impolitely. Dealing with alien species requires exquisite diplomacy.

"It comes," the spokeskiwi says. "And sits like you outside our quarters. We hear its humming."

"Purring," I clarify.

"Humming. It lets us know it waits."

"And you have no description, of course?"

"Only that it is khat, and not pleased. It watches us, and we hear the faint snick of its claws as they flash in and out."

I nod, though they cannot see the gesture. Not only khat waits, I think. I, too, sense the quick in-and-out of a lethal blade even as this carnival of preparation unwinds.

Only it is not an inbred weapon but an acquired one.

"Keewee, Keewee," cries my informant.

You got that right, mate.

Unfortunately, it is precisely my self-appointed job to look up this nail-snicking loiterer.

At least now I know where to ambush it.

My new friends, the Kiwi Nation, are not much fun to watch. Whenever anybody passes, they dive back into the shrubs and vanish.

Of course I cannot blame them. I have never seen such a parade of exotic footwear going by in my life, and I am the roommate of Miss Temple Barr, mind you, an Imelda-Marcos-in-training when it comes to collecting fancy footwear.

Since I am of an analytical nature, I play a game with myself as I lie there waiting for the Godot of the feline world.

A lot of boots go marching by. I call them the Bootbottoms. Some are your ordinary engineer boots, motorcycle boots, combat boots. You know, the casual daytime footwear of the usual urban wuss. There are a bunch of tennis shoes, the new inflated models that look like Goodyear blimps. Even my Miss Temple owns one pair of these pale behemoths.

It is the other shoe fashions that really snag my attention. A lot of them are boots too: some have four-to-six-inch platform soles attached to stretchy knee-highs. *Fee fi foe fum,* I hum to myself as these giant's thumpers go by. I suppose I could get a lift in stature by walking on my extended shivs, except that would compromise my macho swagger. I cannot believe what lengths humans will go to achieve a few extra centimeters of height. Makes me glad to get around on all fours and not suffer from a chronic sense of vertical challenge, like my poor petite Miss Temple or these mighty men and women thundering around on foot-bound falsies.

Then there are a variety of booted, high-rise heels you see a lot of in Las Vegas. These are the thigh-high leather numbers with stilettos of four, five, and even six inches. It is usually dames you find mincing around in these arch-fracturers, and usually dames of a naughty nature. I watch a few of these ankle by.

Then there is the bedroom-slipper brigade. I call them the Softshoes. I do not mean that these folks literally wear bedroom slippers, but their footwear is soft, low, and floppy, ever an excellent choice for sneaking around in. Here they emulate my own time-tested model: dark, leather sole with fur, leather or felt uppers. I notice that the wearers of these shoes sport garb in keeping with their bottom line—cloaks, long loose robes, tunics and tights. When I peer upward to see their faces, I often spot a stuffed dragon on their shoulders. Must be some kind of arcane epaulette.

Then there are the desert rats. Not that they are rats; I have not met them yet to know. But their attire bespeaks hot, arid climates much like Las Vegas. And, in fact, many of them resemble Las Vegas parking valets, particularly from the Luxor, the Oasis, and the Goliath.

These are the Sandalfeet race. Most of the sandal soles are cork or some semisoft material, although some are studded with large, false jewels. Where the Sandalfeet distinguish themselves is in the length, crossing pattern, and substance of the thongs that tie them on. Most laces lattice the lower leg (climbing higher than you have to go to pick a peck of pickled peppers). These thong knee-highs are most favored by the guy Sandalfeet. The girl Sandalfeet tend to wear gold and silver and bronze leather laces that end somewhere above the ankle, although I see a few female Sandalfeet clomping around in studded leather braces like the dudes.

There you have it: a veritable universe of ugly footwear. I have looked upon more bunions, warts, and calluses than I hope to see in the rest of my nine lives.

And still I have not spotted one furred female who likes to go barefoot, except for a gloss of crimson nail enamel on her impeccably sharp shivs.

Chapter 17

Murder by Magic

Temple had a strange, superstitious notion.

She rarely had superstitious notions, so she listened to this one: On no account should Max have anything to do with Lieutenant C. R. Molina.

The last time figurative east met west, Max had become involved in the death of a pathetic young stripper. He already had enough lost causes to chase. Cher was one too many.

So Temple tossed a coin for the privilege of being the one to con information on the Mangel killing out of Molina. For the first time in years, she won something.

"Heads, heads, heads," she chortled, pocketing the tossed quarter as a partial reward.

"I could have fixed it, you know," Max pointed out.

"Start cheating your significant other, and where do you have to go?"

"True." He grinned at her. "At least I don't have to worry about *you* wringing the lieutenant's neck."

"Can't. My hands aren't big enough."

"You could use a garrote, like the killer of Gloria Fuentes and company."

"A garrote is too good for her."

"That's the spirit."

While they were whipping up Temple's battle spirit, the phone rang. She dove for and got the phone off the hook first. Magicians always had to demonstrate that the hand is quicker than the eye, as Max continued to prove.

"Max, not now—!" Temple was laughing as she said "hello."

The laughter stopped.

"Yes?" she said, very originally. "No! Yee-ess . . . It's all right."

She hung up.

"Wrong number?" Max inquired.

"Right party. Molina wants to see *me* downtown about the Mangel murder."

"Don't look so pleased with yourself. You're probably a suspect."

"Even better. She'll never suspect that I'm interrogating *her.*"

"Don't count on it. Damn, I wish I could be there! Duel of the Titans."

"Thanks for the flattery."

"I could wire you."

"I don't think we need to hang on every word she utters. Besides, they might have some detector that would get me in trouble."

"No. Police departments never expect to be investigated, except by their own internal affairs divisions."

" 'Never' is often a famous last word. I'll make notes of the conversation as soon as I get back in the car, okay?"

Max nodded, but Temple could tell that if he had wings, he would be a fly on the headquarters wall for the next couple hours.

* * *

Temple crossed her fingers while she cruised the Storm around downtown. Now that the Fremont Street Experience had roofed the area to provide sound and light shows, some streets were blocked off. Since police headquarters was practically on top of all the downtown action, near the El Cortez, it almost seemed on the tourist route nowadays, especially with the huge half-silo-shaped building in front of it that featured a Picassoesque assemblage of wall sculptures.

Because the building was one of those new-old kind that offered a bland modernism no matter the decade, it wasn't a particularly intimidating place to enter. The desk sergeant noted Temple's name and someone soon came down to escort her up.

At least this someone was her size, an Asian pixie in a khaki pantsuit.

"Detective Su," she introduced herself. *Sue? Or Sue you?*

Temple was surprised to see an extended hand, but the following handshake wasn't the usual hospitable kind. The detective's long, sharp fingernails almost gave her own nails a cuticle trim. It was like shaking hands with a Swiss Army knife or a cat in full claw extension.

Maybe that was how such a petite policewoman impressed people with her danger potential.

They maintained silence in the small elevator car up to the third floor, and until Detective Su knocked on Molina's open ash-blond door and left Temple to her fate.

"Come in." Molina didn't even look up from the folders on her desks.

Temple's modest pump heels suddenly sounded like a woodpecker's raps on the vinyl tile floor. She sat on the institutional side chair and let her feet swing like a school kid's. She always hated having to perch at the edge of chair seats merely to keep her feet in touch with the floor.

"Do you know why you're here?" Molina asked, still shuffling and sticking Post-it notes on forms.

"Professor Mangel's death, you said."

"Murder." The lieutenant looked up. She used her surprisingly intense blue eyes as a kind of laser searchlight, but this time Temple was more surprised by the dark circles that surrounded them like eyeshadow gone wrong.

The lieutenant didn't use eyeshadow and barely any lipgloss.

"Your name was on his desk calendar. What was that about?"

"I went to the university to see his magic exhibition."

"Alone?"

"Alone. I'm allowed."

"Don't get touchy. This is a very serious case. Why were you so interested in his exhibition? As I understand it, it was more of a pet project than anything official."

"I met Professor Mangel when I was dealing with that Halloween séance stunt with all the psychics. He was a fascinating source on the intersection of magic, psychology, and parapsychology. I was particularly interested in seeing his collection of ephemera, and I did see it. That's all."

"Ephemera. The assorted paper collectibles our media-driven society churns out like toilet paper. What sort of 'ephemera' did the professor have?"

"You haven't seen the museum?"

"I've seen photos. I've read reports. I've got a few thousand more things to do than race to the scene of every crime your footprints are all over."

"A visit a couple weeks ago is hardly footprints."

"What did you think of Mangel?" Molina asked abruptly.

"He was the typical academic when you first met him. A little pompous but with a kiddish enthusiasm peeping through. Amusing and philosophical, and unusually open-minded. I liked him, more than I realized, because when I heard that he was dead—" Temple was surprised to find that she had gone as far as she could without getting maudlin.

It seemed a poor excuse for an epitaph, but Molina zeroed in on the one opening it offered. "*Heard* he was dead?"

"I didn't see the item in the paper. A friend called."

"What friend knew about your acquaintance with Mangel?"

"Electra Lark. My landlady."

"Why didn't you say 'my landlady' in the first place?"

"Because she's more of a friend than a landlady, but I thought you'd remember her best as my landlady. As far as I know, you don't know who all my friends are." Nothing like a little righteous indignation when you are caught lying.

"And would you have considered Jefferson Mangel one of them?"

" 'Acquaintance' is the better word."

"How did Ms. Lark know you were acquainted with Mangel?"

"She went along with me on a lot of the séance events."

Molina seemed unimpressed, but that was her usual demeanor. Unimpressed people, especially police people, heard all sorts of overkill babbling from nervous interviewees. Temple did not intend to be a nervous interviewee, which was hard, given that only twenty-four hours ago she had been trespassing on the very crime scene in question.

"Well," Molina finally said, reluctantly, "I'll go along with your story of hearing about Mangel's death from your sidekick landlady. For now." She moved her files around as if each one was a painting that needed arranging. "I'm going to show you a close-up of the body." The eyes looked up to aim a particularly acid beam of blue into Temple's gaze.

It felt like getting a glaucoma test at the optometrist's: You know something invisible is going to press on your eyeball, and all you can do is hold still and take it. And don't blink!

"Since you claim to have some friendly feeling for the deceased, this could be unpleasant."

Temple winced in preparation. The color photo shocked her. All the ones on TV were black-and-white. This looked like a particularly badly composed snapshot. She hadn't expected the bare chest, or the awful, gaping cuts drawn across the torso. The thick, exotic hilt protruding from the center of the photo seemed the least appalling detail.

"The incisions were perimortem, made during or after death. There's some scribing on the skin of the stomach. Either a hesitation surface cut, which is unlikely, or a deliberate marking. It could be the letter S. Do the design of the knife hilt or the letter S mean anything to you?"

Temple had to turn her head away, regarding the photo askance. "It looks like a stage prop," she said of the knife hilt. "So big and exotic."

"I assure you the knife was not a stage prop. It was a seven-inch blade sharp enough to rend flesh all the way past the muscle like a surgeon's scalpel."

"This is awful." Temple knew then that she had to tell Molina everything she and Max had discovered at the death scene, without actually telling her, of course. "The knife looks like something Macbeth would carry."

"Primitive, you mean?"

"Or like a stage prop."

"Stage props don't have intricate metal hilts and surgically sharp blades, do they? I hope not, anyway."

"No, that's true. They look lethal, but often the hilts are just Masonite wrapped in leather, and the blades are poured-plastic metallic stuff."

"Wood and plastic. Mangel would be getting abrasions treated in some emergency room now instead of getting autopsied at the ME's. You remember our friend Grizzly Bahr?"

Temple nodded soberly, wondering how to bring up the Synth without involving Max. She spun the photo back to face Molina, who regarded it consideringly.

"With a knife this large and sharp," she mused with almost hypnotic concentration, "making these mutilations would have been as easy as running a table knife through a room-temperature butter stick."

Why *do law enforcement types always resort to food metaphors?* Temple wondered.

"I can't believe it," she said. "Not only killed, but so viciously. He wasn't the kind of guy to evoke rage in anyone."

"We don't think this"—Molina's forefinger rapped the photographed hilt, making Temple tense, as if the gesture alone could drive that awful weapon in farther—"was a rage killing. It was a staged killing."

" 'Staged?' " Temple tried to sound ignorant.

"Certain killers have agendas. Oh, there may be anger under it, but usually another purpose. These attacks on the body, the entire environment in which the corpse was found, reek of occult, or cult, if you will, symbols and violence." She fixed Temple with a stern look. "This is no time to get coy about what you know or don't know, or even suspect. A lot of evidence at the crime scene was pretty S & M. Just how kinky can magic acts get?"

"That's dark magick, with a 'ck.' Stage magic is something else altogether."

"Let me see, people vanishing and appearing in caskets, women apparently being skewered with swords and cut in half while living, handcuffs, bondage, being chained and immersed in closed water tanks . . . seems to me like all that's ripe for memorialization at the Madame Toussaud's Wax Museum at the new Venetian Hotel."

"Props of danger and death. I wish Professor Mangel were here to explain it to you. Magic has a lot of symbolism about death and rebirth, not much different from religious rites, really. But always, no matter the metaphysics of the psychology, entertainment is the issue in magic."

"So much of entertainment today walks that razor's edge between danger and sadism. Young people are especially vulnerable. I don't like what we saw at that death scene. This was on a university campus, after all. If you think it unlikely that the professor headed up some sick cult—" She paused for Temple's visceral reaction.

"I don't think so! He saw the whole picture too well to dramatize magic. That was just an innocent collection of magical memorabilia. Although . . ."

"Yes?"

"That was where I saw the posters of Gloria Fuentes, the woman who was killed in the church parking lot."

"The former magician's assistant." Molina started shuffling folders and pounced on one.

Temple blanched when she saw it was fat with photos as well as paperwork.

"One Gandolph the Great. You ever hear of him?" Molina asked.

"Only when I saw Professor Mangel's poster collection." Temple followed her blatant lie with a helpful hint. "He had a lot of posters of Gandolph and Gloria's act, from back in the sixties."

"He have posters of anybody else's act?"

"You mean—?"

"You know perfectly well what and who I mean."

"There were . . . several of Max. On the other side of the row. Professor Mangel was a fan."

But Molina wasn't interested in the late professor's good opinion of magicians. She was frowning and rocking her pencil in her fingers so the eraser thump-thump-thumped on the glass desktop. "Several of Kinsella. I asked especially. The detectives on the scene said there were no posters of a 'Mystifying Max' among the display panels."

Temple sat forward, acting indignant, but feeling triumphant. "But there were! Two weeks ago. I saw them."

"I suppose you would remember that accurately," Molina noted sardonically. "I suppose we can consider you an expert witness in that regard." Another thought struck. "Did you tell the magician in question? This town was stripped of representations of him at the time of his disappearance last year. Did he remove those surviving examples? And . . . interesting thought . . . did he also remove the collector? Who better could stage a cult murder than a magician?"

Temple's heart rate outpaced Molina's rapidly thumped pencil. She'd only meant to point out that posters were missing from Mangel's collection, not to nail Max for the crime.

"Um . . . if Max's posters are missing, you'd better check on those other ones I saw of Gandolph and Gloria. I mean, they're both dead, and those are the only likenesses of Gloria, at least as far as anybody knows. She hadn't performed in years. Maybe the murderer was some berserk collector."

"Overkill for posters?" Molina sighed and dropped her pencil to the glass with a ping. "I suppose it's possible. Mangel must have had some listing of his collection. I'll get the forensic computer geeks over there."

"Forensic computer geeks?"

"It's a brave new world, Ms. Barr. Okay, you can go."

"Go?"

"Go!"

Temple stood up, surprised to feel her heels wobbling a little under her.

"There's a link between you and the magician Gandolph and the late Gloria Fuentes. I know there is." Molina gazed at her with a weary certainty. "I have evidence that there is. And when I find a few more connections . . . well, I guess I can't say, sleep tight." She smiled.

Temple did not smile back.

She just left.

Chapter 18

48 Hours

Matt's second date in forty-eight hours was off to an inauspicious start.

Dolores glowered at him through the crack in Molina's front door. The narrow view emphasized, unfortunately, the slight mustache that darkened her upper lip.

Matt felt like the prince confronting the troll.

"Missus said you would come. Name?"

He realized her shortness of speech reflected English as a late-in-life language, not ill temper.

"Matt Devine. I'm supposed to escort Mariah to the TitaniCon at the New Millennium."

Dolores snorted. "TitaniCon. Millennium. Much . . ." She gave up and turned into the darkened house. "Mariah!"

When there was no answer, she reluctantly opened the door to admit him.

Matt had never entered by the front door. It made the place look foreign.

Then two brown bolts of cold lightning streaked across the floorboards, the young cats adopted during the animal blessing at Our Lady of Guadalupe last fall.

"Ah!" Dolores closed and locked the door after him, then vanished down the hall, calling for Mariah.

It was the classic scenario: How long would the young lady keep him waiting? Matt's eyes moved toward the kitchen and the garage entrance he was more familiar with, if a couple of spur-of-the-moment visits could be called 'familiarity.' "

No sign of Mama. She'd sounded pretty harried when she'd phoned to ask him to play substitute parent.

Mariah came dragging down the hall, Dolores shooing the child before her like a chicken.

Primping was not what the kid had been doing. Matt smiled to see the preadolescent uniform in full bloom, a dual gender nonfashion statement: baggy long shorts (longer than what used to be called Bermuda shorts), baggy oversized T-shirt, a fanny pack slug around the mysterious middle, cartoon sneakers with air-cushioned goiters of sole and uppers (looking like clown cars from a circus). The lady shouldn't have put herself out for him.

"Hi," he said.

She rolled her eyes. She was too, too bored by this.

"You remember me," he prompted.

"You came over, and before that, you were at the animal blessing, with that big black cat."

"And we had dinner at the pizza place not too long ago."

Mariah nodded sluggishly.

Despite the sloppy, asexual uniform, Matt noticed that she seemed taller and more stooped at the same time. She must have figured out the taller part, too. He remembered and missed the thick shiny braid down her back he had first seen her wearing months ago. Today's more grown-up chin-length bob fell forward on her face, hiding it. The best undercover agents in the world were preteens.

"I'm not authorized to take the cats," he noted as they dashed through again.

A splinter of smile revealed the glint of braces.

"I'm hoping," he said, "you can explain this TitaniCon to me. I've never been to a 'con' before."

"Really?" She perked up at the admission. Kids ache to be experts on something. "I haven't either, but I've heard all about it from the kids at school, and it's no big deal. I mean, it is. All the cool people in the world will be there, but, you know, it's no big deal."

"Good," he said, nodding. "Thanks, Dolores," he told the hovering housekeeper/baby-sitter.

"Ten o'clock," she growled, a bad-tempered fairy godmother on a much tighter schedule than Cinderella's model.

Matt ostentatiously checked his wristwatch. "Synchronize watches. Ten it is."

Mariah giggled and glanced back at Dolores as they strolled down the front walk. "Dolores doesn't have a watch. You can't synchronize anything."

"There's a watch somewhere. Don't you have a watch?"

She giggled again. "No, but I have all my allowance money with me."

"So do I," Matt confided.

Mariah regarded him sharply. "You don't have an allowance. You're a grown-up."

He bent down to whisper, "I'm not as grown-up as you think."

She didn't know how to take that, so she stopped cold to stare at the Volkswagen. "That's a funny-looking car."

"Well, yeah. But you have to consider that it was given to me by Elvis Presley."

"Elvis who?"

"Presley. The King of Rock 'n' Roll."

"He's not like, like Hansen?"

"He's like a one-man Hansen. Only he's dead."

"Then how did he give you a car?"

"Well, that's the question."

She allowed him to open the door for her, more because she didn't know how to work the handle than that she expected any male/female courtesy rituals. She was only twelve-going-on-thirteen, after all.

"This seat stuff is funny. It sticks to the backs of my knees."

"It's suede."

"Isn't that for jackets?"

"This is custom-made for cars."

"Oh." She stroked the navy upholstery as if it were a cat. "My mom would have taken me except she had to work."

"I know."

"Don't you have to work?"

"Yes, but I'm on a night shift."

"Don't you get tired working late like that?"

"Yes, but if I get you home by ten tonight I'll be all right." He didn't mention that his "workday" began at midnight and ended at one A.M., too strange a concept for a kid with an overtime-working parent. Even Matt couldn't quite grasp earning a year's salary for working five hours a week. Surely it was a sin.

Mariah nodded about his own deadline to get home. She now saw her curfew as a favor for a poor wage-slave. "I have to get up for school at six-thirty."

"That's early. I have to get up at eleven."

"In the morning? I'd like your job."

"Let's hope you won't have to get one for a while."

"Jobs take a lot of time."

"That they do."

"My mom is always working overtime."

"She has a very important job."

Mariah frowned. "Does this car have a radio."

Matt turned it on.

"Does it have seventy-eight-point-five?"

He adjusted the dial. Some frenetic postrap music oozed into the new-smelling car like the rotten odor of chaos.

Mariah nodded to the "music" uncertainly. This was cool in her set. Gotta listen.

So did Matt, unfortunately.

Chapter 19

Icy Fingers

Naturally, I cannot resist returning to the scene of the crime.

I certainly cannot attribute my presence at TitaniCon to a taste for kiwi.

When I returned home last night, I was tired, I admit. And hungry. And more than a bit disappointed that my quarry did not show. What can I say? Like many stressed-out survivors at the start of the twenty-first century, I turn for comfort to the food bowl.

Unfortunately, my food bowl is akin to a shoe. (Yes, I do have footwear on the brain from so much fruitless watching of same.) The sole is a hard-packed layer of Free-to-Be-Feline pellets that have been settling since the last Millennium. The uppers are what is interesting, but Miss Temple has been derelict about ladling the uppers on lately (like shrimp, oysters, sardines, anchovies, and other gourmet seafood delights).

I remember her mentioning "kiwi" now and again, and I believe she keeps this delicacy on the kitchen counter. This is good. I am not able to break into the refrigerator, from whence many of my treats spring, as its door is heavier than the one on a bank safe.

But a countertop raid is no sweat. (Not that I am subject to that disgusting human process. I would rather pant than perspire.)

I leap with one bound to the counter. Now to find my prey. I sniff along the surface, which Miss Temple keeps pretty well wiped down and free of interesting odors.

All I find up there is a roll of paper towels, a pile of unpaid bills, a toaster, and a basket.

Since the basket is filled with balls, it bears investigation. If I cannot eat, I might as well think about getting some exercise to work up an appetite for when Miss Temple comes home.

I do not see colors particularly well, but better than some people think. I recognize the dark balls as tomatoes. They smell both sweet and medicinal, nothing that would interest my discerning palate. I do not do sweet, and I definitely do not do medicinal, as Dr. Doolittle, the vet, can testify.

Then there is the paler ball with the bad case of acne scars, called an orange. I spy one long, very pale shape that I know some pal would like to monkey around with, but not me.

All that is left is a hairy brown ball. Now hairy does something for the old saliva glands. My ancient hunting instincts kick in. This must be the elusive kiwi. Nice of the species to present a neat package for opening. I feel a twinge of guilt for hunting where I have befriended, but these truces between prey and predator are always at the predator's whimsey.

Right now my whimsy says that my stomach would like a nice, fresh kiwi egg for dinner. The kiwi is a bird. I think. And birds have eggs.

So I roll my selected snack out of the basket, set it up before me as if it were a golf ball and I were Tiger Woods. Then, chomp! I pounce, bite, crunch.

The skin/shell/what-you-will gives like thin ice. My fangs dig deep into the soft flesh beneath.

Yeacharghhh! A sweet, thick liquid assaults my mouth, my nose, my very mind.

What alien growth have I been tricked into tasting? As I rear back in disgust, my game color sense tags the awful insides as a deep green color. I have eaten ichor. I do not know what ichor is, except it seems to be the stuff in fine foreign art films like *The Green Slime.* A lot of that cast ended up dead, and I can see why.

I roll around the countertop in anxiety and agony, trying to wash my mouth out with a wad of a paper towel. My rear toenails catch in the paper towels, and soon the whole role is unraveling, wrapping me up in its quilted, absorbent coils.

This is a nightmare!

Then the kitchen light crackles into life above me, looking like an alien vessel about to land amid my titanic struggle with the engulfing, tape-worm-pale coils of paper towel.

"Louie! What are you doing? You're ruining the place. Stop that right now."

What can I say, bound and gagging as I am?

I allow Miss Temple to berate me merely for being curious. I can tell you one thing. I am cured for life. I will never be tempted to sample a rare kiwi bird, which is just as well, as they are an endangered species.

Speaking of which, I roll up into a ball and wonder when Miss Temple will start feeling guilty about admonishing me and feed me something edible. I may have a long wait.

Indeed I did, which was why I slipped back to the New Millennium the very next day.

Some gratitude I get: I risk life, limb, and lymph system to investigate a connection to the deadly events of last month, and all I get is some À La Cat dribbled over my stale Free-to-Be-Feline.

Luckily, I have learned if I present myself, mewling piteously, at Miss Electra Lark's door, I can often reap an assortment of bad-for-you goodies from her stockpile.

It is even worth risking her cat Karma's wrath. Although that psychic sob sister is likely to send me bad dreams for a week after each meal I cadge.

Anyway, I do not let a lack of appreciation stifle my investigative instincts. The she-evil feline we met a few cases back is definitely hanging around this TitaniCon, according to the photo I saw in the paper, and I will find out why or know the reason why. Huh? Sometimes my mind races ahead of my feet. The fact is, as much as I respect and even fear the Sinister Hyacinth, I am also strangely eager to see her again. Perhaps I just wish her to know that she is not fooling Midnight Louie.

I return to the New Millennium at midday. Both chastened and inspired by my culinary adventure on Miss Temple's countertop, I make a dignified, feet-on-the-ground surreptitious entry through the hotel's food service door, hiding under a stainless-steel cart. Back in TitaniCon territory in short order, I take up my post near the Kiwi Nation. I neglect to mention my disastrous attempt to eat their kin. As far as they know, I am not a fish-and-fowl dude, but purely a fish snapper. Since when free they amble by the seashore snapping up shellfish, they have nothing against fish eaters.

Their funny feathers are all in a wad when I arrive. They have spotted the feline who does eat fowl hanging around again.

I take up a subtle position in the swagged shade of a folding-table drapery and wait.

In the room, the feet come and go, wearing shoes by Bandalino. The din rises, for now the public is streaming into the scene. I despair of ever spotting my subject.

Then I hear it. A low vibrato. A deep, passionate thrum.

The Kiwi Nation bumbles back into the bushes.

I look around. I see nothing but the strange-shod humans moving everywhere like random electrons. And then, in the shadow of the Kiwi Nation bushes, I see the red reflection from an azure eye.

I belly-crawl closer to get a good look.

Oh, she is a good look, all right. She has hunkered down, her lithe forelimbs stretched before her and barely touching the grille that encompasses the Kiwi Nation.

Her body is blond and muscular, the way certain athletes, such as ice skaters and acrobats are muscular, but her extremities are sheathed in an exquisite gray-brown purple shade that is impossible to give full due to. I have heard the experts refer to the phenomenon as lilac points, but it does not convey the lethal subtlety of the Awesome Hyacinth's coloring.

The inborn face mask surrounding her eyes and nose looks like silk velvet. I see her front shivs push in and out and feel a thrill of revulsion and fascination. They are painted green now, the light, bright green of alien lights and Kiwi insides.

If her nails are painted, she is still in service to her demonic mistress, the magician Shangri-La, who has caused Miss Temple and myself such anguish and peril in the not-too-distant past.

I toy with the idea of confronting the wench, but then decide I would rather discover where, and what, her mistress is doing at TitaniCon.

TitaniCon. Is it named after the famous ship, I wonder, or simply after the huge elder gods called Titans?

I do not know, but I do know that the ship called *Titanic* was both big and a disaster.

Given the dramatis personae I imagine, I have a feeling that TitaniCon is headed in the same direction as its namesake ocean liner—straight toward impalement on the hidden presence of an icy saboteur.

Chapter 20

Hanky-panky
Hocus-pocus

"Some way to spend a Thursday night," Temple said.

Max turned from the computer screen, surprised. "Some people would consider cruising occult-erotic web sites an adventure."

"Not me. It's not a turn-on; it's a creep-out."

"I agree. But whoever staged that death scene wanted to evoke a creep-out. It's a way of diverting investigators from the real motive and making the victim unsympathetic, at one and the same time."

"That's true. Poor Jeff Mangel dies in unspeakable circumstances. Suddenly everything he was is merely fodder for the sensation mills. Do you think that was part of the reason for the occult stuff, Max? They were trying to debunk everything he'd said and stood for while living?"

He nodded, the eerie light from the screen pulling his features into a cadaverous mask.

Temple knew that in daylight his expression would merely look sober. Now, here, it looked morose.

"Shouldn't we have some light on in the room?" she asked.

"I don't want my neighbors to know we're burning the midnight oil."

"But you have blackout shades, for heaven's sake."

He glanced at her again. "I don't want anyone thinking about creeping up and penetrating my shades to see anything. Some people leave their computers on all night. But not their lamps."

"You think someone would spy on us?"

"Spying is easy. Don't you think someone spied on us in order to know that we'd both seen Mangel, that I had seen him the very morning of his death, or, rather, that his death followed my visit by mere hours?"

Temple's icy hands clasped her opposite elbows. "Does Molina know that, do you think?"

"What do you think? You saw the woman."

"She didn't know that some posters had vanished. I tried to make that clear, while acting like I didn't know what I was saying."

"Good."

"You *want* Molina to know this stuff?"

"I want Molina to know just enough so that what she does will help me. Us. Not her, particularly."

"What about Cher?"

Max pulled away from the computer screen, where a search for Synth spelled backward, Htnys, was coming up empty.

"What about her?"

"Does her death somehow fit in, or is it a coincidence?"

"I don't believe in coincidence. If you really knew what Molina tried to pull on me, you'd see why."

"Can't you tell me?"

"Not . . . yet."

"Listen. Why are we playing this remote-control game of cat-and-mouse with Molina? If we went to her, *I* went to her, told her everything straight out . . ."

"Temple." Max smiled at her fondly. "You think if you're straightforward, everything else crooked in the universe will smooth right out. Besides, Molina can't contribute anything that we can't weasel out on our own."

"You're too used to working alone."

He nodded, a bit regretfully. "It was the only way to stay alive." He eyed her from under dark, Mephistophelian eyebrows. "Haven't you stuck your neck out following your own drummer?"

Temple nodded slowly. "I have, and I can't explain why I did such downright stupid things, except I had this instinct—"

"Instinct is often like an idiot savant: brilliantly stupid. Sometimes that's what it takes to survive, inspired idiocy. Like your most recent example, when you ditched the security of the Fontana brothers because you sensed they would make the situation too secure for anything to happen. Sometimes it takes a crisis to break a fever; sometimes it takes a risk to produce a result."

"Then you don't blame me for that?"

"No. My heart wanted to wring your neck if the perp hadn't tried first, but my gut told me you'd done just what I would have done."

"Really? You would have done the same thing?"

"I'm afraid so."

"Well. Then, I'm a . . . pro. Sort of."

"An intuitive pro. You lack so much experience that even good intuition can't always save you. Which is why I try to hold you down."

Temple glanced at the rather lurid screen. "Not as seriously as that."

Max looked back. "Amazing how much dreck like this is out there. Not so amazing that real life so often tries to live up to the fantasy."

"Poor Jeff. We just can't let him be smeared after death."

"Unless he really was into kink."

"Professor Mangel? No."

"Are you sure?"

"Well, who can be?"

"Exactly."

"We won't know for sure until we prove it one way or the other, right?"

"Right. So, word person, any other rearrangements of 'synth' that come to mind?"

"Synthesis. Synthetic. Hyacinth. Synth you went away—"

"Is that a personal jab?"

"No. Just free associating. Isn't that what we word persons do?"

"As long as you're free associating with me."

"Max, will there ever be an end to it?"

"To what?"

"To the mysteries within mysteries, to the limitations, to the secrets and the subterfuge?"

"An end to life, is that what you're asking?"

"Life is an unfolding enigma, is that what you're saying?"

"Am I?"

"If you don't know, I don't know."

"That sounds pretty realistic."

Temple felt her hands form fists at the irritating formlessness of it all. "I don't want Jeff Mangel left a mystery. Any more than you want Gandolph's death left unattributed. Both of their deaths left them in disguise, somehow, publicly exposed as less than their real selves. That is diabolical."

"Death always is."

"Your cousin Sean died as something other than his real self, didn't he?"

"He was a vacationing Irish-American boy. When he died in that pub bomb, he became an Irish Troubles martyr; he became a man only in dying for someone else's reasons."

"Are you living as something other than your real self because of that?"

"Probably."

Max's face had become the great stone mountain so impressive on stage. Temple depended on that impregnable façade, and despaired of it.

"I can't imagine," she said.

"Don't try. Look. I can't go back in time and fix that. I can only try to fix what's here and now. You agree that Mangel's been given a bum rap. Maybe because of me."

"Or me."

"That's possible. You've managed to entwine yourself with enough of my affairs to suffer for them."

"Then we're doing the right thing. The police don't care about solving our entanglements, only about solving this case or that case."

"And we've got a chain of 'cases' here, Temple. It's getting longer, not shorter. I'm open to suggestions."

She considered. "Why don't you hack into the police system and find out Mangel's personal background. Maybe we've got to prove that he wasn't what he was made to look like before we can find out who needed to ruin his reputation."

"You're encouraging me to hack?"

"We all have our areas of expertise. Mine is obviously inspired idiocy. Somebody has to be left-brained and do the technological stuff. Besides, I'm getting bored by that Black Sabbath orgy routine on the screen. Bring on the faceless, sexless technocrats!"

"Not quite yet, I hope." Laughing, Max turned his gaze back to the screen. "Notice one thing that was present at the death scene that's missing from these scenes from a rock-group costume shop?"

Temple did a quick inventory. "What *isn't* missing? Whips, chains, heavy metal masks, corsets, seven-story-high boots. No knives."

"That's a good catch, seeing that the fatal knife was missing from the scene when we saw it."

"I cheated. I saw a photo of the actual knife, remember?" Even as she said it, a stab of memory pulled Temple's mind back from a mental close-up on a knife hilt to the surrounding pale sea of dead flesh.

Her silence made Max turn around. "Delayed-stress syndrome?"

She nodded without breaking the stillness. It was one thing to view the mere props of violence, another to *know* what a real weapon had done and to know the person at the receiving end of that knife blow.

"The knife bothers me," Max said. "And not the way it bothers you. The elaborate handle you describe smacks of Satanism, yet the scene was more Frederick's of Hollywood than Hell."

"As if somebody had bought a bunch of props from a mall."

"Exactly. It's way too . . . organized for a scene of depravity. We need to track down that knife."

"Break into headquarters?"

Max actually considered the idea for a split second. "No. We can surmise that there aren't any fingerprints on it. What's interesting about it is not evidence on it, but where it came from. I'm guessing it was custom made. I wonder what a cult expert would make of it."

"You're talking the police again."

"Not necessarily. Didn't you say one of the psychics at the Halloween séance worked with the police? I bet some of those cases were satanic murders or kidnappings."

Temple sat up, snapping her fingers. "The psychics were just in town for a convention. Las Vegas is a frequent stop on their rounds."

"I don't doubt it."

"I'll see what I can dig up." Max regarded her until she hastily added, "I didn't mean that literally."

"Glad to hear it. Might break your nails. I've got an idea myself. Let's go our separate ways and see what sources we find."

"Right," Temple said impishly. "It's Frederick's of Hollywood first thing in the morning for me."

"I always thought Frederick's was for the last thing at night."

"In your dreams."

"You let me know when you have something, and I'll let you know when I have something, and we'll follow the leads together.

"Really? We'll work together?" Temple was pleased. Another,

less pleasant thought struck her. "You don't think that this stuff is too dangerous for me to look into on my own?"

"It's too dangerous for *me* to look into on my own."

She caught his meaning. Danger was a non-gender-specific element, but it was the name of the game when it came to the Synth and all its works.

Chapter 21

How Suite It Is Not!

To find my way around this brave new world, I decide to follow my fancy—that is, my nose—which is how I end up in what I learn is called a "con suite."

This is not a piece of musical composition, or a set of furniture, although it comes closest to the set of furniture. It is a set of hotel rooms in which are laid out items of an edible nature. I fear that what humans consider fit for nibbling is only one step above Free-to-Be-Feline. There are many things of a munchy nature, liberally larded and salt-sprinkled. There are dairy products dosed with such abominations as "onion soup mix" and garlic. There are vegetable "munchies." There are chocolate chip cookies by the score.

There is, in short, nothing a reasonable dude would eat. Except possibly the shrimp dip.

Where food for the body is not to be found, there is often food for the clever operative's ears and eyes.

I hunker behind the massive trash receptacle to take stock of the dramatis personae and the unfolding drama, which is distinctly on the couch-potato side.

My observations only confirm what I have noticed elsewhere. There is a whole population of fandom that attends these affairs. They may be a discerning, well-read, and up-to-the-minute cadre on matters of books, films, videos, audios, and such, but they are also imaginative in an extreme degree, going so far as to attire themselves after the manner of their film and fictional heroes and heroines.

Here is where they go dreadfully wrong.

Even I can see that the actors who portray their heroic spacers and barbarian head-knockers are typical of actors: young, fit, and obscenely slim. Any actor who gets a little old and flabby is killed off or wears a really, really disguising alien costume. Like a circus tent with scales. Think Jabba the Hut with a human inside. Come to think of it, there probably *was* a human inside Jabba the Hut.

Anyway, I now am glad that I work out often with Miss Temple's remote control device when she is off working, punching in channels to keep my mitts in flexible condition. Otherwise I would not be the savvy dude I am about such matters. Scanning the series of rooms, I glimpse Bejoran earbobs and Klingon eyebrows, not to mention numerous *Star Trek* uniforms and an assortment of Vulcan and Ferengi ears. Feeling the need of a snack, I search in vain for the Mickey Mouse model.

A group of the robe-clad pretechies, with stuffed dragons on their shoulders and chain-mail headdresses on the female sort, gather around a low table, eating Cheese Puffs and working on a giant jigsaw puzzle of a red-and-green dragon with enough flames to fuel the Mirage's outdoor volcano pouring out of his purely pictorial mouth. Perhaps the dragon-mouth monster is called Halitosis.

Looking at this assortment of homo sapiens, male and female, I again thank my lucky stars that I am not to that species born. I do not have to run around like a Mexican hairless dog with every bone, muscle, and skin wrinkle showing, but am blessed with a nice, camouflaging cover of thick, long, and very slimming black hair. It would really tick me off if that naked breed they call the Sphinx would get my spokescat job simply because you can see its ribs.

There are not a lot of ribs to be seen in a con suite, I conclude, unless they are on a plate, in barbecue sauce.

Far be it from me to be critical of the calorically challenged. I am a pretty sedentary sort myself, eighty percent of the time. But then I leap into intense action. The only thing I can picture the people in this room leaping into, or for, is the remote control device.

Beam me up, Scotty!

Of course, that is not to say that the occasional babe does not stroll through. Babes you have always with you, and I suspect that any babe candidates to be found in this solar system of fans jump on it and ride it for all it is worth.

Hence some lean-bodied females do ankle through, clad in only enough to elude the censors, which in Las Vegas are a pretty endangered species.

I notice that Mother Nature does not tolerate many rivals, however, and those fortunate females with properly endowed bodies often have features better left face down in a bowl of Free-to-Be-Feline. On the other hand, some of the most zoftig ladies to pull a cord into a choke hold around their expansive middles have exceptionally pretty faces.

Life is not fair.

Luckily, I am usually most attracted to bearded ladies and do not have to choose between fairness of face or form.

And in the interests of gender equality, let me point out that the dudes who wander through are not poems of pulchritude either. Many poor things are losing their hair on top. Some sport pretty thin whiskers. Others have paunches even medieval garb, noted for its puffiness, cannot hide.

Poor homo sapiens. Hairless, every flaw is nakedly revealed. A good fur coat would soften all lacks, but they lack even that.

No wonder they almost worship these virtual-reality gods and goddesses of screen and fiction.

I gasp and peek out from behind my garbage can as one of these fully costumed dudes on high platform shoes stomps into the suite.

It is not his not inconsiderable physical presence that enthralls me. It is his resemblance to the dead dude on the catwalk. I have heard of dead men walking before, but usually they wore prison jumpsuits, or even jeweled ones.

A hush falls on the room as the assembled believers try to assess whether the newcomer is the actual actor or a devoted impersonator.

Have I not been through this movie before, in my last case?

In the silence, in which even the rhythmic chomping sounds have ceased, the newcomer pauses, surveys the scene, and burps impressively. Now there is a real man! Imagine eating this stuff day in and day out, and still standing, able to burp.

I almost burp in sympathy, save that I have not eaten in a dog's age.

A buzz starts in the rooms. Is this the real Kaharl, Khatlord of the Kohl Kompendium? Or is it Memorex?

A rather pasty-faced Data from *Star Trek: The Next Generation* edges forward, book in hand. "Can I have your autograph?"

The giant glares down on the lowly android nonlife form. "The proper Earth term is 'May I, Khatlord, may I?' "

A book is thrust, trembling-handed, toward the mighty being.

"No pen?" the Khatlord demands.

The ersatz Data looks around, desperate. In his haste to approach the higher being, he has forgotten the essentials.

A girl with long, flowing hair, a long, flowing robe, and long, flowing fat cells hands him a ballpoint.

Khatlord scrawls a signature.

"What about mine?" a timid voice asks. I expect it to further announce that it is Dorothy, the small and meek.

"Your what?" Khatlord Kaharl booms.

"Maybe he wants my autograph, too."

I examine the mouse behind the machine. This is not a she, but a he, dressed in normal if unexciting street clothes: K-Mart slacks, Target plaid cotton shirt, nerdy ballpoint-pen protector in the concave breast pocket.

"Who are you?" Data asks, quite sensibly.

"I'm the author. I mean, coauthor, of your book."

Data seems as shocked as an android can get.

"See. My name's on it. There."

Even from where I sit, I can see that the type is about the size of Mickey Mouse, er, turds.

Data is at a loss for words.

Obviously, no other signature than the Khatlord's is wanted.

While this bizarre tableau pauses at an impasse, I watch with a predator's eagle eye.

My eagle eye, however, has not spied the interloper at three o'clock low.

He swaggers in from the other room, which adjoins a bathroom, which features a bathtub loaded with ice and canned drinks, some of which, I think, are mildly alcoholic. There is nothing mild about the alcoholic who has just entered the room.

"What a bunch of smug, fat-cat, spineless Judas-goats," he begins amiably.

A buzz runs through the con-suite occupants like a saw slicing deadwood.

The name I catch is "Hanford Schmidt."

Well, that rings about as many bells as a hunchback nowadays.

Hanford is wearing a suit at least, over a Hawaiian shirt. He pushes the suit sleeves up to his elbows. I figure he must be all of Miss Temple's height as he squares off against the Kahtlord.

"You're just a deck of cards," he sneers to the towering figure. "One shuffle and you're a queen of farts. You didn't write anything more than your phony-baloney name on a contract. Timothy Hathaway, author, my clubfoot! You couldn't write a money-laundering list for the Mafia." The guy whirls on Mr. Ballpoint Pen. "And you, you sorry sellout. You'd write your name on Napoleon's syphilis prescription to get a book in print these days. This is a nonbook, bub." Hanford Schmidt slaps Data's proffered volume to the floor and turns on him. "It isn't worth the acid-loaded paper it's written on. Go and sin no more. If you want good reading nowadays, try toilet paper. Or, better yet, ditch the 'droid outfit and get a life."

I blink and reflect that I really resent that "fat cat" crack made many, many cracks ago.

But never fear, Hanford Schmidt has offended every human, animal, and android being in this con suite.

Except possibly the Kahtlord, who laughs.

"Thanks a bunch. I was wondering how my outfit would go over in the masquerade tomorrow night. I'm not Timothy Hathaway, though I sure wouldn't mind being him." He eyes the dazed Data. "You might still want to get Timothy's John Hancock on that book, though. It'll be worth more with both a genuine and a faux signature. And now, I take my leave." He made a sweeping bow, his handsomely spotted features seeming to purr with satisfaction. "So long, mundanes."

Everybody is left sputtering like a fuse that has been dipped in buttermilk.

One of the dragon-shoulders looks up from the jigsaw puzzle. "Nice try, Hanford. But most of the fans at this con are media zombies. They don't care about books anymore unless they're tie-ins, or novelizations, or an endless series of franchise novels for a film world. You used to laugh at us reality-dodging elve-selves, but we're the only fans who care about books written just for readers, like Tolkien's were."

Hanford Schmidt, reeling, isn't down as long as there is a long neck in his hand. "You used to be just obsolete, but now you're obsolete assholes." He looks around for someone else to attack. "Look at you! Wearing your Hollywood knock-off imperial trooper uniforms! And your parasitical, flaming, extinct flying dinosaurs. Don't you care that we're all queuing up at the company store to make the corporate goons rich? Sixteen tons and whaddaya get, another eon older and deeper in shit. I got eight Nocturne awards, and what's it worth? Some idiot like Greg Sellout here writes a whole series of books so some actor can go on the talk shows."

"Seltz," the plaid-shirted author corrects, trying to straighten up to match his pen. "At least I'm getting published, unlike most of the other would-be and has-been authors in this field lately."

"This benighted field. This royaltyless throne of drones. This sceptered slagheap. This dearth of daring. This . . . lost world." Schmidt looks like he is going to cry, except it isn't in his tough-guy contract. "We're all being controlled now. *Them* took over, after all. The earth stood still, and nobody noticed, except the corporate accountants. We are an extinct species, writers and readers. We are a target audience. We will do as the *Vermacht* decides, the bean counters and the double-aught manipulators, and we won't even have the guts to stumble around and mouth the words of the past, like in Bradbury's *Fahrenheit 451,* we'll just let megamerchandising burn up every last independent cell in our barnacle brains."

A silence rules for about a sixty-second beat. Then the slow, lethargic clapping begins.

It is a nice moment, but it does not disprove a thing Schmidt says.

I shake my sagacious feline head. Obnoxious as he is, Schmidt is more right than he is wrong.

For the first time I understand the weird, weird world on display in the con rooms below.

Everything is there to make money, like slot machines. The string of films and related products may look like wondrous worlds created by the mind of man, and occasionally woman, but they are all games. They may produce stars and storylines and multiyear series, but they are cogs in a wheel of fortune that very few play to win. And those battle cruisers and new millennium models of humanoid peace, happiness, and final triumph? They may play like games, but they are money-sucking machines.

Now I understand why murder is the real name of this con game.

Chapter 22

Hyacinth Blues!

At 11 A.M. Friday morning, Temple came back from a trip to the lobby mailbox with her hands full of snail-mail spam. Then her attention was momentarily distracted.

Louie was lying on the kitchen countertop under the phone, as if to point a long, furry black finger—tail, that is—right at it. Might as well have pinned an "Answer Me" note right on it.

Temple went to the office to find her answering machine's little red light a-blinking like Rudolph the Reindeer's nose. When she played the tape back, Max's silken voice massaged her ear and made her toes curl in their Stuart Weitzman steel-heeled pumps. "I have a lead we can follow if you want to go clue hunting."

She called him back immediately and got his answering machine. *Rats and cats and bats! How could someone leave a message seven minutes ago and be AWOL from the phone already?*

Temple voice-mailed right back that *she* had a lead worth following and whose lead did he wish to follow first?

She then walked right out of the steel heels and left them all alone by the telephone. Her bare soles skated across the polished parquet floors, so delightfully cool and ever-so-slightly rough, back to the kitchen. There, Louie got a particularly succulent dollop of wet cat food atop his Free-to-Be-Feline foundation, which Temple dutifully changed every few days, as if not noticing that its level never sank below bowl rim.

She was actually feeling pretty smug. When she and Max had parted last night . . . early this morning, actually . . . she didn't know what she was going to come up with, leadwise. Certainly not a mother lode. She wondered what Max had dug up so fast.

The phone rang just as her cup of hot water for herbal tea was putting the microwave through its wheezing paces.

She punched off the microwave and picked up the receiver.

"My guy won't be ready to see us until late afternoon," Max said, getting right down to cases.

"Well, my gal is ready after one P.M."

"Why don't I pick you up, and we find something to eat along the way? That work?"

"If we chew every bite a hundred times. She's not that far away."

"Fine. I'll start now and drive slow."

"Who are you kidding?"

"The Las Vegas Metropolitan Police. At every opportunity. See you in the parking lot in twenty minutes."

Temple realized after she hung up that she didn't know what seeing "his guy" involved. Should she dress for a formal tea or a Hell's Angels' rally? She presumed a "guy" was closer to the latter than the former, but then, one never did know. Men never told women the really important things.

She settled on wearing red bell-bottom pants with a nautical navy-blue jacket over a sailor-striped jersey: equally suitable for social climbing or riding on the back of a Harley Hog. Temple possessed few platform shoes, but she pulled out some cork-soled jobbies today. Height without wobble.

Max cruised right up as she kept the side door company . . . cruised right up in a bright blue Cavalier convertible.

He stood to alight the moment it stopped, his six-feet-four of height making the Cavalier look Barbie-size. "Want to drive?" He tossed her the keys.

Temple scurried for the open door while he walked around to the passenger side.

"Assume this is the flavor of the week," Temple said, adjusting the side and rearview mirrors to her needs. "Nice of you to color-coordinate with me." They zoomed out of the parking lot, then settled down to a sedate, for Temple, forty miles per hour.

For a non-European car, the Cavalier was spurty, sporty, and nimble, and Temple loved the feel of the wind and the sand in her hair—also, of driving a new car.

"I've got to trade in the Storm," she said as they turned onto the Strip.

"Too bad. It suited you."

"That was a long time ago. It's got a lot more miles on it, and maybe I've changed, too."

Max glanced at her rather piercingly.

"I know. The longer you keep a car the more value you get out of it."

"Kind of like the longer you keep tracking someone," he said obliquely, "the more you find out about him."

"Oh? Had any luck with that creep you think killed Cher?"

Max sighed deeply, as if trying to inhale the wind whole. "No. He's ducked out of sight for a while. I hope that's all. Typical of his sort. He'll turn up again. In the meantime, I can occupy myself with your little problem."

"Thank you, Master Sherlock."

Max grinned at her, his shorter hair blowing back like the mane on an Art Deco lion. "I did think I said that with consummate self-assurance. Are you simmering down enough now to accept directions to our luncheon stop?"

"Only because I'm hungry," Temple growled through her teeth.

The wind picked them clean of any anger she was storing up.

For the next ten minutes, Max talked and she listened.

By then, the Cavalier was idling its motor across from Charley's Old Fashion Hamburgers.

Temple surveyed the pot-holed road that ran between her car and the object of their luncheon appetites. She eyed the wood-sided shack and the hand-painted and misspelled sign.

"Well?" Max demanded.

Max always demanded when he had an illusion up his sleeve.

"Quaint," Temple spit out like a cough. "Where's the beef?"

"Inside the bun, and both are inside the restaurant. We'll have to get out to place our orders. Unless Madame wants to rest. I can put your order in."

"Rest? No, I've got to work off something before inhaling half my fat-and-carb calories of the week. These better be good," Temple swore as her platform-shoes heels met the wooden boardwalk that surrounded Charley's.

While Temple squinted to read the hand-scrawled chalkboard beyond the order-taker's shoulder, Max leaned against the sand-and-wind-weathered wooden clapboard rotting off of Charley's shack.

When she ordered a Jalapeño Deathburger, he raised an eyebrow, then leaned forward to order his own Tabasco Tornado.

They carried the containers back to the Cavalier.

Sitting there, in the not-yet-searing sunlight, fighting the wind for continuing custody of their several flimsy napkins and the crisp tissues that wrapped the food, felt like losing ten suddenly expendable years. Time took the holiday that death was supposed to. It rolled away with the occasional tumbleweed that skittered down the road, its random haste and hesitation eerily like a living thing's.

For once in this toddling town, what was inside Temple's mouth was hotter than the air temperature outside.

Eating under such circumstances felt as much like an achievement and an art form as Olympic ice skating. Every gesture required a nature-borne rhythm. The tissues whipped in the constant breeze like some tutu. Only great skill, economy of motion, and poetry could get their food into mouth-sized bites and safely swallowed without awkward, embarrassing losses.

"Awesome!" Temple balled her napkins and tissues into one orange-sized mass and tossed it dead-center into the open maw of a curbside plastic-lined garbage can.

"Good," Max agreed. His wad of trash lofted dead-on into the same receptacle.

"We're batting one thousand."

"I think that's another sport."

"So what. They're all Zen."

"So what's next, Zen master?"

"I drive us to our mundane appointment. A paltry psychic. What can she have to say on such a fabulous day?"

"A good deal more than the average psychic, I hope," Max muttered.

But Temple was revving the car engine so it bolted from a dead stop into an automotive bound. She wasn't sure she had heard him. And shortly after, she was pulling up in front of the Blue Mermaid Motel.

She put the Cavalier into park and beamed at the sprawling symphony in white-and-blue stucco that lay under the benign surveillance of the huge plaster figure rotating above it all with every gust of wind.

"What are we doing at this dump?" Max asked, leaning to pull the car's white ragtop closed.

Temple scrunched her head low over the steering wheel to keep the Blue Mermaid in view. "Don't shut out the sun! And I can't see the Mermaid."

"Good. Because then *they* can't see *you*."

"Who? Where?"

Max nodded in about three directions at once. Temple followed his indications and noticed groups of hunched young men, all watching them over the humps of their shrugging shoulders.

"Who are they?"

"Hopefully, only nameless drug dealers and pimps who just

want to be left alone. Temple, what are we doing in this ghastly place?"

"Our source is here."

"Who is it? A Gotti family turncoat in the witness protection program?"

"No, just an ordinary citizen."

"With nerve. Okay, but let's make it quick. In case you hadn't noticed, it's 'Hail, hail, the gangs are all here.' "

Temple pulled the room number from her huge tote bag, then did as Max suggested. At least the room was on the ground floor.

She walked with Max to the dubious safety of the second-story overhang, remembering that this was where Matt had tracked down Cliff Effinger. The very late Cliff Effinger.

But Effinger's ghost never said boo as they made their way to the right room.

Temple knocked, tentatively. Max followed up with a knuckle-blisterer.

Moments later, the door cracked open.

Temple didn't know what, or who, Max expected, but she could tell he was surprised.

D'Arlene Hendrix moved back into the shadows of her room as they entered. The room was glowing, not with ectoplasm or other paranormal effects, but with banks and banks of those unscented, short, fat white candles that keep chaffing dishes warm.

"This is—?" Max began, too stunned to finish.

Temple took over. "This is D'Arlene Hendrix. She specializes in finding dead people."

"Well, this is the place to do it," Max said, pulling Temple into the room, shutting the door, and slamming the safety chain home.

D'Arlene Hendrix watched him with grandmotherly amusement.

He didn't waste words. "Lady, what are you doing in a place like this?"

"My job. Won't you sit down? I've furnished the room with my own things. So, a dead man means a lot to you?"

"Dead men usually mean a lot to somebody."

"Not always." She sat on the bedspread, a cheery aqua-and-rose floral pattern that Temple suspected of originating at K-Mart rather than the Blue Mermaid.

D'Arlene was one of those women time had turned on its lathe until she emerged simple, strong, and rounded: tightly curled hair, round granny glasses, and round facial features that worked themselves into matching "O's" or portions thereof: "O"-wide eyes, "O"-shaped mouth, half "O's" from a couple of double chins, and finally flat-tire "O's" formed by the folds of her sweatsuit.

In other words, you couldn't imagine a more unassuming, unthreatening female. Except for the razor-sharp eyes behind the round, trifocal lenses.

Temple had been able to study the psychic so openly because the woman's attention was all on Max. Or seemed to be. You could never tell with psychics.

"*Several* dead men mean a lot to you," D'Arlene was correcting her first impression of Max. "And one dead woman."

He shrugged. She knew as well as he did that the odds of any blanket statement applying to anyone were appallingly high. It was hard work to con a magician.

D'Arlene turned abruptly to Temple. "You are concerned about a dead man. Not exactly a friend, but sympatico." She glanced at Max, nodding. "Two at once, good."

"I don't know what you get paid," Temple began.

D'Arlene's chubby hand whipped upward, one authoritative forefinger lifted. "No."

Temple didn't understand, but Max did.

"We can afford to pay." He meant himself, of course.

"But I can't afford to let you pay." D'Arlene smiled. "I don't let skeptics pay. It compromises my vision. I have a stake in proving myself then."

Max fell silent. Few people turned the tables on him so completely.

"Does the skeptic have a name?" she asked.

"I'm sorry!" Temple realized she had assumed D'Arlene would know Max by sight. Unlike Jeff Mangel, she wasn't a magic buff and would have no reason to. Temple didn't go on to introduce him, because she wasn't sure what name Max would want to use.

"Michael," he said, surprising Temple. "Michael Kinsella. Now tell me why on earth you're living in this sinkhole."

"There are two places I stay in Las Vegas when I'm working. One is the El Cortez."

"It's near police headquarters!" Temple said, catching on.

D'Arlene nodded. "And this place is on the fringe of Freemont Street. Either location suits my special needs. A psychic is just a television set. I need the right antennas. Speaking of antennas, I believe we have . . . not quite met . . . before."

"Be hard to prove either way, wouldn't it?" Max smiled, slid down onto his tailbone in the chair until his legs bridged the gap between the wall and the bed, and folded his long, facile fingers on his midsection.

It was like watching Midnight Louie take a long, luxurious stretch, just to show the world how very relaxed he was. Only with Max, Temple didn't believe the relaxed part for a second.

"I have some refreshments in an ice chest by the bathroom," D'Arlene told Temple. "Looks like you'll have to play hostess." She glanced at Max's Italian loafer-clad feet boxing her on her side of the room.

"No problem." Temple jumped up, a bit sorry to leave this psychic poker game. "Cola, Uncola, or bottled water?"

"Uncola, please," D'Arlene said.

"Water," said Max.

Temple looked around for glasses, but the only ones she spied were so water-spotted they looked like they were etched in a leopard pattern. So she popped one can top and twisted the caps off bottled water for her and Max.

Having delivered the libations, she sat down in her chair and decided to move the showdown along.

"I guess I'm the one with the fewest ghosts to hunt, so I'll go first." Their eyes turned to her. "We don't really want you to try to uncover what happened to someone, or who did it," she told

D'Arlene. "We want to know what you know about the victim. You may not have heard yet—"

D'Arlene stiffened a little, pulling the soft-drink can from her lips. "It's someone I know?"

Temple nodded and started to speak, but D'Arlene hushed her, almost irritably.

"I've been feeling a little restless. Shhh." She turned her head to the side, as if to listen to something better. Her eyes were cast down and to the left.

Max never moved. The silence seemed heavy and pervasive, like invisible fog.

D'Arlene made a faint moan, a "hmmm" to herself. She looked up at Temple through the silly glass frames, her eyes blinking rapidly several times. Her head began moving, small motions, in various directions, as if avoiding or trying to focus on something.

"Jeff. Is it Jeff? Jeff Mangel?"

"Yes," Temple said, her eyes consulting Max.

He remained aggravatingly neutral.

"I should tell you what I'm sensing. Besides death, of course." D'Arlene paused, took a deep breath. "Poor Jeff. Such a nice fellow. It's so much harder, knowing someone. I'm protected, somehow, from seeing relatives and close friends. Acquaintances can go either way. I don't really want to see. . . ."

"You would consider him an acquaintance?" Max asked softly.

"Yes. Definitely. I've felt something. . . . buzzing, but I don't encourage things that come on me spontaneously. Too dangerous. I need a certain distance."

"Maybe this is too much to ask," Temple suggested, squirming to her chair edge, ready to leave.

D'Arlene's plump hand soothed the air between them. "Never mind. Your visit has made my 'tweak' tangible, that's all. Actually, it should help. Ask me your questions."

"Maybe," Max intervened, "it would be best for you to explore your 'tweak' first."

Her eyes sharpened in his direction. "Yes. Of course." Then she reached up, took off the glasses, and set them on the sagging bed-springs beside her. "My own sheets, too," she said, "I'm not *that* otherworldly."

Her face was remarkably unlined for her age, which Temple guessed at between fifty-five and sixty-five, except for the two engraved parallel concentration lines between her pallid eyebrows.

These were the sole straight and harsh lines on her face, and they drove hard for her hairline, only fading an inch from its ragged edges.

"Maybe this is why I've been repulsing these images," she murmured.

"What images?" Max's baritone had become the interrogator.

"Disturbing. Scenes of preparation. Ritual. Symbols drawn. On the floor. Artifacts assembled. Dark. Ugly."

"Sexual?" Max asked.

Her head shook. "No. Not ugly that way. Preparation. Ugly. Premeditation. Sexual paraphernalia, though. But. . . . innocent."

Max's eyebrows lifted as he glanced to Temple. She knew what he meant: There was nothing innocent about that S&M equipment.

"Paraphernalia and one true thing," D'Arlene said slowly, as if seeing it.

They waited.

Her head fell back, her expression pained. "Knife. No. Dagger. Massive. Macbeth. Used, so badly used. As if with passion, but cold. Cold steel."

Her head lowered, eyes blinked. She looked around again in that abrupt, mechanical way that reminded Temple of something.

"That's what I see."

"No perpetrator?" Max asked.

"You're not a cop."

"No," Max agreed.

"Then why talk like one?"

"Killer, then."

"No. I don't see a killer. The killer hides behind a veil, as does the dead man."

"Then," said Temple, "you're suggesting that Jeff Mangel was more than he seemed."

"No, that his death was more than it seemed. Jeff is clear. Like a bell, beneath all this, beneath even his own death. He is truly blameless. Oh, I wish I hadn't had to see."

"I'm sorry," Temple said. "I didn't know where else to get anything. The police—"

"The police," Max said, straightening in the chair, "want to believe the worst of Mangel, because it makes the case clear-cut, if not particularly solvable. Now that you have sensed the circumstances of the death, perhaps you could confirm some information we'd like to know about the victim's life."

She smiled wearily. "I didn't know him well, in the conventional sense."

"But you liked him," Temple said.

The sharp eyes focused only on Temple. "He was impossible not to like, unless you were a very petty person."

"So you could see someone not liking him," Max pounced.

She turned to him again, nodding. "A rival professor, jealous of his popularity. But no such person killed him. Someone who didn't care about him at all killed him. Such a tragedy. So frightening. That we may be killed for something that only one or two persons in the world cares about, and more for what we know, than what we are."

"It was a hit," Max said brutally. "Mob?"

She shook her head. "The hand that welded the knife was not professional. There was passion in it, though none for Jeff Mangel specifically."

"Was there . . . did you sense a syllable?" Temple was grabbing at straws since haystacks wouldn't do.

"A syllable? What a strange question. I see things, not words."

"Did you see anything unusual?"

"Saw only what I told you, the accessories of passion. But not the acts of passion. Oh."

"What?" Temple prompted.

"I did . . . smell something."

"What?"

"An odor. Floral. Forsythia, maybe. Or . . . hyacinth?"

"What made you think it was hyacinth?" Max asked.

D'Arlene Hendrix made her round face wrinkle with uncertainty. "I don't know. I don't really know what hyacinths smell like, come to think of it. That's what happened. I just came to think of it. Hyacinth. But the forsythia I did smell. Very sweet."

Max had somehow managed to drink all his water without anyone noticing. He squeezed the plastic bottle, and it collapsed with a pop like a firecracker.

Temple jumped, but D'Arlene Hendrix did not.

"Thanks," Temple said, rising.

Max stood and collected Temple's half-full bottle, then extended a hand for D'Arlene's soft-drink can.

"I'm not done yet," the psychic said.

"Neither are we," Max answered. He deposited their containers in the motel wastebasket and went to peer through the curtains D'Arlene had paper-clipped shut. "Are you safe here?"

"Oh, yes. I can tune them in, their violent thoughts. They sense it and leave me alone. And here I can tune in the violent thoughts I specifically seek, past or present. This motel is one big receptor. Violence, chaos, evil. It has its own wave length."

"What kind of case are you working on?" Temple asked.

"Child abduction."

Temple winced. "I hope we haven't—"

"No case distracts. They all amplify each other. Make it easier to tune in. If tuning in is ever easy."

D'Arlene sipped her drink. "Thanks for the company. And thanks for telling me about Jeff. Now I'll know I might be getting multiple signals."

"And you'll let us know if you sense anything more about Jeff's death, or life?" Temple was reluctant to leave, as if she had started something she knew she couldn't finish.

Max had cracked the door open and was peering out.

"I'll let you know. I have your card. Him, who knows where

he'll be?" D'Arlene grinned at Temple, as if they were two girl-friends contemplating the mysteries of men.

Temple nodded and went to the door, car keys in hand.

"Get in, drive out, don't look back," Max counseled. He turned to smile farewell at D'Arlene. "Thanks for the game."

Chapter 23

Silicone Valley Girls

"This is so awesome." Mariah stared up, open-mouthed, at the vast, neon-spangled space above them.

"It's pretty big," Matt agreed, feeling his laid-back reaction let the kid down. But what did a realistic adult do in the face of such extravagance? Extravagant display, extravagant expense.

Last night's brief sneak peek was free, but Friday's real deal cost an obscene sixty bucks each for a three-day pass. The "creature" who took their admission money explained that ordinary science fiction cons cost over a hundred dollars for a membership, but since the hotel was cosponsoring this one, the fen cost was reduced.

Matt made the mistake of asking what the "fen" was.

"Were. It's plural. The fen are people like us, of course," the apparition said. "The plural of fan. Let me stamp the backs of your hands so you can come and go all weekend."

Matt had heard of such a practice, usually at dances held in bars with cover charges.

"A spaceship!" Mariah stared at her stamp-tattooed hand with reverence. "That is so cool."

"Looks like a . . . punk octopus to me."

"It's a Shadow ship, silly. It's supposed to look like a spiky octopus, only scarier. I can't believe I've got a Shadow ship on my hand. What's on yours?"

"Um . . . Bambi?"

"No! Oh, gosh, how radical. You've got a Vorlon."

"Is that good?"

"Well, interesting."

Matt nodded. He supposed *not* being interesting at an event like this was the kiss of death.

He looked around, feeling self-conscious. He and Mariah were not dressed for the ambiance, that was for sure. He was relieved, though, to see so many adults patronizing the attraction, the majority, in fact. Kids were a definite minority here, in both age and numbers.

Matt unrolled the two program guides he was carrying for them both. "It says here that there are movies, panels, book and photo signings, dealers' and gamers' rooms. Is it legal to let kids into them? Dealers and Gamers? Gambling is strictly for twenty-one and over in Las Vegas."

"I don't know." Mariah was practically jumping up and down. "I guess if I'm not allowed to do something they'll tell us. They always do. Oh, let's go over there. I see Krell."

"Whales eat it?"

"No. These are from the Khatlord series. There're the Krell, the Kharhud, the Kohl, and the Khatlords, of course."

Of course. Matt nodded and followed. It was all Geek to him.

The stars of the show, which was not one Matt had ever seen, were seated at a long table, barely visible behind a moving wall of fans offering everything but their firstborn child for autographing.

Mariah grabbed her program and scurried into line. He watched anxiously. Her small figure was soon swallowed by the milling adults, many attired as colorfully as their screen heroes and heroines.

He looked for a spot of turf that wouldn't impede the fan feeding frenzy and finally opted for a spot behind a lifesize cardboard cutout of Seven of Nine, the cyber biker babe from *Star Trek: Voyager.* She was wearing—if you could call an aluminum-silver body-paint job "wearing"; he'd seen cars that looked more clothed—the usual futuristic catsuit attached to the usual height-enhancing platform soles four-inches high. Somehow the science fiction film crowd always managed to get women in high heels even if they were half machine.

High heels made him think of Temple, of course, and how charming and feminine her height enhancements made her, without that devil-woman edge that media women had to project. He didn't know why, but that dangerously displayed femininity didn't attract him. He'd think it was too many years in the priesthood, except that Temple could do it without collagen lips, boyish hips, and silicone breasts.

"Well, hi!" exclaimed a voice at his ear.

Was Seven of Nine objecting to his obdurate, heretical indifference and coming to life? No, another woman stood behind him, considerably different in type to Seven, and to Temple for that matter.

Matt had been through so much change since he had last seen her that for an embarrassing moment he couldn't quite place the woman who was such a drastic contrast to the silver-metal cardboard Seven: plain, gawky, wearing a weird band around her forehead, and a strange draping outfit. He knew her from somewhere—his modest after-hours fan group from the radio station?

"Matt! What are you doing here?"

"I could ask you the same thing," he said to buy time, as if anyone could. She knew his name. Not a fan, thank God.

"It seems like ages, although it isn't," she went on.

Who *was* this curly-headed . . . elfette? Please, God, let some name leap into his mind. It wasn't kind to forget people you shouldn't.

Meanwhile, he darted a glance to the fan line. Mustn't let Mariah slip out of sight.

"You're with someone," she said, sounding disappointed.

"Ah, yes."

"Well, I never would have taken you for a fan. Relax. Weirdness is permitted here."

Before he could come up with some polite response, he noticed Mariah's dark head only two rows away from the table.

"You just vanished," the woman was saying. "We heard about you, that was all. It was like you were . . . lifted off the planet."

"Oh." His backward mind had finally kicked into gear. How could he have forgotten? "Yeah. I didn't mean to leave the hotline. Things just happened fast. I still do volunteer but at irregular hours. How are you, Sheila?" His relief at finding a name and place was palpable, like feeling a cool wave washing over him.

"Fine. Don't let the outfit freak you out. I've been an SF fan for years."

"SF?"

"Science fiction. And fantasy. It's always 'and fantasy.' The tech people kind of dominate over the faery folk."

"Oh, they do?" As if Matt cared.

"It's like male principle versus female, future versus past, pessimism versus optimism."

Matt studied her green and brown garb. "Rebellion versus tradition. I'm glad you spotted me. Maybe you can explain things."

Out of the corner of his eye, he saw Mariah fighting her way back through the crowd, her program clasped to what would soon be her bosom.

"Are you married now?" Sheila asked.

"Huh?" He saw she had followed his gaze. "Oh. No. She's the daughter of a friend. Who had to work. You could say I'm out of my element."

Sheila fixed him with a warm brown gaze. "I can't imagine any element you'd be out of."

"This is it, believe me." Without his shield of modesty, Matt felt as stripped as Seven of Nine in her spandex catsuit that revealed everything but her soul.

Mariah came bouncing over. "They let me go down the whole

line without going back to start over for each one. They were so nice! So cool! Look. All their autographs, and we haven't even been here half an hour. You shoulda let me take your program book. They woulda signed it."

"Next time," Matt said. As if he cared. Didn't matter. Mariah did. He smiled at her. She reminded him of her half-grown cats, bouncing off the walls with energy and enthusiasm. Let her keep it as long as she could.

"You like her?" Mariah was asking, a bit pugnaciously.

He thought she meant Sheila. "This is Sheila," he said tardily, but accurately at least. "I used to work with her."

"No, I meant *her.*" A glance to Sheila, acknowledging her presence at least.

"Her." Matt regarded Seven of Nine. "I don't think she's at all likeable, do you? I mean, isn't that the point? She's only half-human."

"All the guys at school say things about her and point at us."

"She's an actor on a show, that's all. Are there some actors on shows you like?"

Mariah sighed, dramatically. "Well, all the girls at school are talking about Angel, but I'm not allowed to see *Buffy.* My mother says I'm too young."

"Youngness isn't a problem," Matt said, "but it may seem like one. See, the opposite of 'too young' is 'too old,' and you don't want to get from one to the other without any space in-between. That's what your mother is trying to do. I'm sure you'll catch up with Angel soon."

"Have you seen *Buffy?*"

He nodded, seriously.

"Is it cool? Is Angel to die for?"

"It's cool. And there's a lot to die for on *Buffy,* mainly evil. That's why your mother wants you to wait a little while. You have to be ready to face evil."

Mariah gave an exaggerated shiver. "Sounds so creepy."

Sheila suddenly spoke. "No, it's not creepy. It's just life."

Mariah's puzzlement at her presence, and at the subject matter, became an earnest frown.

"Hi." Sheila's smile transformed her into a pixie.

Matt began to appreciate her odd garb, even her need to doff her everyday persona to assume the aspect of some sprite or other. Temple, he realized, did that all the time in a less dramatic mode. Was every personality a kaleidoscope of surprises? Maybe. Maybe even his.

"Are you an elf?" Mariah asked. "Cool. I can't decide whether to be an elf or a Klingon warrior."

"Most of us have that problem," Sheila said confidingly. "That's why I have two outfits to wear to these things."

"What's your other outfit?"

Sheila waggled her eyebrows mysteriously. "Stick around and you'll find out."

While Mariah was digesting that, Matt sought professional advice. He opened the program and ran down the list of attractions, soliciting Sheila's expert opinion.

That gave Sheila a chance to tell him that "dealers" and "gamers'" rooms had to do with merchandise and role-playing, not gambling. And that they wouldn't want to miss the celebrity events, the simulation rides, and the media presentations, although the costume parade called the Masquerade might be a little R-rated for the "elfkin."

"What's an 'elfkin?'" Mariah demanded.

"Baby me's," Sheila said without missing a beat. "Are you doing the whole weekend?" she asked Matt.

"Yes!" Mariah answered for him. "My mother said so."

Matt had nothing left to do but agree.

Taken in tow, after an hour in Sheila's wake, Matt had to admit he had learned the lay of the landscape.

She swiftly escorted him and Mariah into the mammoth string of conjoined ballrooms that housed rows of tables of merchandise: books, photos, videos, comics, toy-soldierlike gaming pieces, T-shirts, collectable cards, jewelry, games. Most of the browsers wore

T-shirts that all looked as if they'd just been purchased six tables over: T-shirts memorializing *Star Trek* and *Babylon 5, Buffy* and *Beauty and the Beast, Doctor Who* and *The X-Files*, as well as catchy sentiments related to all manners of belief and enthusiasm from cats to H. P. Lovecraft, the vintage horror writer.

Matt's mundane head was spinning. "Mundanes," he had learned, was the name for those ignorant of or uninterested in all things fantastical, futuristic, or frightening. Then Mariah introduced him to a cable-TV world he had never heard of.

"Isn't he cool?" She stood before her current idol, pictured in a seven-foot-high cardboard cutout.

Matt took one look and concluded that the "good" vampire Angel of *Buffy the Vampire Slayer* would be a better preteen icon than this character.

Imagine a Klingon warrior crossed with the doleful, sensitive Vincent of *Beauty and the Beast.*

Girls always seemed to fixate on these ultra-alpha males with hidden depths and vulnerabilities. Or maybe not. Perhaps that's what they hoped to find in testosterone-ridden teenage boys. Good luck.

He had been the opposite in high school: high on doleful sensitivity and low on alpha. But it had all balanced out eventually. Matt had found that inner strength that didn't depend on bluff and braggadocio. Maybe that's what late bloomers always did.

Meanwhile, to keep the preteen female mind-in-flux occupied, there were always these dangerous video attractions that expressed girls' own ambiguity with their shyly burgeoning sensuous selves.

"Go back in time, sir?" as so many science fiction scenarios tempted?

No way, Chakotay.

"I used to have a crush on Mr. Spock," Sheila confessed, watching Mariah with nostalgia.

"Really?"

Sheila shrugged. "It's a girl thing."

But Matt couldn't help thinking that the science fiction and fantasy worlds elevated the Other, the different, the alien within us all; that "crushes" were really falling in love with a hidden aspect of the Self. Or a secret antithesis of the Self.

Rituals. These were rituals as much as religion was.

Once he made that connection, he could observe the scene with new eyes.

There was an undeniably sexist component, but what was new? Religions made males high priests, and made females acolytes or temple virgins, or prostitutes, or both at once. Seven of Nine.

He looked at Mariah, but she was staring beyond their group, mesmerized.

The King Khatlord, surrounded by a gaggle of fans, had been leaving the signing area when he confronted something amazing: his own image.

Of course there were ersatz Khatlords running around the convention floor, but these were pale imitations with cut-rate costumes.

The newly arrived Khatlord wore full plumage and gear, and he was visibly furious, which made him a figure to reckon with.

"You again!" he thundered, as if playing thunder gods like Zeus or Thor. "Don't tell me you've been duping these poor doofuses with your phoney signature!" He looked around with the vigilance of an angry eagle. "Where's Security when you need them?"

The original Khatlord drew himself up. "You are mistaken, sir," he announced loftily.

Right there Matt suspected he wasn't an actor. That wasn't a Khatlord line.

"Mistaken, no," the second Khatlord said. "What I am is *late*. My limo from L.A. got a flat tire. And here you are, Johnny On-the-Bloody-Spot Gersohn, my personal stalker, waiting to leap into any opportunity to indulge your sick fascination with my role! In the immortal words of a fellow actor, 'Get a life, bud!' And Bill Shatner never had to put up with some would-be Captain Kirk who followed him around always ready to pass himself off as the real thing the moment the opportunity arose. You turn up everywhere, go to every two-bit con that pays to fly me in, pass yourself off as me in grocery stores and gas stations, and now you have the guts to sit in at my signing at a major gig like TitaniCon. I am getting a restraining order, bud, that will put your butt in a sling until halfway into the next millennium. Meanwhile, someone get this creep out of here before I think I really *am* the King Khatlord and tear him into itsy-bitsy pieces to match his brain and stunted emotional development."

When this Khatlord roared, people listened.

In fact, a third Khatlord joined the first two, taking up a custodial position behind the first one.

Matt was fascinated to observe a third level in Khatlord costumery: This was definitely C grade, with a flimsier looking facial appliance and sleazier fabric overall.

There was nothing flimsy about the third Khatlord's grip as he twisted Gersohn's right arm behind his back. He lacked the height the role required, even wearing the usual pumped-up buskins, but his heavier physique made him the match of Khatlord Number One, if not Number Two.

"Shut up," he ordered the first Khatlord in a nasty, intimidating tone that only moderated itself slightly when it addressed the new Khatlord on the scene. "I'll have to see some ID."

"Well, I'm not going to remove my mask. It's not done in public, and besides it's too much trouble getting fitted with one of these things—the real thing, I might add, and not the cheesy imitation you have on your face—but, lucky for you, I always travel with a credit card, and here it is, photo ID and all, sans Khat-face."

The man doffed his heavy-cuffed gauntlet to dig in one of the many pouches and holsters hanging from his broad belt.

From all this aggressive otherworldly clutter came a small rectangle of shiny plastic featuring a holographic dove, such an utterly familiar artifact of the mundane world that Matt smiled to see it flourished as a talisman of sorts among these three freaky-looking guys.

The custodial Khatlord leaned forward to squint at the inch-square image. "Yeah, it's got your name on it, Timothy Hathaway. What do you want me to do with this bozo, Tim?"

"He should be ejected from the con and not allowed back in." The triumphal Khatlord paused, then decreed. "And confiscate that phony mask so he can't masquerade as me again."

The Khatlord guard seemed all too eager. He grabbed the spotted visor and wrenched.

His prisoner screeched and doubled over. "Stop! Part of it's glued on!"

The Khatlord guard, apparently in faithful character to these rapacious spacelords, twisted only harder until the fearsome mask was in his hand and the bare face of its wearer was exposed to the crowd who had gathered.

Pinpoints of blood specked his face, a narrow pale face with a day's growth of beard.

"Take him away," the real Khatlord proclaimed, unnecessarily. The Khatlord guard had twisted the man's arm into a painful grip that had him doubled over again as he was hustled through people who parted like curtains at their approach.

The method of the man's unmasking and handling left a sour taste in Matt's mouth. It was brutal enough to be in a movie, not real life.

He glanced at Mariah, wondering what effect this 3-D violence would have on her delicate psyche, but she was staring at the remaining, and apparently real, Khatlord.

"You mean the signature I got isn't worth anything? It isn't real?"

The Khatlord's sinister spotted face turned her way.

"I mean exactly that, young lady. But come here."

Mariah edged forward.

"Someone give me a pen." The Khatlord snapped his fingers and held up a hairy-knuckled hand.

Someone did indeed dig up a pen and thrust it into his waiting fingers.

The Khatlord snatched the program Mariah held in her hand and scrawled something across the front cover.

"Thank you," she breathed as he handed it back.

"If you want to thank me, Earthling sprout, you will go to the dealers' room and buy at least one copy of my Khatlord Kompendium novel—or, better, several copies to give all your friends—and have me sign them later. All right?" The last phrase was more order than question.

Mariah nodded soberly.

The Khatlord looked around at the gathered crowd. "Well, move along. I'm not going to stand here and re-sign everything you were stupid enough to let a phony autograph. Didn't the voice tell you anything? I have another signing session scheduled in the dealers' room at four o'clock. Come then, and come early, as there'll be a very long line, and I quit exactly one hour after starting. I'm not getting carpal tunnel on your account."

He strode away.

"I do feel we have had an alien visitation," Matt commented to Sheila.

Mariah was studying her alien scrawl. "I can't tell what he wrote, but I bet it was cool."

"Don't mind Hathaway. He's known for an ego the size of Pluto," Sheila said.

"Does this happen often?" Matt asked.

"Imposters?"

"Imposters and this kind of scene?"

"No . . . but it is an alpha-male environment."

"I guess."

"I've heard about this guy. John Gersohn. He's totally fixated on being the Khatlord."

"Like that woman who kept breaking into David Letterman's house?"

"Only Gersohn breaks into the Khatlord's public appearances.

You can see it would be easy to substitute for him, given the concealing costume."

"I'm with Timothy on one thing," Matt said. "He's got an operatic voice. Hard to imitate."

"Maybe Johnny just mumbles and *hmmms* a lot."

"The people here are really that into their fantasy lives?"

"Some of them. You should try it, Matt."

"Dressing up, pretending not only to be somebody else, but some other *species?*"

"It's harmless fun."

"I've heard of cases where role-playing was not harmless fun, and it didn't look like fun for the Gersohn guy. He was humiliated and brutalized."

"That was hotel security, not the con people."

"Whoever it was, the Khatlord guard was enjoying it too much. I know some martial arts, and that guy was a pro. His victim was way out of his league. He didn't require that kind of overkill. And Hathaway is an overbearing bully."

"Shhh." Sheila put a coy finger to her lips.

Matt was about to object when he glanced down at Mariah staring up at him. "They do things like this on the show all the time," she said, almost as if to reassure him about the violent little playlet they had just witnessed.

"But this isn't the show, Mariah. Real life should be better than that."

"But is it?" she asked.

"Sometimes. That's what we aim for. The sometimes."

She shrugged. "I'm so glad I got a real signature. And I even saw his credit card! Wait'll the kids at school hear that on Monday. They'll be so jealous. He does a credit-card commercial, you know, 'cuz he's famous but nobody ever sees his face, so he walks into this phone store and has to show his photo-ID credit card to get okayed. It's pretty funny."

Matt gave up. Everything here was assumed to be larger than life and not to be taken seriously. Still, he saw the fake Khatlord as more to be pitied than despised. That kind of clutching at fantasy was the sign of a disintegrating personality.

Call him a bleeding-heart radio shrink. He'd rather be that than an arrogant Khatlord, the scourge of the Galaxy and idol of millions. What did it say that so many people needed superaggressive icons? Maybe that the meek shall inherit the heroes they deserve.

Chapter 24

Foxy Ladies

Is it not always the case?

Here a dude is searching for a foxy lady of the feline kind, and what does he stumble across but a familiar fellow of the homo sapiens sort?

I cannot believe whose size-ten Hush Puppies I am nose-to-toe with now! Especially not in this otherworldly ambiance, though no doubt my friend has been interested in otherworldly affairs of a completely different nature.

I look up from the fawn suede shoes to discern one of the few humans bereft of inhuman costume touches: Mr. Matt Devine, my Miss Temple's neighbor and sometime swain, although not for some time.

And he is out on the town with another woman.

I do not refer to Spindlelegs, the kiddish sprite wearing those uninspiring duds you see everywhere on her age group these days, called "shorts" and "T-shirt." I stare unhappily at her smudged tennis shoes. Whatever happened to patent-leather Mary Janes? Anklets with rows of lace on the cuffs? Carrying a little purse instead of storing everything in shorts so long and baggy they could cover the rear end of a Mack truck. And sometimes do.

I admit that I spring from another generation. And, my perennial formal black attire lends me a casual elegance that is always with me. Perhaps I long to see a little of it in the appearance of others. Vanished elegance. Fred and Ginger.

No such luck here. The other woman in Mr. Matt Devine's company seems to be wearing baggy green hose with a flour sack over them that is tied around the middle by a rope. The shoes are just fabric sacks gathered at the ankle with another rope.

I can assure you that my Miss Temple would not have visited as imaginative a scene as this without producing something equally imaginative to wear. However, since most of the guest stars have come to be seen and heard, and not emulated, I supposed that a certain predictability in dress does them honor.

I do not wish to attract undue attention to myself when I am undercover, so I back under the burgundy linen hem of the nearby signing-table drapery until I am all but hidden and can see only shoes again.

I do not know why Mr. Matt Devine is with child, not to mention lady elf, but I recall a young person who was present at the dreadful blessing to which I was dragged unwillingly at Our Lady of Guadalupe church last fall.

I am not against some spiritual help, mind you. It is just that I do not like to be confined to carrier, as I was that day, nor to have some cleric, upon introduction, complain that my name is not saintly. As a matter of fact, it is. The Louie part anyway, not the Midnight.

Although, I might point out, "midnight" is mentioned in more than one Christmas hymn, most prominently in the title of "It Came Upon a Midnight Clear."

Someone has obligingly dropped a program to the carpet to be ground underfoot. I skim the listed attractions. Since I am searching for a feline fatale, I must look for her where others of her ilk gather.

It strikes me that female figures are in the decided minority in all these depictions of other species and other worlds. And when they do figure in the scenarios and photos, they are usually femmes fatales, unless they are in the medical or other helping professions, like Counselor Troi on *Star Trek: The Next Generation.*

So my *Midnight Trek: The Next Generation* must take me farther afield.

Slinking from tablecloth to tablecloth, overleaping empty piles of cardboard boxes, skirting monks' robes and Jedi warriors, I head for the booths that feature the two biggest babes in the business cheek by jowl, or perhaps I should say si by bustier.

The lines here are galactic. Luckily, I pretty much match the carpeting, which is the black of deep space sprinkled with stars (which could be the glints in my green eyes), and soon pass up the footwear threesome of Mr. Matt Devine, kid, and elf.

Before you know it, I am playing footsie with Seven of Nine under the signing table.

This gives me an opportunity to measure the height of her platform shoes (four inches, at least by whisker-measure) and to sniff that shiny pewter-colored catsuit personally. Spandex is spandex. Her left hand is balanced on her sleek upper thigh under the table, for the moment, and I lift up to sniff that nasty Borg bracelet of hers. It reminds me of the outfit I had seen pictured on the lady I am looking for, but I smell no hint of feline pheromones. Alas, that would be the only thing to interest me in this semimechanical doll, so I scoot under cover of tablecloth to the open space between tables, then dash forward to ingratiate myself at the very leather-scented feet of Xena, Warrior Princess.

This is no discredit to Xena, Warrior Princess. All human feet, confined to closed-toed boots, are exceedingly pungent to all of my species. Humans apparently do not do the meticulous daily pedicures that we do. Perhaps it is not their fault. They do have trouble putting their feet in their mouths unless they are making a verbal blunder.

This lady's leather quotient is quite appealingly high. I nibble on one of the leather fringes comprising her kilt—or is that overkilt?—but it is too heavily seasoned with steel studs to make a satisfactory munch.

She apparently senses my attentions, as a short sword brushes toward me as if dislodging a fly.

It is only the tip of a very airy whisker, lady! Give me a break. I am here on official business. Well, perhaps it is only officious business.

I was sure my own four-footed siren would be in the vicinity, so I scamper off to the next table.

Here, I am right at home. Those two-faced creatures of the night, vampires, in minor roles crowd all around this table. You have got to admire their saber-tooth canines. I admit to being pretty impressed by humans who sport eyeteeth as long, sharp, and pointed as my own. I do not make as big a production of snarling to display these fearsome features as they do, but I could if I felt like it.

Alas, the canine crowd are the villains of the piece here. The centerpiece is Buffy Summers, the perky, little, blond vampire slayer, and the tall, dark, and angst-ridden wolf in vampire's clothing, Angel. I do not see what dames see in this dude. I have watched this show faithfully with my Miss Temple, and while there are plenty of scenes in which the lady-pleasing Angel removes his shirt, in not one of them do I spot a tuft of nice black hair on his chest. Repulsive! One might as well pet rubber. What do these dames see in this billiard ball with teeth? Beats me. If there is one thing for which I cannot fault Mr. Max Kinsella—and there is a lot I fault him for, including wandering off and leaving my Miss

Temple without a protector until I came along—it is that he has always been nicely haired, even though I have never (thank Bast) seen him with his shirt off.

There are some things even a house detective (formerly) does not Need To Know.

Although I have rubbed kneecaps with several of the most in-demand guest celebrities, I am still stymied in my goal of tracking down the babe that made the papers three days back.

Given that unwanted guests and fish reek after three days, her trail should stink to the stratosphere by now.

Chapter 25

Cut to the Quick

"What did you think of my gal?" Temple wondered when the Blue Mermaid Motel was a distant image floating in her rearview mirror.

"Useful for Christmas presents," Max said, nodding judiciously.

She took a hand off the steering wheel to punch him in the arm. "A roundabout way of calling her a fruitcake."

"I don't believe in Santa Claus, or psychics."

"She nailed you: several dead men and one dead woman on your mind."

"Anyone who knew my profession could figure that out."

"Who's supposed to know your real profession?"

"No one," he admitted, grinning. "One thing's clear. She didn't see Mangel as a closet debauchee. I'd trust her personal judgment far more than her psychic one. Anyone trained to read other people is a pretty good judge."

"Anyone including magicians?"

"I hope so. Take a left next corner. We're heading north."

"How far north?"

"Out of the city. My guy is the rugged type."

"Oh, goodie, I get to take this baby out on the freeway."

"It's not the Firebird; it's peppy but not powerful. And you don't want to attract police attention."

"Listen, I could use attracting something besides dead bodies."

"Really." Max turned to her. "We have some time to kill. If you know a convenient turnoff—"

Temple wrenched the wheel to the right. The landscape here was flat scrubland. They jolted into it for about one hundred yards before Temple braked the car to a stop.

"I was thinking of something more formal," Max confessed.

"I wasn't."

"Well." He twisted back to study the freeway. Distant trucks and SUVs and limos raced by, supremely oblivious. "I don't think we'll attract the highway patrol, unless someone decides we went out of control and crashed."

"We should be so lucky."

"Luck," he decided, "has nothing to do with it."

It was one of those impulsive, unpremeditated occasions where the stick shift made an interesting ménage à trois. A nice necking session in a car not made for it, which made everything interesting. Temple ended up spanning both the driver's and passenger's sides along with the dashboard.

"This is more like it," she said at last.

"Like what?"

"Like it used to be, in Minneapolis."

"Improvised, you mean."

"Improvised, nuts, dangerous, fun." She gazed up into his eyes. "I can't decide whether I like you better with blue eyes or green."

"As long as you like me."

"I always will, Max. That's the Kinsella curse."

He flinched, and she regretted. "I only meant—"

"You meant what you said, and meant nothing by it. That psychic made me antsy."

"You believe her?"

"That's not the point. She's believable. Who knows why? I know something about needing to be believable. That's the curse."

"I wish—"

"Don't stop."

"Wishes are weapons, aren't they? I'm happy, Max. Right now. Okay?"

"Okay." He thought for a moment. "Am I the reason why?"

"Yup."

"Then it's worth it."

She nodded, not asking what "it" was. Happiness was not asking questions. True happiness was not needing to.

She had stopped the car on the brink of a dried-out wash and now noticed that there was no place to turn around.

"You think I can back up straight in reverse all the way to the highway?" she asked.

"Honestly?"

"What else is there?"

"If you have to ask, no."

"Then you drive for a while. I don't know where your 'guy' lives anyway."

The guy lived out where the rattlesnakes and the survivalists dwell about six feet outside Hell, Nevada.

Temple stared at a landscape from the dark side of Mars. Barbed-wire fence had been the only sign of civilization for three miles. Of course everything was fenced these days, the sign of distant ownership even on these forsaken acres.

The shack looked unfit for human habitation. Only the sand-savaged ancient jeep outside promised occupation inside.

"Air-conditioning? Temple asked.

Max spread his hands to encompass the desert. "Wind, sun, sandburn."

The car top had been up since they'd taken the dusty road off the highway. The radio had been tuned to a soft rock station but was off now, so the wind whistling through the ragtop was their only music.

"Minneapolis, land of ten thousand lakes, where are you?" Temple asked rhetorically as she got out of the passenger side and slammed the door shut on the eddy of sand her exit created.

"No mosquitoes," Max suggested optimistically.

She gave him a piercing look before lowering her sunglasses from their position atop her head. "Why do I feel like I'm Scully and you're Mulder?"

"You have red hair?" Max hazarded. "Okay. This is my interview. I kept a straight face through yours."

"Straight face," she repeated, putting one on and feeling like an alien behind her dark glasses.

After they walked up to the shack, Max stared at the ramshackle door, then shrugged, and knocked.

It shuddered to every blow.

"Mace?" he asked. "Mace Jones?"

No answer, except Temple incredulously mouthing the name "Mace." She looked down at her sensible wedgies, and frowned.

Max reconnoitered, disappearing around the rear of the shack.

Temple fidgeted at the front, er, door. Why did this feel like a made-for-television movie? All except the sex scene. She leaned against the splintery wooden doorjamb and smiled.

The door opened, and she fell inside. *Max!*

No Max, just "Mace." *Ohmigod!*

Sweat. Muscle. Sawdust. Tequila.

For a few dollars more, she'd head for the Mexican border.

Except she seemed to be in the room with him.

"Hey, pretty lady."

Mace was dressed in tattoos, a leather vest, and leather pants. Mace was, to her best guess, an arresting blend of black and Hispanic. Must have a hell of a personality conflict.

He was one tough hombre. Uh, dude.

"Come on in," he invited.

"Not without me." Max stood in the hot light of the open door, tall, rangy as barbed wire, and about as dangerous.

"You the knife-thrower dude?" Mace asked.

Temple raised her eyebrows, but in the shaded interior of the shack, no one noticed.

"Yeah. This here's my knife throwee." Max nodded at Temple.

Mace let his hand drop from her upper arm, but his eyes registered appreciation. "She must have some nerve."

Some nerve. Temple tried to convey that sentiment to her knees. They really didn't need to knock; the door was open already.

"Where can I see the merchandise?" Max asked.

"Out back," Mace said. But first he smiled at Temple. "Macedonia Jones. Pleased to meetcha."

"Macedonia? Quite . . . classic." Temple extended a hand. "Nice to meetcha, too."

Mace lifted her hand to his lips. She rolled her eyes like Mae West, finding Max's eyes. One psychic, they said, equals one psycho.

Max came up fast, and it was hard to say if Mace released her, or Max claimed her. Or if Temple extracted herself from the middle of both.

"You seen the shop?" Mace asked.

"The corrugated shed out back?" Max queried in return.

"Right. It's where I work."

Temple ground sand into her soles en route to the shed, which, once they were inside, proved to be huge and, thankfully, air-conditioned.

"Nice," she couldn't help proclaiming once the chilled air hit her.

Since the rest of the place looked like Vulcan's workshop, "nice" would hardly describe it.

It was much larger than the residential shack up front. Temple saw ovens, and forges, and what looked like grinders and buffers.

Mace was less interested in showing them the elements of manufacture and more interested in showing off the products.

Temple had never seen so many large, decorative knives in her life, outside an infomercial.

Max and Mace talked Asian methods versus Spanish methods, talked steel, talked hilt, talked signature, talked inlay, talked edge, talked collectibility.

As far as Temple was concerned, they could have talked Urdu.

What she saw was knifery raised to a lethal and elegant art. Bowie knives, commemorative knives, Native-American knives, Asian knives . . . she had no idea that so many variations on the simple steak knife were possible.

"Tell him what you saw, honey," Max urged, breaking into her reverie.

Mace was pretending to look interested.

"Gee," she said. "It was an awful big knife."

Mace seemed to take this personally, and positively.

"And the . . . hand part, you know. The whatever—"

"Haft," Max said.

"Hilt," Mace said.

"Yeah. Whatever." If only she had a big wad of gum to chew. While she paused, both men hung on her very breath. If only she were blond. "It was . . . sharp, like the blade itself, you know? I never seen anything like it." She hadn't, if only she could remember every detail from the photo she'd seen in Molina's office. "Kinda like a big figure eight, or a cleft, you know, like a *musical* cleft, all swirly. Only sharp, too. Am I confusing you?"

Both men were quick to say no.

"It was like the handle—I guess you call it haft, or shaft, or hilt, or something—so the handle was like one of those Meedy-evil weapons, if you know what I mean. Anyway, it'd make a great stunt. Can you think of one like that, Mace, huh? I hope you know what I mean."

Temple batted what she assumed were her eyelashes. *Think Savannah Ashleigh,* she told herself, *and all will be well. Hell!*

Mace rubbed a grimy hand over his grimy chin. "Frankly, folks, I think you're talking pretty kinky here."

196 • Carole Nelson Douglas

"Really?" Max asked, interested. "I'm not averse to a little kink."

Mace winked at Temple. "I bet not." His voice lowered. "I got some very hot numbers. A little on the satanic side. You interested?"

"I imagine anything on the satanic side would be hot," Max responded.

"Got all these signs and symbols inscribed in. Bunch of hokum, but the flakes like 'em."

Max nodded.

Mace swaggered over to a metal cabinet and pulled out a manila envelop stuffed with papers. He began to shuffle through them.

Temple glimpsed knives with naked male and female torsos for hilts, and assorted symbols. But it was an abstract design she had seen, and finally she spotted its twin.

"There!" She thrust her hand out to stop the riffling process.

The knife design revealed was bizarre but not ribald. The longer she looked at it, the more certain she was that it was the right one.

An elegant power invested its odd yet striking shape.

Max nodded once, not happily.

Mace smirked. "The little lady seems to know what she wants. I also make chain-mail bikinis to order. Right to size."

"We like this," Max said. "Give us an estimate and a copy. We'd be interested in . . . a dozen, I guess."

"A dozen?"

"It's a knife-throwing act. I do a dozen at a time."

"Whatever you want, but I ain't got a copier out here. This was a one-off, for a very particular customer."

"Maybe it's copyrighted," Max said. "Maybe we should deal with the guy who commissioned it."

"Who said it was a guy?" Mace responded, grinning.

Temple couldn't tell if he was negotiating or telling the truth. Odd that she assumed one precluded the other.

"You got an address on it?" Max asked.

"Confidential," Mace snapped.

Temple swallowed and played her part. "Gee, I really like it, Mace. Doncha think you could help . . . me out? Maybe we do need a chain-mail bikini."

Mace wavered. "A dozen, you say?"

"At least," Max said.

"And a metal bikini?"

"For sure," Max said, with irritating fervor.

"I copied the sketch myself, for production. I could let you have that one, if you bring it back."

"For sure," Max said.

Mace handed Max the paper and Temple a swatch of linked brass metalwork. "So you can see the workmanship. Feels like icy butter."

Oh, joy.

"Thank you," Temple gushed.

"Right." Max grabbed her elbow and hustled her back to the car.

They managed to drive away, Max steering; Temple studying the sketch.

"Initials," she pronounced.

"Of the person who commissioned it?"

"One hopes. Let's see . . . 'S' . . . 'N' . . . 'H'."

Max shook his head. "It's a code. 'S', skip the 'Y,' 'N,' skip the T,' 'H.' "

"Gee." Temple stared at the dead-end insignia. "I thought it looked like short for SavaNnaH. You think?"

"Sorry. I suppose you could sell her a used chain-mail bikini."

"I suppose so, but what I really want to do is sue her uplifted ass off in *The People's Court.*"

Chapter 26

Someone to Watch over You

Matt stood on his tiny, triangular, third-floor patio, staring down at the icy blue rectangle of the Circle Ritz pool.

It was too cool yet to swim, but he longed to go down, pull out the blue mats, and move through his Tai Chi routine. Mostly, he longed to rinse away the exotic hubbub of TitaniCon.

No such luck.

This was only a rest break in what was sure to be a full week-end of wall-to-wall mania, given Mariah's energy and enthusiasm for all things science fictional, heroic and imaginative, and, apparently, for expensive reminders of the historic occasion.

The momentary island of peace had been won by his suggesting a pizza break somewhere less hectic. Not quite knowing where to go for this, he had headed home. His number-one social advisor, Temple, had been out, but Electra Lark had been decidedly in and up for a spontaneous kids' night out.

Right now she was giving Mariah a tour of her penthouse, since she had read Matt's glazed look in an instant and arranged for a few brief moments of solitary R&R.

He shook his head in bemusement. Mariah veered from pre-teen flights of fancy to sudden spurts of girly maturity laced with a giggling, nervous interest in way-too-old-for-her male media figures. She couldn't decide if she resented his adult presence and tacit supervision, or if it was cool to be escorted by someone who could pass for a media heartthrob.

Matt supposed a fatherless upbringing might intensify the typical teenage-girl attraction to older men and authority figures. And the science fiction world was full of male authority figures, captains and alien kings from *Star Trek*'s bald Captain Picard to the King Khatlord.

Matt's meditation on the teen years, single-parent families, and what Sheila called "fandom" was interrupted by a car driving into the corner of the parking lot visible from his third-floor balcony.

The convertible that pulled to a stop was bluer than the pool. Its white interior was like the showy velvet inside of a jewelry case, putting a spotlight on the contents, Temple and Max Kinsella.

Matt should have felt a jolt at seeing them together, but the distance made it seem like he was watching a movie.

Temple had been driving. Her wavy red hair looked more tousled than usual. Kinsella, he noticed, did not seem to be regrowing the ponytail he had shed for some reason the last time Matt had seen him, when he had been so upset over the death of a stripper he had run into during his mysterious doings.

Kinsella got out and went around to open the driver's door for Temple, who seemed reluctant to give up the wheel.

Apparently, it had been a madcap outing.

But she got out and moved in front of the door as Max slammed it shut. They stood by the car, talking.

Kinsella suddenly lifted Temple to sit on the bright blue hood, a tiny doll-like figure from above, dressed in red and navy. She put her hands on his shoulders. They kissed.

Matt's movie suddenly zoomed into flashback and closeup, to a dark, desert scene: Temple sitting on the hood of her aqua Storm in a purple taffeta dress, and Matt standing there like a department-store mannequin, doing nothing except freezing in dread and desire.

He didn't feel jealousy at what he saw now, only a profound sadness at how little he had been equipped to deal with any of this as far back as—what, last summer?

He was unable to stop watching or punch through his deadened emotional distance to the present, after the turmoil of reliving the past when he had done the fatally wrong thing: nothing.

The kiss ended. Kinsella helped Temple hop down from the car. She was walking toward the Circle Ritz, disappearing into the building.

Then Max Kinsella looked up. Right at him.

For an instant, a bolt of adrenaline melded the shame of the past, the regret of the present. Matt didn't pretend not to have been looking. Meeting someone's gaze over such a distance gave him an odd, alienated feeling.

Kinsella didn't prolong the moment. He just opened the car door and drove away. Anticlimax.

Matt remained looking down at the vacant pool and empty parking lot he had seen so often. Max Kinsella was a now-you-see-him, now-you-don't kind of guy, courtesy of his magician history and his razor-edged past. He wondered how Temple felt about having the equivalent of Janice's "Invisible Man," though he could no longer decipher his own feelings toward Temple and had given up trying to.

Did God ever manage any kind of dispassionate interest toward humankind? Culture after culture placed Him high above, looking down. His eye is on the sparrow, but His hand in the actions of the higher animals was harder to see. The Old Testament God sent angels and prophets, punished and commanded. The New Testament God sent his Son to change water into wine and taste vinegar while dying alongside criminals on a cross. Was God in his heaven, dispassionate then?

Perhaps God was looking down on Matt now, looking down,

seeing past, present, and future . . . and feeling sadly distant. As Matt himself felt now.

The doorbell rang, startling Matt back into the real world, which at the moment were several: the Federation, the Empire, the Kohl Kompendium.

He went to admit Electra and Mariah, who stood beaming on his threshold. He smiled at their incongruous partnership. Maybe this was his future with women: over sixty and under fifteen.

"It's so cool up there!" Mariah declared, glancing at Electra with a conspiratory giggle. "Such great *Karma*." Obviously, there were secrets a mere male couldn't share.

Electra winked at Matt as Mariah dashed into his living room and pounced like one of her half-grown kittens on the red sofa.

"I love this couch. It's so cool"

She sprawled in undignified disarray, all legs and arms, like a kitten.

"Brother," Electra said under her breath, "you have your hands full. What were you thinking of, taking on a kid for a whole weekend?"

"Her mother needed a break, and I didn't know much about kids."

"You will now. Call me if you need another break. Maybe Temple can help, too."

"No!" He hadn't meant to sound so negative. "We'll be fine. All I need to know is the way to a good pizza place. Now that I've got a car, we can all go."

And there was always Sheila.

Chapter 27

Foxxy Lady

Max decided to get some mileage out of the Cavalier before he turned it in to his friendly neighborhood parking-lot drop-off point.

He hated to follow the fun afternoon with Temple with a walk on "Sleazy Street," but he was used to treading very opposite sides of the avenue in quick succession.

Then, too, maybe guilt kicked in. What right had he to fun afternoons—if you could term calling on a psychic and a knife-maker fun—when Cher Smith would have no afternoons at all for eternity?

Time to pull a lowlife out of his own psyche, throw it out there, and see what it could learn.

Max frowned at himself in the mirror-lined Romanesque bathroom that he had inherited either from the late Orson Welles or the late Garry Randolph. It was hard to say which previous occupant of the house had ordered the black marble and mirrors.

It was a pity that "Vince," one of his favorite sleazeball imitations, had been the persona to aggravate Rafi Nadir, the strip-club bouncer Max suspected of being Cher's killer. Max had grown rather fond of Vince, as an actor would relish a favorite villain role. Plus, the look was easy to do. Only it was sure to set off Raf Nadir.

But why not tick off Nadir? Might get some answers.

Max reached for the pomade to grease up his hair. Hello, Vince.

Life went on at Secrets, if you could call what went on there nightly "life."

Max parked the Cavalier, top up, in a dark corner of the parking lot.

Even the asphalt seemed to throb to the deafening music inside. Max could only hear the primal base thumps as he approached the single door in the boxlike building.

The sign blinking and nodding and winking atop a long pole was bigger than the entrance to this joint.

A tangible wall of smoke and sound made Max hesitate for a split second. Then Vince shouldered through the thick atmosphere, swaggering toward the bar. Tonight he was wearing a satin jacket embroidered with the name of a long-gone hotel-casino, the Dunes. Green and pink palms grew like glitzy mold on the jacket's black satin back. A black sleeveless "Tee" beneath it permitted the display of a chunky lump of cheap gold on a chain.

As he approached himself in the murky mirror, he lifted his hands to smooth the sides of his hair. Talk about greasing palms.

The usual number of lethargic men were sprinkled around the tables, the long bar-cum-mosh-pit along the lip of the stage, and at the bar proper, where a couple of bored girls were pretending to copulate with a pair of metal poles.

"What'll you have?" asked the man named Rick.

They were always named Rick.

"Boilermaker." Max laid a twenty on the dewy surface. A couple of liquid drops trembled as Rick snatched it up. Nobody let money lie long at a strip joint.

He got a shot of whiskey, a tall glass of beer, and ten bucks back.

Strip joints were better at stripping customers of their money than the girls were at dropping clothes.

Max looked around nervously as Rick moved bottles and glasses around behind the bar. "Guess it's early yet."

"Yeah."

"You still got that hair-trigger bouncer?"

Rick paused, looked at Max, shrugged. "Don't know who you mean."

"You'd know. The girls were scared of him."

"How'd you know that?"

"Man, you could see it in their eyes. He was a little scary. Not that I scare easy."

Rick grunted. He was used to customers with points to make, like how tough they were, or how much the girls liked them. Fact was, any man who came into a place like this was a mark, pure and simple. If things went smoothly, he'd leave thinking he'd gotten something for his money.

Max drank and sipped, and let his ten bucks sit on the bar soaking up booze and water and somebody else's sweat.

His carelessness said he was a veteran, that maybe he had enough money to be interesting to someone who was looking for a mark.

He looked around, still edgy. "He don't scare me, whoever he is."

"That's nice."

"Just wanted to check if he was on."

Rick nodded to the matching bar on the other side of the cavernous room. "That your guy?"

Max took in a thick-necked kid who probably played halfback for the local team. Moonlighting. Big but green. Big enough to intimidate beefier guys than he was, but brute strength had never been Max's long suit.

It was a fact, a factor, and often a disadvantage. He knew his own deceptive, trained, tenacious, tensile strength was a match for all the muscle in Las Vegas, including the muscle-bound gray cells in the brutes' heads. Thin steel wires held up bridges; thick ropes didn't.

"Naw, the college letterman ain't him. Guy I'm thinking about could eat him for afternoon tea. Don't see him. Guess I can have some fun without cracking my knuckles."

Max crammed a fistful of salty, fatty crackers intermixed with the rare peanut into his mouth and chewed noisily. "Got any good new girls?"

"Gal from Reno. Goes by Redd Foxxy."

Max "hmmmed" appreciatively. "When she on?"

"Later. Want another?"

Later. Want another. The name of the game.

"Sure," Max said, draining both booze and beer in a few gulps.

Rick looked happy, but he also looked like he wished somebody more imposing than the junior weightlifter across the way were here.

"Guy you're asking about," he said casually, dropping off another weak shot of whiskey and another watery, bland glass of beer at Max's post. "He'll come in later. He has a fancy gig up at one of the Strip hotels. Pays a bunch. But they close down early. Don't want those green felts to be neglected. So he'll be along, after midnight. Raf, I think you mean."

"Raf. Like Riff-raff?" Max offered a semidrunken laugh. Some people can't hold their chug-a-lugs, and Vince was one. It was a very convenient failing. "Hell, I ain't afraid of him. I just wanted to know when he'd be around. What Strip hotel would hire a strip-joint bouncer?"

Now Rick's nose was out-of-joint, where it would lead his mouth right where Max wanted it. "New place. High-toned. The New Millennium. Secrets isn't the dive you think it is."

"Sorry, pal. Didn't mean anything by it. Here." Max peeled off a ten-buck tip then clumsily gathered his disparate-sized glasses and rambled toward the stage-lip seats. "Redd Foxxy, huh? Got to check that out. Sure it isn't 'Reddy Foxx?' "

He spent the next hour grinning vacantly at a lot of T&A aimed at his face while itching to head for the New Millennium.

Raf Nadir was moving up in the world, at least this week.

None of the strippers who did their five-minute stints were the same ones he'd seen a few weeks ago. They moved around from club to club.

He needed to move around, too. After an hour, he lurched up, wove out to the parking lot, and reclaimed the Cavalier.

Time to ditch it, and its clean, blue-white afternoon memories.

Time to find out what Raf Nadir was doing when he wasn't intimidating forlorn strippers, and maybe killing them. And for that, he would need outside inside help.

Chapter 28

Louisiana Joyride

Day Two.

Mariah came bouncing out of the house before Matt could get out of the car, ecstatic that her mother had got her sprung from school as a surprise. Otherwise, a color shift in her T-shirt and baggy shorts was the only change from yesterday.

She jumped into the front seat. "Mom says I can get a Bab Five T-shirt."

"Great."

"That's where I want to stop first, the dealers' room. Is your Vorlon-hand tattoo still good? Don't tell Mom, but I didn't wash my hands, just in case."

Matt flashed the top of his right hand. "Well, I did, and the whatchamacallit is still in one piece."

"*Okay!* I wanta go on the Wormhole ride. You don't have to go."

"What if I want to?"

"You do? Well, I guess you can. I've seen old people lined up for it, too."

"Hey, I hate to tell you, but most of the people attending the con are 'old.' "

"I didn't mean *old* old." Mariah flashed him a glance. "I mean, even some of the actors are old, too, if you think about it."

Matt didn't answer, wondering when kids finally crossed the chasm to realizing that they themselves were in the process of becoming old. Probably the late twenties.

The drive to the New Millennium wasn't very long, but Mariah kept silent during most of it. Only as he was turning into the long winding driveway to the hotel's rear parking ramp did she speak again.

"I want to be older. Not much older, but some. Twelve is such a dorky age. I mean, you're almost in junior high, but everybody treats you like a baby still. I want to be just old enough so I can do what I want to do without anybody stopping me."

"That's another thing I hate to tell you: You never do get that old."

"People tell *you* what to do, and then make you do it?"

"Well, the police do, so you don't want to break any laws. And then there are the general rules of courtesy just in getting along with strangers, and all sorts of unwritten rules in getting along with the people you work for or know."

"You mean you never get to do exactly what you want?"

"Sometimes you do. But most of the time you have to adapt what you want to what will work with the world around you."

"Bummer!" Mariah hopped out of the car the minute it was parked. "I'm gonna go get that shirt before someone says I can't do it."

Matt let her skip ahead on the open second-story walkway to the hotel. Kids ran on energy and impulse, and every year those fuels diminished a little, until without even noticing, youngsters had become oldsters.

He decided that merely watching a twelve-year-old who seemed to locomote on hidden pogo sticks was an aging activity.

He picked up his pace to catch up to her before she melded into the crowds already pouring into the TitaniCon area.

In the dealers' room, she ran from booth to booth, torn between a T-shirt with a roaring, coiling, flame-throwing dragon, or one depicting an array of sinister-looking spaceships dogfighting near some neon-colored planet.

He remembered Sheila's comment about the division between high-tech and low in the science fiction and fantasy scene. Mariah was a living battlefield between the two extremes of imagination.

"Do you have the time?" she asked Matt, the first query of what would be several, to judge by yesterday's pattern.

"It's a little after eleven. What's the hurry?"

"Well, I promised to meet Sheila by the Wormhole."

"Oh? Isn't she a little old for that?" he teased.

"Yeah, but she promised to buy me Nimbus of Narnia."

Multicolored cotton candy, by any other name, Matt knew by now.

"After the ride, of course," Mariah said.

"Maybe we'll all get Nimbi of Narnia after the ride."

"Nimbi?"

"That's the Latin plural of Nimbus. If you take Latin in high school, you'll learn that. Or don't they teach Latin anymore?"

"I don't know." Mariah bit her lip and headed back to a table piled with T-shirts. Today, the dragon had won.

Matt stood by while she pulled a selection of worn five-dollar bills from her fanny pack to pay for the purchase. Another few years and she'd probably be doing this at rock concerts. He trembled for her mother. Baby-sitters wouldn't be available then.

They began weaving through the flow of aliens and ordinary earthlings starting to immobilize the constant traffic through the vast ballroom.

"Oh, look!" Mariah squealed.

Matt decided that these were the two most common words in the preteen vocabulary.

A table featured upright boards of black felt swagged with

exotic-looking costume jewelry. Mariah had stopped at one to fondle the pearl-and-crystal-threaded chains.

A woman wearing a cap of fine chains and beads that lay over her long brown hair like a spiderweb came to stand behind the display.

"What are these little ones?" Mariah's glittering dark eyes were hypnotized by the exotic baubles.

"They go like this." The woman lifted one off its pinhook and pushed her heavy hair and lightweight headdress over one shoulder.

She slipped the thing over the top of her ear, so the chains hung down in both front and back.

"It's an earring?" Mariah asked.

"An alien earring."

"And you don't have to have your ears pierced to wear it?"

The woman removed the earring, shaking her head no.

"Can I try it?"

A hand mirror levitated at Mariah's height. It had been lying on the black felt behind the jewelry board. In an instant the woman had tucked Mariah's short bob behind one ear and slipped the jewelry over it.

"How neat! I can wear it without having pierced ears. I want it!" Her head snapped around as she remembered Matt. "I can get it? Please!"

His first *in loco parentis* dilemma. He remembered Mariah arguing for pierced ears over pizza recently. He remember her mother saying no.

"They're not pierced," Mariah was urging, alert to every nuance of his expression.

Matt knew what his face was giving away: disinclination, hesitation, wavering. It was his call, darn it. He didn't want to countermand her mother. On the other hand, the dangle-thing was a noninvasive compromise. A costumey noninvasive compromise meant for an adult, not a kid.

Holy cow.

"Here." Reaching past him, a pair of long, green-tinted fingernails plucked an earring off the board and held it up to the mirror. "This is nice."

"This" was one of those pearls on fishline thingamabobs Matt was seeing on women everywhere as necklaces, bracelets, earrings. Airy. Delicate. Perfect for a preteen.

"It all floats," Mariah cried, enchanted. "Cool. This one. Can I have this one, please?"

"Like planets in space," the green-nailed one said.

She reminded Matt of a cross between the Evil Emperor Ming and the Wicked Queen in *Snow White*—big silver lace collar, close-fitting head-and-neck cap sewn with jewels, elaborately painted eyes. He wasn't sure if he should recognize her from a specific film or show, if she were a major player guest-starring at TitaniCon, or simply a fan planning to enter the costume competition they called a masquerade.

Whatever, she was his savior. He nodded an okay at Mariah and even reached for his wallet. "This one's on me." He turned to the exotic diplomat. "Thanks for the suggestion."

"No problem, handsome." She winked, blinking incredibly long, silver-metallic false eyelashes. "Enjoy," she intoned to Mariah, like a smarmy sales clerk and turned to vanish into a crowd crammed with creatures just as bizarre.

That last "enjoy" sounded a bit too much like "Come, bite" for Matt's taste, ruining her exit.

Mariah was regarding herself in the mirror, the delicate solar system on an invisible string circling her cheek. "Thank you, Matt! You are so cool. Not even hardly old at all!"

He noticed with a twinge how pearly the beads looked against her olive skin and emphasized the whites framing her dark eyes. Vanity, and growing up, and inevitably, danger.

Well, he'd discuss this little transaction with Molina after this was all over. Presumably her killer schedule would slow down eventually. *Killer schedule*. Macabre choice of words . . .

"There you are!"

Sheila was threading through the crowd in her wren-brown robe, her drab coloring lost in the swirl of more exotic costumes.

The green-nailed woman was nowhere to be seen, not even her massive collar.

Sheila took several deep breaths after she reached them. "The crowds are getting brutal. Listen, I'm afraid I can't go on the Wormhole with Mariah like I promised."

"Why?" Matt and Mariah asked as one.

She shook her head in disgust. "Stupid accident. After we split up last evening, I was on the moving sidewalk, and it was wall-to-wall people. Some stupid tourist pushed me into the rock garden as I was about to get off." She lifted a foot. Matt looked down to see a very out-of-period flesh-tone Ace bandage wrapping her ankle above equally unelfin cushioned sneakers.

"I'm told you need to brace your feet on the floor during simulated motion rides, and this ankle is unhappy enough just gimping along. I'm sorry, honey," she told Mariah, her eyes truly regretful.

"That's okay," Mariah said. "Matt can go on with me." She tossed her head, as if to shake her hair out of her face, but actually it was to shake it back behind her ears so Sheila could see the dangling ear decoration.

"Oh, hey. That's out of this world. How pretty. I wish I had one like it." Sheila made all the right feminine noises that Matt couldn't provide.

"You can't. It's the last one. But there are some others here," Mariah said generously.

"Thanks. I'll wait to gussy up until tomorrow. Maybe then I can ditch the dopey shoes."

"Are you going to be able to get your money's worth here?" Matt asked her.

"Oh, I'll go sit down in the con suite. You two go ahead. Explore the next dimension. Maybe we'll cross paths again."

Matt felt torn. Sheila had obviously enjoyed crossing paths so far, and he'd appreciated her presence since he felt so awkward with Mariah. On the other hand, she had been relishing her role as part of a family triad enough to make him a bit nervous.

"We'll check the con suite after the ride," he suggested. "Where is it anyway?"

Brightening, she told him.

Mariah, meanwhile, was jumping from foot to foot in impatience.

Matt was devoutly glad that he had been able to be a "father" for so long without any real fatherly duties or conflicts.

"We'll see you later," he told Sheila, realizing that Mariah had been very patient with the banal adult conversation going on over her head while tantalizing goodies like more solar system ear-dangles and Wormhole rides awaited.

She knew right where to find the ride entry and led the way on prancing feet.

There was a long line, of course, in which she jiggled, burning energy as if it were a renewable resource.

"Gosh, this ear-thing is so different. No girl in school will have one. Do you think it's too weird?"

She clasped her hands behind her neck. (They were a bit grubbier at the nails and knuckles than her mother would have permitted, had she been home to oversee Mariah's departure, Matt bet.)

He smiled to see insecurity rush in where overconfidence had trod not five minutes before.

"It looks very nice. Sometimes you want to be different from everybody else. And sometimes you don't."

She frowned. "That's true." She seemed amazed that he should make sense. "How do you know what you want to be when?"

"You just have to play it by . . . ear." He tweaked the one she kept pushing her hair behind, so the tiny pearls shimmied.

"Oh, fun-nee!" But she giggled. And then she looked ahead at the nearing entry to the ride. "It won't be too scary, will it?"

"Don't know. Haven't been on it."

"Are you scared?"

"A little. Anything you haven't been on before is scary."

"But you're big."

"Are you sure you don't mean 'old.' "

"I never meant *old* old." She bit her lip. "How old are you?"

It was rude to ask, but he sensed she was trying to put things in a perspective that was constantly changing these days.

"As old as my mother?" she persisted.

"About that old."

"You don't seem as old."

"I'm not your mother. Mothers always seem older than they are to their own kids." Actually, he suspected Molina did have a few years on him.

"Does yours?"

He nodded.

"She must be really old. I mean, being your mother."

"Actually, she's pretty young for a mother, and she's getting younger every day."

"That doesn't make sense."

"Yes, it does. My mother had a lot of worries when she was young. Now, things are better, and she's getting younger."

"I guess my mom has a lot of worries."

"Yes, she does."

"It's really kinda—"

"Kinda what?"

"Everybody at school knows she's a policewoman. The kids all say she's gonna get 'em, like she's the neighborhood bogeyman. Sometimes I wish . . ."

"You wish your mom weren't a cop?"

She nodded, unconscious of the decoration waggling in her ear for the first time. And said nothing more.

Matt supposed that being a cop's daughter was as bad as being the preacher's kid. You had the ultimate authority figure to rebel against. And so did all your friends and enemies.

"Your mom's pretty neat." Did kids today even know what 'neat' meant? "It's a tough job, you've seen that. She's one of the first women to do it. You should be proud of her. I know she's proud of you."

Mariah stared at him with the clear, testing gaze you don't see after a certain age. He tried to meet it.

She nodded. "Maybe she'll get younger when she's older. And I'll get older when I'm not as young."

"It generally works that way."

"Really? Uh-oh. We're gonna be in the next group on. Will you . . . hold my hand if it gets scary?"

"If you'll hold mine."

She bit her lip, looking like a kid that would face demons before holding anyone's hand. But she wanted to know the possibility was there.

Didn't everyone?

Matt was glad he had been through this simulated movie before, with Janice, who had not asked to hold his hand.

After hearing the standard warning that kids under four-feet high—Mariah had shot up way past that in the last year, to the best of his memory—pregnant women, and heart patients, plus people with head, neck, back, and joint injuries should immediately bail out, they shuffled into the line that led them directly into the row of seats.

Once buckled in, Matt leaned down and whispered in Mariah's ear a bit of inside information he had learned on the previous ride. "If you disconnect the seatbelt, your chair will quit moving. It's supposed to be like a roller coaster, so if it's too rough, just unbuckle."

She nodded, too nervous to speak. Fear of the unknown was finally penetrating that fearless young faith. She slipped him a sickly grin, sideways.

He gave the thumbs-up sign.

And then . . . lights, camera, action, they were bucking and swerving and skidding and twisting in their expensive seats while the screen ahead of them plunged them through black tunnels of space and swirling, psychedelic birth canals of wormholes into exotic sound-and-light-show realms beyond. Spinning galaxies and alien constellations and ships swooped under, above, beside them, shooting fireworks at them, missing, exploding dead ahead like stars gone nova.

Now he knew what to expect, and heard himself laughing, and shouting, and felt himself dodging and blinking the phantasms that came from all directions and assaulted all senses.

It only lasted minutes, but they seemed like breathlessly long minutes. Some of it was scary, and he wondered a couple of times when it would be over. And a couple of times he wished that it would never end.

Then all the chaos quieted. They were a bunch of strangers belted into a dream machine together.

He glanced at Mariah. She was laughing, but her hands were still white-knuckling it on the armrests. "Okay?"

"That was . . . fun. Can we . . . do it again?"

"Right away?"

"Well, maybe not right away."

He unbuckled and stood, surprised to feel the floor—or the soles of his feet—still throbbing a little. He took Mariah's hand as they edged out in a jam-packed crowd to make way for another round of joyriders.

She didn't object.

Chapter 29

"A" Is for Anonymous

"Fancy meeting you here," she said.

Temple smiled as Matt and company almost walked right past her.

"Oops. Sorry," he said. "We're still a little discombobulated from the Wormhole."

Matt looked more than discombobulated to see her. He looked shocked. "And company," which was a preteen girl, looked green around the gills. Maybe it was the Wormhole ride. Maybe it was encountering any competition for Matt's attention. Temple thought the twelve-year-old was a little mature to be holding onto his hand for dear life.

Matt shook the girl's hand to get her attention as he introduced her. "You remember Mariah Molina," he told Temple.

Mariah's face squinched in embarrassment. "You don't have to use the whole name," she muttered. "I'm thinking of having everyone call me Mari with an 'i.' "

"Why not use the whole name?" Temple said, swallowing her own shock. Having endured a long, dark night of the soul regarding her unusual first name when she was in seventh grade, she was eager to ease anyone else's discomfort with a first name. Even if the last was one . . . grrrr . . . Molina. "It's a lovely name," Temple insisted. Mariah disagreed by making a face. "I can see it on a diploma or even on a book cover."

"Everybody tries to call me Mah-*ree*-a, like Latin for the Blessed Virgin."

Temple couldn't tell whether Mariah more feared being known as blessed or a virgin. "That's not who you're named after," she said promptly.

"Who am I named after? Nobody I know."

"Well, it's not exactly a person."

"I knew it was stupid."

"It's not stupid. It's the wind." Mariah's face showed puzzlement. "The wild west wind. 'They call the wind Mariah.' Mah-*rye*-a. It's a song. A very good song."

"I bet you don't know how to spell it."

Temple assumed a classroom performance position, eyes up at the ceiling as if the secret answer were written there, hands clasped behind the back. "M-a-r-i-a-h."

"That's right!"

"Thank you. Do I get an A?"

"Nobody gets an A for spelling just one word right."

"True. I'll have to spell something harder for an A. How about co-in-ci-dence?" She smiled at Matt.

He had relaxed during her byplay with Mariah, and now he looked not surprised but relieved.

"Her mother is mile-high in overtime," he explained, "and had promised to take Mariah here, so I, uh, volunteered. But why are you—?"

"The simulated motion ride. As a freelance employee of the Crystal Phoenix, I thought I'd investigate what the other hotels are doing now that the Phoenix Action Jackson attraction is getting ready to open." Temple's glibness at inventing excuses for her unofficial undercover work amazed even herself at times. "Maybe this, um, Wormhole thing is only here for TitaniCon, but I wanted to give it a test drive."

"Really?" Mariah was no longer nervous about the red-headed woman who was distracting Matt's attention. Instead, she saw another sucker. "I want to go on again. Go with me?"

"Sure," Temple said, noting that her cheerful sangfroid annoyed Matt a trifle. "Let's queue up, kid, and show those worms what we're made of. Say, radically cool earring." She snapped her fingers into the dangling sections so they swung.

Mariah, won over, pushed back into line, pulling Temple with her.

"I'll get the tickets." Matt reached for what was obviously his most useful accessory here at TitaniCon, his wallet.

"Oh?" Temple grinned. "You coming, too?"

"Not this time." He vanished into the crowd. She hoped he'd be able to get tickets by the time they'd inched their way to the entry area.

Temple screamed. She gasped. She wished she'd never signed up for this mission. She wished she could do it all over again. She and Mariah came lurching stiff-legged out of the Wormhole exit like zombies, blinking at normal light, sound, and gravity, buddies born in the eye of the simulated motion storm.

"How old are you?" Mariah wanted to know as they shuffled along with the crowd.

"Why do you ask?" Now that Temple was past thirty—just— she felt unaccountably sensitive about the subject of age.

"Matt says my mother isn't as old as she seems."

"How old do *you* think she is?"

Mariah thought and thought, then took a bold chance. "I don't know. Thirty-two."

"Relax. I'm not as old as your mother."

"Are you older than Buffy?"

"Buffy? Oh, you mean the vampire slayer."

Mariah nodded.

"Maybe. That is the cutest earring. Where'd you get it?"

"They don't have any like this left."

"Don't worry. I won't steal your thunder. Gee, you guys get competitive young. Isn't Matt too old for you?"

Mariah blushed. "He's way too old," she said with feeling. "How old do you think he is?"

"Waaay past thirty-two."

Mariah digested that distressful news. "Maybe he'd be all right for my mom."

Temple tried not to choke at that idea, wanting to laugh, and then suddenly finding the idea very unfunny. What *was* Matt doing squiring around the homicide lieutenant's daughter anyway?

Didn't matter. She had her own secret mission here, and Mariah made a terrific cover.

"You're much cooler than Sheila," Mariah volunteered.

When in doubt, ask simple questions. "Sheila?"

"That funny elf-lady Matt knows."

"Elf-ladies are good to know," Temple said judiciously. "You never can tell when one will do you a good turn."

"Kinda like fairy godmothers?"

"Right. Kinda like fairy godmothers." Temple smiled. Mariah was taller than she, when she was barefoot anyway, but emotionally she was still a midget. *Ah, kidhood.*

"You're prettier than Sheila."

Thank you, wind-named girl! Odd how stupidly competitive you could be when you were out of the game, Temple thought. *Maybe especially when you were out of the game.*

"Wanta show me where those wild ear-things hang out?" she asked Mariah. The kid really didn't resemble Molina and certainly didn't have her mother's odd blue eyes. *Must take after her father.*

"They wouldn't show up the way you wear your hair anyway."

"True. But a girl can dream."

"Can she? Really?"

"Really."

"I think he's tired of me."

Temple didn't have to ask who. "Oh. Well, maybe he's tired of me, too." Temple regarded Mariah, trying to find the real person under the age group. "But, hey, we've got each other, right?"

"I don't even know you."

"We've got to start somewhere."

Matt was waiting impatiently for them to clear the Wormhole crowds and rejoin him.

"I thought we might want to check on Sheila in the con suite," he told Mariah.

She looked highly unexcited.

After Temple asked and was told what a con suite was, she sided with Mariah. "Look. We girls really want to shop. I've got to see this way-out dealers' room where Mariah got those cutting-edge earrings. Why don't we meet you up there?"

Matt, whose eyes had glazed slightly at mention of the dealers' room, nodded quickly.

Mariah looked hesitant as he walked away. Temple could understand; she herself was dying to meet this Sheila.

But, first, she needed to slip away from Matt.

So she nodded a "lead on" gesture to Mariah, who perked up at the idea of guiding an adult to something she had discovered. They were off to see the dealers' room, the wonderful world of Awes, Temple feeling oddly transported to another planet.

After several circuits of row after row of T-shirts, books and comics, photos of actors in alien drag, chain-mail jewelry, et cetera, Temple turned Mariah loose at a book dealer's table and dug her cell phone out of her tote bag.

Max answered on the third ring, wherever he was.

Temple hunkered in the space between two dealers' tables. "It's me."

"Learn anything good?"

"After a couple of hours wandering around, I realized that Security was nowhere in sight."

"So?"

"So I left the TitaniCon area and hit the main hotel venues. Found a genuine, pistol-packing security man in a New Millennium space suit and asked some questions. As a delegate of the Crystal Phoenix, of course."

"Of course."

"And . . . there *is* no visible security at TitaniCon. That's the whole point. It's a fantasy world, Max. You oughta know about that. Even Security is in disguise. Your guy might be masquerading as a Cardassian, a Bajoran, or an Odo shapeshifter. It doesn't matter if I have an updated sketch of an old photo of him. He's in deep cover."

Max's long silence grew alarming. Had her cell phone lost its signal? "I can keep looking—"

"Never mind."

"Speaking of never minding, guess who's on site? Matt and Molina spawn."

"Molina spawn?"

"Didn't you know? Pre-acne kiddo. Not a bad kid, really. We did the Wormhole together."

"Molina's child is there?"

"Mariah's older than a child. Girl, eleven or twelve maybe. Awkward age, really. I find myself annoyingly sympathetic. I haven't felt this protective since Louie entered my life."

"Oh, Jesus."

"Max? You never take the Lord's name in vain."

"I'm not now. I'm asking for outside assistance. Temple, listen very, very carefully. That guy I wanted you to spot, he mustn't know, see, recognize what's-her-name."

"Mariah."

"Mariah. I am not kidding. She must *not* be recognized. That's now more important than any other reason you're there. Disguise her."

"Max! How do you disguise a twelve-year-old?"

"Temple, you could disguise a watermelon. Just do it. If *he's* in disguise, I hate to think—"

"She could be in danger? A kid? Come on . . . Molina's kid? What do you know that I don't?"

"Too much. Trust me on this. And if you manage to spot this Raf character, no matter the disguise, well, you're James Bond material."

"I don't want to be James Bond material. I want to be me material."

"You're a pro. Hide the kid, number one. Find the guy, number two."

"And number three?"

"Take good care of yourself."

"What are you going to be doing?"

"Reevaluating the whole situation."

"From a distance."

"From a distance. It's all that's possible at the moment. Sorry."

"Me, too." Temple glanced at Mariah avidly reading vintage *Wonder Woman* comic books. Hide the kid. Max never overstated anything. Imagine. Her safeguarding Lieutenant C. R. Molina's kid. It was a weird, weird world, just like they always said.

Chapter 30

Louie Goes Out in the Garden to Eat Worms

In desperation, I cruise by my shy friends, the kiwis.

They edge out to snag a worm or two, despite my presence. I pride myself on making pals where other operatives would alienate. You never know who you will come to count on in a pinch. And these are pleasant, harmless chaps and chapettes. (It is hard to tell which is which, so in these politically correct days, it is best to hedgehog your bets.)

"You limeys see that hot-blooded carnivore around lately?" I ask.

"We are not limeys. They are from another island entirely."

"I know, I know. You lot are from that land down under, the merry old land of Oz, as they call it."

" 'Oz' is a nickname for Aussieland. Australia to you. We are natives of New Zealand."

"Right. Next-door neighbors to the Aussies. What is the diff?"

Feathers, if you can call the wimpy barbs these critters sport feathers, bristle en masse. Zounds, I have riled the natives again!

"The 'diff,' as you put it, is extreme. New Zealand is, for one thing, an up-and-coming film location, the home of *Hercules* and *Xena*," the ruffled kiwi announces with something like assertiveness. "Surely you have heard of these notable entertainment phenomena?"

I at least can take pride in goading a notoriously shy and mild breed to high dudgeon . . . although these birds will never fly, not with that set of stumpy wings and tail.

"I am familiar with Hercules and Xena."

"Besides our burgeoning international film industry, we are noted for a wild and varied topography," puts in another kiwi.

Man, these birds are so highfalutin they are candidates for those spectacles that perch on your beak and hang from a long black cord, except that they are too blind to see better even with the aid of fancy glasses.

"And opals," I put in, thinking of Miss Temple's missing ring.

"That is the other place," a kiwi darts from behind a bush to hiss at me.

"No 'crocs?"

"Please. We thrived so long because our native island was free of predators . . . until the people came."

"Every place is free of lots of bad things, until the people come. On the other hand, they do bring Dumpsters."

The kiwis make with the *keewee, keewee, keewee.* Obviously, they have never hung behind a MacDonald's to good effect. Poor little maggot-mashers. Not much fat, salt, and sugar in *those* slim pickings.

Speaking of which, the head kiwi takes a nosedive and comes up with something pale and wriggling.

Disgusting! Now I know why they say it is not polite to watch other species eat. Unless you happen to be eating the other species at the time.

"You are an odd duck," a kiwi says to me.

Whatever. "True. I am civilized beyond the majority of my kind. I no longer have to rely on what I can round up on the street to eat. I am a self-employed entrepreneur, I have an upStrip condo in which I reside, a lady partner who is one foxy chick, all the take-out sushi I can eat, and a cushy job, not to mention my own exclusive lounging area, attired in zebra print."

"And yet you wish to find that nasty egg eater?"

I am not sure about the consumption habits of Miss Hyacinth, only that they are probably highly sophisticated.

"It is my job," I say modestly.

"As it is our job to be guest stars," a lone kiwi puts in from behind the cover of the bushes.

"Exactly. You guys have done quite well for yourselves, being out-country cousins and all."

"It is not just for the money and exposure," the head kiwi puts in fiercely, toddling to the barrier to push his long, nostril-toting snout practically down my throat. "We have a mission for our kind."

"Admirable. And what is that?"

"We must draw attention to our plight, our diminishing numbers, the sheltering forests that are being hacked down to serve humankind at the cost of all other kind. The only way to do that is with a media presence."

I nod sympathetically. "Frankly, my own species is being cut down by the millions each year here in the good old U.S. of A., and there is darn little being done, and we have a pretty good media presence. It is just that it is all too easy to forget about those of us who are not safe at home during these troubled times."

The kiwis nod and kiss turf. They apparently must gather food from the soil while they may, even when major survival issues are being discussed. I do not say so, but in terms of media presence they are some eons behind we Felidae, not being graceful, elegant, soft-furred, and purr-capable. But before I start patting myself on the back, I must remember that no matter how attractive the species, it is still way too easy to end up as road kill in the modern world's constant path of progress.

"Keewee!" cries a small brown bird. "She comes."

"She" can only be She Who Must Be Obeyed.

"Cheese it! The cat!" cry several kiwis.

I do not waste time feeling honored that I have not been lumped in with my kind.

I do not want to lose this lead. So I flatten on my belly as the Kiwi Nation fans into the bushes to vanish. Then I creep toward the back of the compound where the bushes grow thick.

In a moment, I spot the pale motionless form I am seeking.

She lies as flat as a wet bath mat. Despite the unfortunate pale blond coat that draws light like an arctic fox, she has pushed her five dark-swathed extremities so low, along with her brunette facial mask, that her torso seems to float on shadow, like a reflection. These two-tone dames are a bit schizoid, no doubt.

Her nails are extended, I see, and painted a poisonous green.

My hunter's eyes catch the glimmer of silver. She wears the harness I saw in the newspaper photograph, part battle gear, part adornment. As such, she is in perfect sync with the human/semihuman cast at this TitaniCon. Or should I say perfect *Synth?*

For I have heard that word bandied about in Miss Temple's and my quarters. I do not doubt that Miss Hyacinth could enlighten us both on the subject. I do not doubt that Miss Hyacinth could enlighten a lot of people on a lot of subjects, should she deign to converse with them. But that is not possible. She is feline in the extreme. I am the only one with a prayer of prying some information from those tight-lipped fangs.

My only hope is in winning her over.

I belly crawl close and give a scouting chirrup.

Her belladonna-bright blue eyes snap to my presence like a plumb line. I hear a savage sigh. "Louie. So we meet again."

"I would not exactly call it 'meet,' " I say. "I was hoping our tails would lash time together soon."

Her thick, mink-brown extremity is the antithesis of the airy plume of *mon amour,* the Divine Yvette, a shaded silver Persian of exquisite coat, but it makes an exceedingly good club, as do her boxer-brown limbs. I do not underestimate the athlete's tensile strength in every limb, the superbly female, feline strength in every hair.

The kiwi do not fear for nought.

As I edge nearer, I spot an enhancement to the exotic leather and metal-stud harness not present before: A dangling headdress that circumnavigates her pert, upright ears to dangle like temple bells around her sharp, piquant face.

"That hardware," I note, "must make it difficult to sneak up on prey."

"Challenge," she purrs, "is everything."

"What are you doing here?" I ask. Okay. It is not an original question, but I have to start somewhere.

"Working," is the startling answer.

It is startling only in that I did not expect her to be so frank.

"And you?" she asks.

"Working," I answer, so she is aware that we are on the same wavelength, if on possibly different sides.

"Ah, Louie. I have never met a male of my species who is also dedicated to work. Most often they are pampered layabouts or sad homeless castoffs."

"That is not our species' fault," I growl.

"You would excuse them on the basis of circumstances? You, who make your own circumstances?"

"Yes," I snarl. Snarl is the only thing this dangerous dame will understand. At the moment. "There is us, and there is the species. And without the species, there would not be us."

Okay, it is gibberish. Any port in a storm. Interestingly, my gibberish has got her goat. Big time.

Her tail slashes now, rather than merely lashes. "I owe allegiance to no one or nothing."

"You seemed attached to your last boss, that two-faced lady magician called Shangri-la."

Now her tail is into rug-beating, big time. "What makes you call her two-faced?"

"She may like to pose as one who is capable of kidnaping and possibly murder, but she is no better than a sneak thief. She made off with my roommate's brand-new ring during her so-called magic show at the Opium Den. Not that I was exactly crazy about that ring, considering the source, but possession was nine-tenths of the law until Shangri-la's greedy little long-nailed hands showed up."

"You do not like long nails?" Hyacinth purrs, snicking out her own personal supply of Japanese-chef-sharp shivs. I notice that their enameled green color looks well against the lavender-brown hose she wears, although it clashes with her eyes as blue as the skies over Siam, which we call Thailand nowadays. Leave me not think of Thailand at the moment.

"It depends where these nails are pointed," I say. "I see you do not defend your erstwhile associate." I am pushing the issue, but Hyacinth is not answering my questions fully and frankly.

She shrugs her pale blond shoulders, then bites suddenly at an errant twist of hair until the incipient snarl is subdued. It cannot be fleas, surely. I have never seen a less flea-bitten dame.

"She disappeared," Hyacinth concedes in a languid drawl as she draws her long pink tongue along the glistening hairs of her shoulder. "I had to find another gig. Luckily, that is not hard to do in this town."

"Yeah, what is this 'Phssst, the psychic Kir-khat of the Kohl Kompendium' I read about in the papers?"

"My new role. I play a twenty-third-century hybrid between feline and human."

"And the harnessry?" I glance askance at her outerwear of black leather and silver studs.

Hyacinth yawns, showing ragged teeth. "Humans have such limited imaginations. They think future beings will love to run around in creations you could hardly get a self-respecting horse to wear today. It is their little fantasy, and apparently it stimulates their erotic imaginations. What do you think, Louie?"

"I think that my erotic imagination is not about to react to anything that resembles a collar used on Spike, the pit bull, thank you. Besides, I do not have to rely on imagination. I am into the real thing."

"I see." Her eyes narrow to slits. "I would discuss that with you at greater length, depth, and width, but I am required to participate in a presentation here in a couple of hours and must save my strength for my performance. Will I see you at the Khatlord Kompendium preview?"

"Very likely," I say, despite not having heard of this event until now. It would never do to let a dame like this think that she knew more than you about anything, trust me.

So we each bare our teeth in what passes for a friendly grin and back away from each other without turning away.

Neither of us was born yesterday, though it would not be polite to point that fact out to a lady.

Besides, I think she knows it already.

Chapter 31

Novel Ideas

Temple and Mariah ambled into the con suite an hour later, Temple's credit card reduced in credit line. But they both were as unrecognizable as Temple's personal bottom line.

Temple hadn't expected several adjoining rooms filled with strangers, none of whom were Matt.

"Have you been up here before?" she asked Mariah.

The kid shook her head, which shook the shoulder-length plastic-bead-and-elastic-cord headdress reminiscent of Bo Derek's dreadlock coiffure in the racy movie *Ten*, which Mariah was too young to have even heard of. Temple was almost too young to have heard of it, but she had, being a with-it PR woman.

Temple herself wore a much costlier version of the headdress in shining black metallic mesh. With imitation black pearls. Very Theda Bara. Frankly, after seeing this twenties-style, heavy-metal frippery, she had become quite enamored of the idea of dressing up, even if disguise had not been the prime directive.

She noted with approval that several much younger, much larger women in the suite were similarly topped in much cheaper versions of her own exotic headdress. In the mirror behind the wet bar, as she ordered Mariah a Diet Coke and herself a Sprite, she noted with even more approval that the accessory had effectively dampened her red hair. Nothing like red hair to attract unwanted attention. She felt like an odd combination of a nerd and a showgirl.

This, apparently, was the wonderful world of science fiction and fantasy fiction, film, and fandom. The word "fandom" was a new addition to her vocabulary, just acquired at a dealer's table below.

She and Mariah clutched plastic glasses of soft drinks and took shelter against an unoccupied wall to survey the scene. The suite was the usual Las-Vegas grandiose: acres of terrazzo flooring, cushy modular seating pieces upholstered in something from your Aunt Hortense's Key West tapestry handbag, and huge, heavy, stone serving tables suitable for a Renaissance banquet. Temple noticed that the savvy management had jerked the fancy area rugs from under the food-laden tables. When she saw the imported edibles, she saw why. She checked out her latest camouflage job.

Amazing how the shoulder-brushing headdress gave Mariah a long-haired look—also way more adult than her mother would have liked, but the kid had the height to masquerade as a Temple contemporary, since Temple usually passed for fifteen.

There they were, two con girls on the town, ignoring lascivious glances from severely overweight computer geniuses. Genii?

"This is so cool," Mariah said. "I feel like I'm in senior high. They serve beer, you know."

Temple glanced toward the infamous wet bar. She could definitely use a beer. "I know. But we're underage."

"You are not!"

"You don't know that, do you? And don't forget who bought your goldilocks."

Mariah subsided. She loved the bronzy-golden sheen of her headdress better than the forbidden beer. Girls always yearned to be the opposite of what they were, for some perverse reason most useful to marketing directors. Temple couldn't remember what she had considered the perfect antidote to red hair at Mariah's age. Maybe . . . blond. Maybe black. That was her: drawn to extremes and hamstrung between the difference.

Temple studied the suitescape. Tons of T-shirts, many familiar from the dealer tables below, most memorializing film and story: *Star Trek, Star Wars, Space Trooper Bazaar* and its khatlords. A lot of people immersed in books. This was a comforting sight.

And a lot of comforting snacks lingered on coffee and side tables, featuring the main food groups: carbs, fat, sugar, and an occasional veggie media for balance.

This meant that chips, pastries, pretzels, M&Ms, bagels and cream cheese and fruit preserves, cheese squares, and cold pizza triangles predominated. Also fat rolls and zits on the assorted fans. Not to mention thick lenses all the better to see the aforesaid with, my dear.

"I don't see Matt," Temple told Mariah. "And I doubt he'd recognize us. Do you see Sheila?" *Do you know Sheila, like Matt knows Sheila?*

Mariah squinted into the panorama. "No. She doesn't have a dragon on her shoulder today."

Temple nodded. A dragon on the shoulder would have been a help. "Let's cruise the rooms then."

Mariah held back. "Are you sure these temporary tattoos on my face aren't too . . . dorky?"

Temple pulled away to study the heavenly constellations she had set loose on Mariah's physiognomy.

"Let's see. The rings of Jupiter on your left cheekbone is *tres chic, cherie.* And you definitely needed the Big Dipper on your chin. Is the holographic Saturn on my right cheekbone too . . . much?"

Mariah shook her head. "My mom——" she began.

"Isn't here." Temple finished the thought, and the conversation. "Let's find Matt and see what he thinks of us."

That gave Mariah pause, but Temple grabbed her elbow and hustled her along. "Come on, girlfriend."

234 • Carole Nelson Douglas

They sighted Sheila first.

"There she is." Mariah pointed.

Temple pushed her hand down. "Don't want to upset the natives. Are you sure?"

"*She* looks the same."

Temple didn't miss the stress on "she" and was satisfied. "Let's sneak up on her."

They materialized beside the empty sofa that Sheila commanded, one tennis-shoe-shod foot lifted to rest upon the littered, glass-topped coffee table before her.

"Hi," Temple said. "Can we sit?"

"Sure," said Sheila, studying them cautiously. Finally, she zeroed in on Mariah.

"Mariah?" She pushed herself upright in the smushy cushions. "Is that you?"

Mariah giggled. "I fooled you, didn't I?"

Sheila instinctively looked at Temple, as if sniffing a responsible adult. Well, semiresponsible. "Temple Barr," she introduced herself.

"Where's Matt?" Sheila asked.

"You don't know?" Temple responded. "We came up here looking for him."

"He was here, but he wandered off." Sheila suddenly shrugged. "That's cons for you."

"Cons?" Temple sat down beside her, feeling oddly like Mata Hari in her headdress.

Of course Sheila was wearing a full costume, if only accessorized by her own plain face. And she was plain. Temple was torn between feeling sorry for, and envying her.

"Fell on the moving sidewalk yesterday," Sheila continued, waggling her Ace-bandaged foot on its cocktail-table support. "The only thing you really do at cons is stand, and here I'm sidelined. Oh, well. Say, Mariah, you don't look like the same girl. You look older."

Mariah giggled happily, and Temple breathed relief. For a preteen, maybe older was the best disguise, even if it brought the threat of beer.

"Can I go get some food?" Mariah asked.

"Again? Sure, I'll just sit here awhile." Temple did.

"Do you know Matt?" Sheila asked Temple when Mariah had attacked the buffet table like a starving locust.

Innocent question. Not-so-innocent answer. Did she know Matt? Not in the Biblical sense, for sure. And maybe not in any other very meaningful way, after all. So she nodded. Effective operative always gets her information, if not her man. "We're neighbors," she said.

"Oh." Sheila looked relieved. "We used to work together."

"At ConTact?" Temple asked.

"Right. We just ran into each other here." Sheila glanced at Mariah.

"She's a mutual . . . friend's daughter," Temple explained.

"Umm." Sheila nodded. "And you two—?"

"Ran into each other here."

"Small world."

"Actually . . . very large world. I've never been to one of these sci-fi cons before. It's pretty impressive. Lots of people, lots of attractions."

"First: don't say 'sci-fi.' The phrase goes back to the fifties when hi-fidelity sound was coming in. 'Hi-fi,' they called it. Isaac Asimov coined the phrase 'sci-fi' for science fiction and it stuck, and stuck, and stuck, like a record needle in a groove. Frankly, Asimov was a breast-fixated, old-style sexist, but even he came to hate the sci-fi label. It's denigrating. 'Hi-fi' is long gone, but we're still stuck with 'sci-fi' in the *New York Times* crossword puzzle definitions."

Temple nodded. "It's easier to coin a phrase than to demystify one."

Sheila waggled her bound toes, impressed. "Exactly! Thus spake nerddom. We're all asocial eggheads here or dorks or nerds. Pick your put-down term."

"Really? I hadn't noticed."

"Thanks, but we kinda like our pariah status. Somebody's got to do it."

Temple, who'd been keeping one eye on Mariah so steadily that she felt she was morphing into some alien with multifocus pupils on stalks, suddenly detected violent sound and motion heading in their direction.

She bounded off the sofa to Mariah's side in an instant, startling a would-be Wookie who was engaged in trying to scrape sour-cream onion dip onto the broken potato-chip shards that remained in the bottom of a huge wooden salad bowl.

The eye of the storm barreled into the room in the next instant, although it was definitely not quiet.

The two men were arguing as one tried to outstride the other, trailed by a third man who looked ready to wring his hands with exasperation.

As they charged through the clots of talking people, they bumped elbows and tipped drinks down T-shirt fronts. Heads turned their way in annoyance, and mouths opened to protest. Then the victims' faces recognized the perps'. Talk silenced as onlookers turned to watch, as if the quarreling men were a sideshow that had been scheduled for their entertainment.

Temple had never seen sheer rudeness given so wide a berth before. *These guys must be really mean,* she figured. So she whispered, "We've got front row seats over there," to Mariah and gently pulled her toward Sheila and the couch.

"What you do mean it's not the end of the world?" one man was shouting. He was tall and thin, with receding blonde hair and round tortoiseshell glasses that made him look more baby-faced than hawkish.

"It's not the end of the world if you don't mind slapping up a tombstone inscribed 'Here lies Gutenberg's last. Read the inscription, if you still know how to do that archaic process, and weep.' "

The second man was almost comically opposite to the first: short, dark, bushy-haired. He was wearing a knit sports shirt, pale yellow, to the tall guy's T-shirt. Maybe that and the wiry silver strands in his hair made him seem older than his debater, perhaps fifty-something.

"They're shouting like a couple of kids," Mariah noted in amazement.

Sheila just nodded. "Nothing new. The guy in the golf shirt is Hanford Schmidt and Mr. Tall is Alan Dahl. They're both well-known writers in the field."

"The field?"

"Science fiction novels. The old-fashioned kind. Conceived by writers, not filmmakers. What the field used to be before it became dominated by hundreds of books set in film worlds."

"I read the Buffy books," Mariah volunteered.

"That was a movie and then a TV show," Temple realized, getting the idea at last. "You mean it used to be a book-to-movie, but now it's a movie/TV-show-to-book world?"

"Books, plural. Writers who can't sell their own ideas end up writing for the various media-tie-in series. It's changed the face of the field. Luckily, I like fantasy novels, and that hasn't been such a big hit in film, so I can find books by my favorite authors."

"Xena," Mariah pointed out.

Sheila regarded her with a nod. "That's right, I guess they do novels on *Xena* and *Hercules,* too. I don't read the tie-in series, what they call 'franchise' books. They're just not as imaginative, don't have as much real fire, as individually written books."

"Wow." Temple was amazed. "You're telling me that 'individually written books' are passé? No wonder these guys are getting overheated about it."

"This pathetic squid," Hanford Schmidt was enunciating with gusto, jerking an arm toward the third, silent partner in the altercation, "is undercutting real writers by taking that lousy Hollywood money, the piddling pittance the studios and filmmakers are letting authors get, 'cuz the more money those series going-on-book two-hundred-aught-oblivion make, the more they cut back the writers' percentage to one-thousand of a yak-turd percent. And no royalties, no foreign sales cuts. These self-abusing sellouts aren't writers, they're pissant wonders, gutting themselves, as well as every other writer, not to mention the readers who are too dumb to do anything except lap up the mindless formula fiction the schlockmeisters are shoveling into their three-celled brains. They might as well announce their neutering to the world and write romance novels."

Having insulted everyone he could think of, including Temple's absent, romance-writing Aunt Kit Carlson, Schmidt paused to take a deep breath. Even then he wasn't silent: his thumb kept pumping the top on a retractable ballpoint pen so fast it sounded like Morse code.

"It's fine for you to talk," piped up the "squid" in question, his high-pitched, nasal voice shaking with feeble fury. "You're an 'old pro.' You get flown gratis all over the world to be a guest author at these things, even if you haven't written, much less published, a new book in years. You can live off what you used to be until death do you and the world you've made a career of looking down on part. I have to make a living, and at least I'm writing."

"And," Schmidt went on, clicking furiously, seeming to ignore him, "who do I hear is running for president of our esteemed science fiction writers' association. Some *woman* I've never heard of. The science fiction writers used to be a respected organization with clout. Now we're eunuchs."

"And sexists." Temple was surprised to hear herself speak. She was supposed to be guarding Mariah and keeping a low profile.

As Schmidt glared in her direction, his face curdled with scorn.

Temple remembered too late that she was wearing a rather extreme and frivolous and feminine disguise.

He didn't bother to respond, turning back to the towering Dahl, who had used the distraction to resume his side of the argument.

"Oh, sure, Hanford Schmidt, hero of the working-stiff writer. How about those of us who are working with reality instead of in some self-serving time warp? You know you're chuffed because you, Mr. Literary Sci-Fi standard-bearer, can't get published anymore because you can't bullshit the world into thinking your every snotrag is immortal. The free lunch is over, yes; it's not enough to bombast your way into winning nebulous awards. Publishers demand bottom-line performance nowadays, not the ego-boo of book beauty contests. WOSF is working to help the in-the-trenches writer."

"What did he say?" Temple asked Sheila. "It sounded like an acronym. WUSS?"

"Close. Writers of Science Fiction. W-O-S-F. There are supposed to be two "F"s in there, for Writers of Science Fiction *and* Fantasy, fantasy writers being added a few years ago, but the SF guys have never accepted having their beloved logo reflect that almost half the writer-members write fantasy and dark fantasy, and half are women. Actually, Temple, I kinda like your interpretation. WOSF: 'Remember, folks, it sounds like WUSS.' That's really funny when you remember that a few years ago, a male member—in the strictly general sense of the phrase—actually advocated the creation and sale to members of a . . . get this. A WOSF necktie."

"A necktie? But you said half the members were women."

Sheila lifted her eyebrows significantly. "Right. You know how much we girls like to throttle ourselves with neckties, the favorite weapon of serial killers."

"Well . . . I suppose someone, some woman, could have countered with a proposal for the creation of a WOSF kilt. Unisex, you know."

Sheila collapsed in snickers at the idea of all the big bad boys of WOSF in kilts.

The two prime specimens in the center of the room glared at her, suspecting they were the butt of the joke, but not exactly how much the butt. The third guy already wore plaid, but no doubt it would clash with the imaginary kilt.

In fact, Temple pictured those two dueling titans of testosterone in pretty pleated plaid kilts well above the knee, and joined Sheila in her laughing fit. Mariah, caught in the middle, contracted the contagious germ of humor and joined in.

They were laughing so hard they hardly heard round two begin.

"I'm not talking to you," Hanford Schmidt said. "At least you write books in worlds you've conceived, pathetic as they may be. I mean, your fantasy-quest hero's name is Esalen, as in the flaky institute in California. How hopelessly seventies can you get? That's as bad as naming the poor bloke Alanon, after the AA group Al-Anon. But quality control is *your* problem. I'm talking about financial control, which these franchise writers don't have.

"You like being used and abused?" Hanford screeched, his pen punching the third writer in the chest right on the name tag, which Temple read as "Greg Seltz." Bang! The "Seltz" took another blow on the "S." "You like adding characters and whole worlds and solar systems to some half-baked screenwriter's maunderings and getting paid less and less for it, because if the writer makes more than fifty thou a book, he must be getting way too much? You like knowing that the guy who dreamed up the original story and characters is taking a bigger and bigger cut of your puny someteenth of one percent as you're banking your fifty Gs and getting used to it and are having less time to write your own, original book? Why bother? You're just a hack anyway."

"My last *Space Trooper Bazaar* book got a starred review in *Publishers Weekly*." Greg, backed into the wet-bar counter, was fighting back. "They said that I had transcended the genre of the franchise novel with richness of characterization and imagination."

"So much more the waste," Schmidt clipped out.

"He's right about that," Temple muttered, remembering what the essayist Sidney Harris had said about lavishing talent on too-simple projects. He had noted that the pianist Paderewski could probably invest the tune of "Three Blind Mice" with dazzling invention and embellishment, and that the more magnificent Paderewski could make it sound, the greater the waste of his talent would be.

On the other hand, a novel dealt with characters and issues, and no matter the genre, the writer could always invest the material with underlying significance. That was the beauty of a book.

Temple caught herself. Was she actually getting interested in the issues over which these puerile debaters were flexing their machismo?

She glanced at Mariah, worried that the scene would be disturbing. *Hah! Kids today are all too used to simulated violence.* Mariah was gazing as raptly at the three contentious men as if her TV set were tuned to the *Jerry Springer Show.*

But then Greg Seltz, tired of being pounded in the name tag, grabbed something off the countertop behind him, suddenly becoming the mouse that roared "enough, already."

"Keep your creepy little fists off me, Schmidt. You're really just mad at yourself because your big mouth boxed you into a philosophical corner, and you can't get in on the gravy of media tie-ins because you'd be backing down from a public position. Maybe you could write one under a pseudonym, like Cecil B. 'Cess' Poole. *If* you could write a book that tells a real, coherent story instead of being a string of rants and raves about how us lowly hack writers won't let you save us from ourselves."

The object Greg's fist was waving around? A steel bottle opener that made a nasty weapon.

But Alan Dahl caught Greg's wrist on a pass and quickly peeled his fingers from around the steel shank. "Save it for some useful work. Cool down, Greg. Hanford. There'll be a WOSF meeting Sunday morning. Why don't you save some of your precious breath for making points where it counts, instead of making scenes in the con suite? Huh? All right?"

Schmidt backed up, inadvertently doing a bump and grind on the mammoth trash container.

This time, even Temple and company managed to quash any giggles. Schmidt's natural pugnacity had hardened into icy fury. His small brown eyes glittered like BBs. He suddenly grabbed for the bottle opener, wresting it from the taller man's grasp. Then he sneered, reminding Temple of Crawford Buchanan . . . if he had venom.

He stalked out, his heels hitting the con suite terrazzo like iron weights. The bottle opener hit the floor, bouncing in an eerie echo of Schmidt's clicking pen.

Alan Dahl turned to Greg Seltz. "You all right? Don't take it personally. You know Hanford."

The other man shrugged. "There's room for everybody in our field. I don't know why he has to act as if he's top dog all the time."

"Sometimes gadflies are useful, but you can't count on them to do the thankless background work that really gets things done. I see you've started a new series as coauthor with the head Khatlord. How's that going?"

"The usual. I do all the work, he gets all the talk shows and the credit. But I do have a small percentage of foreign royalties on that project."

"Good." Dahl picked up a plate of chocolate chip cookies. "Just have a bite and forget about Hanford. He's a case of arrested sanity." Leaving, Dahl's foot kicked the bottle opener into another stuttering fit of clicks on the hard floor.

After Dahl left, Greg Seltz stared at the plate of cookies as if they were cobras.

A dressing-down from Hanford Schmidt gave the job title "drill sergeant" a whole new dimension, Temple thought.

"They sure acted stupid," Mariah commented. "And is that guy going to, like, eat a cookie or just stand there forever? 'Cuz I want one."

"Me," Sheila said, "I could use a breath of fresh reason. I'd like to go down and attend some of the panels."

"Panels?" Temple inquired.

"Didn't you get a program book when you paid to get in?"

She frowned and began digging in the tote bag always at her side, like an unseparated Siamese twin. "Might have tossed something in here . . ."

"Never mind." Sheila waved her own booklet, which she pulled out of a capacious pocket in her robe. Worry wrinkles creased her muddy complexion. "Where is Matt, though? I'm sure he wouldn't just leave us up here and go off someplace."

"Yeah," Mariah said soberly. "You'd think he woulda heard everything that was going on."

Temple jumped up when she saw Seltz put down the cookie

plate. In an instant, she had passed the plate to the others, and chocolate chips were melting on the backs of tongues.

At that moment Matt walked through the door. "What's been going on in here?" he said, spotting them on the couch. "That guy in the hall really was steamed."

They chewed gummy cookies like guilty kids, unable to answer, but exchanged pointed glances.

"Boys being silly again," Mariah finally answered. Cookie crumbs clogged her braces, but she was the first free to talk.

Matt nodded, not really understanding.

"Where were you?" Temple managed after a rewarding swallow.

His head jerked toward the hall. "Across the way. There's a no-smoking lounge. I got involved in this hot discussion of whether *Star Trek* or *Star Wars* was the more spiritual concept."

"Did anyone come to blows over it?" Sheila asked.

"Not noticeably. Have I missed something in here?"

"Just a performance-art piece on the wages of a big ego," Temple summed up. "We were going downstairs to attend some . . . panels?"

Sheila nodded to answer her questioning glance. "You should like that," she told Matt, smiling faintly, an expression that transformed her plain face. "More of the same sort of discussion you were having up here, only they use panels of writers and editors. And I'd bet Mariah would love to attend a presentation on the new Khatlord movie."

"There's going to be a movie!" Mariah was big-time excited. "I gotta hear about that."

She had inadvertently proved the obnoxious Hanford Schmidt's point, Temple noticed. Unfortunately, obnoxious people can be right about things; that's part of what makes them so obnoxious.

Temple pushed herself out of entrapment by sofa. Mariah effortlessly bounced to her feet beside her. That left it for Matt to extend Sheila a hand and pull her upright.

"Oh. My foot was asleep and doesn't like being waked up. Give me a minute."

"Temple," Matt said, "why don't you take Sheila down in the elevator, and Mariah and I will head off for the moving sidewalks."

"No," Temple said.

Matt seemed startled by her outright refusal.

Temple rephrased the plan. "I'll take Mariah down, and you can help Sheila. I wouldn't be able to do a thing if Sheila lost her balance, but you're a big, strong man and can handle that better than I."

Matt remained speechless. He seemed to be waiting for a southern-belle drawl to issue from her mouth next, as she added that "poor little me" just couldn't tie her own shoelaces.

But Temple kept a deadpan expression, and he could only agree graciously to what she had suggested. Sheila, she noticed, shot her a surprised but alarmingly grateful look.

I didn't want to do it, Temple ached to confess. She couldn't get the appalled tone in Max's voice out of her head. For some reason, the moment he discovered Mariah Molina was on the premises, she could feel his anxiety level escalate. That sent hers skyrocketing. Better that Mariah be with someone who was on her guard.

When a master magician like the Mystifying Max was worried about something, it behooved ordinary mortals to watch out.

Chapter 32

Lost in Space

Matt explored the back halls of the hotel until he found an elevator and held it open while Sheila hobbled aboard.

All the while he felt vaguely finessed and oddly wronged.

Though the patience to help the handicapped had been ham-
mered into him since kindergarten, he was a bit annoyed at having the role of Boy Scout doled out to him while Temple trotted
off with Mariah firmly under her wing.

Matt couldn't tell what irritated him more: Sheila's ever-more-
mooning attitude toward him or the uneasy feeling that he was
Mariah's designated adult, and he shouldn't let her go off with
someone else—anyone else, even Temple.

"Thank you." Sheila gazed up at him in the otherwise empty
elevator with cow-brown eyes. "I'm sure you'd rather be off with
the able-bodied."

Matt was sure, too, but of course he was trapped, in more ways than one. "No problem. You didn't ask to twist your ankle. How's it doing?"

"Great . . . now."

The implication in both her voice and eyes was that his presence alone was a healing influence. This was more power than Matt cared to have ascribed to him, in the priesthood or out of it.

"Maybe you need to get home and put your foot up on something."

"I really can't drive until it feels better." She caught at his arm as the elevator subtly jerked to a stop.

Matt fought the urge to shake off her clinging custody. He was appalled by his lack of sympathy, except that he'd rather have been with Temple and have known what was happening with Mariah. First of all, what would her mother think of that Halloween getup? Maybe that's why Temple had dashed off, leaving him with the cumbersome Sheila. She didn't want to face the music about corrupting a juvenile, although a gaudy Mardi Gras headdress could hardly constitute corrupting a minor. Could it?

"You seem distracted," Sheila noted, patting her tightly permed hair that would hardly respond to a currycombing, much less gentle feminine patting.

"There's a lot to take in here," Matt explained lamely, trying to figure out where they were when the elevator disgorged them.

They seemed to be in the main part of the hotel and would have to walk back into the TitaniCon area.

"You have your hand tattoo so we can get in again?" he asked.

Sheila's look of dreamy delight grew more unfocussed. "What tattoo?"

"Didn't they stamp the top of your hand when you bought your weekend pass?"

She looked blank but brightened when he lifted her hand to examine it. "Was I supposed to get stamped?" she asked.

"If we've left the TitaniCon area, they won't let us—you—back in without one."

"I'm sorry, Matt. I didn't know I was supposed to get one. I guess I got overlooked."

Not hard to do, Matt thought, *when you're wearing a dumpy brown robe in this array of exotic plumage.*

"Maybe we can slip by them." Ordinarily he would have tried to explain, but he felt an odd, escalating sense of haste. He wanted to catch up to Temple and Mariah, almost as badly as a kid who'd been left behind.

As they neared the entrance to TitaniCon, "them" turned out to be two six-and-a-half-feet-tall Klingon guards glowering under their corrugated foreheads, their costumes bristling with alien military insignia and weapons.

Sheila shook her wide robe sleeves down over her knuckles as they skirted the traffic jam of attendees lined up to pay their way in. Matt flourished his stamped hand under the guards' aggressive, ultra-acquiline noses.

Beside him, Sheila gave a feeble, palm-up wave.

Perhaps the guards weren't about to challenge a limping woman, or they thought the pair looked too honest to question. For whatever reason, Matt and Sheila moved into the space-station ambiance unquestioned.

Matt stopped the minute the Klingon-types were far enough behind them. "Do you have a ticket receipt?"

"Yes." Sheila started digging in her robe pockets.

"Just get in line here and explain that they neglected to stamp your hand with a weekend pass. I'll go find Temple and Mariah so they can hold seats for us at this presentation, whatever it is, and come back for you."

Sheila nodded uneasily, already looking abandoned.

"You'll be fine," he told her, turning and pulling the rolled program book out of his back pocket as he went.

It was almost three P.M. He scanned the program and found an entry: *Khatlord Kompendium: The Motion Picture.* In the Neptune Ballroom. He squinted at the badly reproduced floor plan (everything was done in dotted lines, including solid walls) and hurried ahead.

Other people trotted alongside him, all rushing to be somewhere. People farther ahead had stopped, he saw, forming a semicircular wall of padded shoulders, robed backs, and oddly capped heads studded with the angled thrust of phony weapons here and there.

Matt forgot politeness and began worming through the circling rows of people amid the breathy reactions of an enthralled audience—ooohs, aaahs, gasps, and choked cries, followed by indrawn sighs.

Then he heard the clatter of real wood and steel on wood and steel. Ignoring the indignant stares of those he squeezed by, he pushed close enough to see.

The crowd encompassed a large circle of space, almost like a set for theater in the round: a couple of rough wooden tables, a small footstool, some props reminiscent of a tavern Attila the Hun might have patronized.

On stage at the moment were two of the larger-than-life people he was growing accustomed to seeing here, offering a display of film fight scenes. One was a long-haired man in a sleeveless leather jerkin and leather trousers. The other was a long-haired woman in a studded leather kilt, knee-high boots, and a heavy-metal breastplate-cum-bustier that made Wonder Woman look like a high school cheerleader.

They jumped, thumped, shouted, and spun as the smaller, wooden, tavern props around them shattered under their energetic leaps and bounds.

Matt relaxed suddenly. He knew enough martial arts to see that this was not a fight but a tightly choreographed display. The woman's circular chakra's steel edge seemed blunted, and the man's club bounced off the set pieces it skimmed against.

The crowd roared approval as the woman flipped backward to elude the man's club. "You go, girl!" a chorus of female voices urged. "Get her, Hercules," shouted the men. "Xena!" cheered the women.

Matt doubted these were the series stars. This kind of demonstration was too dangerous, and they moved too much like an acrobatic team. Stunt doubles. These must be the stunt doubles.

He couldn't help enjoying the show. They were drilled to perfection, masters at making rehearsed moves look spontaneous and deadly.

Still, letting even experienced martial-arts experts loose among a watching crowd was dicey. The mob seemed to understand that it had to ebb and flow constantly to give the fighters room. Moving with the fighters they watched made them part of the spectacle.

Matt couldn't help thinking of the repugnant annual running of the bulls in the Spanish town of Pamplona, in which the goaded, maddened animals formed a dark, thundering wave that the maddened crowd of running men tried to ride like suicidal surfers. People sometimes craved these moments of dangerous intuition, when their instincts were the only thing that kept them safe from life's raw edge, even if they had to manufacture the circumstances by brutalizing animals . . . or watching the simulation of humans brutalizing other humans.

Still, he couldn't help admiring the fighters' concentrated grace.

Hercules had leaped atop a trestle table, his weight tipping it over. He thundered off before the table could fall, and it rocked back into place. Now Xena was advancing, slashing with her circular metal chakra. Their complicated "pas-de-battle" evolved until each swung the weight of the other around in turn, making them a centrifugal force, each jerking back into the other's orbit only to fling the opponent outward again in turn. It was a clockwork move, generating its own imperative pull, so the fighters themselves couldn't stop their crack-the-whip motion.

Matt saw something low and pale flash along the floor toward them, some small living thing racing toward incredible danger.

Among the opposite onlookers, he saw the swing of garish beads near the ground. Something leaned out of the crowd after the running object. Behind that, something taller yet reached forward to pull the figure back.

These impressions jumbled together like millisecond film cuts. Behind and just after these quick flashes of movement, in the crowd, something large and diaphanous as a dragonfly darted in to push the taller figure forward, into the ring of contention.

The glimpses resolved into images he could put identities on: a strange pale animal running among the stomping boots of the barbarian warriors; Mariah Molina in her absurd headdress reaching to save the animal that so resembled one of her manic tiger-striped cats; Temple, wearing what resembled a black, heavy-metal nun's wimple, grabbing for Mariah's shoulder to keep her from falling into the field of battle, and something . . . someone . . . behind Temple knocking her forward, off balance, pushing her right into the fray with Mariah and the creature.

The combatants were fixated on each other and their intertwined motions. The darting creature (a strange, flightless bird? a Chihuahua?) dodged one of Hercules's huge boots as it stamped the floor with tremendous force.

Mariah, scampering after the fleeing creature, suddenly saw her own danger and stumbled sideways to avoid the human whirlwind heading toward her.

Temple came diving after her, using the impetus delivered by the enigma in the crowd to catch Mariah's T-shirt shoulder.

But they were both off-balance now. There was no place to go except cower where they were and hope to dodge the human cyclone headed their way.

Matt pushed between two startled audience members, barely aware of faces frozen in horror all around him, and thumped flat-footed atop the trestle table in imitation of Hercules. The table tilted and, for a moment, balanced perfectly under his weight like the crest of a wave. Unlike Hercules, he did nothing to keep this wave from cresting. The table crashed over on its side; Matt jumped away only as it hit. He had just enough time to grab Temple and Mariah as they scrabbled toward him. They all dove onto the hard floor beneath the overturned wooden tent.

The heavy table jolted as the whirling dervishes, still at it, careened around it. The woman's fierce yells sounded like a cock fight. Matt peered over the table's thick edge to meet another object hurtling toward their trapped position: a cat, black and bristling. It mounted the insecure perch of the tilted table edge, yowled a challenge to match Xena's best, and leaped onto the nearest higher object . . . Hercules's beefy, now-shirtless back.

Another yowl was heard, low and furious. Human.

As the fighters' momentum paused, the crowd pressed inward to keep them from moving and to end the danger. Smothered by people, sweating performers looked around, startled, to find three audience members in their midst.

Relieved onlookers rushed the three and helped them up.

"Where did that cat come from?" Xena demanded, wiping her dripping forehead with a fairly useless metal-cuff-clad wrist.

"Cat? Felt like a cat-o'-nine-tails," Hercules complained, pressing a hand to his back. "Did that same something fly through my feet earlier?"

"Something snarled at me over the edge of that table," Xena added, directing her warrior princess gaze to the onstage trio. "How did you people end up here? Don't you know it's dangerous?"

They had no chance to explain. The crowd, in many voices all at once, testified to what each had thought they saw. They were unanimous on only one thing: Matt had heroically turned the tables on possible tragedy.

"I told the organizers this was a dangerous stunt," Hercules grumbled. "We should have been on stage. Interactive everything, that's what they want today. We could have ended up with interactive hash with these three as the ingredients, including a kid."

"You okay?" Xena bent down to ask Mariah.

"Sure, Xena." She gazed at the supersized woman with the same wonder that Matt had seen in Sheila.

Sheila! He'd forgotten about her. At least she hadn't witnessed his spur-of-the-moment heroics, which were earning him pats on the shoulder from people in the crowd . . . then he looked up and saw a familiar brown figure watching from the fringes. *Oh, no—*

"What . . . how?" Temple was regarding him with awe, but more for his sudden appearance on the scene than for his derring-do.

"I had a feeling." He knew it was more than that. "We have to talk. I thought I saw someone push you."

"I know I felt someone push me—hard." She looked at Mariah. "Did someone push you?"

The girl shook her head, putting the beads into glittering motion. "No. I just saw the yellow cat streak by, like at home, and I was worried. Where is it? What happened to it? Is it all right?"

They looked around. "I don't see any injured cats lying around," Matt said after a moment. "But I could have seen injured people."

Mariah made a contrite grimace. "I'm sorry. I didn't think. I was just so worried about the cat."

"For nothing. I saw its dark-masked face as it came back to nail Hercules. That cat knew how to take care of itself," Temple said severely. "You don't. You stick by me, and you don't make a move without asking first, okay? This place may look like a playland, but it's full of risks, especially for people who step over the line."

Mariah's face grew so serious that tears seemed close. Being bawled out in public was always humiliating, especially in front of the media goddess Xena, even if she was only an imitation. Matt had never heard Temple sound so severe, but he understood why. He'd felt the awful gut-wrench of watching a child falling into harm's way, too. Suddenly, being a responsible adult human felt like being the most helpless creature on earth.

"Good save." Hercules slapped Matt on the shoulder, flashed supernaturally whitened teeth, and ambled off with Xena, still patting at his own savaged back.

Everyone was dispersing. Matt searched the shadows beyond the people, even as Sheila limped over.

"I didn't see everything," she said wistfully, "but it looks as if you all played an accidental part in the show. After that excitement, going to a presentation will seem tame."

"Tame?" Temple digested the concept. "I like it."

"Wasn't Xena super?" Mariah asked Sheila. "I love that silver circle she carries. Then she throws it out like this way-cool metal Frisbee. Boom! You're nailed."

"It's a chakra," Matt told her. "The disk is a martial arts

weapon, but it's also symbol of one of seven mystical centers of spiritual or ethereal energy in the human body, according to Hindu philosophy."

Temple was chakraed out. "While we're chatting, can we all sit down in a row on our little chairs and stay there for a while?"

Matt nodded, grimly. He didn't want to sit and watch another fanciful and possibly dangerous exhibition. He wanted to go somewhere quiet and ask Temple what the heck was going on.

But he had a feeling he wouldn't find that out until Mariah and Sheila were not present. And he had an even stronger feeling that there was no way either Temple or himself would let Mariah out of their sight for a moment now. Or Sheila let him out of hers.

What a miserable idea this was turning out to be.

Bite or Be Bitten

I do not stick around to take a bow, although I deserve one.

It is not every day the little guy gets to stick sixteen fully extended shivs into the back of a behemoth like Hercules and bring the big guy to his knees.

Lucky that I did. Then I did not have as far down to the ground to jump off.

I am in and out of there so fast I look like smoked lightning. In fact, I cannot resist slinking back and around to the audience's gathered ankles to wait for my reviews.

"Did you see that black thing that flew onto Herc's shoulders?"

"I think it was a bird, crow maybe."

"Naw. It was some bit of costuming that fell off in the fray. Looked like some ratty yak fur or something."

"I think it was that piece of paper that was blown into their legs by all the wind the battle scene whipped up. It had a dark side."

Boy, that last observer sure got it right: That pale interloper has a dark side, both actually and figuratively, which makes the moon look like a piker.

Amazing how so many witnesses can all see the same thing and observe roughly nothing.

I confess to being torn between two courses at the moment.

On the one mitt, I am itching to know who—or what, this being the kind of place where lots of whats are running around—gave my Miss Temple the dangerous bum's rush onto the fighting ground.

On the other mitt, I have a bone to teethe, pick, and suck dry with the instigator of it all.

All it will take is finding same.

So I slink away before my notices are completely in. Now that Mr. Matt Devine, he of the flying feet and postprandial balancing act, has his three little ducks in a row, I believe I can trust that nothing too terrible will happen to them while I am off on a mission of my own.

My instincts were right: Where that murderous-minded minx with the neon-blue eyes turns up, something evil is afoot.

The question is where the minx has gone now.

I begin by prowling in wider and wider circles around the scene of the crime, hoping to pick up an other-than-human scent. It takes several circles before I find a trace of her perfume. I am not kidding. This kit wears perfume, like a human female, and it is the delicate scent of a flower called hyacinth.

I fear that is the only delicate thing about her.

Needless to say, I am seeing red at seeing my roommate and her charge endangered. This is the second time that brown-masked babe has been responsible for putting our lifelines on the line, for I do not doubt that she was deliberately seeking to lead little Mariah astray.

All right. Little Mariah is not so little. What would you expect with a homicide lieutenant for a mother? Not to mention that said mother is also a giantess compared to the petite perfection of my Miss Temple. (You can see that I am slightly biased in favor of me, and also mine.) Nevertheless, in terms of years, Mariah is still a bit wet behind the behind the perked appendages. And I do not like the fact that the person who was actually shoved by the lurker in the crowd was my Miss Temple.

I am not the noseman that my associate Nose E.—the drug-and-bomb-sniffing Maltese dog—is, but I can follow an obvious trail. And that Hyacinth is nothing if not obvious. What is she doing here, I ask? "Working," she says, licking her long pink tongue over her long white teeth. Working to put my people in jeopardy, as she has done before.

Well, she will not lull my senses with that Panama Purple catnip she favors again.

I must say that I enjoy being on the trail in an environment where anything goes. There are enough people in strange guise here that one black cat on the prowl looks like something too boring to notice. Besides, most of them take me for a living mascot, rather like those stuffed dragons you see everywhere. In fact, I could use hopping a ride on a shoulder, but I must keep my nose to the ground, so it is no rest for Midnight Louie.

I must also tread carefully, lest I be trod upon. Here my dark coat not only makes me easy to overlook and thus step on, but there are many TitaniCon attendees with industrial-strength stepper-oners upon their feet.

I finally track down my prey.

She is lounging on a velvet-draped box like a posterbabe for a kitty porn site on the web, her tail lashing lazily.

I see that I have trailed her to a huge chamber into which people are pouring in dribs and drabs, mostly drab, to judge by this crowd. We seem to have left the costumed contingent behind to prowl the halls. Perhaps they could not bear to be sequestered away in this limited venue.

I waste no time with small talk.

"What are you really doing here?" I demand.

"Working," she says again.

"You do not look like you are working at anything other than being a loose cannon. What was the idea of racing across that battlefield?"

"It seemed like it would be fun."

"Your idea of fun is other people's idea of hara-kiri."

"Hara-kiri? No, I don't know the name. Any relation to Mata Hari?"

"Why do I think you know a thing or two about the spy game?"

"I do not know, Mr. Midnight Louie." Her eyes slit to laser-light hyphens. "I have traveled internationally, it is true, but now I work in Hollywood."

"Now? Like in 'right now?' "

The tail does a mazurka flourish. "As a matter of fact, yes. As soon as these tiresome directors, writers, and actors assemble and bore the audience into a stupor, I will be called upon to make an appearance to mark my film debut."

"You mean you really have a legitimate part in something?"

"I was a stage performer when you met me, after all. Now I have gone multimedia. There is a syndicated series, there are a series of novels and audiobooks, there will be a film, and CDs, e-books, whatever the future allows."

I admit that my green eyes go greener. My brief TV commercial gigs with the Divine Yvette begin to look a trifle . . . trivial.

"So the thing in the newspaper was real? You are this Phsst, psychic Kir-khat of the Kohl Kompendium?"

"Read it and weep."

"But you are not really psychic," I answer slyly, for I know one truly psychic dame, name of Karma, and it is hard to fool me on this issue.

Hyacinth shrugs her lean and lovely shoulders. Her bones are sharp as shark's fins, or boomerangs. Both items make me think of those poor kiwi birds she has been hanging around. But I suppose they would tell me huffily that the shark and the boomerang are Aussie icons, and not a rare and remote Kiwi thing. Let them eat worms, and let Hyacinth eat them.

My momentary snit ebbs fast. I would not wish being eaten by Hyacinth on anything. And the kiwi are actually amiable birds, much less pushy than your average parrot.

I settle down to keep her company. As long as I am watching her, she is not doing mischief in the vicinity of Miss Temple and associates.

Of course, to do my duty in this regard, I must make myself the object of Miss Hyacinth's attention.

And that is not a very safe position to be in, I can state from past experience.

Chapter 34

Big Bad Worf

Temple found her toes tapping on the small-scale pattern carpeting. Not much of it showed under a massed army of folding chairs holding a myriad of TitaniCon attendees.

The atmosphere was noisy, crowded, and headily ripe. She wondered again what she was doing here. She sat toward the end of a row. On her right sat Sheila, staring raptly up at Matt. On her left was Mariah, staring raptly up at the stage, where a large, black-maned being she had been informed was Kharal, King Khatlord of the Kohl Kompendium, occupied center stage.

Not that there was much stage: just a raised platform with a long convention table covered in the usual white floor-length tablecloth. The table bore the usual, boring convention accessories: four mike stands with microphones and the gleaming centerpiece of a clear plastic water pitcher surrounded by six upended drinking glasses. Behind the ordinariness loomed a Last Supper–size neon pictorial and sign that read "Khatlord Konquers" and displayed spontaneous combusting atoms or whole worlds in explosion.

Except for the lordly presence of the King Khatlord behind one of the mikes, ordinary humans sat along the table, itching and chatting among themselves while the audience strained to get comfortable on the unpadded metal torture devices upon which they were sitting.

For once, Mariah was the only one in the place who wasn't squirming. She clutched the promotional papers available at the ballroom entrance and often looked up at the exotic spacescape suspended from the ceiling. The alien solar systems and galaxies twirled like old-fashioned mirrored balls above the audience, casting splinters of neon and laser light on the walls, floor, and faces of the gathered throng.

In a few moments, one of the men on the podium knocked his pen on an open mike to get the crowd's attention. Temple cringed at the assault on her ears, but maybe she was just edgy because she'd nearly been taken off at the knees by Hercules and Xena not too long before.

As the five panelists took turns introducing themselves, Temple discovered that she would undergo the Khatlord experience in stereo. If Mariah on her left weren't offering running commentary on who was who in the convoluted storyline involving numerous races and members thereof, Sheila on her right would be tutoring Matt on similar complexities from quite a different point of view.

Temple tried to scratch her head under the heavy metal wig but found it an impossibility. No wonder a headache was starting to throb behind each eye and at the base of each ear.

While the discussion onstage considered the difficulties of deep space communication between alien races, Temple longed to pull out her handy-dandy cell phone and call Max to find out what was really going on here besides interstellar conquest.

She knew Matt wanted to talk to her about something, but she dared not let her attention wander from Mariah for a second, and she doubted Matt could lose Sheila's doting eye for even less than that, so they were all trapped.

And maybe that was just what someone wanted, for she *had* been pushed by a powerful hand. It seemed such a petty thing, pushing a woman into a child and thereby hurling them both into what amounted to a wrestling ring. But petty didn't mean the intention hadn't been lethal.

The combatants were trained martial arts experts, trained to keep their blows from hurting each other. It didn't mean that any innocent bystanders thrown in the way of those blows would survive just the right kick to just the most vulnerable spot.

Temple couldn't believe that all these people, most of them grown-up, would sit here like zombies agog at this blatant promotional session hyping yet another Hollywood space epic.

Apparently the Khatlord saga was a successful syndicated space opera that was going to the big time with its first feature film "crossover." This she gleaned from Sheila.

Apparently, the Khatlord himself was a sort of Byronic hero/villain who kept fans in a turmoil of trying to decide if he was a good guy or a bad guy. This was Mariah's analysis of the character anyway. And, she added, he was really cool because he was kinda like a cat.

Kinda like the Beast in the old *Beauty and the Beast* show Temple had never "got" years ago either.

And, Mariah explained, cats were cool because you can never tell what they're thinking.

Temple could not disagree. She had glimpsed a bit of flying black fur during their brush with martial arts that reminded her of Midnight Louie. What he was thinking of by showing up— again—at an event like this was too terrible to contemplate. She would prefer to think that he didn't think at all, but, frankly, too many recent events did not justify that conclusion.

The alternative was even worse, for if Louie didn't turn up merely because he used to wander this town and still craved to haunt the Strip, then he had a purpose. And usually when he turned up, things went from bad to worse. Temple hated to be so blatantly superstitious, but Louie was a very bad omen.

She started fanning herself with the freebie papers. Didn't anyone else notice how crowded and hot it was?

The Khatlord himself had stood up to enthuse about his forthcoming flick. He was another of those looming bassos who belong in grand opera. Temple had noticed that Klingons and Darth Vader were often portrayed by African-Americans whose voices were deep and resonant enough to shake listeners to their souls.

Given the dehumanizing outfits that made them taller, wider, and wickeder than life and their masklike facial embellishments, they did indeed embody larger-than-life beings.

The Khatlord disdained the microphone as he boomed out into the three-thousand-some seat house, "And I am proud to announce that the first Khatlord film"—he paused for applause, which came in a resounding wave—"will be based on my very first Khatlord novel, so this is an especially pleasurable and personal project for me."

More applause, a tidal wave this time.

One audience member was so carried away that he stood, and stood so abruptly that his chair tipped over behind him.

Temple wondered if they were about to witness speaking in tongues, perhaps Khurses.

But the man drove through the several people blocking his way to the aisle and went charging up the side of the ballroom and out the rear doors.

He didn't look like the charging type. In fact, he looked like Wilbur Wuss. In fact, as he passed parallel to Temple's row he looked a lot like . . .

"Greg Seltz," Sheila hissed in Matt's ear. "He's the guy who cowrote the Khatlord books." She gave Temple a quick glance. "Remember? He was the guy who got between Hanford Schmidt and Alan Dahl when they were arguing in the con suite."

"I think he was the *reason* they were arguing in the con suite." Temple craned her neck to watch Seltz's complete exit. Ow. Her neck hurt. Kriminy Khatlord! Where was Max when she needed him for a massage? Only a cell phone away, but she didn't want to use it, except in private, and she didn't see any privacy coming until she left TitaniCon after having seen Mariah off the premises in Matt's custody.

She leaned forward. Matt was looking as grim and bored as she felt.

His glance crossed hers, and she read his own urgent need to talk to her. She had an awful feeling that the current impasse in communication was assisting everybody but them.

Inside her tote bag, the visage of the man Max sought reposed, useless. He could be anybody here . . . a passing Klingon . . . the Khatlord on the podium, although not likely, as he was an actor named Timothy Hathaway . . . maybe even one of the occasional Mr. Spocks who floated through the con in their elfin ears and "Very Fifties" short-trimmed, glossy black bangs. No, she didn't see that brutal face on the portrait passing for Mr. Spock's aloof asexual Sherlockian persona.

Maybe he had come as the Big Bad Worf.

Chapter 35

Call Notes

Max sat at home, staring at the telephone.

Why didn't Temple call?

His fingers itched to dial her, except he suspected that might be the wrong move.

If not her, then who you gonna call?

Molina?

No. Not yet.

He hated being out of touch, helpless, but, for the moment, there was no help for it.

He stood. He had to do something, even if it was the wrong thing.

Chapter 36

The Last of Sheila

"It's getting late," Matt said, checking his watch.

They stood in the hallway, people flowing around them as if their foursome were rocks in the stream.

No one answered him or made a move.

His eyes skimmed Temple's. She seemed to be thinking on the same track he was: *Let's talk, but let's do it privately.*

He turned to Sheila, ashamed that he had to work to produce a smile. "I need to talk to Mariah's mother when I take her back. Are you okay with getting yourself home?"

The question seemed to wake Sheila up to the fact that she had an existence outside TitaniCon.

"Sure," she said valiantly, disappointment thickening her voice. "I'm sure I can drive. The ankle's okay if I don't put too much weight on it. Well. It was great seeing you again." She glanced at Temple, troubled. "And meeting you."

In a spasm of group guilt, Matt, Temple, and Mariah watched Sheila's solitary figure vanish into a sea of T-shirts and costumes.

Temple shook off her angst. "We need to go someplace quiet and less crowded," she said.

"The con suite," Mariah suggested.

If Temple still wore glasses, instead of invisible contact lenses, she would have been gazing schoolmarmishly over their frame tops at Mariah. "Not quiet and uncrowded enough."

Temple was thinking. Matt could see her public relations brain scanning the scene. She knew public events. She knew crowd control.

"The ballroom!" she told them. "It's the last place anybody'd be right now. They won't have it set up for anything else yet. There's too much junk to move. And you," she told Mariah, "can look over the cool props to your heart's content while Matt and I sit down to rest."

And talk was a given.

So they pushed the heavy entry doors open again and barged on through.

Into emptiness. Into silence.

Both were unbelievably welcome.

Above them, still moving in the Space Odyssey: 2001 ballet of human toys in eternity, swayed the imagined planets, stars, novas, black holes, solar systems, galaxies, and undiscovered Milky Ways that people kept hoping were out there . . . somewhere, and populated.

Ranks of empty, expectant folding chairs spoke to all the unplumbed possibilities on Earth, and far beyond Earth.

The long table sat empty on its platform, its now-unlit backdrop still the hubris of neon proclaiming "Khatlord Konquers." Seen in an empty ballroom, the phrase was both a sobering and hilarious comment on the ambitions of carbon-based life forms from a puny planet with vast delusions of grandeur.

This space has the huge, hollow, serene aspect of a cathedral, Matt thought. His imagination translated the secular furnishings into pews, aisles, an altar, even a dimmed vigil light—the great neon billboard now unlit behind it all. What man might imagine God might be.

Science has moved man from the false idols of the primitive past to a secular self-worship in the present, he mused. *Isn't it odd that the science fiction worldview that is considered the most logical, the least God-dependent,* Star Trek, *has always addressed the thorniest human moral issues? And the science fiction phenomena that is considered most mystical,* Star Wars, *is considered the most God-friendly, and yet is less idealistic and more dark than* Star Trek?

He saw life as the reverse: God offered hard choices. God was not the good and evil inside every human: the Force versus Darth Vader, the anti-Force. God was the attempt of mind over matter, to find the human in the alien. And the alien in the human. And to be humbled by them both.

After the past hour's hype and screaming, how amazing that they could retreat to this now tranquil stage set for another, entirely imaginative view of the universe. Did religion require a suspension of disbelief, as theater did? Was the secret simply a letting go of everything the human fist had been trying to clutch onto since the moment of birth, when those infant fists first flailed at their very existence?

He could tell that Temple and Mariah beside him were experiencing the same blessed sense of sanctuary here. Such a medieval concept. So needed in the hurly-burly, hectic modern world.

They moved toward the empty altar, the voices only memories, even the massive neon sign behind the empty microphones darkened, blank, empty.

Except that it was not.

Chapter 37

Time Warp

At last!

Relief forces have arrived.

First I hear the big doors at the far end of this gigantic room whoosh open and shut. Then voices, small and wee, echo in the vast chamber.

It has been so quiet in here for so long that I wonder if my ears still work. They do! I cannot see who has entered, but my sharp ears soon tell me they are friendlies.

Thank Bast.

Now it is time to study my embarrassing situation.

I cannot see because the lavender velvet curtain that drapes my prison grille obscures everything.

The astute observer will realize that I am inside the cage reserved for Hyacinth.

When last we saw me, I was outside the structure, and the dangerous but lovely Siamese was lounging atop the velvet and the barbed wire beneath. All right, it is not barbed wire. But it could be!

So. How did I get in and she get away?

Quite a magic trick, is it not?

I am not quite sure, except that I am not pleased about it. Here is what I remember.

I am watching her, and she is watching the doings on the platform where the Khatlord is the center of attention and a lot of duller-looking men in suits are discussing cinematic wonders and such. They drone on and on, like bees with vocabularies.

Naturally, I am bored, and begin to doze off.

Things are foggy after that. Perhaps Hyacinth has nicked me with a Valium-bearing claw. Perhaps the earlier excitement with Herc and Xena has just been too much for me. Apparently, Hyacinth has been brought onstage to make her bows, because the next thing I know, the cage is being lifted and the velvet cloth falls over me, and a stagehand scoops me into the prison saying, "This one's time out is over. Put the drape over the cage. The trainer says it quiets the animal."

I yowl to high heaven at this suggestion, but then am given a drubbing as the cage tilts and shakes. The velvet cloth covers my prison and me, then we are finally set down and left alone.

Here I realize that the clever Hyacinth has seen to it that in the shadowy confusion of the offstage area, I have been confined in her place!

Naturally, I am furious and make the cage shake until it almost tips over. But no one comes.

I am forced to conclude that I have been positioned in some forgotten corner.

And there I stay as further droning and self-congratulation emanates from the platform. Finally, an ear-splitting aria of endless applause echoes and echoes in the ballroom, until one would think those fictitious planets revolving on high would be shaken free of their guy-wires.

That is how they do it, you know. It is always either done with mirrors or wires.

I am pretty steamed, but at least the decadent Hyacinth has a purple velvet, down-filled pillow in her cage, not to mention a Pretty Paws commode at the far end. I make a point of using it in a fairly indelible way.

Cheap revenge, however, gives little satisfaction.

And I soon recognize the mass creaks and shuffles in the wider world that signify I am being deserted in this quandary. The audience is leaving. Even the panel members are leaving. Hyacinth, obviously, is long gone.

I will be marooned here until such time as I can free myself or find some sucker to do it for me.

With the mass desertion of the room, finding that sucker looks like a slim chance.

In the dimness, I pat down the prison door. If it has one of those lift-style latches, I am out like gangbusters. If it has one of those pinch-type latches, that even humans curse and break their fingernails over, I am just a bird in a gilded cage. Call me Kiwi.

After several digital explorations, I discover that I am trapped behind a dreaded pinch latch to which has been added the dire precaution of an extra twist of heavy metal holding it closed.

Apparently Miss Hyacinth has been a naughty girl in times past and requires extra security. Grrrrreat, as my huckster idol Tony the Tiger says. I must pay for her misbehavior.

Resistance is futile, and protest is fruitless. No one is here to hear it, and they would ignore it if they did. I am savvy enough to know that. Sheer physical force is not enough for the steel trap door on Miss Hyacinth's lodgings. It occurs to me that the twelve-gauge latch is there as much to keep Miss H in as to keep anyone untoward from getting at Miss H.

No wonder she arranged for the change. She is off and up to no good, while I sit in for her. And where is her trainer? Off and up to no good, too? Apparently she has left the magic show of the lethal and larcenous Miss Shangri-la for a screen career, but I cannot doubt that she still partners some human in nefarious deeds.

Well . . . I examine a set of matched porcelain bowls inscribed with her name, may it be stricken from every stele in the great Gobi desert! Hmmm. Could this fish gumbo be Japanese blowfish in eel sauce? A great delicacy on the side of the planet where the rising sun first casts its rays each day. Of course it can be fatal. I decide to go on a diet. As for the water bowl, it is filled with either cologne or some adulterated spring water from someplace where they do odd things to canine coats, like France.

I decide I am best off entering a meditation mode and eschewing food, drink, and negative emotions. I think of my acquaintance Karma and hum softly to myself. It is handy sometimes to be your own lullaby machine.

So I wait.

And dream.

And have nightmares.

My ears twitch back, offended.

By what?

Is it the tick, tick, tick of the clock? The drip, drip, drip of a leaky faucet? Or the click, click, click of a safe dial?

But the sound is not that regular. It is more like a drum beat: *whoosh-click, whoosh-click, whoosh-click.*

It is just predictable enough to make my ears itch with irritation. Having nothing better to do, I picture what could be making this sharp, metallic sound. Probably a weapon on a costume, moving as the owner walks. That is why it misses a beat. It is on the owner's right side and only jostled sufficiently when that limb takes a step.

Brilliant deduction, Louie. Look, ma, no eyes!

Now that I have figured out the likely source of the sound, I am ready to go back to sleep again, and do.

Except that next, I hear hissing. An ophidian in the grass? Rasping as it goes on its hidden path? By now I am fully alert. And fully irritated. If seems as if I will be made an unwitting, unwilling, and unseeing witness to something that clicks and hisses as it goes. Maybe a Uthrellian Lionx.

No. Voices. Human. Whispering. Soft. Hissing. Anger.

Two voices.

No good ever comes of two hushed voices. At least not among humans.

I fan my ears to and fro, striving to catch every syllable, every nuance.

I also insinuate a mitt through a square in the grille— *ouch!* this is a very fine grille—and try to hook a claw in a velvet fold so I can pull it askew enough to see something.

But my prison is set on the floor, curse it, and I see nothing but chair legs and tablecloth and feet.

And all around in the great empty hall with the heavenly bodies twisting slowly in the air-conditioning high above, I hear the hissing voices bounced back and forth, a hushed volley of anger that moves faster and faster . . .

I get another mitt through the grille and try to patty-cake the velvet between both mitts, and then pull.

Often, I and my brothers and sisters have done this same thing and have been accused of being so cute as the humans twitch some tantalizing plaything out of our reach time and time again. Torture masquerading as fun, if you ask me! We are very serious about our motor skills and our mitt-to-eye coordination. These are survival techniques, and no matter how domesticated our lot, we must keep them in fighting form should we ever be suddenly cast on our own in the cold, cruel, toyless world.

I have almost lifted a corner of the velvet when I hear a tremendous impact.

Then the buzzing of a million bees and the crackling of a thousand grackles.

Nasty birds. Nothing like the gentle Kiwi Nation. Of course, even nasty birds have their uses and, no doubt, mothers who love them.

My poor ears flatten right to my skull. The racket is so awful, especially that sharp, shattered scream at the beginning.

I push my face against the grille and search the small bit of scenery visible. *Whoosh-click.* Footsteps thump down from the wooden platform to carpet and grow mute over the long distance to the far doors.

Meanwhile, I am left in the dark, smelling singed hair and flesh and a small amount of leather. Is it possible that the deceitful Hyacinth has truly become a cat on a hot tin roof?

I would not wish such a fate on a dogcatcher.

Chapter 38

Rain and Wind and Fire

Matt was used to approaching altars with reverence. This one he approached with dread. They all sensed the taint of human sacrifice, even Mariah, who made a furtive sign of the cross. As they came closer, the dimmed neon letters revealed what had dimmed them.

Not a stagehand.

Not a breaker lever on a light board.

Not a lightning strike.

No, the sign itself had been broken.

By the crash of an alien body against it.

They moved nearer, neither Temple nor Matt thinking to shield Mariah against the truth: A figure stood seared into the vanished brilliance, crucified on the dimmed cross fire.

The Khatlord, hurled somehow, onto an electrocuting field of lighted neon, into the excessive voltage of imagination and hype. Killed by a billboard.

"Is he dead?" Temple breathed.

Matt nodded, then shook his head. No theologian could ever answer that question yes or no. He stopped thirty feet away. Some mysteries required distance. His hand stopped Mariah. He couldn't shelter her from this, but she didn't need to confront it any closer. He sensed an adult acceptance of the death scene. Maybe her mother's profession had taught her that death came unexpectedly.

Temple couldn't stop, and he wouldn't stop her.

"My God," she said, mounting the platform by the side steps. She was staring at the Khatlord as if she recognized him. But she had recognized something else. "I *thought* I'd seen that weapon before."

Matt didn't try to understand her. The death weapon had been a carnival of light, a grid of voltage, a lethal divining rod of electricity. And behind it, as with so many things people were often urged to accept as God's will, was undoubtably the twisted hand of man, of the human.

Chapter 39

Mother of Invention

Carmen Molina was glad that detective lieutenants didn't have to drive.

She would have been breaking every traffic regulation in the book, and then some.

The uniform at the wheel was pushing it anyway. He sensed her urgency.

Send your kid off because you couldn't be there. Work to do. Cases to open, close, too many to leave suspended in limbo.

Limbo. Her kid. Leave your kid off. Let someone else baby-sit. Not a baby. A twelve-going-on-twenty young adult. Lots of years between twelve and twenty. Everything happened then. Or, worst-case scenario, nothing.

Matt Divine. Salt of the earth. Couldn't find anyone more twisted up in the right thing to do. Not enough. Not in the face of murder. Why? Her kid. This event?

She was there. Mariah. And nothing heard from her. Or Matt.

And a spectacular murder on the very same premises. So what if six thousand other people were present? That was five thousand, nine hundred and ninety-nine too close to Mariah. It had sounded so innocent, so kiddish.

Oh, my God. Couldn't he drive faster? No. The courts were coming down hard on unjustified pursuit speeds, and they were pursuing nothing here but her maternal imagination.

Her job. Do the job. Doing the job would solve the problems. Mariah would be found. Watching some space fantasy film. Eating popcorn with Matt Devine. Six thousand people. No reason her daughter was anywhere near what had happened.

"Want me to use the siren, Lieutenant?"

She thought he'd never ask.

It was getting dark enough that the parking lot looked like a cherry-top convention. A man was dead; they didn't need all the uniforms. Alch and Su met her as she left the Crown Vic.

"What are you doing here?" She hadn't meant to bark. She was glad to see them. What was the matter with her?

"Had a mortality to check out here before. Apparent accident. This one's no accident." Alch was midlife mellow to a tee.

"This one is very interesting." Su's bizarre Dragon Lady eyebrows, plucked into twin peaks, looked like Swiss-chalet roofs. "Most macabre."

Alch chuckled at his petite partner. "You know how many homicide dicks use the word 'macabre?' "

Avuncular Molina didn't need now. "Shut up, Morey. What's macabre?"

He was hurt. All right, she'd been insensitive. How many times had insensitivity been used toward her? Dammit.

"Sorry, Morey. I've been stressed out lately. What's the story?"

They explained: a man in a bizarre costume electrocuted against a gaudy neon sign. Neither one was gaudy anymore. Bizarre costume. It rang a bell. Only all the alarm bells in her head were going off at once. Where was Mariah? Why hadn't she heard a word about Mariah? Surely Matt Devine knew something deadly had happened at this hotel, this event? Why hadn't he tried to call? Where was he?

"We'll check with the crime-scene team," Su said. Or Alch. She didn't know which had spoken.

After a moment's numb contemplation, she noticed they were heading away and moved to follow them into the hotel.

A walking shadow blocked her path, having intersected her on an angle from the sidelines. One of those science fiction freaks, six-and-half-feet tall and wearing the face of a jungle animal.

Molina stiffened. Idiocy would not stand between her and her child. "Out of my way."

"No."

She reared back. She was not in the mood for nonsense, and this figure from a kid's TV show was nonsense.

"Get out of my way," she repeated, through her teeth. "I'm the police." She started reaching into her jacket pocket for the clip-on ID so idiots like this wouldn't accost her.

"You don't want to go in there, Lieutenant," the thing said.

"I don't?" She was ready to unload. Then it hit her. How did he know her rank?

The creature pushed closer between her and the uniforms, forming a wall. He was big enough for it. That didn't worry her one bit. The "lieutenant" worried her.

"Lieutenant?" she repeated.

"Good. You're thinking again."

"You son of a . . ."

"You recognized me."

She pulled back. Grew deadly calm. Focused. Remembered her back holster. Remembered more. This was the shadow suspect she'd been chasing for months through a maze of unsolved murders and mysterious scams. The now-you-see-him, now-you-don't magician she'd tried to use as point man on a touchy problem from her past. Her archenemy and Temple Barr's significant other. The Mystifying Max Kinsella.

"What are you doing here?" she asked. "Dressed like this?"

"Still working for you."

"For *me?*"

"You gave me a name, a history, a sketch. He gave me a dead girl. I'm here. He's here."

"What do you mean . . . he's not dead?" She hadn't meant to sound hopeful.

The ludicrous maned head shook. "I mean he's here. So is your daughter."

The last word drove her forward, toward the hotel. "I know."

He stopped her with a bar of pseudomailed arm, metallic waffle-pattern stuff, glittering like reflective safety tape.

"Listen," he said. "You gave me a job. Let me do it."

"I told you to forget it."

"If you could make me do that, Lieutenant, I would in a heartbeat. But you can't."

She didn't like that. She had unleashed him on a possible enemy. Now she had a certain enemy chasing a possible enemy, and she had no allies at all. And her daughter was in there.

"You're not thinking. *He's here,*" the man-beast repeated.

"He?" She had to be sure.

"Your man."

Oh, those two words stung, perfectly professional now and perfectly personal once. There, but for the grace of God, would be no Mariah. She began to appreciate why some of the poor souls she took away in handcuffs had gone completely berserk.

She ran a hand through her hair, amazed that it had not been torn out yet.

"Listen." He spoke softly through the feral mask, a voice of reason in gothic guise. "You can't go in. He's in disguise, like I am, but I assume he would recognize you."

"I've changed," she argued.

"I'm glad to hear it." He could sound amused at a funeral, she didn't doubt. "But those eyes haven't."

She glared at him. Damn her eyes! Damn her father's traitorous eyes. His curse. At least Mariah didn't have that: Nordic eyes in a Mediterranean face. Lord deliver us from the fury of the Northmen . . .

Of the Khatman . . . no, Khatlord, that's what the dispatcher had said.

"You like this!" she accused, falsely, knowing even as she said it that she simply needed to discharge fury she dare not feel.

"No more than you," he said, cryptic. "Listen. Temple and Devine are there. They'll get your daughter out eventually."

"Why not me? Why not now?"

"Because," he said, "you can't. I can't. She witnessed the discovery of the body. They found the dead man, all three. Your detectives will have to take your daughter's statement and release her. You know the procedure."

"They can do it tomorrow. I'll order it."

"And tip *him* off? You'll wait. She'll be out in an hour or two. You'll wait. And then you'll let them take her home, and you'll have set up a tail to make sure that nobody follows them. Or you. It's just procedure, just discipline, Lieutenant. Routine discipline."

"As if you ever had any," she managed to snap before she choked on the words. Any words.

But she returned to the back seat of the Crown Vic to do what she did worst of anything in the world. To wait.

Chapter 40

Hung Up

Temple nervously watched the Cardassian, Klingon, and Khatlord security forces isolate the ballroom.

She, Matt, and Mariah were confined to their one small circle of hell, hemmed in by these overarmed behemoths in platform shoes.

Temple had never wanted to use a cell phone as much in her life. Where was Max?

She and Matt and Lieutenant Molina's daughter sat on the edges of their folding chairs, waiting for the detectives to finish orienting the forensics teams and turn to interviewing the folks who found the body.

Mariah was hunched and quiet, although her thick sneaker heels kept drumming the skinny metal legs of her chair.

Matt's profile was bleak. Temple had never seen his face so sharpened by concern, not even in the darkest days of his personal quest. She supposed being responsible for a child while discovering a dead body was not a happy place to be.

But the victim hardly looked dead. His costumed persona was so much larger than life that the lack of life didn't seem much of a change. He was still an icon, slumped against the sign's metal fretwork like a disconnected Borg.

This was all so much like an episode from your favorite sci-fi show. Oops. She remembered Sheila's lecture on how outmoded that term was.

Sheila. Hey. She was out of this. Matt should be pleased about that.

She glanced at him. No, she wouldn't mention that bright side.

Sadly, nothing shook her about this situation as much as the close-up look she had gotten at the Khatlord's waist-holstered dagger. The overall impact of the Khatlord costume was so bristling with exotic and intimidating uniform and weaponry details that it had been easy to overlook what she now considered obvious.

She supposed it would be called a dagger. It was a heck of a big knife with a heck of convoluted handle. Haft. Hilt. Whatever.

When she had casually mentioned it, Mariah had told her the Khatlords called it a Kohlian Klaw.

She called it one damn coincidence too many.

Her stomach did a sickening double axel, even as her mind skated off in another direction.

Max needed to see this thing in the flesh. The metal. The pseudo metal, whatever it was. Where was he?

Poor Professor Mangel! What had he done to get himself skewered by a lethal duplicate of a prop from a syndicated TV space show? Now if that were Jeff's body up there, pinned against the gray and broken glass tubes. . . . Temple felt a stab of the guilt that must prickle Matt's thin skin. She had meddled. She had gone to Jeff to discover the identity of the woman killed in the church parking lot. Later, Max had gone to him. And then, only hours after Max's visit, amiable, enthusiastic Jeff was dead. Spectacularly stabbed by a weapon as mythical as a unicorn's horn.

Now that weapon had reared its ugly head and horn again. As a prop! A plaything! A mock weapon!

Temple really wanted to examine the dead man's dagger. And of course the police wouldn't understand.

"Don't worry." Mariah's soft voice came thin and sweet in the chamber empty of sound except for the noises of recording, dismantling, and body-bagging. "My mother will come and take care of it."

Temple smiled at her, but a nagging thread jerked at her subconscious. That's right. Where was Molina? Normally, a murder scene without Molina was a free ticket for her. But this was one place the homicide lieutenant should be, up close and personal. And she wasn't. Why not?

"How we doing over here?" The jovial question was addressed to Mariah, not to the adults who flanked her.

The man with the graying mustache squatted down before Mariah, wincing as his knees jackknifed. "I hear your name is Maria."

"Mariah," she corrected. "It ends with an 'H' "—she glanced at Temple—"like what they call the wind in some song."

"Oh, that Mariah!" He pulled out a notebook. "All right, Mariah. Your friends here can move off with Detective Su while you and I talk. Okay?"

"Do you work for my mother?" the girl asked as Temple and Matt moved away.

"Ah . . . we all work for the police department. But, yes. Your mother's the boss."

"I know." Mariah sighed.

Detective Su's job was to interview and distract the adults while Detective "Mustache" tried to interrogate Mariah.

Temple could tell that the tiny Asian woman performed any job with clockwork precision.

"Why did you come in here after the presentation was over?"

"Mariah," Temple said quickly, afraid of what Matt had been about to answer. "She's a kid. She loved the ceiling stuff. We were going to show her one more time. After the crowd had gone. It is something, isn't it?"

Detective Su glanced up at the glittering cosmos. "Maybe. I want to know what happened here on earth. So the billboard lights were dead, along with the guy when you came in here at . . . ?"

"Seven-thirty," Matt said, quite truthfully, and therefore quite convincingly.

Obviously, the best plan was to let him answer when facts were called for. When interpretation was at stake, Temple would take over and put the proper spin on things.

Temple cast a glance sideways. Detective "Mustache" was a teddy bear type. If anybody could tease the truth out of Mariah, he could. Why did she think the truth had to be teased out of Mariah?

As she wondered this very thing, the detective bent his head to his notebook to write something down. Mariah looked at Temple and winked.

Once Temple and Matt had testified to the state of the body being just as it was when they had entered this ballroom, the time, their actions after realizing a dead man was in the room, Temple calling the police on her cell phone, and Matt going to notify hotel security, Detective Su snapped her narrow notebook shut and stood.

"I understand one of you is to take Lieutenant Molina's daughter home."

"Me," Matt said quickly.

"I'll get an officer to escort you and the girl to your car. I'm not sure what the plan is after that. Wait here."

Su minced off on the chunky-heeled sandals that peeked from beneath her tailored pants, while Matt stood and ran his fingers through his hair.

"I could use a bathroom break."

"Go ahead," Temple told him. "I'll watch Mariah." She didn't envy him reporting to Molina on all that had happened.

She wondered how much he'd tell her. She wondered how much Mariah had or would tell anyone.

They were partners in crime, with none of them having any idea where the others stood.

"Detective Alch," Temple said, recognizing him way too late, as he brought Mariah to her in Matt's absence. "We've met."

He nodded. "You going to take care of this big girl for a minute?"

"Sure."

Mariah made a face as he moved off. "He treats me like a little kid."

"Sometimes that's kinda nice. You'll miss it someday, believe me."

"I do," Mariah said. "I've heard about you."

"Anything good?"

"Not really." She gave Temple a sideways glance. "I hate it when people don't tell me things for my own good."

"Me, too. But I've got a few years on you; I've earned the right to be told."

"There's being told . . . and there's telling."

"And—?"

"What did you tell *your* detective?"

"Only about finding the Khatlord here."

"Me, too. Do you think Matt will squeal if they get him alone?"

"I don't know. He's a pretty straightforward guy."

"That's a problem."

"I don't think so."

"Well, I like him. Kinda," she added quickly, so Temple wouldn't get the wrong impression. "But we know what's going on. So I didn't tell."

"Tell who what?"

"Detective Alch. Anything much. If I told him about the Xena and Hercules thing, I wouldn't get to come back here again, would I?"

Temple was shocked. "Mariah, no convention is worth—"

"We'll have to come back if we're going to catch the murderer, won't we?"

"We?" Temple asked.

"This is way too complicated for the police. I mean, somebody's been after us for the whole convention, but who'd ever believe it? Who'd be after you, or Matt, or me? Or even Sheila?"

"After us? What are you talking about?"

"It's obvious. I could tell you'd been pushed after me into the fight scene. And there's Sheila saying someone shoved her on the moving sidewalk, and she hurt her ankle. And Matt could have been creamed by Hercules and Xena if he hadn't done that cool trick with the tilting table. I know it sounds stupid."

Out of the mouths of babes, or babe wannabes. "No . . . it doesn't sound stupid. But it's hard to believe—"

"I wouldn't believe it if I hadn't been here," Mariah agreed. "So it's up to us to figure out who and why. And we need to keep this between us."

"Oh, really. Don't you feel a little guilty about deceiving your mother? And Matt?"

"Maybe. But you don't. I can tell."

"Mariah!"

"That's all right. I understand. Sometimes you have to do it for their own good."

Chapter 41

Kitnapped!

Temple was relieved that Matt and not she had to deliver Mariah to her waiting mother.

Detective Alch had offered to escort Temple out of the ballroom, past the POLICE LINE DO NOT CROSS tape the color of bumblebees. Su got the happy chore of bringing Goldilocks Matt and Baby Bear to Mother Bear.

Temple would just have been happy to spot a Papa Bear, although she didn't really think Max would relish playing that role.

She declined Alch's escort, saying that her feet were killing her, and couldn't she just sit here and rest.

It crossed her mind that the man sketched on the paper inside her tote bag could be the dead man. Was anybody sure the corpse was the real Khatlord? A lot of Khatlord troops were running around the convention, some of them security people, some of them extras from the television series, and a few of them fans practicing for the Masquerade tomorrow night.

Alch looked dubious at letting her stay, but he also had the sympathetic look of someone whose feet killed him from time to time. And she could tell he didn't think she could kill a fly, unlike his superior officer.

So he left her there to contemplate life, death, and where Max Kinsella was . . . oh, my God! When had she last talked to him? Could *he* have possibly—? She gazed at the tall, anonymous figure being lowered to the floor for bagging, tagging, and more invasive procedures.

Temple's mental health took a drastic plunge.

It would be just like Max to go undercover here, and the Khatlord guise was perfect for his physique. Everyone was assuming that the dead man was the famous actor Khatlord, because he had been doing a presentation in this ballroom earlier. But Hercules and Xena hadn't been the real thing.

So the man on the neon grid could be anyone. Did anyone even know what the real Khatlord looked like?

She pulled out her cell phone and punched in Max's number.

It rang. And rang. No answer.

Not good.

Temple shut her eyes. She was tired. And her neck hurt. And she had no business telling the police how to do their body identifying. But someone should suggest . . .

She was up and moving toward the platform.

The body had only been lowered to the floor after its original position had been videotaped. Cameras were old hat—forties fedoras, she supposed—on crime scenes nowadays. Now it was live action of dead bodies.

She also supposed the crime-scene crew had seen people who had been electrocuted naturally. And who was to say the Khatlord just hadn't backed up with too grandiose a gesture into the neon circuit board of light behind him?

But after the session? For an absent audience? Why? Why be there? Had he been threatened by someone? Forced to backstep into death? What a clever way to kill without even touching the victim. That remote but lethal-touch idea reminded Temple of someone, or something, but she was too tired to pin the tail on the donkey with any accuracy.

The forensics people were absorbed in their work. Another moving figure, another set of footsteps, especially at the fringe of the action, beyond the DO NOT CROSS barrier, would not be, like certain truths, self-evident.

No one noticed her approaching the scene of the crime.

The end of the long table was in shadow. No spotlights had been trained here.

Temple crept closer, straining to see.

She smacked her shin on a nasty metal table leg.

And she didn't dare hop around, curse, scream. It always hurts worse when you can't articulate your pain. The aptness of that thought vis-à-vis psychic pain crossed her mind, but this physical pain was too sharp, too intense to allow her thoughts to wander. It hurt! She had absolutely no padding on her poor shin. And, being where she wasn't supposed to be, she couldn't even whine out loud.

She sank to the carpeting, cradled the wounded leg, rocked, bit her lip, stifled any moans.

A brush of velvet soothed the savage shin.

Velvet?

The cloth on the panel table was the usual scratchy hotel linen.

She discovered a low rectangular box beside the table and lifted a pale fold of velvet. It didn't conceal a table leg but a low metal box.

Two burning gold irises glared at her from beneath it.

The box is alive! It's . . . R2D2, disassembled. It's . . . the head of Frankenststein. No. This head was black, with pointed ears. Mr. Spock? Oh, and a familiar, though faint, yowl.

She started pulling lilac-colored velvet away from the metal cage that provided its shape. She felt like a magician for once, like Max, drawing the scarf of endless possibility from the sleeve of deception.

She finally unveiled the cage door, and a latch—one of those awful pinch-together things that required more tensile strength

290 • Carole Nelson Douglas

than the female fingers are capable of exerting. Grimacing and grinding her teeth in silence, she finally sprung the mechanism.

Sprung none other than Midnight Louie from durance vile. He came lurching out of the sheltered dark like a punch-drunk boxer, ears flattened, dazed dark pupils overwhelming his usually green and glorious irises.

"Shhh!" she said. As if a cat would know what that meant.

She'd wanted to know where Max was, but here she had found where Louie was when she hadn't even known he was missing.

Poor fellow! Locked in this squinky cage. How and by whom?

He seemed inclined to rub and purr on her, but this was not the time or place for public displays of affection.

She crawled over to her deserted folding chair, grabbed her tote bag, crawled back, and stuffed the still punchy Louie into it.

There wasn't a lot of room, but tote bags are used because they are accommodating, especially the giant economy size. Plus Louie's weight sunk him to the bottom like a stone.

She hefted the straps over her shoulder. Trying not to hunch over like Santa, she made for the side aisle outa there.

"Miss Barr?

She turned, beaming innocently.

Detective Alch had noticed her departure.

"You all right?"

"A bit fagged, thanks. You know where to reach me." She turned and trotted insouciantly up the aisle to the exit doors.

Oh . . . *ouch!*

Chapter 42

Home Ground

"You've got to get a new car," Max complained from the back seat when she slung Louie and her tote bag on top of him.

Temple decided not to have a heart attack in favor of peering closely into her back seat. Two dark and feline-faced somethings were getting overfamiliar with her drive-shaft hump.

Temple didn't even want to know how he had managed to conceal himself in her locked car.

"Max! I'm so glad to see you like this. I mean, you *are* wearing the Khatlord costume. I was so afraid of that."

"How did you guess? I'm only asking because I pride myself on being unpredictable."

Temple sat in her own passenger seat, aware that her knees as well as her neck were hurting. " 'Pride' is a particularly catlike word. It had occurred to me that the dead man could have been anybody, wearing that Khatlord suit, that fake face, that mane of hair. And knowing your propensity for disguise . . ."

"I've been too busy to get killed," Max said drily, "though not too busy to know about the murder. Now drive me home so I can peel off this loathsome likeness to Midnight Louie and get to work. You're Miss Inside, I'm Mister Outside. We need to compare notes."

"I'm just so glad you're all right."

"Me, too. Watch your rearview mirror. We could be followed. Your leaving here has to look normal."

"What about when Matt took Mariah home?"

"It looked normal, but it wasn't. I persuaded the maternal unit to leave the driving to Matt but to put a tail on him."

"She was here in person?"

"Here and fit to chew tungsten. Don't worry. I kept her out of the way."

"Now that's a feat."

"Is everybody okay?"

"If you mean me, Matt, and Mariah, yes. If you mean the guy crucified on the Nevada Power Company, no."

"Any sign of the subject?"

"Dammit, Max, we've just been interrogated by the police, which I'll tell you about later, and we've seen fire and we've seen rain. Where the hell the 'subject' is, I don't know. What I'm most worried about is the weapon."

"What weapon? It's obvious the victim was electrocuted."

"Probably, although I don't know an ohm from an ooomph. But that's not it. Not the dead man, it's what he was wearing."

"A costume?"

"Yes. And part of it was a weapon. A fictional, fantasy weapon. A knife."

"Knives are big in futuristic scenarios, don't ask me why."

"Not any knife. *Our* knife."

A very long pause from the backseat. "Our knife? Or *the* knife?"

"*The* knife. The one that killed the professor that I saw in a photo on Molina's desk. She's not going to miss this."

Max expelled an audible breath. It might have been impa-

tience. It might have been indecision. Knowing Max, it was probably two and two adding up to fourteen.

"Temple, don't dawdle," he said. "Drive us home. I'll take care
of it. Don't worry."

Don't worry. Be happy. Temple felt as if she were trapped in some
weird scenario, like the starship *Voyager* in the Delta Quadrant.

"Your place?" she asked. "Or the Circle Ritz?"

"If nobody's following us, the Ritz, yes, Jeeves."

"How will we know about the following?"

"I'll be able to check discreetly after I unload this cat. Oooof."

"Good luck," she wished him, heaving herself over the shift
console and into the driver's seat. She felt a charge of mental
energy, a sense of puzzle pieces lying hither and yon begging to be
slipped into dovetailed neatness. A sense of profound relief. If
Max had to be undercover, she had hoped it would be in one
piece.

But he was taking no chances. Even when they arrived at the Circle Ritz, Max remained wedded to her floor boards.

She was instructed to take Louie and her tote bag in; he would
follow when safe.

The dead man was behind them and probably being unloaded
at the medical examiner's facility. This exaggerated care seemed
out of place, but Max was King of the Forest when it came to
subterfuge.

He slithered over her balcony half an hour later and adjourned
to the shower.

Louie had felt the same need of a thorough cleansing, and he
lay on the loveseat licking his sleek black coat sleeker.

For Louie, she opened a tin of sardines to garnish his Free-to-
Be-Feline. For Max, she uncorked a rather nice Beaujolais and
slipped into something comfortable from her bedroom closet while
he was steaming up her bathroom.

Max missed no nuance when he came out wearing a bath towel

for a loin cloth and drying his hair on a hand towel. "You were worried."

"Weren't you worried about me?"

"Not particularly."

"You should have been. First poor Sheila—you don't know her, she's a ConTact buddy of Matt's—was run into the moving sidewalk. Then Mariah had to chase a loose cat into the martial arts ring, and I had to try to stop her, which got us going a round with Hercules and Xena in full battle cry until Matt leaped in where angels fear to tread and tipped a table into a shelter for us."

"Dare I ask what else happened?"

"We ended the day going back into the ballroom where we'd seen a big media presentation on the forthcoming Khatlord movie, figuring it would be deserted and give us a chance to catch our breaths . . . and there was the King Khatlord himself tangled in the neon billboard. That's when I realized he was wearing the duplicate of the dagger that killed Jeff, and then it suddenly occurred to me that a lot of people wore Khatlord gear, and that the dead man could be you! And then I found Midnight Louie locked in a velvet-covered cage on the floor. How did you end up in Khatlord guise, anyway?"

"Talk about a movie-poster day: Murder weapon found on a dead interstellar dignitary, Khatlord found apparently electrocuted, a housecat found caged nearby. . . ." Max sat on the sofa beside the laving Louie and continued to towel dry his equally dark and lustrous hair. "No, I'm not dead. Getting the outfit merely meant appropriating the appropriate costume from the security-guard changing area. I noticed the popularity of the Khatlord costume and chose the same outfit to blend in better. No, I did not see our target. By the time I got oriented to the layout, Dorothy, the Good Witch Glinda, the Strawman, and the Tin Woodsman, not to mention the Cowardly Lion"—here Max glowered at his sofa partner—"were off to see the Wicked Warlock of the East skewered on a billboard for the Emerald City. I only had time to head off the Wicked Witch of the West, who was etching 'Surrender Dorothy' onto the parking lot asphalt."

"So. Mariah is Dorothy, I'm Glinda, Sheila is the Strawman?

Matt the Tin Woodsman? Louie the Cowardly Lion? What does that make you? Toto?"

"The Wizard, naturally," Max said, grinning. "Pay no attention to the man behind the Martha Stewart towels."

She shook her head and poured them two incorrectly brimming glasses of wine. "I thought cats didn't like water, but you and Louie are wet enough for a litter."

Max sipped, then leaned back. "I'm sorry, Temple. This was my little crusade, and now everybody's dragged into it."

"This guy I have the sketch of, you mean?"

He nodded.

"You think he's—"

"I think he's the one who killed Cher, the poor little stripper girl I ran into while looking for something else. I shouldn't have asked you to try to track him, but you were on the spot, and I had information that he was working security for this charade."

"He really has nothing to do with anything, then. He's just a man who likes to kill women?"

"I don't know what he is, except dangerous. I got between him and his imagined territory. I can't let him go. Not until I know if I'm right. I'd rather be wrong."

"So your reason for being there is totally unrelated?"

"Unrelated to what?"

"To the Synth. To Jeff Mangel's murder."

"Are you saying that both of those are related to TitaniCon?"

"I'm saying that the Khatlord's death certainly is. Where's your costume?"

"In pieces on your bathroom floor."

Temple got up and trudged into her bedroom.

Her bare feet enjoyed hitting cool tile, but steam still filled the small bathroom. The coarse black mane hung from a hook, along with an interesting spandex headpiece/mask. The boots slumped against the white tile walls, large enough for a giant.

The tights and padded jacket hung from towel racks, and the ersatz armory lay in a thorny pile on the floor.

Temple lifted the massive belt with its dangling implements as

Max followed her in from the living room. "You ever check out your gun belt, Marshal Dillon?"

"It's all just plastique and metallic tape."

Temple unholstered one item. A knife whose blade and hilt were molded silver rubber.

The design angles, however, were sharp as steel.

Max's face registered shock and dismay. "I never paid attention to the cheesy props."

"The actual Khatlord had less cheesy props. I saw the dagger hilt the minute we saw him dead. It was really metal and was the same design as the knife that killed the professor, and as that creepy knifemaker made for person or persons unknown."

"Mangel was killed by a TV weapon? What would an obscure professor interested in magic and the mantic arts, and maybe a little ESP, have to do with the Khatlord Kompendium?"

"Don't know." Temple picked her way over the litter of the Khatlord's costume. "I'm going to microwave some dinner."

"Uh, do I have any clothes here still?"

"Check it out. My closets are an open book."

"Right. *War and Peace*," he called after her.

He came into the kitchen soon after, wearing black slacks and a blue, lightweight wool sweater.

"Delighted to find some shreds of myself still in your closet, along with an old poster," Max said.

Temple smiled over her shoulder as she did what she did best in a kitchen: bustled. "Don't sound so smug. That poster may be the last of its kind, and this sweater was what tipped Molina off to the fact that your natural eye color was blue, not green."

"What was Molina doing in our—your—closet?"

"She was all over me about you, especially right after you vanished. She's been all over me ever since. And they call criminals 'hard cases.' They should look at the law enforcement types."

Max picked a slightly bruised apple from a countertop basket. "She's had to be that way. To get where she is in a macho field like law enforcement she'd have to be three times better than the male contenders around her."

"Better means meaner?"

"Tougher."

"I guess I've worked in mostly female-type fields. Besides, I wouldn't make a convincing hardnose."

"You're resilient," Max consoled her, biting into the apple.

"Speaking of mysteries, what was Matt doing taking Mariah to TitaniCon?"

"What did he say about being there?"

"That Molina had promised to take the kid but was swamped with work this weekend."

"Sounds reasonable to me."

"Well, yeah, but why ask Matt to baby-sit?"

"Match made in heaven?"

"You've got to be kidding!"

He shrugged. "Catholic backgrounds. She's probably a few years older, but nobody's counting much nowadays."

Temple shook her head. "That'd be the day."

"You did mention he was there with a friend named Sheila."

"Former coworker. And I got the impression they'd run into each other there." Temple paused in midbustle, rustling up a salad at the moment. "You know, Mariah is the one who twigged it. All of us had mishaps at the con. Sheila turned her ankle on the moving sidewalk; said someone bumped into her. And Mariah and I were almost pounded into next year's vintage by barbarian boots."

"How was Devine injured?"

"Well, he wasn't. But he was certainly in danger of it during his race to our rescue."

"Interesting," Max conceded, checking the under-the-sink cabinet for the wastebasket—it was there as always—and tossing the apple core inside.

"What about the bouncer whose picture I carried close to my heart all through the con? Well, it was actually in my tote bag, but I always carry that on my left shoulder and clutch it to my chest."

"What about him?"

"Could he be harassing us? Or one of us?"

"Why?"

" 'Cuz he's a mean dude?"

Max looked sober as he considered the idea. "Hard to believe. I'm the only one he'd have reason to recognize, and I was in more thorough disguise than usual."

"I know." Temple stopped tearing Romaine long enough to shiver. "After seeing that poor man dead on that neon billboard and realizing you might have adopted his costume . . . I really, really wondered at first. . . ."

He wrapped his arms around her from behind so tightly she couldn't shred a fingernail. "No one knew I was there."

"But there's something about Mariah. Why did you have me disguise her?"

Max's sigh reverberated through her rib cage. He kept her in close custody. She felt cozy and safe in his sweater-clad arms but didn't think it was an accident that she was unable to see his face.

"You know what kind of lethal loyalty system I ran afoul of in Ireland," he said.

"That was long ago and in a galaxy far away."

"Time and distance don't matter. Loyalty is the virtue—or weakness—you live or die by in my line of work. I need to keep my borders very strict. Protect my sources. An ex-journalist should understand that."

"So there's more going on here than your tracking down a man you suspect killed Cher?"

"There's always more going on everywhere. But in this case, it's nothing that should affect you and yours. I suspect Molina will keep *kinder* to home from now on."

"You haven't met *kinder*. That kid wants to be at TitaniCon. And Mother promised."

"That's another thing her line of work, and mine, have in common. Sometimes promises have to be postponed."

Temple kept very still. He wasn't just explaining the parent-child dynamic, he was referring to their own situation. What promises postponed, though? Living together? They hadn't shared quarters since he'd vanished more than a year earlier. The tacit notion of his getting out of undercover work, of being safe enough to marry someday?

"It's dangerous not to know things," she said finally.

"And sometimes, paradoxically, safer." She felt his lips brush her hair before he released her and produced a plump red tomato from the basket. He moved it from the palm of his hand to hers. When she started to pick it up to slice it for the salad, it fell into perfect sections, like an instantly opening rosette.

She couldn't help laughing, her worries receding in the face of wonder. "That's what I've always needed. Kitchen magic. Practical magic."

Chapter 43

Grounded

The beefy veteran officer who escorted Matt and Mariah to their car took one look at the silver Volkswagen shining like a giant mercury gumdrop in the high-intensity, parking-lot lamplight and shook his head.

"This car at night, avoiding a tail? It's as bad as driving a zit any time, but at night—jeez." A rib-rattling sigh underlined his disapproving head shakes.

Matt was ready to cop out. *It's not mine,* he wanted to say. *It belongs to Elvis.* Except that sounding crazy would be worse than driving a high-profile car, he guessed.

"Just drive her home, same route you'd always use. We'll handle our tail."

Matt wanted to point out that he didn't go to and from Molina's house often enough to have a "same route," but he doubted the cop cared about the fine points.

"I don't get it," Mariah said once they were weaving their way through the rows of parked cars to the exit. "What's the big deal about you taking me home? I thought my mom would be here."

"That's just it. She probably *was* here." He leaned forward to inspect Mariah's face as they passed under a street light. "I thought you were going to wash off the outer-space tattoos before you went home."

"Gosh!" Mariah's palms slapped to her face. "I forgot. Mom will kill me."

He grew even glummer. Not only was the trusted kid-sitter returning a child who was an accessory to finding a dead man, but she had been accessorized like a sideshow performer. "Where's your headdress?"

"In my fanny pack. It's collapsible."

At least something about this outing was discreet.

He tried to settle himself in the still-stiff-feeling seat. Driving the beetle felt like sitting under a mushroom, cozy but confining. He lowered his head to peer through the rearview mirror. All that he could see behind him in the dark were pairs of headlights like animal eyes. Why the precautions? Being the first to see the body shouldn't require this rigamarole, even if a homicide lieutenant's daughter was involved.

Matt fidgeted in the seat again, uneasy, boxed in. Could he be missing the Hesketh Vampire? At least on a motorcycle you never felt trapped in steel and traffic.

Mariah was leaning forward in her seat to fiddle with the radio dial. Bursts of music and talk flared and faded, doing nothing for his nerves. "What are you looking for?"

"A cool station."

"It's not far," Matt suggested, "and I'm not familiar with the way in the dark. Maybe some peace and quiet would be nice."

She sighed as pointedly as the policeman had and threw herself back in the passenger seat.

Matt decided nobody was going to be happy with him this evening, including himself, so he better give himself a break and forget about worrying.

But he wasn't sure, when he finally pulled into Molina's driveway, whether he was happy the unhappy ride home was over, or worried that the confrontation with the parental unit came next.

"Boy, will mom be jealous that I found a body," Mariah said before unlocking her door and jumping out.

Matt doubted that. Her schoolmates would be jealous, but her mother would be something else.

He followed her around the attached garage to the front door, glancing over his shoulder at the street, which remained deserted.

Mariah twisted the doorknob impatiently. A moment later the deadbolt snapped off and the door opened.

"Hi, Mom! It was terrific." Mariah charged in like a talking machine. "There were all the *Star Trek* and *Star Wars* and *Babylon Five* types walking around, and Hercules and Xena, and some really cool *X-Files* stuff you could buy, and even cats. One wore a harness like a dog and is in the new Khatlord movie, which maybe will be in trouble since the Khatlord's dead, although anybody could be the Khatlord, since he wears a mask on his face."

Mariah was all the way to the dining room, still talking, before Molina could lock the door behind her, nod at Matt, and catch up.

But catch up she did, pretty darn fast. "What's this on your face?" She tilted Mariah's profile toward the overhead lighting fixture. The tattoos looked like bruises in the softer lighting.

"Don't freak, Mom! It's just temporary. The red-headed lady got them for me."

While Molina was staring speechlessly at her daughter's celestially decorated cheeks, Matt gave her a quick inspection. She wore her usual dark-colored, tailored pantsuit, that matched her straight bobbed haircut, but her face was twisted tighter than barbed wire: taut-set jaw, fine lines narrowing her eyes.

Suddenly the facial tension relaxed. "Cool, huh?"

Encouraged, Mariah unzipped her fanny pack and flourished the beaded headdress. "And she got me this really radical thingie for my head." She plopped it on, askew.

Matt braced for maternal disapproval. Molina's wholesome preteen daughter looked like Little Egypt.

Molina's laughter was genuinely delighted. She glanced at Matt. "I take it the 'red-headed lady' was Our Miss Barr?"

He nodded. "You're not. . . . mad?"

The lines around her morning-glory-blue eyes crinkled again, this time with amusement. "Not mad, glad!" Her expression softened in a way he'd never seen before as she smiled down at Mariah and smoothed her dark hair behind one ear, revealing . . .

"What's this?" she asked.

Mariah was ready for her. "It's not really an earring, Mom. It's Bajoran. Like they wear on their ears on *Deep Space Nine*. It's not permanently attached, see? I can take it off. Matt said I could have it."

"Oh, he did?" The laser eyes zapped his again, this time their expression hard to read. "Well, you better take your treasures to your room. And you could think about washing your face before bed."

Mariah scampered off, reminding Matt just how young she was.

She paused in the hallway, uncertain for a moment. "Aren't you working late tonight?"

"I am, but not at work."

Mariah didn't get it, instead resuming her race to the bedroom. The soft patter of feline feet darted from somewhere in the kitchen and pursued her down the hardwood-floored hall.

Molina turned to Matt, the aftermath of tension around her eyes still marked. Before she could say anything to him, or he to her, the phone rang.

Molina was at the kitchen phone before Matt could blink.

"Yes? Nothing. You're sure. Circle the area for the next half hour, just to be safe. Any positive ID on the body? I want the ME to treat it like a celebrity death. Full and visible security. Don't want these scummy tabloid photo freaks getting a morgue shot, like they always try. Use the secured autopsy room. And let me know anything new, any time."

She hung up, turned to Matt again, lifted her eyebrows quizzically, smiled. "Well. What have you got to say for yourself?"

"Obviously, I'm sorry. There was no way we, I, could have known there was a corpse in that empty ballroom until we all had come too close to avoid seeing it. She handled it well, for a child her age. . . ."

"I'm not worried about the damn corpse!" Molina interrupted. At the stunned expression on Matt's face she calmed down as abruptly. "Mariah knows what I do for a living. She can even tell when I've witnessed an autopsy. I've never tried to disguise any realities of that sort."

She leaned against the snack counter, bracing an elbow on her other hand and beating a fist softly against her chin. "No, the body is the least of my problems." She frowned and regarded him again. "So. You took Our Miss Barr to the convention."

"No. We ran into each other there. Temple was checking out the simulated-motion ride on behalf of the Crystal Phoenix," Matt said in answer to another upraised eyebrow. "In fact," he added, "it was Temple who took Mariah on the shopping expedition in the dealers' room—it's a kind of bazaar. I okayed the ear thing earlier, but Temple was in charge of . . . the rest."

"And when was this?"

"You mean, what time?" What could it matter?

"Humor me."

"I don't know. Late afternoon, I suppose. Am I being interrogated on a baby-sitting job or a murder?"

Molina shook her head, more at herself than him and went to sit on the well-used sofa in the main room. "Sorry. It's been a long week."

"If you're upset with Temple for buying Mariah junk—"

"Upset? It's the first useful thing that woman has done as long as I've known her."

"I don't get it."

"You won't either, because it's nothing I can tell you about."

Mariah came pounding down the hall. "Face washed, but I'm gonna wear my Bajoran earring to bed, 'cuz you sure won't let me wear it out of the house."

"Maybe on Halloween," Molina said. "You get any dinner?"

"Oh, yeah, they had this con suite, and it was full of food. Really good stuff. I don't need to eat until Monday. I'm gonna go back and call Yolie, okay?" Mariah had almost vanished before anything human could have responded.

"She has her own phone line," Molina explained. "I can't afford to have teenage talking rituals tying up mine."

Matt came and stood over her. "Whatever's going on, you look exhausted. Have *you* had any dinner?"

She closed her eyes. "Nope."

"Lunch?"

"Nope."

"Have you got anything ready to eat here?"

"Nope."

"Why don't I call out for something before I go?"

By then he was heading to the phone. Molina raised a limp hand. "Takeout menus posted on the cupboard door above the phone. Chinese, Mexican, or Italian."

"What do you want?" Matt perused the rows of small bold print accented with discreet grease spots.

"Surprise me."

He dialed the pizza place and ordered a large special. Mariah could breakfast on any leftovers for days. Then he went through the cupboards until he found two bottles of wine. Grocery-store screwtop, closed.

He opened a white zinfandel but couldn't find any footed glasses, so he poured some into a juice glass, hesitated, and poured a juice glass for himself.

When he presented the glass to Molina back at the sofa, the eyebrows lifted again. He realized that was about all she had the energy to move at the moment.

"I don't think I dare," she said, wistfully studying the light shining through the pale-rose liquid.

"I don't think you do not dare."

She took the glass he extended, sipped, and made a slight face. Matt sat down beside her.

"So," he said. "You're not mad at me? Or Temple? Or Mariah?"

She shook her head.

"Then what's the trouble?"

"First of all, I'm going to have to tell Mariah she's not going back to that damn TitaniCon. She will not be a happy Bajoran, or whatever."

"But if none of us did anything wrong—"

"Something went very wrong there. Nobody's fault, but I can't have Mariah exposed to . . . to those kind of problems and still keep my mind on my job. All right?"

"You said it had been rough lately."

"Gang shootings, animal killings by a self-described Den of Doom at a high school—and you know what gets killed next after animals—two of those 'she left' murders unsolved, if they were in the same cycle. . . ." Molina shook her head. "And . . . I was worried about Mariah."

"She'll be heartbroken if she can't go back to the con. The big Masquerade is tomorrow night."

"I know. She'll think I've grounded her for no reason, or worse, for something she did. And she didn't do a darn thing wrong."

Matt could have sworn he heard Molina's voice almost break, but she sipped the wine before he could be sure.

He put his own glass down atop a *National Geographic* magazine on the battered coffee table. "Listen."

She shifted her head and eyes away like a headstrong horse.

"Carmen."

Face still averted, her eyes narrowed as if she were taking aim at something. Maybe soon it would be him. He sensed frustration, fury, fear.

"Carmen," he repeated firmly.

He wasn't just invoking the name she sang under, one of the few expressions of personality she allowed in her life. He was recalling a long ago conversation, in which he had slipped into his role of counselor without either of them knowing it, into his old role of priest.

Invoking the name she was almost never called by meant he

wasn't going to accept the barriers she used in everyday life. He wasn't going to accept her as authority figure, or policewoman, or consummate professional.

"I respect that you can't tell me everything that would explain yourself to me," he said. "But if you're going to handle whatever this is alone, you have to recognize the cost. Give yourself a break. Or you'll crack."

Her head snapped back to face him, eyes burning. "I have never cracked."

"Doesn't mean it can't happen. You have never had a child in danger."

The fury discharged. "You've never faced losing a child!"

"I've never faced even having one. But I know severe stress when I see it." He smiled gently. "If you don't share it with someone, you'll take it out on everyone."

"So. They'll take it then."

"We don't all work for you, you know."

"Great! I ask you to do me a favor, and now you're turning on me. Okay, fine. Your assignment is over. Good-bye."

He didn't move.

Her arms were crossed over her chest, and her face was a steel trap. There was the smallest hint of a pout at the corners of her tight-lipped mouth.

"Playing the tough professional isn't suitable for all occasions. How long since you've gotten to the Blue Dahlia to sing?"

"What the hell does that have to with anything? I haven't felt like going over there, that's all. And with all these cases, there's no time."

"I suppose the death on site is kind of off-putting."

"Don't be ridiculous! I'm a professional. Do you think that a dead body showing in one place over another is going to put me off my own life?"

"I think if it doesn't, you're in trouble."

She glared at him, her eyes so stunningly blue he was struck speechless. She'd always had the kind of electric blue eyes that often strike people dumb, he was used to that. He wasn't used to the intensified effect of a phenomenon he'd never seen before: the sheen of unshed tears.

They stared at each other, Matt a little shocked by how deep her trouble ran; Carmen appalled by how exposed she had become.

"Mom?"

Mariah stood in the archway to the hall, wearing a Buffy the Vampire Slayer sleep shirt and fuzzy elephant slippers.

"Don't be mad at Matt. I made him buy that ear thing. I told him you wouldn't mind."

"Oh, baby." She held out her arms, and Mariah came over, cautiously. "I wasn't mad at Matt. Or you. I'm just upset because . . . because I was worried about you being where someone was murdered, and because sometimes I have to tell you 'no.' "

Carmen pulled her daughter down beside her on the couch. "Let's see that ear thing; I didn't really get a good look at it. Hey, that's pretty clever, all right. I guess you know how to get around the letter of the law, huh, kid? It's not a pierced earring, I'll give you that."

"You're not going to let me go back, though, are you? Sometimes I get so tired of being safe all the time. I'm the most safest kid at school."

Mariah's face lowered until her curving wings of hair covered the revealed earring and her face. Carmen was silent for a long moment. Matt watched her bite her lip, blink, and then her head jerked up.

"Yes. You *are* going back. With Matt and the red-headed lady and all your new gear on." The look she flashed Matt was electric with challenge.

Carmen sipped her second juice glass of white zinfandel alone.

Mariah, ecstatic, had gone to bed as meekly as the proverbial lamb. Matt, troubled by her sudden decision, had visibly refrained from interfering before he left. She shook her head. Being a counselor sometimes was almost as thankless a job as being a police officer.

She hated to consider what Max Kinsella would think of what she was planning to do. He'd figure she had looned out.

Lieutenant Molina set down the half-full glass, eyes narrowed, picturing all the possibilities. From the moment the costumed man had fallen from the artificial sky, this TitaniCon had reeked of links with past cases and conspiracies within conspiracies. That first death could never be proven as murder, but this second one was a different matter. Very different, according to what Grizzly Bahr had just reported from the morgue.

TitaniCon was the perfect setting for a confusing melange of masks and mixed identities, with reality on an extended vacation. It even sheltered Rafi Nadir, whose presence in Las Vegas was personally threatening to her, and to Mariah. Kinsella suspected him of one of the unsolved murders that plagued her case files. She suspected Kinsella of telling her only what suited him. And why not? That's all she told him. Or anyone. Including the darling Mr. Devine.

But, now, talking with Matt, assessing her vulnerabilities and the risks, Lieutenant Molina had made a daring decision: she would not deny her daughter a harmless pleasure, and at the same time she would play the same "con" game that had been going on to unmask a killer.

For a moment, Carmen resurfaced, on a wave of maternal dread, then subsided. Molina rose to pour the wine down the sink. She had a lot to do.

Chapter 44

Cranky Thanky Call

When the phone rang, Temple got to it first. It was her place now.

"I know who you are, and I know what you did," the female voice said without identifying itself. "And thank you."

Temple thought for a moment before she deciphered Molina's cryptic shorthand. She was glad Max was in the bedroom fiddling with the stereo.

Molina meant Temple's improvised disguise job with Mariah.

"Thank Max," Temple responded promptly.

"I don't think so."

"You're a stubborn woman."

"Thank you."

"Is she okay?"

"Okay. I'm, uh, letting her go back tomorrow."

"You're what . . . ? I admit I don't know what's going on, but—"

"Maybe you could help Matt keep an eye on her, hmm? That's not too hard an assignment, is it? Helping Matt?"

"What do you think?"

"That you're a crazy woman."

"Better crazy than stubborn."

"Time will tell."

"I guess it will."

"So you'll help?"

Temple sighed. "What else are little girls made for?"

"Much more, but it's a start. Thanks."

Molina hung up. She always came and went like that, a force that didn't need to introduce itself or sign off. That's when Temple found herself really envying her for a few seconds. Most of the time, she didn't, and especially now.

Mariah was going back into the eye of the storm, with innocents who knew nothing to defend her. Temple sure hoped the professionals knew what they were doing.

Neither Max nor Molina was confiding in her, but they were both counting on her. It was an impossible position, but she supposed it was a major vote of confidence.

Chapter 45

Lockout

Alone at last!

I cannot say that I am thrilled by the reason for my sudden solitude.

Suffice it to say that I finished bathing in my own good time only to find the master bedroom occupied by another master.

Ah, well. I have learned to be philosophical in my middle years.

This gives me the living room loveseat to myself, on which I can recline and contemplate the day's events. I can contemplate particularly the murder I overheard.

Of course I cannot testify in any court of law, but I know that the hissing sounds that preceded the final executioner's hiss of electricity were the last words both victim and perp said and heard.

If only they had not lisped with secrecy! If only I had not

been trapped within a lavender-velvet-draped cage! I am quite good at reading lips; it comes with the territory. My kind has been reading lips, and profiting therefrom, for thousands of years.

But I was blinded in this instance, so must depend on other factors to solve the crime.

Somehow, I am sure, the Sinister Hyacinth has a role in the unraveling events.

I sense a grander plan behind the immediate crime.

From the bedroom comes the swelling orchestral sounds of Vangelis' *Cosmos*, the theme music from the television documentary helmed by the late Carl Sagan billions and billions of minutes ago. Now there was another dark-favored dude with charisma, although his was in the academic field.

The thought reminds me of my Miss Temple bewailing the recent loss of a professor friend of hers. Who would kill an academic dude? I cannot think of a more harmless sort, unless they are moonlighting as critics. This is the only time these spectacularly wimpy types get lethal. The pen is sneakier than the sword.

It could be the late professor was snuffed for postdoctoral theses offenses, but I do not think so, from what I have overheard.

Somehow the murder in academe is reflected in the murder in multimedia.

What a conundrum! I will have to survive a night's sleep on this lumpy, lonely sofa, and then hie off at the break of dawn to the New Millennium to crack the case.

It is too bad that MY MISS TEMPLE cannot read thoughts, otherwise SHE WOULD KNOW that I am about to sacrifice my safety, sanity, and sacred honor ON HER BEHALF.

But she could not hear a five-ton weight drop over those swelling chords of Vangelis.

The science fiction types celebrated at the TitaniCon would have us believe that We Are Not Alone.

But we are, and I have never been so alone as on this night when I am evicted from my own room by a former tenant.

I suppose, from his point of view, I had evicted him.

Sometimes there is no winning for losing, and Las Vegas is full of moments like that.

Chapter 46

Prisoner of Literature

"I'm a suspect," Hanford Schmidt chortled in the hallway, loud enough to wake the dead.

Unfortunately, no resuscitated Khatlord came striding down the hall.

"I've been told not to leave town." He rubbed his hands together with glee.

"Feel free, anybody with incriminating details, to rat on me to the resident flatfeet. Meanwhile, I demand to be taken into public custody. Bring forth the chains, so I can write. I feel inspired for the first time in years. I will be in the dealers' room, where I will set up a typewriter—get that, Luddites, I will use a retromachine—and I will write the Khatlord tie-in novel to end all tie-in novels, about how a heroic writer wrings literature from the evil empire of one-dimensional characters created by media milquetoast hacks."

Temple and Matt watched him taken away by accommodating dealers, everyone laughing.

Temple had the odd notion that these people lived so deeply in a fictional world that even a real-world murder wouldn't shake their fantasies free.

The morning paper had been quite explicit: Well-known actor Timothy Hathaway, beloved portrayer of the equally beloved and loathed Khatlord, had perished of excessive voltage at the Titani-Con convention now running at the New Millennium Hotel and Casino. A lengthy obituary listed all of Hathaway's acting history and credits, as well as a summary of the Khatlord world and mention of the forthcoming film, which could either massively benefit or massively suffer from its star's extravagant and untimely death by person or persons—or species—unknown.

Given the environment, the actual death didn't seem any more real than a televised one.

Temple shook her head at the departing "suspect."

"I'd better take Mariah to the dealers' room for another redo," she said.

Mariah already had donned her headdress, but the temporary tattoos awaited. She wanted Yoda and Princess Leia today.

"I can't believe my mom let me come," was Mariah's mantra on the way to the wonders of every description that awaited them.

Temple herself was wearing a blond wig she'd picked up at K-Wigs on Charleston earlier that morning. With her too-small, spaghetti-strapped top and pale satin jeans she thought she made a pretty credible Buffy, but Mariah hadn't noticed the resemblance. Temple had brought a pair of nonprescription, tortoiseshell glasses she had salvaged from a community theater production years ago and a beige cardigan sweater of Max's for Matt, and told him he was Giles.

"Giles?" he had asked. "Why would I need props to play somebody normal?"

She had exchanged an exasperated glance with Mariah.

"That's it," Temple told Matt. "That was a very Giles thing to say."

She turned to Mariah. "What do *you* say? Shall we boogie on over to the Bronze?" She was referring to Buffy the Vampire Slayer's fave teen hangout on TV, but the hip reference was lost on this kid.

Mariah curled her upper lip. "What are you talking about?"

"The dealers' room," Temple said more directly. "More fab things to buy, vampires to spike, charge cards to max out."

"Oh, right."

Once there, Temple loaded Mariah up with facial tattoos of all the coolest media characters and even got a likeness of Angel for her own Buffy-bare shoulder.

Mariah stopped to buy a small ceramic candleholder in the shape of Saturn for her mother, something Temple doubted Molina would have much use for, but the thought was sweet. What had Midnight Louie ever bought for her, besides some untimely interference in her lifeline?

"Matt's nice, but he's not very good at taking girls out, is he?" Mariah observed during one of their few quiet moments.

Temple nearly choked on her Nimbus of Narnia, which was hard to do, because it was mostly blue-dyed air, aka cotton candy.

"Why do you say that?"

"Well, he worries about everything."

"He's not used to escorting girls your age, who keep getting into trouble."

"What's trouble?"

Temple remembered Mariah's wink yesterday and realized that she was talking to a homicide lieutenant's daughter. "Walking into a ballroom with a dead man in it. That should be a pretty traumatizing thing."

Mariah shrugged. "It wasn't bloody or anything. Now, if it had been one of my cats—" Mariah swallowed hard at the very idea. "Besides, I loved the Khatlord series, but the guy who played him, well, he was kinda stuck up. He really threw a tantrum yesterday when that other guy pretended to be him. Kinda immature, you know?"

"Actors can be that way. I've known a few. And other actors can be as mature as Methuselah."

"Methuselah? What show is he on?"

"And oldie but goodie called the Old Testament."

"Neat name, but you can't fool me. That's just that churchy stuff."

"You'd be surprised how far out that churchy stuff can be. But, anyway, have you bankrupted your mother yet?"

"Nope. I've got some left. Besides, Matt bought me this earring." Mariah gave it a finger snap so it swung.

"I thought he wasn't good at taking girls out."

"Well, sometimes. Except when he says no."

"That's his job."

"He's a baby-sitter." The tone was sarcastic.

"You're still a baby sometimes," Temple said firmly.

"Am not!"

"Are so!"

"Says who?"

"Says Buffy. All right?"

"You're silly for a grown-up."

"Thank you."

"When are we gonna find the murderer?"

Temple took a deep breath. "I don't think that's our job here."

"What is our job here?"

"Keeping the murderer from finding us."

Matt had hardly had time to don his new Giles guise when he was snagged by a pair of roving detectives.

"We were hoping Miss Barr would be with you," Detective Su told him undiplomatically.

Nothing like being unwanted by the police to give a person low self-esteem. "Anything I can do?" he asked.

"As a matter of fact," Alch, the senior member of the team began, but Su made an impatient gesture. "He might have some insight," Alch persisted.

"We wanted Miss Barr," Su explained, "because of her public relations expertise."

"She certainly has it," Matt agreed.

"Then she'd know about this crowd?" Alch asked, eyeing the passing slipstream of T-shirt-clad attendees liberally blended with assorted aliens and elves.

"Not personally."

Alch's face puckered. "Did you always wear glasses?"

"Uh, no. Not . . . always. What were your questions?"

"Well." Alch scratched his mustache, "We've never interviewed tougher subjects before."

"Tougher?" Matt was surprised. Except for outstandingly temperamental writers like Schmidt, and occasional opinionated outbursts by obsessive enthusiasts, he found this crowd more pacifist than most.

"He means we can't get through to them," Su explained, lifting her exotically shaped eyebrows. "Earth to Pluto problems."

"They won't cooperate?"

Alch was paging through his narrow spiral-bound notebook. "Oh, they seem cooperative enough. There was this fellow in a robe who lingered after the film presentation and saw a Khatlord go into the ballroom. His testimony was, 'Forsooth, and my eyes not deceive me, I saw yon dead man walk to his own demise all unawares. If only I had known to belay him.' When I asked what time he had seen this, he answered that he was not wealthy enough to own a timepiece, but he supposed by the rumbles of his stomach that it was nearing the hour to sup, perhaps five of the clock."

Matt tried not to laugh. "They come here to live in another world, Detective. I suppose they don't know how to leave it when reality intrudes."

Alch, having found a sympathetic ear, flipped some more pages. "So we start looking for people in Khatlord costumes who might have gone in, and we dig up this other guy—"

Detective Su snorted in disgust at the mention.

"—named Tom Snell. He says a Khatlord answers only to the King Khatlord and now that the King is dead, long live the King, and he must wait until a new Khatlord is prided before he can deal with alien investigators."

"He can deal with us downtown," Su said. "A few official interrogations ought to snap these idiots out of la-la land."

"This isn't a limited phenomenon," Matt said. "Have either of you ever been to '*Star Trek: The Experience*' at the Hilton?" His answer was their looks of extreme incredulity. "I was just there with a friend, and when she tried to ask the Ferengi host—you know, the Ferengi; the bald, big-eared creatures from *Star Trek: Deep Space Nine?*"

"I am so sick," Su said, "of hearing the words '*Star Trek*' in italics with colons after them."

"Anyway," Matt went on to the sympathetically nodding Alch, "my companion couldn't get Word One out of him about costume and makeup. She's an artist who's interested in the massive changes in physiognomy these alien-mask makeovers achieve, but he wouldn't even admit that he was in costume, or that everything about him wasn't perfectly normal. So I can see you'd have a hard time breaking through these people's fantasy zone."

"Great!" Su's exasperation was boiling over. "We have to go back downtown and tell the lieutenant that all our witnesses and suspects are reality-challenged. Why bother pursuing the case? Get a change of venue to Mars and let the little green men take care of everything!"

Alch was chuckling.

Su wasn't through. "And that nut who just went off to the dealers' room, tickled pink that he might be a suspect. Harry Schmidt or whoever. These people are too deranged to kill anyone."

"Hanford Schmidt," Matt corrected. "And I hear his writing career has been in a stall. A little notoriety might be up his alley."

"Say," Alch suggested to his partner. "Maybe we should run him in. Help the guy out. He might actually confess. I hear writers like solitary."

"Solitude," Su corrected acidly. "Although *I'll* probably end up in solitary on a homicide charge if we don't make some headway with the mental fender benders around here."

Alch gave Matt a one-finger salute in thanks and farewell as Su stalked off on her chunky heels.

He reminded Matt of a man walking a very ferocious Pekingese. No doubt her intensity and his sagacity made a good detecting combination, when their variant personalities weren't driving each other nuts.

Having nothing better to do, Matt edged into the dealers' room to kill time and mull over the investigation. He didn't envy the detectives trying to tease testimony from people who had come here to forget reality, not witness it.

He idly paged through some large, mounted posters in a bin, trying to figure out what Molina had in mind by returning her daughter to the scene of the crime. Luridly colored images of Flash Gordon and Dale Arden flashed by, along with planetscapes and sinister machines.

The passing of Timothy Hathaway was now fact. The morning TV news shows had all announced the puzzling and sudden death. They hadn't said murder, but the police hadn't said that it wasn't murder.

Still, Matt knew, more than Hathaway's death was going on here. Whatever it was, it had made Molina go icy with fear, then had led her to take a risky gamble. He had watched her decide to throw the dice. Whatever she planned was so out of character that if he saw the full picture, he'd be scared white-knuckled himself.

But he didn't know, though he guessed that he, and Temple, and Mariah were all a part of it.

Should he even be here now? Or should he be with Temple and Mariah, although he'd sensed he wasn't particularly welcome on their shopping expedition? Tonight was the big costume Masquerade. Was that when a murderer would be unmasked? Or would strike again?

"You like that?" a soft voice inquired over his shoulder.

Matt focused on the posters he was flipping past. Long-legged space girls in racy costumes, or mostly absence of same.

"I hadn't noticed," he started to say, realizing how lame that sounded. Any guy who failed to notice these would be blind or gay.

He turned to confront a masked female in a shiny-burgundy spandex bodysuit with holes cut out at the shoulders and sides, the living embodiment of the fantasy forms in the posters.

"Just passing time." His equilibrium switched wildly between fantasy and reality. Hard to believe a real girl could embody the exaggerated form celebrated in the drawings.

Then he realized something even more astounding: He knew her. "Sheila?"

She shrugged, which did a lot for the catsuit. "I don't usually wear this where anyone really knows me. I guess it's not professional."

Now he couldn't ignore it. Her. And he couldn't just whistle, like the guy who was passing behind them was doing at the moment.

"You look . . . marvelous. Gosh, I sound like Billy Crystal. Fantastic, I guess, would say it."

"Thanks." She took a deep breath. Also good for the catsuit. "I'm really nervous doing this. Maybe you can understand—"

"I get it. I truly do. We were given unwanted gifts, right?"

She nodded, relieved. "I feel so split. Ever since I passed puberty. God is cruel sometimes. Great body; lousy face. Sometimes, I just feel I've got to show it off. And here, I can wear a mask."

"We can wear masks anywhere. So, what happens at these things when you—?"

"Oh, the guys drool. Guys who'd never look twice at the woman behind the mask lust after me like they've got no chance. Maybe it's revenge. I don't know. I always feel like a fraud, no matter what I do. I have some fun here, though. I'm like a minicelebrity. You watch."

"I can believe it. You give Seven of Nine a run for her silicone."

"Mine's all natural," Sheila sniffed. "Will your friends be ashamed of me like this? I can change."

"Let's see."

"It's funny. You hate your looks, and I hate my body."

"I'm getting over that looks thing. It's how we use our gifts, not what they are."

"Then I shouldn't be playing this game."

"Maybe you can remind people that their fantasies aren't totally unrealistic."

"I feel so shallow for enjoying my little game."

"I don't know, Sheila. As long as it doesn't hurt anyone. Does it?"

She shrugged again, and three guys behind her ran into each other.

Matt let the racy posters flip back against the vintage movie stills. He didn't know where to look, of course, but was that his problem, or Sheila's?

He wondered what Temple would make of this.

Max stood in the wings of the New Millennium's massive theater, feeling more nostalgic than he could afford to.

The petaled ranks of empty crimson-velvet seats made the immense house into one full-blown rose of a space, ripe for filling. The black, wooden stage floor tempted his feet and legs with its unique spring, a surface made for leaping, bounding, disappearing on.

At the proscenium arch's sides, the curtains fell from somewhere high, beyond seeing. Their heavy, textured folds bunched, like a forest of giant sequoias with velvet trunks.

The backstage was as deserted as the auditorium, but Max had hopes his asked-for audience would take place anyway.

Echoes of a single set of footsteps came from the opposite wing area. A tall man wearing magician's black emerged from the backstage darkness, pausing just as he became visible to Max. Had an audience filled the empty seats, not even someone seated on the front row's most extreme edge would have been able to spot the man, he was that careful.

Max moved toward him, crossing the empty stage, exposed to the empty house. His own measured footsteps echoed like a Spanish dancer's played at thirty-three-and-a-third speed.

The man nodded. Or, rather, his mask did. Like a ninja mask, it covered his head and neck, fashioned of flashy spandex fabric that mimicked a leopard's spots. From a distance, it resembled an all-over tribal tattoo.

"My bodyguards are twenty feet away," he told Max, speaking through the same hidden device he wore in performance, a tiny lavalier microphone attached to a voice-altering unit, also tiny. The eerie "protected witness" effect only enhanced his performances. Max doubted it would do much for his social life, though.

Not that the man had any social life, any more than Max did.

"Would I really know you?" was Max's first question, asked with a smile that admitted he already knew he wouldn't get a straight answer.

"You might. I know you. You've done your own disappearing act. Professionally as well as personally."

"For my own reasons. This"—he nodded at the man's bizarre mask and mike setup—"is more than an act, isn't it?"

"Oh, yeah. The death threats haven't stopped since I began turning the magician's bags of tricks inside out five years ago. But those TV specials got me this star gig."

"Is it worth it?"

"How much is several million a year worth? It can buy me wall-to-wall protection."

"There are always chinks."

"There are chinks crossing the Strip."

Max had to listen hard to decipher the harmonic double-talk that came from the masked face's high-tech vocal scrambler. He was reminded of Darth Vader. No wonder this guy was cleaning up. He was tapping into moviedom's mythic unconsciousness just by trying to stay alive.

Max also felt he was looking into a distorted mirror. They were both magicians. They were both something more and paying for it with threats to their lives. Max was an avocational antiterrorist, or had been. The man opposite him had become a professional debunker, perhaps after his own magic career had piddled out. Now he was an entertainment phenomenon, revealing secrets to decades-old magic tricks. He wisely avoided spilling the beans on current magicians' illusions—they were his neighbors down the Strip, after all—but a lot of second-rate magicians out there still worked the old chestnuts, and they didn't like his act one bit.

"You ever hear from the Synth?" Max asked.

"The Synth, the Brotherhood of Prestidigitators, the kids with magic kits. They all hate me."

"You fear any of them more than the other?"

"Nope. Anybody could be nuts enough to make good on a threat. Look at kids nowadays. Look at Columbine."

"And the Synth?"

"Sounds phony. Sounds pretentious. But what do I know?"

"Ever hear of a Shangri-la?"

"Magician? Female?"

Max nodded. Twice.

"No. I don't really pay attention to what the legitimate charlatans do, you know? Sorry, didn't mean to get personal."

"I don't let things get personal with me. That man who fell from the TitaniCon catwalk early this week. He was working for you, wasn't he?"

The antimagician started, jerked like a puppet on a string. "What makes you think that?"

"The paper described him as being dressed as a Khatlord, but he was wearing one of your masks, wasn't he? There isn't much difference between your leopardlike mask and a Khatlord's. Especially in the dark. On a catwalk."

"Son of a bitch!" The voice garbler made it sound like Donald Duck was swearing, not a very Disney thing to do. "You're saying Barry didn't just fall?" he garbled on. "He was pushed?"

"Or was killed and then pushed. What was he doing way up there?"

The Cloaked Conjuror began pacing, careful to walk north and south instead of east and west, careful not to put himself in view of anyone who might be lurking in the supposedly empty auditorium.

Max moved into the wings's shadow, too. He'd proved his good intentions by exposing himself; now he didn't have to. Especially now that he knew for sure that the first man had been murdered.

326 • Carole Nelson Douglas

"Damn," the eerie voice said. "You put your finger on it. My mask is their mask. I've been using this for five years. The Khatlord empire is just three years old. They ripped off my persona."

"So sue them."

"You know it's easy to sue, but hard to win."

"So you were planning to upstage the King Khatlord's guest appearance at TitaniCon?"

The Cloaked Conjuror stopped moving. "How did you know?"

"I'm a showman, too. What was it going to be? An unannounced appearance from on high by the Cloaked Conjuror in the middle of the King Khatlord's signing session? Maybe with a big cat conjured out of nowhere at the same time? A leopard? That would point up the too-close resemblance in the masks as well as get you and your million-dollar show lots of ink. Except now the head Khatlord is dead, too. So what does that make the motive for your man's death?"

"Hey. I didn't have anything against Hathaway. All's unfair in love and multimedia franchises, but the actor who played the King Khatlord was just a tool. It's the so-called writer-producer who ripped off my face, so to speak, and he isn't even at TitaniCon. Those guys always hide behind accountants and avoid the line of fire."

"Apparently a lot of underpaid authors are about as happy with those guys as you are."

"See. People like that would be much more likely to resort to murder. I mean, I get paid a Khatlord's ransom, and you just said they get cheated with peanuts."

"True. But I don't think your man died because of the Khatlord stunt."

"Then what for?"

"I think he was mistaken for you."

The man's masked jaw dropped, accentuating the feline muzzle that covered his nose. Even his bizarre voice was stilled. "I've got bodyguards," he said finally.

"So did JFK, MLK, and Princess Di."

One of the magician's gloved hands balled into a fist and slammed into the opposite, leather-clad palm. The sound was as sharp as a whip cracking on the empty stage.

Max regretted a lot of things, but right then he wouldn't have traded his relative freedom for the cage the Cloaked Conjuror now saw assembling around him, as if he were a big cat at the center of an illusion.

Max was still a one-man band, relying on himself to save himself. He was still the master of his fate. The Cloaked Conjuror wasn't, and he was just beginning to see how little choice he had.

Max, though, was just beginning to see how hard it might be to nail whoever had killed the Khatlord. And the leopard-masked magician's apprentice.

Chapter 47

Disorder in the Court

Temple took one look at who—what—Matt was standing with in the hall, and knew that the discreet teenage cleavage of her Buffy the Vampire Slayer outfit was totally outclassed.

Unfortunately, she had stopped dead to survey the competition, so Mariah had time to sum up the scene with preteen prescience.

"Wow. Look at the babe with Matt! Where'd she come from? And him in his Giles getup. I wanta look like that when I grow up."

"No, you don't," Temple said, although she couldn't think of any logical reason why not at the moment. *These so-called cons,* she thought glumly, *allowed far too many fantasies out of the closet.*

Of course all the males passing within two feet of Matt and friend were doing the modern equivalent of a goose-step parade: jerking their heads to attention so fast their necks threatened to leave their shoulders. Was this the epitome of the outer-space New Millennium female?

Temple mused that one of the biggest filmmakers today, George

Lucas, made movies where the women were feisty at first, but were progressively transformed into revealing-outfit-wearing pawns of the dominant male society. In the Steven Spielberg-directed first Indiana Jones film, the Tibetan-tavern spitfire becomes an irritating, backless-dress-wearing tag-along coveted by the villain, and spunky Princess Leia ends up wearing a chain-mail bikini for Jabba the Hut in the second *Star Wars* movie. Sure, a director might be influenced by twenties and thirties film adventure serials, but he didn't have to put modern women back in those unthrillingly sexist days of yesteryear. Under the mysticism or the adventure, they were just New Age-brand male chauvinists profiting from pandering to macho wish fulfillment. When Spielberg produced angst-ridden films on the global female condition, she would respect him. And, to hear the talk around TitaniCon, Lucas was waxing ever richer off the labor of progressively more underpaid writing talent.

Having mentally cleared the decks, Temple approached Matt and Megafemale.

She was usurped by a six-feet-seven dude wearing a Hawaiian shirt that outgarished even one of their landlady Electra Lark's muumuus. He sported an undernourished goatee and grease-slicked curly hair, and his round, amiable face was drawn with anxiety.

He didn't even notice Seven of Sexty.

"Somebody told me you're somebody," he burst out when he was within hailing distance of Matt.

Temple joined the group in the nick of time. "Of course he's somebody. Who are you?"

"Gary Fischer. I'm TitaniCon cochair for the fan events. Now that the King Khatlord is dead, we're short a celebrity judge for the Masquerade." He turned to Matt again. "Could, uh, whoever you are, fill in?"

" 'Whoever he is?' Where have you been?" Temple was waxing redhead-indignant, even though she was a temporary blond. "This is Mr. Midnight, star of radio, national talk show, and the chicken-slash-pea dinner speech circuit. This man knows Elvis."

"Ah, that's nice."

"And . . ."—Temple was not slow to discern when she was in the wrong arena—"the eminent Hanford Schmidt."

"Oh, terrific." Gary Fischer rolled relieved eyes at Matt. "Great that you know him. That helps with Hanford, but not always. Hanford's on the judging panel. He's agreed to stay on so long as we move his typewriter and his chains to the judges' table tonight. You two should hit it off like gangbusters."

So far, Temple thought, *Matt has not met Hanford, but "gang-busters" could well describe a meeting of the twain.*

"Temple could judge," Matt started to say, hoping to pass the buck.

But Gary had by now noticed the spandex female and was lost to intelligent discourse in this solar system.

"Hi," he said.

She turned her masked face aside.

He fell apart, sparing Matt a glance. "Seven of Nine. I mean, seven o'clock tonight. Main ballroom. Be there." Matt was history. "So. What planet did you come from?"

"Uranus," she articulated with the overprecision of Marilyn Monroe in a movie she had never wanted to make.

Gary Fischer moved on to the next TitaniCon emergency, a bedazzled if confused young man.

"I don't believe we've met," Temple told Seven of o'clock.

"Yes, we have." Seven lifted a spandex-swathed gam that needed no endless leg lifts on a gym floor for toning. The lumpy profile of an Ace bandage shone through.

"Omigosh, Sheila?"

"That's me. Omigosh Sheila. The Wonder from Down Under."

Mariah let her mouth drop and remain in the "duh" position. "Gosh. Can I look like you someday?"

"Not without genetic alteration," Temple advised her. "Sheila. You . . . look really buff."

How nonplussing to find the plain Jane you had spent the last twenty-four hours pitying metamorphosed into the con siren, Temple thought.

Matt, bless him, checked his watch. "Seven o'clock tonight.

You may have to fill in for me if Ambrosia can't extend her hour into mine. I'd better call the radio station right now. Is the main ballroom the one where we—?"

Temple nodded, while Sheila allowed a fan to guide her to a potted plant for a photograph.

Mariah jerked Temple's satin pants leg, her notion of being discreet. "What happened to Sheila?" she asked.

Temple shrugged.

"She is so wicked cool."

"Wicked?"

"It's what all the senior high girls say. My mom is so dull. What's the matter with her? Even you look more interesting since you came here."

Temple narrowed her eyes at that 'even.' "Your mom's a working woman. Sheila isn't working here."

"But everything my mom wears is navy or black or something. She doesn't own anything I'd want to dress up in."

Temple guessed that Mariah knew nothing of blues singer Carmen's vintage velvet wardrobe. But even the midnight-dark thirties gowns were too subtle to impress a Millennium chick.

"Your mom has to work for a living in a man's world." Temple found herself an unlikely apologist for Lieutenant C. R. Molina. "Her position has a certain authority and dignity. She doesn't need to doll herself up like a sex symbol to get cheap male attention."

"Oh. But can't she be a little bit cool?"

"It's cool to be serious. It's cool to be real. Me and Sheila, we have a theatrical side, but it isn't real life, and it isn't going to save the world."

"But it's fun!"

"Yes, it's fun. But you've got to watch fun. Fun can fool you."

Mariah shrugged. She would have another decade to figure out "fun" and "serious" and "unfair."

Matt returned, glum, to announce that his producer was delighted to fill in for him while he was on his celebrity judge gig. In fact, she'd announce his whereabouts on the air.

Sheila returned from her moment in the flash cube. "That guy said that Hanford Schmidt is conducting a murder investigation in the dealers' room, from his typing chair, like Nero Wolfe. Want to go see?"

"Yes." What would this nervy blowhard come up with next? She nudged Matt. "Besides, you should meet your fellow judge."

"I don't need to meet any of them. I know nothing about a Masquerade or what goes on at one. I'll just agree with everybody else, and that'll end it. But if I have to stay for the Masquerade, which starts at seven and must run to all hours, how am I going to take Mariah home?"

"I'll take care of it," Temple said. The public relations professional leaped into every breech.

Of course she didn't relish broaching Mama Bear when she brought Baby Bear home. Perhaps she would call first to let Mama Bear know that Goldilocks was coming.

Odd, Matt hadn't commented at all on her Buffy outfit and babe-blond hair. Maybe he was finally losing interest, as she had so devoutly hoped. So . . . drat!

So they migrated to the dealers' room to congregate around the raised dais on which King Schmidt the First, the One and the Only, held forth.

Temple darted into a harem-girl skirt concession. There, concealed among the sheer silk draperies, she pulled her trusty cell phone from the pink canvas backpack with the picture of Lucille Ball that she had taken instead of her trusty tote bag in a bow to Buffy's teen persona.

She was surprised to find the phone answered after the first ring.

If she had been calling Max, she would have thought he was on the move. But Molina was putting in all her time downtown these days, which was why Mariah was here unshepherded, except by unrelated amateurs.

"Yes?" Molina barked gruffly enough to indeed be Mama Bear.

Temple filled her in on the evening's coming turn of events.

"Isn't this Masquerade a costume contest?" Molina asked.

"So I hear, but otherworldly."

"And Matt will be a judge? I wish them luck. But don't bother to take Mariah home. Keep her there."

"It could go very late. I've heard midnight."

"She's always begging to stay up late. Humor her."

"But only I will be able to keep an eye on her while Matt's doing his judging gig—"

"Always the eager amateur operative. You think you're so smart. Act like it. I don't want Mariah coming home unless Devine's in the party, no matter how late. Got it?"

"Yes, but—"

The phone was dead, but before it had given up the ghost, Temple had heard a strange, high yip in the background.

Perhaps a police dog was on the case. Some case. Whatever, it kept Molina at the office this late on a Saturday, and kept Temple in the role of baby-sitter.

Guiltily, she ducked out from under the silken rainbow of fabrics and looked for Mariah. There. With Matt and Seven of Double-D Cups, or whatever *nom* Sheila was masquerading under.

Sheila had attracted her own crowd, a sort of wart on the general wen of fen clustered around Schmidt and an ancient manual typewriter he was banging away on like a two-year-old pianist.

He had donned a pair of unfashionably oversized tortoiseshell-framed glasses, from which the gray-brown hair around his ears stuck up like shafts of hay.

Schmidt cultivated an air of uncool, halfway between seedy professor and gone-to-seed nerd. Driving it all was his own angry ego.

"All right!" He banged an empty long-neck beer bottle on the shaky typing table that upheld the black metal Royal typewriter. "Quiet in the court."

The long-neck banged again, even though alcoholic beverages were forbidden in the dealers' room. Of course, Schmidt's was empty. Where it had been emptied was a matter for conjecture, but Temple would bet that it had been drained right here, where it should not have been.

"This is," Schmidt announced, "in honor of our guests from the land upon which the first rays of the rising Y2K sun sprayed like Liquid Plumber, a kiwi court." He reached down to lift up a bird cage, in which apparently grew a fern, under which was sheltered a funny-looking brown bird.

"Not a far cry from a partridge in a pear tree," Temple whispered to her party, "if only the season of the year were right."

"I wanted this to be a kangaroo court," Schmidt went on, his bellweather voice carrying farther than most of the con panel members' microphones had managed. "But I am told that kangaroos are unpredictable beasts prone to fisticuffs, and we can't have that ilk running around TitaniCon unchallenged, can we?"

From the wicked won't-you-come-home-Bill-Buckley twinkle behind Schmidt's glasses, the most unpredictable beast prone to fisticuffs in the vicinity was Schmidt himself.

"Bring on the first witness," he bellowed, banging out a few sentences on the typing paper rolled into the Royal while he waited.

In a minute, a towering Cardassian and a cowering Ferengi escorted a fair-haired, balding man before Judge Schmidt.

"Found him in the bar, eh?" The judge demanded, pushing his glasses down on his stumpy nose as if they were meant only for reading instead of being Clark Kent–size, disguise-big spectacles. "Where else would you find a writer?" Schmidt picked up his makeshift gavel and looked hopefully down the empty neck. "Ah well, I shall have to reverse the Hemingway formula and write sober, with hopes of editing drunk.

"All right. Let's see. Why would Alan Dahl, author of two-bit— I think that actually characterizes the power of his computer programs—nonselling sword-and-sorcery epics want to kill a TV science fiction icon like the King Khatlord? Could it be genre envy? Well?"

"This is ridiculous, Schmidt. I've heard that the law is an ass, but you've outdone yourself here."

"Then you won't mind telling a legal ass where you were right after the Khatlord of the Kohl Kompendium film presentation. Or producing witnesses."

"I don't have to answer to you for anything, but I was in the con suite. I never attended the Khatlord thing. I'm not interested in these film-oriented worlds, and I don't have to write for any of the franchises, thank God."

"You're welcome." Schmidt took on a dignified air as he bowed slowly.

Then his head snapped up, like a revivified ventriloquist's dummy suddenly possessed by an alien and even more obnoxious personality than the original. "Minions, bring on the next suspect, whom our helpful previous witness has just fingered. Greg Seltz!"

The next victim still wore plaid, the same plaid shirt as yesterday. Talk about a starving writer.

"Now," shouted the judge, "was this witness discovered in the bar?"

"No," answered the Borg guard, the only creature with a pastier face than the man in his custody. "He was found in a hive of his fellows. Resistance was futile."

"Yes, yes, yes. I know your catch phrase, you anemic bundle of exterior synapses. At least the Tin Woodsman responded to being well-oiled." The judge examined his empty gavel, snorted, and pulled a sterling silver flask from his back pocket. "Try some of this for fuel," he said, thrusting the flask at the impervious Borg.

The Borg glanced right, then left, then said in a mechanical voice, "We do not partake of fermented organic substances."

"No. Then why do you goose-stepping gizmos think you can make solid cubes do the two-step? They may be able to fly, but dancing is a physical impossibility!" Schmidt took a long swallow from the unseen contents of his flask and returned it to his back pocket.

"All right, wormhole," he addressed Greg Seltz. "I happen to know you sold your soul to write a Khatlord Kompendium book. What was it? The twenty-thousand-dollar advance? The thrill of seeing your name in eight-point type under a photo of an actor in a costume designer's version of a limp character created by a filmmaker who's recycled every cliché since Buster Crabbe wore tights? The sure knowledge that you were producing a deathless word-for-hire work worth about one-sixteenth of a percent of the cover price in exchange for all further rights in the product of your loins . . . ? That is, of course, where you keep your brains and your writing soul. Well?"

"This is ridiculous," Seltz said, "but what else can anyone expect from a blocked writer with a twenty-five-year jones? You've had your fifteen minutes of fame, Schmidt, and it was called the sixties. We are on the cusp of the Millennium, in case you hadn't noticed. The written word is in eclipse. The world has passed you by. WOSF awards mean less than the metabolized contents of your ever-present flask or your self-aggrandizing tantrums. I got more money for being exploited than you ever got for doing hack work for long-gone TV shows that show their age, as you do. Get a life!"

Temple, a passive audience member for a change, blinked. Seltz showed more spunk than she would have expected. She had encountered Schmidt's type of intellectual bully before: alcohol-fueled anger, all sound and fury, cutting down everyone around him so he would look taller.

Generally, it was better to let them rock and rant, and save your energy for the real things in life.

Schmidt was also taken aback. "Well. The louse that roared. Can you tell me that you didn't want to kill your esteemed 'coauthor,' the King Khatlord, at the presentation when you learned that your own Khatlord novel provided the inspiration and plot for the new Khatlord feature film with not one iota of further payment going to you? Nada. Zip. Zilch. Zero. But the stupid actor would get a cut. You can bet his 'celebrity' book contract didn't freeze him out of film and foreign rights."

"It isn't exactly my book," Seltz began.

The beer bottle thumped wood. "The hell it isn't! You think I'm washed up, you Jell-O-spined toad, but I'm trying to save the field from sellouts like you. For every few grand you take when the film franchise is making millions, you admit that ideas are cheap, that writers are expendable, that we are moving to a world of special-effect, blockbuster epics that don't have squat to say about the human condition. How plead you? Guilty? Accepted by the court. Now stew in your own right-to-work juices. I'm sure the Khatlord empire would be happy to accept a twenty-thousand-dollar plot and book for their next hundred-and-ninety-million-dollar movie, not to mention merchandising and fast-food tie-ins."

Next to Temple, Mariah tugged on Buffy's arm and squirmed. "That man is right. We all rush to get the latest thing, and two months later, it's a new latest thing. My mom says that, too."

"Imagine. Your mom has something in common with Hanford Schmidt."

Mariah took another look at the irascible, and potted, judge, then giggled. But Temple noticed that her fingers rubbed over the Yoda tattoo on her cheek. She was beginning to feel had.

"So," Schmidt said, leaning over his typewriter to fix Greg Seltz with a well-oiled eye, ballpoint pen in hand again and clicking madly. "You were seen rushing out of the Khatlord Kompendium presentation. Was it when you realized that your book was the blueprint for the forthcoming film, but that you would reap not a dime more profit for it? Did you come back to kill your coauthor, who, having written nothing, but being the embodiment of the King Khatlord, would still stand to make millions from the film when you'd be eating celluloid? Well?"

"I knew what I was signing," Seltz said quietly. "I thought it was worth buying time so I could write some of my own books."

"Listen to yourself. 'Write some of your own books.' You have to prostitute your talent to Hollywood doofuses in their twenties who will send you forty-page revision letters of total idiocy to be able to afford to write 'your own books.' My only quarrel with you, dear doofus, is that you struck at the wrong target. Forget the egotistical actors who put their names on your books and go for the jugular. Go for the gutless producers who wouldn't know creativity and talent if they took a lunch with it at Spago at four in the morning."

"He's a totally dysfunctional narcissistic alcoholic," Matt whispered in Temple's ear. "And he's got a point."

She nodded. Sheila was standing too close to them for what she wanted to say next, so she went on tiptoe to whisper in Matt's ear. "If he's so right, and such an angry young-old man, could he be the murderer?"

Startled, Matt snapped a glance her way. "Murder to make a political point?"

She nodded. "I've heard of worse motivations."

The crowd behind them pushed them forward together. Had to give Schmidt credit; he knew how to grab an audience.

Temple grabbed Mariah's arm, even though that could be construed as uncool. Matt had fastened onto her elbow. Dear Giles, so protective.

That left Sheila on her own, and Temple felt a twinge of unease to see her sleek, unmistakable figure separated from the trio by a welt of people.

"Now," Schmidt was saying, standing, swaying, waving his pen, the maestro to the bitter end. "The kiwi court is in recess for the moment. Go forth and sin some more. And anybody who buys the judge a beer is off scot-free!"

The crowd was undecided as to whether to disband or dispense beer.

In the overwhelming eddying motion of people going in all directions at once, Temple lost touch with both Mariah and Matt.

Panic slipped in. Was this planned? Oh, Lord. Where were they?

She trod other people's feet until she spotted Matt's blond head. Found him, and found Mariah. He had stuck to the kid like glue, like a Watcher who knew who the real Buffy was.

"What about Sheila?" he asked when he saw Temple.

But she wasn't to be seen.

Given the outfit she was wearing, that was either a significant achievement, or a very sinister fact.

Chapter 48

Disorder in the Closet

Under fluorescent lights, the wardrobe room offered an unframed long mirror leaning against a wall and a maze of racks holding the carapaces of some of the most repellent life-forms in the galaxy.

It was actually a large storage room next to the locked room where the hotel stored clients' baggage. For now, like many people attending TitaniCon, the room had taken on an exotic new role: wardrobe room for the security guards masquerading as science fiction extras.

Max studied rows of rubber alien masks from such shows as *Star Trek, Star Wars, Babylon 5, Star Trooper Bazaar*. They sat on Styrofoam heads lining wire shelves atop the clothes racks. It reminded him of the classic scene in Mel Brooks's *Young Frankenstein* when the doctor's assistant, Igor, was brain shopping for the unfinished monster.

Max wondered what unfinished monsters were masquerading behind these representations of modern nightmares. One he knew by name. Another one might be a killer who had figured out, as he had, that the security wardrobe was ripe for easy picking. Or, the killer might be a two-in-one deal, a solution that Max would prefer but doubted was reasonable.

Why would Rafi Nadir—strip-club bouncer, rogue ex-cop, bully of women—kill a relatively well-known actor?

Murder for hire?

Max regarded his pacing image in the mirror. He made a pretty formidable Khatlord. In fact, he had removed the platforms from the requisite boots. He wanted to be able to move well, and fast, if he had to. And, at six-four, he didn't need extra height.

He had to stay fully dressed, even though the poor air circulation in here turned his costume into a rubber-and-spandex wet suit from the inside out.

Nadir had seen Max, or a disguised approximation of him, and Max couldn't risk reminding the man of that.

Max didn't mind the isolation, the wait, the discomfort. Magicians endured all that, over and over again, first in rehearsal and then in performance, for the sake of an illusion.

This was for the sake of a solution to a murder. Maybe two. Then, and now.

He shook his head, with the big-cat nose and jaw built into the otherwise elastic mask.

A Khatlord's "whiskers" were stiff, lethal-looking barbs. Amazing how the dangerous and sinister fascinated the human being, like some species that needed to produce special effects to intimidate its prey, which—most often—was its fellow humans.

He smiled beneath the mask. He had previously checked out Temple and company on the con floor. Mariah was already concealed beneath the cheap effects of "Con Girl," with every garish accessory for sale in the dealers' room. Temple made a fetching Buffy. He only wished he could be there to help her find out if blonds had more fun. And Devine . . . the Giles-style professor accessories didn't do a thing for him, although Giles supposedly had secret powers. Max was glad he'd killed a lot of time lately working out in front of the TV. Got him up to speed on all the media action figures available at your friendly neighborhood comix store.

Why on earth had Molina gotten involved with some past incarnation of a guy like Rafi Nadir? That was the biggest mystery in this whole morass. Had a kid by him. Some strange story there. What? Twelve, thirteen years ago. Must have been in her twenties, and a lot dumber than she seemed today.

He paused as he remembered her call last night. Temple had given her one of his numbers a bit back; now she was using it. Probably because her daughter was in danger.

She never identified herself when she called, and she didn't have to. The rich contralto of her torch-singer alter ego, Carmen, flavored her speech, though she wouldn't want to know that. Magicians needed good ears as well as eyes and quick hands.

"You say you're at TitaniCon because you're working for me," she began.

"Although I'm now also working for me."

"You're working for me as long as my daughter's there, and you need to know I'm sending her back in."

"You're what? For God's sake, why? I won't have another Cher on my conscience."

"You're a criminal. You don't have a conscience."

"You know that's not true; that's why you're calling."

He didn't say which of her accusations was not true, the criminal or the conscience part, but it was pretty obvious. More obvious than Max liked other people, particularly police people, to know.

"All I'm saying," she answered, "is that I want you to find Nadir. You know he's there. You've seen him before. You're in a better position than any man or woman I've got."

"What about the Khatlord death?"

"Forget the Khatlord death. That's my concern. I want you to find Nadir, then watch him to make sure he doesn't find my daughter. Simple, right?"

"You can't order me to do anything."

"No. But I can hold you responsible for my daughter's safety, and I will."

"That's not fair—"

"That's the way it is."

She had hung up, of course. Delegating authority brooked no argument. She had the superior officer part down; too bad the human being part always lost in that conflict.

It was absolutely insane for her to return her daughter to this scene. She wasn't insane. That meant she had more in mind than he knew. He hated outguessing someone he knew so little about, and she had made certain that anyone tracking her would find too little to use.

Well, he would do what he was ordered—because he wouldn't forgive himself if anything happened to Mariah—but that didn't mean he couldn't do a lot more.

Chapter 49

Cut to the Chase

If it wasn't surprising that Sheila would attract a crowd in her current getup, it was unnerving that she could totally vanish in a crowd.

Matt, Temple, and Mariah moved through the eddying bodies, looking for their lost cybersheep.

"Maybe she got abducted by a berserk Bajoran," Mariah suggested. "Or the Borg. They want her back."

"We don't see many Borg here," Temple pointed out. "The costumes are too complicated."

"The Borg are creepy," Mariah agreed. "Listen. I bet somebody lured her away for a photo op."

Temple nodded. "Good idea. But where?"

They ended up in the central spaceport area where ceilings soared, spaceships spun above, and the mobs were truly huge.

Matt finally spotted her, not unforeseen given his superior height.

They found her cowering under a tall potted plant, not unlike a kiwi beneath a fern.

"Sheila!" Matt was both solicitous and shocked. "What's wrong? Why did you disappear?"

"The wages of popularity." She laughed shakily. "I've never done this at such a big con before. The . . . fans just swept me away. Wanted signatures, wanted to sign my bodystocking. And this one fan, done up as a cyber QE One, she just shoved me until I fell off my platform boots, which are built into my catsuit legs, so I got all twisted up and people started to walk over me."

"Sheila, are you all right?" Temple wanted to know, keeping a fist curled into Mariah's T-shirt.

"No. My ankle. It's worse."

"You should go home," Matt decreed.

Sheila turned the eyes behind her mask on him. "No, I . . . you think so?"

He nodded, torn by divided duties. "Can you . . . drive yourself?"

"I guess so. It's walking that's hard."

"Why don't we all walk her to the car," Temple suggested.

Only Mariah groaned at the idea. "I'm tired."

"You can't be tired," Temple said. "You're a kid. Come on, some fresh air will do us all good."

Temple sat right down against the wall to show her game spirit and to make Sheila feel better about abandoning her glamourous persona. She switched her modest navy Buffy pumps for the air-cushioned tennis shoes she carried in her pink Buffy backpack (or Big Temple tote bag) at all times now. Made one understand where the word "gumshoe" came from.

In moments the quartet was heading for the up escalator and the bridge to the parking ramp. Sheila hobbled along gamely, unmolested within a three-person buffer zone. Of course the touted fresh air lasted only as long as the twenty-yard-long sky-walk to the neighboring parking ramp. These three-story open-air bridges between buildings reminded Matt of a Venice without the shadows, and provided a terrific view of the "topless towers" of Las Vegas.

"Topless" in Dr. Faustus's sense of endless height, not in the modern-day vulgar Vegas connotation.

Unfortunately, the sun-washed bridges didn't offer good photo opportunities. Waist-high stucco walls were topped with sheets of Plexiglas, smudged safety barriers high enough to make picture taking iffy. Once inside the parking ramp, it was like exchanging the airy angel food cake of architecture the eye could feast on outside for a multilayer cake with carbon monoxide filling. Cars idled in and out, spewing fumes visible and invisible. Sheila, flustered by the unwanted end to an unexpected day, couldn't remember where she had parked her vehicle.

Time for Giles to take over. Matt sat Sheila, Temple, and Mariah down on a concrete wall. "Tell me what model, year, and color to look for," he told Sheila. "I'll run up and down a couple levels to spot it."

She complied, her mask dangling from her wrist, smiling wanly, not only because she was tired and her ankle hurt, but because she was hurt that they seemed tired of her company.

Matt trotted off, wondering how he'd ended up escorting three females instead of just one-in-training.

He found the aged Toyota Tercel two levels up, then wished he had taken Sheila's keys so he could drive it down to her.

He retraced his steps, dodging a continual stream of ascending cars. Some of their drivers idled hopefully in place when they spotted him. Was he on his way to dislodge a car from a precious parking space?

Nope.

"Two levels," he told the trio when he returned to them. "Want me to take the keys and bring it down?"

"No, I can walk." Sheila stood to demonstrate her readiness.

Temple stood, too. "There must be an elevator."

There was, and it turned out to be reasonably close, so they all hiked or hobbled over to it. After the press of a button and a two-minute stroll, they finally saw Sheila into her car.

"She's a nice lady," Mariah said, watching the car back out as far as it could. An idling Prizm was panting to slip into its parking space. "I thought she was kinda dull, until I saw her outfit today."

Temple pulled on Mariah's false, beaded braids. "Well, anybody'd look dull to a girl with temporary tattoos on her cheeks."

Temple glanced at Matt, realizing that she'd usurped the care and supervision of Mariah, but he couldn't know why.

"Can you two wait here while I make a quick phone call?" She asked Matt, not Mariah. "The reception will be better out here."

He watched her scoot—Temple was one of the few humans over three years old who could scoot—to the ramp's open-air edge. She perched on the low wall, then pulled out a cell phone from her tote bag, and punched once on the faceplate. Preprogrammed one-touch dialing. This was a number she used a lot. He could guess whose it was, and that added a whole new dimension to what might really be going on here.

"She's okay," Mariah commented as Matt sat beside her on their own slice of concrete buttress. "But she's kind of a party pooper."

Better that Temple take that rap than he. Amazing how kids always cast the adults around them as extremes: either heros or villains.

He wished he could read lips. Temple looked puzzled, then exasperated, then shut down the machine and rejoined them.

They started trudging toward the skywalk again.

They were about forty feet from the skywalk when a sound like a bagpipe in extremis reverberated from the concrete surfaces around them.

They stopped just as an aggressive grille came grinning around the tight corner of the up ramp.

Black, with a feral glint to the design of grille and headlights; heading toward them faster than a bowling ball coming all the way from Detroit.

They all scrambled, Matt gripping Temple's and Mariah's clothing and pulling them like grocery bags atop the trunk of the nearest parked car.

The vehicle missed them but slammed into the rear of the

neighboring minivan. Glass tinkled to concrete as the van shook on its springs.

"Out of here!" Matt shouted, propelling them toward the skywalk.

"What about the damage to the van?" Temple objected. "We're witnesses."

"We want to be live witnesses." He pushed and pulled them onto the walkway, not wasting time in looking back.

The minute they were on the bridge he realized that it was wide enough for a car, should anyone be demented enough to try it. He could hear the jerky squeal of brakes being applied, released, applied again. The car was turning around.

"Come on!" he bellowed. Sound was a weapon. He had learned that in martial arts classes. It could also be a goad.

They ran onto the deserted bridge in the sky, blinking in the sudden searing daylight, running toward a distant row of dark-glass rectangles glinting with the brass of fanciful door pulls.

Beyond those doors lay the dim, overpopulated wonder of the New Millennium hotel and all its works.

Behind them came no more squealing, just the thrum of a motor revved to the max.

They ran, miraculously keeping together. Matt glanced over his shoulder.

A black automotive grin was cresting onto the skyway. The maniac was driving right after them.

"Run!" he shouted again, "and don't look back."

The doors grew into a reflective wall clear as the sheeted water of a tidal wave. In the tinted glass depths he glimpsed a motorized demon like a great black shark growing larger.

"Be ready to spring to the sides," he shouted, panted.

The watery glass wall loomed dead ahead. Everyone took a door, yanked a brass planet Saturn out of its ordinary orbit, and dashed through.

They kept running.

Behind them came a roar, a crystal cataract of falling glass like glaciers dying.

Ahead lay the escalator mouths, one up, one down.

All three crowded onto the down escalator, losing footing as the teethed surface slid into molehills under their feet. They ended up straddling two or three steps, trying to grab onto the handrail, trying to hold each other up.

Brakes screamed like a banshee behind them.

Matt turned to look.

The car's front was wedged in the bank of shattered glass doors like a vintage Ford grille embedded in a retrocafé's lunch counter.

The impact had tilted its demonic grin into a lopsided smirk.

Matt thought he heard faint footsteps running back over the skywalk.

"Did anybody get the license number of that driver?" Temple gasped.

After a silence, Mariah began giggling.

They started walking down the steps, hurrying again until they hit level ground, then Matt and Temple started running again.

"Wait!" Mariah dug her heels in like an anchor, resisting their grip on her arms. "We're leaving the scene of an accident. We can't do that."

Cop's kid, Matt thought. *As bad as a minister's kid at all the wrong moments. But you have to admire the results of training done early and often.*

"We've got to keep moving," Temple said. "There might be more."

"More cars?" Mariah was unconvinced.

"They were after us," Matt said, wondering even as he said it who "they" were and which one of "us" they were after. "Our first job is to get to safety. We can always testify later."

Mariah allowed their logic to sweep her along in their flight.

They ran onto a second down escalator. A few obliviously happy tourists were taking the first up escalator toward the shattered doors.

Matt wasn't worried about them. The fading footsteps would be long gone. The car was unpiloted, dead, mired in broken glass and twisted metal.

A man in Cardassian guise was at the bottom of the up escalator, a walkie-talkie pressed to his alien ear. He began leaping up two and three steps at a time, pushing, passing tourists on the left.

Security was impressive. Temple had turned to stare at him, hard. Matt breathed easier as their party passed him like ships in the night, innocent little trawlers they, a family of three—man, woman, child. Not worth noting when something was going terribly wrong.

He felt like they were escaping into Egypt, and then there it was before them again—the exotic dress and sights, the throngs of foreign people, the crowd in which they could lose themselves.

"Let's move it." Matt grabbed Temple's sleeve to slow her up while he whispered in her ear, or what he presumed was her ear beneath the disconcerting blond wig.

His mind boomeranged back to the prime question. *Who was that behind the wheel of the rogue car? A random maniac? A determined attacker? Why?*

The crowd was all flowing against them, going to some mass attraction they were ignorant of. Like salmons leaping against the elemental flow of water, they pushed deeper into the direction everyone else was deserting.

It made them stand out, Matt knew. But the danger was behind them. It was natural to flee as far from it as possible.

Unless greater danger awaited them ahead.

Chapter 50

Close Quarters

Max hated being in the closet.

There was nothing to do here but act busy every time someone entered.

Then it was fiddle with his Khatlord outfit until the newcomer had come and gone. Max must have buckled and unbuckled the same weapons belt three dozen times, while each newcomer had arrived, exchanged his mundane clothes for the exotic skin of costume bearing his name tag, and left again.

None of the remaining tags bore the name "Nadir," but Max didn't expect it to. His man would have used a pseudonym; Max had.

He waited for just one man to enter: one man whose face he knew. Then he had to stay just long enough to see which costume the guy used. After that, he could finally leave this windowless box and merge into the mob outside and wait to track his prey.

But identifying the man came first.

If his man showed up at all.

Meanwhile, the watch beneath the Khatlord gauntlet showed late afternoon creeping into evening.

What if his man wasn't working today? Or what if by some odd-ball chance he had recognized Mariah, maybe even before Temple had put her in deep coverup? What if he were stalking Temple and Mariah even now? Molina was demented to send the kid back in, knowing Nadir was on the premises. True, the odds were very long that he'd ever connect Mariah with her mother and himself . . . but blood will tell, they say, and Max had seen blood spilled on much longer odds than this before.

The door cracked, catching Max bracing a lace-up boot on the wall and cursing the knotted laces.

"Those are a bitch, aren't they?" a rugged voice asked. "Makes you realize why they had serving wenches around in the good old days."

"Damn right," Max muttered through the muzzle of his leopard-snouted mask. "Damn stupid thing to ask security guys to do."

"Security guys!" Rafi Nadir snorted as he stripped off his cam-ouflage jacket. "Most of these guys are college Joes and limp-wristed, would-be actors. Wanta get discovered for the movies."

Nadir sat on the lone locker-room bench provided to remove his hiking boots.

"Movie gig wouldn't be too bad," Max said, "but I'm used to regular security."

"Yeah?"

"Yeah. Worked the Aladdin before they imploded that sucker down to the sandline."

"Hotel security is okay, but the action's somewhere else."

Max sat down on the bench's other end to untangle his lace knots. Black chalk dust darkened his knuckles and nail rims.

"Where's that?" he asked.

"Well, I almost got a great gig here. Had to, uh, remove some wimpo freako who likes to dress up like one of these weirdo actors. I bounced him good. The big-cheese actor was real impressed. Was talking about putting me on the payroll. Liked my style."

"Say, you've seen more action at this thing than I have."

"It's knowin' where to be."

"That's for sure." Max cursed his bootlaces, stood and cursed the cumbersome, weapon-hung belt. "This mother's bigger than a World Wrestling Federation championship belt. Who do they think we are? Jesse Ventura?"

"Right." Nadir laughed with genuine relish. "Bunch of lily-livered politicians. Jesse'll show 'em. Politicians. That's what cost me my last job."

"So when do you start?"

"Huh? Start what?" Nadir stood, finally looked at Max the Khatlord. "Say, you must have extra high lifts in those boots."

"Took what they gave me. So you start—?"

"Start what?" Nadir's face was the harsh-handsome kind some women—it was hard to imagine Molina as one of them—liked: dark hair, eyebrows, lashes, and swarthy skin, but already starting to look fleshy and dissipated at forty.

"Your flush new job with this big-actor type."

Nadir pulled the leopard mask over his head and face. The vaguely reptilian, leopard-pattern, stretch fabric fit his physiognomy like a glove. Max could have told Nadir from the Cloaked Conjuror in an instant, but most people wouldn't be able to see the subtleties beneath the spandex skin.

"It's kaput." Nadir struggled into the stiff intricacies of his Khatlord costume, his voice muffled, but not quite muffling his disappointment and anger. "The guy died. Yeah. Right here. Yesterday. Went waltzing with a high-voltage sign. Or maybe somebody took him dancing, if you know what I mean."

"Hey, I take a day off and miss the main event. So he was fried. Any idea who might have been tempted to tango?"

"I'd say that wimp I busted, but he didn't have the *cojones* for it. Especially after I escorted him off the premises. *Capisci?*"

Max spoke Spanish, as it happened, and everyone who watched TV spoke Mob.

"I get you." Max boxed the man lightly on the shoulder.

He stiffened, then decided to accept the gesture of camaraderie.

Human powderkeg, Max noted to himself and smiled behind the concealing mask. He'd left a trail of oil-based iridescent powder on the massive Khatlord-costume shoulder pad. No one would notice it except the person looking for it.

"See you around," Max said in farewell, with some irony, and left the confining room.

At last! Now he could look up his party of three.

He started toward the spaceport entry area. The place thronged with people it hadn't attracted before. Many, if not most, were in costume, representing every alien being in the galaxy of science fiction, and fantasy-based books, TV shows, movies, games.

Max stopped, people never even pausing, just flowing around him like an endless river.

He thought waiting for Raf Nadir to show in the costume room had been a pain in the neck. Now, finding Temple and Mariah in disguise in this moving mob would be a worse pain.

They were the ones he should have used his fairy dust on. How could he protect someone he couldn't find?

Chapter 51

Judgment Daze

"I'm supposed to be a judge," Matt shouted at the green-skinned, toga-wearing person guarding this particular set of closed doors to the Neptune ballroom.

"You *are* a judge," Temple shouted at Matt in turn. She repeated herself to the greenskin.

"Mattie Vine? I don't have that name on my list."

"The cochair asked me," Matt hollered over the roaring-crowd noise, "after the Khatlord died and couldn't make it."

"The coach? The cat cried?" Greenskin shook his/her head, which was also green, and quite bald. It was as if Temple and Matt stood under Niagara Falls, the roar of two-thousand-some voices pent up in the hallway waiting to be admitted to the ballroom for the Masquerade was that deafening.

Temple stood on her tippy-toes and reached for the top of her voice.

"He is a judge. A substitute judge. Let him in!"

Greenskin wobbled from foot to foot. "You should have gone to the other entrance."

"Other entrance?" Matt shouted. "Where?"

"Out through the hall and around."

"He won't get there in time for Judgment Day," Temple repeated, keeping her hand twisted in Mariah's T-shirt to make sure she didn't get lost in the crush.

"If I let you through, the others might rush the doors."

"Not if you shut them right after us," Matt insisted.

"Only you."

"They're with me. I don't judge without them."

The creature stood aside to crack open the door.

The crowd behind them drew in a breath, then pressed forward like hungry lions scenting Christians.

"Just you." The gatekeeper stepped in front of Temple and Mariah as Matt started through.

"They're with me," Matt said, stepping hard on the gate-keeper's foot.

He jumped back. Temple rushed forward, dragging Mariah with her.

Matt had turned to push the door shut after they were through, but several folds of exotic clothing were still caught in the crack.

"What a mob," Temple said, discovering suddenly that it was no longer necessary to shout.

Through the door, they could hear the greenskin bellowing, "Judges, they're judges, judges."

"You've been awfully quiet," Matt told Mariah.

"It's like the lunch line at school, only twenty times bigger. I've never seen adults acting like that before."

"These aren't adult adults," Temple explained. "They're adults playing at being kids again."

Mariah wrinkled her upper lip. "It's not so great being a kid that you'd want to go back."

"You will once you can't," Temple predicted. "Or you'll think about it."

Matt had moved into the aisle between ranks of empty folding chairs to stare at the huge room's distant end. "At least they changed the configuration."

Temple and Mariah joined him to gaze silently at where the King Khatlord had died.

"Why couldn't they use a different room?" Mariah asked.

"It's too hard to change the site of an event as complicated as this Masquerade," Temple said, speaking from long experience in PR problems. "There's no other space this large. The dressing rooms are set up off the ballroom, the stage and runway were probably in pieces in the side rooms even yesterday.

"And," she added, "in Las Vegas the show must go on. There are way too many people who've bought tickets to let anything stop the parade."

"It's not like we really knew him," Mariah said.

"If anybody here did, you did." Matt put a hand on her shoulder. "He was a favorite character in a favorite show."

"I liked the way he roared on TV. And everybody listened. But I didn't like the way he roared here, at that man who dressed up like him, at me."

"He was an actor, Mariah," Matt pointed out. "Part of what you see on TV is real and part of it isn't. And part of what you saw here was real, and part of it wasn't."

"What part wasn't real?"

"Oh, I suppose those tantrums he threw. If he had been really happy with himself, he wouldn't have had to act like such a big shot, right?"

"You mean he was kind of like a bully at school?"

"Yup. Throwing his weight around."

"Somebody finally threw it around for him, I guess."

"I guess," Temple said. "I don't think the murder was premeditated, though."

"Why not?" Matt asked. "Someone could have asked to meet him here after the panel, planning to push him into the sign all along."

"Death by neon? Kind of iffy, isn't it? What if the glass tubing didn't break? Or the victim didn't come in contact with the electricity where it did break?"

"Accident or design, who did it?" Matt pushed her.

"Honestly, you guys!" Mariah put her hands on her hips, the first sign that she had any under the loose T-shirt. "It's so obvious. That plaid-shirt guy from the con suite that everybody was yelling at. That other wild guy kept saying 'Plaid Shirt' had been taken to the cleaners over the book he wrote for the Khatlord. It's like he knew the new movie was based on it. But I don't think the plaid-shirt guy did until he got to the panel and heard what the movie was about."

"Seltz did run out," Temple admitted. "And he looked pretty green."

"Too green to do much about anything," Matt said. "Besides, what was done was done. He didn't have any pull in getting the Hathaway guy to see him."

"But if he did," Temple said, "maybe demanding that Hathaway share some of his acting loot with him to pay him for the book idea. . . ."

"Hathaway would have laughed him off the dais. He was a big man, even without the Khatlord gear. I can't see anybody who wasn't pretty strong pushing him around."

"Unless the pusher was absolutely maddened with rage. And the writer guy left the ballroom because he couldn't stand to hear another word. Maybe it had nothing to do with TitaniCon and Hathaway's professional life," Temple added. "Maybe he'd done a girlfriend wrong, and she had a brother in the merchant marines."

Matt shook his head. He brushed at his hair but had forgotten he was wearing the Giles glasses and knocked into them instead.

"I don't know what we're wearing these things for." He folded and stuffed the glasses into the second-hand cardigan's pocket. "I'm going to the stage area to find out where they want me. We might as well settle before the mob rushes in. Looks like this is going to be a long, loud evening."

Thanks to Matt's pull as a judge, Temple and Mariah were soon perched on seats in the very first row, near the judge's table at stage left.

The assembling judges proved to be a combination of local celebrities and writing eminences. Hanford Schmidt was the only writer Temple knew, and he really did have some fan-slaveys tote his typewriter and chains to the table. A couple of younger men in jeans and T-shirts were apparently successful writers.

Matt had to sit right away and scribble down a bio for the announcer to read. Temple asked to see it and rewrote it in a more immodest manner.

And then all the doors burst open at the room's opposite end at once, as if admitting a parade of elephants, and the mob flooded in. The roaring chatter of a couple of thousand people crashed forward like the surf as they rushed for the best seats along the T-shaped, raised stage.

In half an hour everyone had found a seat. By then it was minutes past the announced starting time. Even a couple of judges slipped into their seats late.

"Hey, there's Xena!" Mariah announced after turning from staring at the crowd. She waved at her friend from the martial arts display. "It is the real one, isn't it? I saw a few in the crowd, but they didn't look this good."

"Well, it's the real fake one," Temple said. "The Hercules and Xena we saw fighting were the stunt doubles. You know what stunt doubles are?"

"I know. They're the ones who really do all the cool, dangerous stuff. Maybe it's like that writer who really wrote the book. Maybe they should be the stars of the movie. Hey, look! Xena waved back at me. And Matt did, too."

"She probably recognized you as the rug rat who nearly tripped her up," Temple warned Mariah.

She hated to tell an impressionable girl that Xena was just another babe in amazon's clothing. As if every woman could be a towering martial arts expert with long raven-dark hair and sky-blue eyes, a bustier body, and a possibly inappropriate relationship with her girl apprentice. How come when it was two guys, like Hercules and Aolus or Butch and Sundance, it was just a buddy movie, but when it was two girls, there were lesbian intimations? Unless it was Thelma and Louise, of course. They did take a suicidal dive like Butch and Sundance, which she guessed made them two of the guys.

Temple's ruminations on media-female role models ended abruptly when the last celebrity judge slipped into place. And slip in he did, appearing as if by magic in a seat between Matt and Xena, who both looked a bit startled. The man's mask amazingly resembled a Khatlord's, except it wasn't. And he wore dramatic but definitely late-twentieth-century street clothes: black tails, black leather gloves, black tie. The only thing missing was a top hat, which wouldn't have fit over his leopard-spotted mask. He was only lacking a Khatlord's Klingon-style mane to pass for one of the Kompendium aliens.

The sudden appearance technique was awfully like Max's. Temple wondered if he'd decided to ditch the Khatlord outfit. That would be so like Max! Sitting next to Matt judging this costume-orama . . . and nobody suspecting a thing.

When the Cloaked Conjuror's eyes grazed the crowd and they passed the place where Temple sat, she winked.

He didn't wink back, but then he couldn't. Not with that spandex mask on.

While she was watching to see if the leopardman had changed his spots, Matt had been getting acquainted with Xena. Or vice versa.

Temple saw him pantomime some sort of martial arts move. She nodded and pantomimed back. Must be discussing yesterday morning's fracas, when all Temple could do was jump into the fray and become another potential victim.

Didn't judges have better things to talk about?

"I wouldn't call her pretty," Mariah said to Temple. Aha. She too had noticed the judges getting chummy.

"Striking, more like it," Temple agreed. "Awfully tall. I guess you'll get there yourself, though," she added quickly. "I'd like to be taller."

"I just cut off my hair," Mariah said.

"That long hair is way too much trouble to keep up. I bet it's a wig."

Mariah fixed her with a look that said, *Don't humor me because I'm a kid.* "No, if being Xena's stunt double is her job, I bet it's her own hair. You can't have a wig flying off in those fight scenes."

"True. A bald Xena would look a lot less attractive."

"Matt seems to like her."

"Well . . . he has to be polite, and she is stunning. And that outfit is a walking oxymoron: warrior princess."

"What's oxymoron?"

"An oxymoron is words put together that separately mean the opposite of each other."

"It'd be a great name for an alien race: the Oxymoron."

"And you could have the Synecdoche and the Iamb and the Trochee."

"Oh, cool. Let's write it!"

"First we watch the show," Temple said as the formalities began with the huge, Hawaiian-shirted cochair stepping up to the mike stand at stage left.

He introduced the writing guest of honor, which allowed Hanford Schmidt to stand up and wave his long-neck beer bottle high above his head. They were going to bypass his speech for the moment, but he vaulted on stage and commandeered the mike for ten rambling minutes during which he repeated his despair for the future of the science fiction field, interspersed with comments on major female Hollywood sex symbols, that were supposed to be funny but just came off as wishful thinking.

"Xena's better looking than all those ladies," Mariah whispered to Temple halfway through, with a frown.

"Yeah, but she's better-armed, too, so Hanford will stay away from her."

The artist guest of honor, it turned out, was to be the emcee.

He was a balding, short, pear-shaped guy in his forties who spoke with some emotion on how much the support of the fans really meant as he was building his career. He went on to confess that he once thought the peak of becoming a really successful fantasy and science fiction artist would be reaping the most notorious benefit of such fame: One day a female fan would approach him on trembling legs and ask him to autograph her breast.

Ribald laughter started in the vast room, but the artist hadn't hit the punch line.

"It finally happened," he admitted, "only nobody told me I'd have to use a roller."

It took thirty seconds for the meaning of that to sink in, and when the laughter came, it was distinctly lacking a soprano register.

"Poor man and his blasted ideals," Temple muttered.

"I don't get it," Mariah complained.

"Be glad you didn't. He'd better watch it. I think Xena did."

This deflected Mariah from other awkward questions and focused her attention on her heroine, who was indeed listening with her head cast down, rhythmically beating her chakra on the judge's tablecloth.

"She looks mad," Mariah said admiringly.

"Or bored. And look at Matt. I think his eyes are crossing."

Mariah giggled. "Mine can do that, too."

Next came the introduction of the judges.

Schmidt had already wrested his fifteen minutes of fame from the emcee this evening, so the other judges were given short shrift. Temple sat impatiently through the endless bibliographies of the two writers she didn't know, and the startling news that Xena's stunt double had started her performing life as a ballerina and later worked as a female wrestler in the Philippines. She stood up and waved her chakra, principally in the direction of the artist guest of honor at the mike. The Cloaked Conjuror was credited with demystifying magic for fun and profit, and barely stood to take his bow.

Matt, or Mr. Midnight, was introduced last. Temple listened carefully to make sure that the spiel was properly read. He stood and nodded his head as the applause washed over him in turn, stronger than before, probably because his was the last intro the audience had to suffer through.

362 • Carole Nelson Douglas

Before Matt had even sat down, the ballroom lights dimmed. A bank of specialty spotlights switched on, bathing the stage and the long tongue of runway that extended into the audience.

Thence commenced a spectacle as lavish in its way as any Broadway or Las Vegas revue. While it took a while to introduce the entries, once the lights came up on their living tableaux on stage, breaths were taken in and gasped out at regular intervals, all the while strobe flashes exploded in the audience.

The entrants had obviously been working on their outfits for at least a year. Some were groups representing whole casts, each garbed to represent the human and alien dramatis personae. Others were solos, and even a peacock would have envied the imaginative, massive, and bizarre show of glitz and glory.

Some costumes were triumphs of recreating in person what the television and movie worlds did with special effects. The monster from *Alien* was a huge, bio-robot that lurched across the stage to threaten the judges.

One man entered in perfect C13PO guise.

Other acts were more mundane but always politely applauded. There was the three-hundred-pound man in the Wookie suit who padded on like Pooh-bear, just stood, and padded off. A two-hundred-fifty-pound woman in a belly dancer's outfit, with a coin-heavy belt around her hips comprised of all her tips, did a brief monologue about the time Conan the Barbarian came into her tavern. When the warrior scanted on her tip, she "belted" him with one swing of her hips and the gold-heavy belt, and bumped-and-ground the hero off his bench to the floor.

There was a multiple Vorlon transformation and a Borg collective "freeing" that was choreographed like a modern dance as the drones shed their mechanical attachments.

And there were an awful lot of nearly naked ladies with *Playboy*-perfect physiques, wearing only boots and jewelry and looking no more alien than the showgirls in the hotels down the Strip.

Despite the genuine variety and imagination, Temple started checking her watch. Mama Bear had said to let Mariah stay as long as it took, but her watch was pushing midnight, and Temple's rear was going numb on the metal folding-chair seat.

"We have one last surprise entry," the emcee said finally, sounding as weary as the audience.

No doubt, Temple thought unkindly, *he is anticipating hours of using his roller on bared breasts after the show.*

"We don't normally make exceptions, but in this case . . ."

He stepped aside as the lights went suddenly dark.

One faint spotlight focused on the center curtain.

A huge, stiff arm poked through, then another.

Frankenstein? What was so hot about that?

The huge figure on platform boots stomped out like a mechanical zombie. As the spotlight intensified, the figure glowed with a green phosphorescence.

Eeriest of all was the face, its green-background pallor interrupted by the regular pattern of a tattoo lacework . . . not tattoos, leopard spots.

This was the ghost of the King Khatlord.

He stomped forward, all his armaments clicking and rattling like silverware.

Temple had never heard a Khatlord approach except during the noise and bustle of a crowd. This one was a walking Swiss Army knife, cutlery clanking. A perfect ghost. He could have been Hamlet's father, or the Monster, or the Mummy gone high-tech, or . . .

Chapter 52

Fatal Entry

Well, I will be an ape's uncle.

In fact, the whole human race would be a lot better off if one of my kind had been.

Anyway, this is the most startling resurrection in the sci-fi world since Mr. Spock.

I have been lurking about unsung, keeping my ear to the ground. Literally.

Once I realize that the only evidence I have is the evidence of things not seen, I realize that I must *hear* my way to finding the killer.

I have been listening to every click and snick and tsk I can discern at TitaniCon, and, believe me, there are quite a few. Nothing has quite rung true, however, until I am dozing backstage here preparing to feast my eyes on the Masquerade and possibly on the Sinister Hyacinth in her latest S&M (Skintight and Masked) outfit.

The Sinister Hyacinth has been disappointingly absent, but I do suddenly find my right ear pricking at a sharp clicking sound that is all too familiar.

I immediately open my eyes to scan the back-stage crowd for the source. All the entrants have gathered behind the curtain, except I don't see any Wizard of Oz, or even of Aussieland.

I do spot the kiwis, who tell me that they are to appear, but not with one of the many Herculeses and Xenas present, as one would think, them all having New Zealand in common, since the shows named after the respective superheroes are filmed in N.Z. No, the kiwi are associated with the alien beings from the planet Enoziwt, where they are a prominent feature, with their green-dyed quills, of the native animal life. In fact, they are the only animal life, as it is a very low-budget show.

I work my way behind endless '*Trek* uniforms and various trailing alien appendages (a popular costume ploy) made from feathers, scales, silicone, rubber, and what appears to be gummy-bears stuff.

I do not have much time. I can see the curtains trembling preparatory to being drawn open to reveal the chorus line of invented denizens of galaxies far and near for a final look before the judges choose the winners.

Once that curtain is whisked away from this display of feminine pulchritude, earthly and alien, and of masculine extremes of warriorhood and monsterhood, I know the flash cubes will go nova all over this place. They have already provided a twinkling Milky Way as each entry paraded down the runway.

And once the applause begins at the revealed mass of Masquerade contestants, I will have no chance to hear a single click in the tsunami of sound.

Then I get a reprieve.

The emcee announces a final entry.

I hear the entry's advent first, simply because I have been concentrating on ear power.

Thump, thump, thump. Not a click in a carload of thumps. Rats. Perhaps it was expecting too much for the perpetrator to announce himself to one and all, at least by his clicks. I always hope for the happy ending, though, being an old-fashioned kind of guy.

I fear it is another one of these heavy-booted types. I will have to watch my tail. One misplaced thump and my rear is in a splint.

I edge away but do not allow my view to be obstructed.

Well.

Well done.

When I see the eerily glowing figure push through an opening break in the line of masqueraders to the front of the stage, it is all I can do to restrain my applause.

A radioactive Khatlord ghost. Part Frankenstein, part Swamp Thing. And the mask . . . more leopards should come in hologram-green with black spots. The kiwis will fade in the shade next to this electric dude.

Oops. "Electric" was a tasteless choice of adjectives for the late bearer of the Khatlord crown.

Who, I wonder, did they get to impersonate the corpse?

Chapter 53

Unmasked

If Temple had offed the guy, she'd be pretty unhinged by now.

Apparently Timothy Hathaway's killer was made of sterner stuff.

No one stirred in the vast room. Everyone sensed that this ghastly figure had come to accuse, and they couldn't wait to hear what he would say, presuming this walking mummy could speak.

Hanford Schmidt had propped up his feet at the judge's table, was rattling his chains ostentatiously as he flourished his snapping-turtle pen, and was looking around for a mike.

But the only mike at the table was in front of Matt, and his clasped hands around the base indicated that he wasn't about to give it up to a man who'd already used up his fifteen minutes.

The King Khatlord thumped to the very lip of the stage. There he stopped, looking over the entire audience and even turning to view the gathered contestants forming a fabulous chorus line at the stage curtain.

His out-thrust arm swung from side to side like an accusing pendulum, the gesture wooden and laden with significance.

What a ham, Temple thought, and then: *Is it Max? No!*

She glanced at the Cloaked Conjuror.

He was tilting back in his folding chair, arms crossed over his chest, the leopard-spotted mask an eerie twin to the face of the creature on stage.

The Cloaked Conjuror had killed the Khatlord? No, *he* was Max. Right?

The Khatlord lifted a hand to his neck, twisted it, and then pulled back, ripping the catlike mask from his face in one, long, smooth pull.

Temple winced, remembering how the monomaniacal fan John Gersohn had been unmasked so brutally by the security Khatlord, who couldn't possibly have been Max. Where had that fan-guy been, anyway? No one had seen him since the confrontation. Could he have killed his idol and skipped town?

No . . . because as the Khatlord's head rose from doffing the mask and as his natural features lifted to the warming spotlights, they became unmistakably and clearly . . .

. . . Timothy Hathaway.

Chapter 54

No Takers

Or was that a Timothy Hathaway mask under the Khatlord mask? Temple wondered.

In this special-effects crowd, anything was possible.

The Khatlord tucked his displaced mask underneath his arm, as one of Henry VIII's wives was said to have done with her head, and began a grand tour of the stage, circling so even the contestants could view his resurrected, and smug, features.

Every dog must have his day, and Timothy Hathaway obviously loved to lap up all the attention he could muster.

It struck Temple that he was a high-profile target right now.

Who had arranged this? Why? Obviously to startle the killer into the open, but why would anyone think a murderer would fall for the old resurrected-corpse trick?

The walkabout was clearly designed to show that Hathaway was the real thing, but Temple couldn't be sure, because nothing was what it seemed to be at a convention for which everybody was pretending to be somebody else.

The reappearance was spectacular, but Temple was betting it would be a spectacular bust as well. No killer in his or her right mind was going to look at a figure in Day-Glo green paint and break down and confess.

Nice try, whoever concocted this finale, but dead end.

Chapter 55

Torn Between Two Killers

I am afraid that I must admit that if I *had* been an ape's uncle, the human race would not be in any better straits than it is today.

For while I realize that this Khatlord revival has been engineered to tip someone's hand, it is obvious that the hand in question, whosoever it belongs to, is not tipping.

Obviously, it is up to me to turn the tide, but how?

I look frantically up and down the assembled feet and legs of the Masquerade contestants. Even the poor little kiwi are in the line, uncaged, but on almost-invisible fishline leashes held by their alien masters from the planet Enoziwt, who are not even going to be finalists, in my opinion.

The kiwi are out of their cages.

I forget about hunting a human miscreant with my ears and look around with my feline eyes.

She is hunkered behind the Khatlord Kompendium contingent in the shadow of a platform boot. A twinkle ricochets off her iridescent snakeskin harness like faint starlight. It catches on the sickle moon of one bared fang.

The kiwi are feather dusters!

I hunch down, measuring the many feet to my right I must spring to avert a massacre.

My left ear flattens. I hear the faintest of clicks, the merest suggestion of unpremeditated motion to my far left. The Khatlord appearance has discomfited someone. I immediately calculate how many feet to my left I must spring to literally nail a murderer.

One will kill. One has killed.

Who to stop?

It is a lose-lose situation.

Dead kiwis will decimate an already brutalized population.

The human killer has already done his or her worst.

I am torn.

Then I receive a bolt of inspiration from an event I have already participated in. My eye falls on a genuine steel sword a weary vignette member has set on the stage floor.

I leap for it, pulling back the last moment, so my rear feet kick into it with full force and with the motion pool players call English. The sword goes spinning down the slick stage floor toward my target. Like Hercules and Xena in their chain-reaction spin, it is lethal and inevitable.

I glimpse Hyacinth's eyes widening to the whites.

I have no time to watch more. I am bounding left.

In the stir the spinning sword leaves in its wake, my prey has decided to slip away.

Click, click, click.

Not a weapon, but a crutch.

Click, click, click.

Still behind the lines, as it were, I find the one person shuffling off stage behind the chorus line of contestants. Undercover. Luckily, the costume is a standard Federation uniform and not particularly impenetrable.

I catch up with the boots, overtake the one boot with the steel brace under the arch to correct an impediment.

I leap up, sink my fangs canine deep into the smooth flesh of the bulge called a calf, just above the boot top.

Satisfying screams of frustration reverberate simultaneously from my right and from my left.

Curses, foiled again, folks.

So sorry.

Chapter 56

A Kiwi Chorus Line

"*Keewee, keeewee, keewee,*" came the eerie call from the far side of the contestants' line.

A gaggle of luridly green birds scurried like guinea pigs through the feet of their captors into stage center. Even Timothy Hathaway, basking in his King Khatlord persona's triumphant return from the dead, stopped strutting at center stage to gawk at the scene-stealing kiwis. A man in a *Star Trek* uniform moved forward in slow motion to corral the kiwi birds. No, he was staring at Hathaway as if the undisguised actor's features were a mask. Hathaway returned the stare. The other man shrieked suddenly and dove off the stage, hitting the floor hard and limping toward the side aisle.

Temple heard the faint click of Hanford Schmidt's damned pen, but her attention was more abruptly jerked to the judges' table by something louder and more violent. A heavy crash.

Matt was standing up, hands reaching out. The judges' table lay

on its side. Schmidt wasn't clicking his pen, but his chains were
swinging.

The science fiction writers sitting at the table's far side had
vanished behind the Cloaked Conjuror, who crouched behind the
upended table like a hunter in a blind who was now the hunted.
Xena was leaping the overturned table edge in superhero fashion,
her flying forward motion making the studded leather blades of
her kilt clash like crossed swords.

Mariah had grabbed Temple's elbow and was jerking it like a
pump handle. "There it is! There it is!"

Their little corner of the world was a far cry from the hubbub
on stage as kiwi birds scattered in all directions.

Temple watched Xena bowl over a figure in a far-future uniform
not twelve feet in front of them: ancient fantasy versus fantastic
future.

The figure scrabbled to its feet and lurched away.

Xena was up, launching her feet in a double kick at its knees.

It toppled. Xena dove atop it, then reached into her knee-high
boot and pulled out something that shone metallic silver.

Temple clapped a hand over Mariah's eyes.

A dagger was definitely PG-13 and probably an "R."

While Mariah struggled to avoid Temple's grip, Xena kneed her
victim to the floor, pinned one twisted arm to the small of the back
with one hand, and swung her weapon into play with the other.

Temple cringed.

Oh. Not a dagger.

Bracelets.

No.

Handcuffs.

Handcuffs?

Before Temple—or Mariah—could blink, the figure, hands
bound behind its back, was dragged upright by . . . well, what else?
By Peter Pan and a middle-aged male fan wearing a T-shirt featuring a painting of a plate of spaghetti with a severe mold problem and a banner of strange device: Cthulhu. Their prisoner,
looking like the Phantom of the Opera at first glance, proved to

be wearing a simple mask, half black, half white. So he was still an enigma, as was Xena, Warrior Princess.

She tossed back her long black hair. Her bright blue eyes flashed the lightning of the gods.

Temple polled the people left at the judge's table. Still no writers were visible. The Cloaked Conjuror was peeping over the edge. He was not Max, and Max was not him.

Matt was shoving the table aside to reach her and Mariah. "Are you two okay?"

Temple nodded. Mariah nodded.

"What happened?" Temple asked.

Xena, breathing a tad hard, approached them, gear rattling. "An arrest. Everybody okay?" She surveyed the three, then turned to crane her neck to see the people still behind the table.

Nearby, T-shirt fan and Peter Pan bracketed a figure with a lowered head.

Temple nodded greeting to Detectives Alch and Su. Su was not Peter Pan, but an elf. Close enough.

Mariah's grip on Temple's elbow tightened, then loosened.

"Mom?" she said, and her tone was priceless—half wonder, half horror.

Temple guessed that this is what fantasy is all about.

"Shhhh." Xena put a finger to her lips. "Can you two"—she looked at Matt and Temple—"take Mariah home and put her up for the night? I'll explain later."

"I don't want to go home with them, I wanta see my cats—"

"I've got a cat," Temple said. "I think."

"Mo-om," Mariah protested.

"Shhh," Xena said. "We're all undercover."

"I can't believe it," Matt said as if he couldn't help himself. "What ever made you think of—?"

Xena's blue eyes glanced into the ancient distance. "Someone told me I couldn't disguise my eyes. So . . . I decided to let my eyes be the disguise."

"But," Temple began.

Xena put her hands on her hips. "Hey. This isn't so different from the outfits I wore when I was working vice in L.A. Only thing I'm going to miss is these boots. I guess in Las Vegas, naked is the best disguise." She tossed her hair and holstered her chakra. "Take good care of the sprout." After tousling Mariah's cool haircut, she was gone.

So were Alch and Su with their prisoner.

"We don't even know who—" Temple started to storm at Matt.

"You have the big, fat, lazy, black cat, right?" Mariah was asking. "My cats sleep with me. Do you let him sleep with you?"

"Sometimes," Temple said, smiling although she was still exasperated with everybody. "When he's good."

Molina was pleased. Kid outa here; suspect nailed; no one the wiser.

A Khatlord blocked her path.

She stiffened.

"You done with me?" he asked.

She sighed and recognized the ghostly green paint. "Yeah. Thanks. We'll be in touch tomorrow."

He didn't move out of her way, although with her platform boots she probably had two inches on him.

"You did a wonderful job," she said.

Honey dislodged him like lighter fluid-loosened masking tape.

She moved on.

The Masquerade was in shambles. No winners had been declared. She looked back to see that Matt had been delayed by a tall guy in a Hawaiian shirt who was dredging the shell-shocked judges up from their bunker.

Mariah and Temple Barr were waiting for Matt to finish, but they would soon be gone. She knew Alch and Su would see that both the suspect and those two got off the lot safely.

Meanwhile, Wonder Woman had to get back to wardrobe to trade in her bullet-repelling wrist cuffs.

Molina felt pretty good. Mariah had been goggle-eyed. Impressing her daughter had not been the point, but it wasn't an unwelcome side effect. Devine hadn't been totally surprised, but she'd been forced to chitchat with him at the judge's table. The look in Barr's eyes was worth the bruises.

A hand reached out to her upper arm and stopped her head-long progress. Cinderella had to get her battle gear back to the fairy godmother pretty damn quick.

Another Khatlord! Would the species never end?

"Hey!" he said. "I like your style. I used to know a woman with eyes like you."

"Yeah?" she said. "Crossed?"

But her heart had stopped. She looked into the eyes peering through the mask and saw the past. Where was Mariah? Not yet out of here. Suddenly triumph, motion, breathing were things of the past.

He had found her.

"Odd color," he was saying. "I wanted to forget a lot about that woman, but I couldn't forget the eyes."

Speechless. Her voice. Two words she could bark out, but how many more would no longer fool him?

Another gauntlet clapped heavily over her shoulders.

Don't freak. Knee-jerk martial arts would only tip him off. Apparently he hadn't seen anything but her walking along, and that was enough.

"Hey, Sheila-bird," a voice vibrated in her ear in a down-under accent. "A bunch of us are getting together for a bit of kiwi beer before we head off to that long flight back to New Z. Ready to party?"

She turned to look into the eyes of another Khatlord. The Khatlord standing in front of her dropped his hand from her arm, confused.

"We've done enough stunts for these Yanks." The arm around her shoulder tightened and shook her as if to shake out her brains, her agreement. "Right? Save something for the cameras back home. You don't want to lose your edge on this kiwi-shit convention. It's TitaniCon, all right. Big and disastrous."

He laughed and pulled her away with him, into the crowd of milling, chattering fans.

"That was—?" she started to say, then couldn't finish.

"Him. Yes. Where are you headed?"

"Xena's room. Stunt double. Promised to return the outfit."

"Where's Mariah?"

"With your Miss Barr."

"Good idea."

Max Kinsella slung her around as if she were a paper doll, and at the moment she was.

"I'd like to hang with you, babe," he announced for the benefit of the crowd, although it likely no longer sheltered the likes of Rafi Nadir. "But I've got to get some shut-eye before our flight tomorrow. And someday," he added for her ears only, "I've got to find out the reason for *that*." The Khatlord jerked his head in the direction of the man they'd left behind. "Got to run. Plan to follow a fox to earth. Tally-ho."

He was gone, with the wind.

Xena looked around, hunting with her eyes.

Carmen was not pleased, but too unnerved to do much about it.

And Lieutenant Molina was madder than spit.

Chapter 57

Auld Acquaintance

The judges were disgruntled.

Xena had walked off and left them one short.

The cochair was bugging them for quick decisions on twenty categories.

Worst of all, they couldn't leave to tell everyone about the incident they'd witnessed until the judging was done.

Matt and the Cloaked Conjuror righted the table, but the magician seemed nervous about sitting behind it in plain view.

The writers gathered up the scattered notes. It took the panel five minutes to sort out each other's jottings and to eliminate Xena's by default.

"Let's move," Hanford Schmidt decreed, tossing his chains aside. "Ten minutes and I want to be out of here."

So they pulled their folding chairs closer together and named Grand Champion Group, Single, Fantasy, Science Fiction, Media.

The major awards were most obvious and most easily dispersed. The devil of dissension was in the minor ones.

Matt was in concert with the others until they reached the last category: Most Clever. The three writers wanted to award this to the three-hundred pound Wookie. Matt could agree that the costume was professionally accurate and even costly, but no way could he—or the Cloaked Conjuror—see wearing a furry suit as particularly clever.

Matt proposed the buxom serving wench who turned the tables on Conan the Barbarian for being such a cheap tipper, with the Cloaked Conjuror's eager second.

"She was a dog," Schmidt said. "A woman that weight should never wear a belly-dancer's costume. It's visual pollution."

"Wait a minute," Matt objected. "Why should a guy that weight, and more, wear a Wookie costume? The Wookie in *Star Wars* was extremely tall and thin, as well as hairy. The tavern wench arranged the veiling very cleverly to camouflage her weight, and, besides, the whole point of the piece was that she was a woman of substance and didn't have to take what Conan was dishing out."

"Feminist crap," one of the other writers said.

"And who just jumped out to stop that guy who probably murdered someone here two days ago? One of us guys?"

"The tavern bit was funny and well-acted," the Cloaked Conjuror said sharply. "And I need to get out of here." He looked over his shoulder. Matt realized that the two men in civilian clothes holding up the wall behind them were his bodyguards.

"It took a lot of nerve for the overweight guy to enter at all," one writer said stubbornly.

"So this is a sympathy category?" Matt was glad Molina wasn't here. Apparently all women contestants were judged on their Perfect Ten bodies, period. "There's room for three-hundred-pound guys who just stand there covered in hair suits, but not for two-hundred-fifty-pound women who not only make a revealing costume work for them, but use it to make an amusing point about big guys, and big girls? A clever counterpoint to the rotten attitude of the emcee-artist, who was disappointed because the only breasts he might get to autograph at a science fiction con were so huge he'd need to use a roller."

"So what is it?" asked Schmidt, who literally sat in the middle of the two sides. "Three votes for the fuzzball and two for the fat girl? Simple math makes the answer plain." He rapped his empty beer bottle on the table. "The award goes to the girl in the industrial-strength garter belt."

"Hey," the writers said in chorus.

"I changed my vote," Schmidt answered. "Fat girls don't do a thing for me, either, but the radio shrink and the magician have a point. Besides, the Wookie is from one of those damn media empires, and Conan and the bar girl are from a bunch of books written by an actual novelist. Let's reward originality and the written word while we still have some left."

And that was that.

The judges handed the emcee a final sheet and were abandoning the table even before the winners could be announced from the stage.

"Got to avoid being trapped by the crowd," the Cloaked Conjuror muttered to Matt, rising to join his bodyguards, who hustled him out.

Schmidt bailed next. "I gotta find out what pathetic worm got grabbed by the 'feminazi.' "

"I've got a kid to get home." Matt nodded at Temple and Mariah to follow him in a quick exit.

Mariah looked longingly at the stage, wanting to stay until the last award was announced, but Temple whispered something to her and she came along quietly.

"What were you judges arguing about at the end?" Temple whispered to Matt when they were sidling discreetly along the side wall on the way out.

Already other attendees were rising to get a jump on the forthcoming mob-departure scene.

"Sexism and female body image," Matt said.

"Good thing Xena was gone by then."

"That's what I thought," he said. "Let's try to stick together. This crowd is going to cause a traffic jam all the way to the exit doors."

It was too late. By the time they reached the back row of doors, people six deep were pressing forward in an almost unmoving mass. Triple that number pinned them into the mess from behind.

Temple and Mariah linked arms, while Matt shepherded them forward from behind.

Inching ahead in the chatter and the crush, Matt wished he had left the judges' table sooner. This meltdown would take at least forty minutes to clear.

Each immediate goal seemed endless: funneling through the narrow neck of the doors, edging over the hall carpeting toward the escalators.

A heavyset woman of the type Matt had just championed pushed between him and Temple and Mariah. He didn't like that, taking his responsibility for the girl even more seriously now that her mother had consigned her to Temple and himself for the night. And wasn't that a curiosity?

Two burly Klingons pushed the people next to him aside, and behind the first woman. He could still glimpse Temple's blond wig and see flashes from Mariah's plastic-bead headdress.

He tried to push ahead, but too many people were pushing in from the sides to get onto the escalator. They were all body-to-body, front-to-back and back-to-front, the mindless kind of crush that could kill people if anything happened to make them panic and run.

Before he knew it, Temple and Mariah were completely invisible.

He kept pushing, forcing himself forward. Finally he got a foot on a top escalator step it was too crowded to see. People all around him were tripping and grabbing at other people's body parts as they tried to stabilize themselves at the top of what was now an avalanche of moving flesh and bone.

Matt used the view from the escalator top to scan the heads below—there! Temple had Mariah by the shoulder and was at the bottom of the long, long slope, looking back and up for him.

Don't look up too long, he wanted to yell. *The bottom's coming at you.*

Someone behind Matt swayed close and curled a hand over his left shoulder. Hard.

Something pressed into his right kidney. Harder.

Some idiot wearing a sword in this melee . . .

A strange scent made his nostrils flare. A woman's perfume, but like no perfume he'd encountered before. Elusive.

The head of the person on the step above lowered to offer an apology.

"Sorry, Mr. Midnight." The voice was low with a silken undercurrent of warning. "Just remember that I'm not done with you."

He glanced at his shoulder. The graceful strong fingers grasping him ended in talons painted a delicate poison green.

The object at his back jabbed, just as he wrenched sideways.

He felt a numbing pain and sensed something dropping to the escalator step. People ahead of him turned to frown, then stumbled for their lack of attention as the moving steps vanished into the main floor.

Matt stumbled off the escalator with them, still trying to twist to look behind, to spot whatever had jabbed him.

He was shoved to the side with his fellow sardines to make room for more riders fanning out from the escalator.

"Here!" someone shouted.

A hand grabbed his elbow and pulled him back, along the escalator's solid side. Temple, Mariah still glued to her.

People were all pushing forward like lemmings, so the shelter of the escalator wall offered breathing room.

"We thought we'd lost you," Temple said. "What were you looking for just now?"

"Something jabbed me and fell."

"There it is!" Mariah twisted loose and bent down to pick up something that someone's foot had kicked into a small open spot of floor.

"Mariah!" Temple sounded exasperated. "You could get trampled."

"Look! How neat." She held up a strange object of silver metal, with a handle and a bulbous end. "Is this what poked you?"

"Could be." Matt now had room to run a hand over the small of his back. The muscle felt sore, as if slightly bruised. That was all. This time. He took the object from Mariah. He had been afraid of a syringe. Kept it.

He studied the faces still streaming down the escalator, masked visages mingling with the unmasked.

"You take Mariah home," he told Temple. "I'll come along later."

She didn't argue, having read trouble in his eyes.

"And, Temple."

She hesitated, awaiting instructions.

"Take a very circuitous route home."

She nodded.

He knew he planned to.

Chapter 58

Buffy-Slayer

Max deserved a break today.

It was two A.M. Sunday. Empty streets were a welcome change from the carnival-style overcrowding of TitaniCon. He enjoyed not wearing spandex and a leopard muzzle as a second skin.

He felt leopard-smug, though. He had tracked Rafi Nadir back to his den, a residential motel on the downtown's unfashionable fringe a couple notches up from the Blue Mermaid and less likely to be patrolled by the police. Know where an opponent lived, and you had an inestimable edge.

Even better, Nadir had gone straight from the New Millennium to his own rathole. He hadn't followed any of the principals in the action at TitaniCon home, including Max's personal principal, Temple.

Max smiled at her gaudy efforts to disguise Mariah Molina and her own transformation into Buffy, the Vampire Slayer. Max thought Buffy deserved a postmidnight visit from her boyfriend, Angel. And she would get one.

He parked around the corner from the Circle Ritz and kept the Big Cat persona to move from shadow to shadow as he approached the building. He paused by the apartment building's foundation.

Temple adored its fifties design and details, even if that meant putting up with the tiniest tiled bathrooms on the face of the planet. She loved its round exterior shape and black-marble facing, its triangular patios, the odd-shaped rooms, the private entry halls and doorbells to each unit, the arched ceilings.

Max relished all that, too, but Temple would have been disappointed to know that when he saw the building he fell in love at first sight with its easy exterior footholds. The Circle Ritz was a second-story man's dream, which is why he was always nagging Temple to put better locks on the rank of French doors to the patio. She resisted replacing the vintage hardware. One of these days he'd slip over while she was gone and do the job himself.

But for now, the vintage hardware was man's best friend. Max started climbing the black marble, whose blocks obligingly canted out here and there because of the round construction. From the first-floor balcony he stretched up to the next, caught onto an upright bar, then pulled himself up and over onto Temple's patio.

A rustle in the overhanging palm tree made him look over his shoulder just in time to see a small black shadow fall like a coconut to the patio tile. Except it made no impact noise.

"I suppose you were out trailing prey, too," he whispered to Midnight Louie.

The cat rubbed against his black trouser legs, more to pick up and deposit scents than to display affection, Max guessed. Then Louie inserted a paw under one of the French doors and began jiggling it.

"Not that way." Max used the ever-handy credit card to push back the lock. Before he could do more, Midnight Louie leaped up to depress the lever. This was a joint operation. The door sprung slightly open, then more so as Louie eeled inside.

Max paused again. The damn cat was taking all the fun out of this.

He moved inside silently, then shut and locked the door as soundlessly.

As he turned into the room, the moonlight and streetlights reflected off the arched white ceiling, highlighting the pale sofa.

The pale sofa bed.

Who's been sleeping in my sofa bed? Papa Bear wondered, creeping over to look.

Ah. Ravenlocks. He smiled down at Mariah's features glimpsed through sleep-tossed strands of hair.

Like most kids, she would be almost impossible to wake. Light sleeping only plagued adults. He hadn't the faintest idea why she was here, and she had not the faintest idea of what danger she'd been in for the past three days, or how frantic her mother was at the thought.

But it was over now . . . for now, and Max seldom had the chance to see those he protected sleep the sleep of the untroubled.

It was enormously satisfying. While he watched, Midnight Louie jumped up on the covers and settled in at her feet.

"You watch her, old man," he softly told the cat. "I'll take the bedroom."

The bedroom door creaked slightly when he opened it. Max always made sure that doors and windows in any place he ever lived were never oiled. He liked to hear things go bump, or creak, in the night. It kept him alive.

He knew when this creak would come and steadied the door to disarm it before opening it further, then shutting it, and then turning, so slowly, the deadbolt lock. All his bedroom doors had deadbolt locks, the better to buy time to reach for and find a weapon.

This room was darker. He moved slowly, aware of Temple's penchant for walking out of her shoes where she felt like it. Barefoot girl when she wasn't on high heels.

The zebra-stripe comforter revealed itself to his dark-adapting eyes first, then the lump under it.

He sat near the foot, carefully, so the springs didn't tremble, and leaned forward in inches until he could hear her breath.

"Hello," she said, sounding neither sleepy or startled.

"Did I wake you?"

"Not really. I was too excited to sleep."

"Oh?"

"I noticed that the Masquerade costumes could easily have provided the props for Jeff Mangel's death scene."

"True. Another tie-in."

"But mostly I've been wondering who the murderer is. Wasn't it nasty of Molina to rush off without telling anyone?"

"She had a lot to think about, including your young visitor."

"Yeah. Isn't that weird? She sent her kid home with us."

"Us?"

"Well, Matt followed us home, but he said to take a very circuitous route."

"He did, did he?"

"He did, and I did, and we're all right, aren't we?"

"Perfect." Max did what he had been resisting doing with Mariah and tucked the twisted covers under her chin.

"You came to tuck me in? Get real, Kinsella! Where were you anyway? For a minute I thought you might be the resurrected Khatlord, and before that the Cloaked Conjuror, and before that—Hey, give those covers back!"

"I thought you didn't want to be tucked in."

"There's tucking in, and there's . . . tucking in."

He moved up, tucked himself in beside her. "I was there."

"Did you see Molina?"

"Yes."

"Incredible. And then palming her kid off on us. Me." Temple sat up. "She'll hear."

"Not likely."

Temple settled down again. "So you were there and saw it all."

"I saw your Buffy imitation. Fairly fetching. You make a cute blond."

"Really? You think so?"

"I'm here, aren't I?"

"You saw me there? You were watching me?"

"I was watching a lot of people. But I liked watching you best."

"Oooh. Isn't this a little . . . risky? I mean, with the kid in the other room?"

"Uh-huh."

"I see."

Max turned her face to his in the dark.

"I mean, I don't *see* that way, but I see the other way." She paused because she had to. "And, I suppose, Buffy had Angel stay in her room when her mother was in the house."

"We hope so."

"And you can come and go as quietly as any vampire around. . . ."

"We know so."

"We're not ever going to be angsty about this, are we?"

"I hope not. At least not until the second season."

"Good. I am not in the mood for angst."

"What are you in the mood for?"

"Whatever you can come up with."

Chapter 59

Faceoff

"Dolores is there," Molina told Temple over the phone at nine-thirty A.M. Sunday morning. *At nine-thirty* A.M. "You can drop Mariah home as soon as possible and then come downtown."

"Downtown?"

"My place. The police station? Are we tracking yet?"

"Okay."

"And bring Darian, the Librarian."

"Huh?"

"Giles. Mr. Devine. Everything went all right?"

"Went?"

"With Mariah last night."

"Oh. With Mariah. Fine. I put her on the hideabed and Louie slept beside her all night long."

"Louie." Molina sighed. "Don't take too long."

So Temple called Matt and made Mariah wash her face in the

392 • Carole Nelson Douglas

spare bathroom. Then she fed her some dry cereal with milk that neither of them liked.

"Maybe Dolores will give you a good breakfast," Temple suggested halfway through, "when you get home."

"Mom won't be there?"

"She called from her office. Guess they're busy booking and grilling whoever she tackled last night at TitaniCon."

"You don't know who?"

"Nope."

Matt knocked five minutes later, looking fed and rested. He refused the cereal. Temple couldn't blame him. He commented that she looked a little tired. Temple couldn't comment back. Being a Slayer, even a retired one, involved an intense commitment and a lot of late nights.

They took Matt's Volkswagen, Mariah bouncing around in the back seat like a restless kitten.

The dour Dolores welcomed Mariah back into the house without question, and they soon were on their way downtown. Being a passenger put Temple to sleep, so there wasn't much time to discuss the events of the previous day and night.

By the time they had been escorted into Molina's office, though, Temple was alert and eager.

Seeing Molina as Molina was hard after accepting her as Xena, the Warrior Princess, just yesterday. Temple kept expecting her to pull a chakra out of her desk drawer.

Instead, she had been eating lunch out of a takeout white Styrofoam container. She set it aside the moment they arrived. "Su and Alch are interrogating the suspect. Would you like to watch?"

"Would I?" Temple tried to contain herself. "Would we? Sure."

"Follow me."

Molina led them down a nondescript hall to a nondescript door. Once behind it, they faced a very nonnondescript piece of plate glass that gave them a fairly full view of interrogation room.

There was so little in the room—drab walls, floor, a bolted-down table and chairs, tape recorder, ashtray, Su, Alch, Hanford Schmidt.

"Hanford Schmidt?" Temple burst out, then covered her mouth.

"They can't hear us," Molina reassured her, "though we can hear them."

"But. . . . he was at the judges' table. He can't be the killer. He can't be the guy you tackled. Or is that the other way around? He *is* the killer, but he isn't the guy you tackled?"

"Relax. He's the suspect's lawyer."

"Hanford Schmidt is a lawyer?"

"He's licensed to practice."

"But who—" Temple strained to look past Hanford to whoever was sitting on his other side. Apparently the Invisible Man.

"You mean you really haven't the slightest idea?" Molina was looking more cheerful by the minute.

"No! I don't even know how you managed to mislead the press that the victim was Hathaway and then got Hathaway to lay low until you were ready to have him make a shocking reappearance."

"Wasn't hard," Molina admitted. "We only found out it wasn't Hathaway when the victim was stripped of his costume for the autopsy. I figured if we were deceived, the killer might have been. So we roused Hathaway at his hotel and convinced him to go underground because someone might be after him and would soon know was still alive. Plus, Hathaway loved the idea of coming back from the dead; figured he'd get some good publicity out of it."

"He will." Temple frowned. "So if you knew early on that the victim wasn't Hathaway, then the killer could have meant to kill Hathaway . . . or have known that the Khatlord he pushed into the neon sign *wasn't* Hathaway and wanted to kill *him,* if it was a him, given that even women can wear those height-enhancing boots and pass as men; look at you—"

Molina looked at Matt. "You've been quiet. Any theories?"

"Only that I think it was a mistake."

"The murder? Don't you believe that murder is always a mistake?" Molina gave Matt a challenging smile.

"This one was a tragic mistake, I think. I don't know anything. Just that."

"Give the boy a gold star." Molina stepped away from the glass so they both could see. "Behold the man."

Matt, more puzzled than shocked, sat on one of the armless chairs provided. Temple, her sight line still blocked, muttered, "Apparently an unthinkably low-profile killer."

"Murder is unthinkable," Molina commented, "and sometimes the murderer is, too." She smiled as Schmidt unrolled some righteous spiel on the other side of the glass. "One thing about those militaristic alien-race costumes. Leather takes a heck of a hand print. Except we didn't know whose hand to look for."

"That's why the hokey Khatlord resurrection at the Masquerade," Temple said. "You were betting the murderer didn't know he'd killed the wrong victim and that you could flush him out."

"Hokey, yes. But let's say I was in good company, Buffy. And Giles." She favored Matt with a wink.

"That hand print told us the murder was unpremeditated," she went on. "With all the elaborate gloves and feature-altering costumes around TitaniCon, a prepared murderer would have disguised his presence better. But with so many suspects all over the place, and such weird ones, and the fact that the victim was wearing a costume like dozens of other attendees . . .

She looked into the room. "Now that we've got him, we've got him cold. Whorls never lie. This case will be decided in the courts on motivation, intention. And motivation and intention, not guilt, are what made the guy bolt when the Khatlord appeared in person and revealed that Timothy Hathaway was not dead. That's when the play became the thing to snare the conscience of a . . . not a king, in this case. Far from it."

"Jeez, Lieutenant," Temple whined. "Give us a break. Who is it?"

"We'll have to wait for Mr. Schmidt to sit down and stop declaiming."

"Never, you mean," Temple said morosely. "I have seen his shtick."

Molina sat beside Matt. "I do love to see my detectives sink their teeth into a suspect."

"All right!" Alch, driven to his limit, bellowed that phrase inside the interrogation room.

Well, Alch *was* a nice guy, so he only snapped wearily, like a tired basset hound. "Sit down, Mr. Schmidt. Your client has volunteered to answer some questions. Why don't you let him?"

"Sit," Su decreed in a dog-obedience-school tone.

Schmidt looked at her as if for the first time, blinked, and then sat. Obviously, he was in love.

Temple sat forward as she finally saw the man sitting at the table on Schmidt's left. "No. Mr. Cool? Mr. Intermediary? Mr. Fringe Person? Alan Dahl?"

"Let him tell it," Molina advised.

Alan Dahl was a writer, the pale drinking straw of a man who had tried to calm down Schmidt as he had attacked the Khatlord coauthor, Greg Seltz.

He looked scholarly, and now he looked confused. And terribly, terribly sorry.

"Thanks, Hanford," he said to his frenetic defender. "I guess I'd reached dead bottom. When I learned that Greg Seltz was furious that his book was the blueprint for the first Khatlord film, all I could think of was that Hathaway would need a new coauthor. A new ghost writer. I . . . hadn't been able to sell my own work for two years. You were right, Hanford. Nobody wanted to read about Esalen, the Elven adventurer, anymore. And, at my age, trying to reenter the job market . . . well, it wouldn't have been pretty. I wasn't treading on Greg Seltz's toes. I could see by the way he'd stormed out of the presentation that he hadn't known his right-to-work book had inspired the movie. He already knew that he wouldn't get any more money. But, you see, I really needed the advance. The up-front money. I wouldn't feel ripped off, because I just needed another few thousand to help support my wife and kids. I didn't care if I was being exploited. Not surviving is worse. Selling hamburgers at some fast-food place is really worse than writing for a few dollars, Hanford. You can ride on a reputation. I never had one. Just a bunch of books that sold decently enough to not be noticed by anyone until they raised the bar on the bottom line. So . . . I hung around after the presentation, hoping to catch Hathaway alone. Just to offer my services. To promise that

I wouldn't make any trouble. I'd be happy with what they could give me—"

"You poor, benighted sot," Schmidt began.

"Shut," Su said.

Temple noticed she only used words with sharp "T" sounds on Schmidt, as one was advised to do to capture the attention and compliance of dogs.

Rrrrightttt.

Schmidt shut.

Alan Dahl ran a tremulous-fingered hand through his thinning hair. "I went in after everyone had gone out. I hadn't seen the Khatlord leave. I never thought about him leaving by a back way.

"Anyway. There it was. An empty ballroom. An empty dais. That . . . massive neon sign blinking, and the Khatlord strutting in front of it, bigger than life, like Patton in the movie, declaiming something about, I don't know, the future empire and sovereignty and whatever.

"So I went up. He never noticed me until I stood before the stage. And I addressed him quite respectfully. Asked if I might have a word. Said I had a proposition.

" 'Approach, vassal,' he thundered. I understood. Actors get carried away by their roles. I understand they can't be a strong on-screen presence without some ego. So I came closer. Explained myself. Explained I wouldn't be a problem. He was striding back and forth in front of that Khatlord Konquers sign. It was so confusing, the neon blinking at me like a strobe light as his body moved back and forth, back and forth.

"And I just kept saying I'd be happy to cowrite his next Khatlord book. On any terms. I started to tell him about my publishing history, but he waved one of those gauntleted hands.

" 'You'll have to have your people talk to my people,' he said.

" 'People,' I said. 'I'm just a midlist author. Or was. I don't have "people." You and I can work it out,' I said. I went up the stairs to the stage, tried to get some sort of one-on-one situation. But the closer I came, the more he paced, like he was running in place. 'Away,' he said. 'I can't talk about it now.'

"But . . . you're the star,' I said. 'What you say goes. I'm just asking for a personal commitment here—'

"He went berserk. He ordered me to stay away. Said he couldn't talk about it. When I wouldn't leave, he started blustering and stuttering. Said I was not a writer he'd care to associate with. Said he was going to get somebody big next. Cormac McCarthy or somebody. Stephen King. I don't know. What he was saying was nuts, but all I heard was those household names, and I got so angry, and I . . . I hated the way he had just brushed me off as if nothing I had ever written or had to say mattered. So I . . ."

The hand was raking through his scalp like a metronome, drawing blood, but he didn't seem aware of it.

"I was just trying to make a point, that I existed, I was a reliable professional, I needed the work and knew better than to make any trouble, and he kept moving away and talking and not looking at me, not even through that stupid mask, and I got mad, madder than I've ever been, and I put up my hands, and I pushed him, pushed him against the wall so he'd have to listen, even though he was so much bigger, and I hadn't pushed anybody since kindergarten, and he . . . he pushed. He fell back. Against the wall. Only it was an . . . exploding wall of light, and he just stuck there, like a bug in an insect trap."

Dahl let his hands fall to the tabletop. "I guess he was dead. I guess I ran. I knew I'd killed the King Khatlord, but it felt like an episode, you know? On TV? It didn't seem real. Even when he came out on stage at the Masquerade, it didn't bother me. It wasn't real either. Not until the mask came off, and I saw that Timothy Hathaway wasn't dead, that he was alive. And then it was real. Because I didn't know then who I'd pushed. Because it couldn't have been a character on a TV show who deserved to fry anyway. It had to have been someone else, and I never wanted to kill anyone real. So I had to get out of there. I almost felt this spur, in the back of my leg. Had to get out of there. I wasn't running. I was trying to think. And then someone knocked me over and tied me up. For trying to think. That's all."

No one spoke in the interrogation room, which was quite a record for Hanford Schmidt.

No one spoke in the observation room.

"Who did he kill?" Temple finally asked. She was surprised to hear her own voice come hoarse and ragged, as if she had been confessing, not Dahl.

Molina glanced at Matt. "You gave the key testimony."

"I did?"

"When you tried to make Su and Alch feel better about interrogating people who weren't in the same timeline as the rest of us. You explained how the *Star Trek* performers wouldn't forsake their 'characters' for anything. That was the key to the murder. That's what got the guy killed. He wouldn't give up the character until it was too late."

"John Gersohn," Temple said. "The fanatic fan who kept showing up where Timothy Hathaway appeared. He was in the ballroom because he needed to take the stage in his hero's footsteps. He wouldn't promise Dahl anything, because he couldn't, and neither could he forsake the notion that he was the real Khatlord because his whole personality was tied up in it, so . . . he drove the Dahl guy nuts and fell into the impromptu electric chair for the sake of his obsession. Which of these two were the more deluded? Victim or killer?"

"That's for the courts to decide, and Hanford Schmidt, I'm sure, to argue endlessly." Molina stood and glanced into the other room. "I see Alch and Su are done for now. They've got a lot of transcript to go over. Shall we?"

She gestured to the door.

When the three emerged, only Su and Alch were leaving the interrogation room.

They nodded, grudgingly, at Matt and Temple.

"You need us for anything, Lieutenant?" Alch asked.

"No, just do your paperwork. I don't think that Schmidt guy has much to fall back on but the quality of mercy."

"Kinda pathetic, though," Alch commented.

"Nuts!" said Su.

They passed a pair of uniformed officers, who grinned and clapped their hands. "I do believe in fairies," they chorused.

Su did a rapid burn. "Idiots! They still can't tell an elf outfit from a Peter Pan."

"I'm sure glad I found that funky T-shirt," Alch congratulated himself. "Nobody here can pronounce Cthulhu."

"Not yet," Molina said as she peeled off into her office.

Matt and Temple followed.

She went to her desk, examined the residue of the Styrofoam container, and grimaced.

"What are you two still doing here? You have no corroborative statements to make. Skedaddle. And you never heard of Xena, right?"

"What do you take us for? Teenagers?" Temple asked indignantly.

"By the way," Molina said in farewell, "Mr. Dahl had a rather deep animal bite on his left calf. He wears a brace on that leg from a childhood surgery. We gave him some first aid on his arrival here. The doctor said it was definitely a domestic animal bite. He will have to undergo a series of rabies shots unless someone can produce an animal whose dental impressions match the bite that is up on its rabies shots."

"The only animal we know is Louie," Temple said, "and he had his rabies shots only a couple of months ago. Are you saying you need a cast of his teeth?"

"No. Only that you could spare Mr. Dahl some painful injections if you could prove that Louie bit him."

Temple thought. After hearing Dahl's testimony, she was betting that Hanford Schmidt could get him off with a manslaughter plea bargain. Painful shots? Well, he had killed a man, and they did rather extreme things to animals suspected of rabies, such as cutting off their heads. Better to not expose Louie to heartless bureaucrats.

They left.

Matt was smiling.

"What are you thinking about?" she asked.

"Besides Molina as Xena? I'm thinking that it's been quite a weekend. But I did learn one very valuable thing, what with everyone running around in Khatlord costumes and killing the wrong person, and other stuff."

"What's that?"

"That it's no good being an Invisible Man."

"Is that supposed to mean something to me?"

"It might. Someday."

Chapter 60

Sunday, Sunday

"What happened to your Xena costume?" Mariah asked, sounding disappointed.

"Give me a breather. I just got in the door." Molina sat on the nearest chair that wasn't occupied by a snoozing cat. "I had to give it back."

"It was really Xena's? And it fit you?"

"Close enough to fool a few people. It belonged to the Xena you saw doing the martial arts demonstration earlier in the convention."

"Is she really the real Xena's double?"

"One of them."

Mariah nodded sagely. "You could be another, I bet."

"I've got a job."

Mariah's nose wrinkled. She was wearing her ear thingie. She had sworn to wear it everywhere except where she wasn't allowed to: school on Monday morning.

There were times when Carmen thought a school uniform saved the sanity of half the mothers of the world.

"You don't mind not going back to TitaniCon today?" Carmen asked gingerly.

"Oh, no. What else could happen better than last night? I've never seen a criminal nabbed before. And wait'll the kids hear my own mother did it, in a Xena outfit."

"Uh, you don't have to mention the costume, Mariah."

"Are you kidding? That's the best part. Is it okay if I call Yolie?"

Carmen nodded. Hours on the phone giggling. What would come next would be minutes of awkward silence on the phone. With a boy. She leaned her head on her hand and enjoyed the sudden silence in the living room, the peace of cats asleep. She could use a few dozen catnaps herself.

Except that her brain was not asleep. It wasn't even the latest arrest that kept the mice running in double-time on the exercise wheel her mind had become lately. Although . . . she had an itchy feeling about the Khatlord killing. That first death, the man who might have fallen accidentally, or jumped to his death from the catwalk. It bothered her that he had never been identified, much less been tagged as a victim of deliberate death. Of course those science fiction costumes don't allow for carrying much twentieth-century ID, but his fingerprints came up clean, which only confirmed he likely was some innocent civilian dead through mischance rather than murder. Still, the coincidence of *two* Khatlord-attired men dying in the same week at the same convention . . .

She was getting a backlog of suspicious deaths as long as the lengthy arm of the law is supposed to be. And she had thought that the long-ago Goliath Hotel casino death—the one revealed the very day magician Max Kinsella had finished his engagement with the Goliath and celebrated by vanishing for almost a year, leaving Temple Barr flat—had been an annoying unsolved case on her record.

Now there was the magician's assistant, Gloria Fuentes, found in a parking lot, perhaps part of the "she's gone" sequence tied into the Blue Dalhia murder in Molina's own back yard. And now there was the professor who died in lurid ignominy, knifed on campus, a specialist in magic, of all things. And Cher, just the latest death to have a link to Max Kinsella.

Max Kinsella. And Rafi Nadir. Death and danger. Their names ran around and around the fringes of her sanity until their images appeared to blur and melt into each other.

Why Las Vegas? What was Rafi doing here? Did he suspect something about her? Did he have any notion of Mariah's existence? Was his presence here raw coincidence?

And what would Kinsella do now? He wouldn't leave Rafi alone; that was certain. The more he intruded in whatever game Rafi was making his own, the more likely he was to lead Rafi right to her. And to Mariah.

She replayed Raf's words to her Xena-self. He said he had *wanted* to forget a lot about a woman who had eyes just like hers. Wanted to, but had not been successful. She didn't take that as a compliment, but a threat. The Rafi Nadir she had left years ago in self-preservation had become a sly, bitter man with a volcanic temper. Seeing him again was her worst nightmare. She winced to think that it had taken Kinsella's intervention to shake her loose of the shock of confronting Raf again after all these years.

Raf had wanted her pregnant. He probably hadn't wanted a child. He had simply wanted her caught in circumstances beyond her control that he had created by sabotaging her diaphragm. Then he would have manipulated her guilt, whether she had gone through with the pregnancy or not. Either way she would have been guilty.

So she had left him. Vanished. Not unlike what Max Kinsella had done to Temple Barr, only his vanishing act had been a noble attempt to protect Temple. Hers had been an ignoble attempt to survive Rafi and to deprive him of the one thing he needed more than anything else. Control. If he found her, found Mariah, he'd want control back with a vengeance, and he'd be in a position to grab it. The last thing she wanted was Mariah confronted with a man who was her father in name and genetics only, who would see her merely as a tool to use against her mother.

How to defuse the possibilities?

The dead stripper, Cher, might be one way. Kinsella had his own addiction to guilt. He suspected Raf of that sad death and wouldn't let go until he was sure. Therefore . . . she needed to work that case. Find the killer. Kill two birds with one stone: get Kinsella off the Raf connection, remove Raf from suspicion, ironically.

She didn't think he'd killed the stripper. He liked control too much to let the objects of it escape so permanently. Unless his temper had exploded.

For a moment she remembered the young police officer she had met so long ago. Nothing like the man he had become, and yet . . . the poison had to have been there.

If he found them, what would he do? What would a court do? Give him anything? Like it or not, he was the father of her child. She liked it not.

Molina glanced up at the small wall mirror near the door. She was framed in it like a most-wanted fugitive, her vivid blue eyes visible even from across the room. Damn her eyes! She'd never liked them despite compliments over the years. They'd always marked her out as different, almost alien to the Hispanic culture she grew up in. And now they threatened to betray everything she had wrested from a life that guaranteed a long, steep uphill path.

Maybe she'd be forced to take a page from the Mystifying Max's book, and resort to color-changing contact lenses.

Matt got home Sunday evening from a solo dinner at a Mexican restaurant to find a message waiting on the answering machine he had been forced to invest in. Janice had called to invite him to dinner at her place Monday evening.

His eyebrows lifted as he heard her recorded voice explain that the kids were out of her hair for the day and she would have time to actually cook up something interesting. She hoped he was free. Did he have any culinary dislikes he wanted to register?

Matt found himself trying to remember if he had told her he had Monday and Tuesday off from the radio show and wouldn't have to be leaving by midnight.

His fingers felt a little cold, if not his feet. Janice wasn't the manipulative type . . . but she wasn't stupid either. *Why not?* he thought. Temple was hand-in-glove with Kinsella again. He'd seen it for himself when they got back to the Circle Ritz from some joyride somewhere. He was entitled to his own life. He'd been told to go forth and socialize. Maybe that meant putting himself in the path of possibility.

Thinking of possibilities, or impossibilities, there was something he had to do. He picked up the notepad, found the phone number for his former boss at ConTact and dialed.

"Glad I caught you in," he told him. "I hate to bother you on a Sunday, but I need Sheila's number. . . . Sheila. She's still volunteering for ConTact? . . . Oh, not as much since I've been gone. . . . Yeah, I've got a pencil. Thanks."

He looked at the number on his notepad. He had written it on a new page he could tear out. He hoped there'd be no reason to keep it. Matt dialed quickly, trying not to practice what to say.

She answered on the third ring.

"Sheila? It's Matt. Just checking to see how your ankle is. Good. And it's a good thing you left the Con early. The police got the person who killed the Khatlord. Yeah, right on site. It'll be in the papers in a couple days, I imagine. Timothy Hathaway wasn't the victim, after all. It was a fan in a Khatlord suit."

She expressed appropriate shock and wondered if he'd had a good time at TitaniCon.

"I had a time of it; that's for sure. At least the little girl wasn't hurt. Not so little, I know, but age-wise. . . . No, just working. I have a lot of out-of-town speaking engagements. They go with the on-air life. I just never know when I'll be in town, and of course I'm working every night . . . yeah, maybe we'll run into each other again. Take care."

He hung up. He was sorry, but he just couldn't take that kind of mooning attachment, not even to be nice. The fans outside the radio station after his show were enough. Unfortunately, their ranks were swelling. Leticia had paid for a couple more billboards after Elvis.

He supposed he should be grateful for his sudden worldly success, but guilt was a much more familiar companion. *Get over it.* He remembered Carmen Molina's terse advice. She'd been referring to Temple's reunion with her returned significant other. At least he'd only glimpsed Kinsella from a distance this week. The less seen of him, the better.

Now.

He looked at his watch. Only nine o'clock. Only a couple of hours to kill before he had to head to WCOO and listen to everybody else's problems on "The Midnight Hour." Mr. Midnight on the job, solving all problems, easing all heartaches, offering all empathy from midnight to one A.M.

What was he going to do to kill time until then?

The phone rang at about nine-thirty. The booming voice on the other end warmed him.

"Frank. I'm surprised to hear from you." God the Father, Matt thought, would probably sound like Frank Bucek, his ex–seminary instructor/father-confessor turned civilian FBI agent. Talk about authority figures.

"Been busy, Matt. Sorry to take so long getting back to you on that little item."

"What little item?"

"Don't tell me you've forgotten? Elvis."

"Who could forget—?"

"Anyway, I had the voice wizards go over the tapes of your conversations with the King of Never-say-die."

"And?"

"It's the darnedest thing. We're figuring a technological breakthrough. Someone has managed to splice, maybe digitally, we're thinking, actual tape of the King talking, syllable by syllable, into a darn convincing facsimile."

"You're saying it's Elvis?"

406 • Carole Nelson Douglas

"Of course not! The FBI doesn't believe in Elvis. Dead is dead. We're saying someone went to a lot of trouble to make believe he wasn't. Dead."

"Then the tape is a fake."

"Yeah. But the voice . . . well, it's pretty real, Matt. Sorry. Can't explain it any more than that. We'll be keeping an eye on any other state-of-the-art audios coming out of Vegas. Somebody out there has a very sweet setup. You hear from 'Elvis' again, let us know. Maybe we can track the con artists down. We could use 'em on our team."

Matt made a few lame personal inquiries and finally hung up.

The FBI had just officially refused to comment on his tapes of himself talking to Elvis—*live!* That fact was scarier than talking to Elvis. Live.

His eye fell on an object on the clean gray cube he'd bought for a living room end table. K-Mart? Or Wards?

It lay there, bright and shiny silver, like an elongated sterling silver baby rattle.

Mariah might have recognized it when she picked it up at the base of the escalator, where it had fallen. But she was too dazzled by the alien artifacts of TitaniCon to notice something exotic but familiar from her own world.

And Temple, the self-described fallen-away Unitarian Universalist? She hadn't a prayer of recognizing this artifact from rites she'd never observed.

He picked it up, remembering occasions he'd had to use it. *Asperge me. Wash me, O Lord.* Wash away sin; wash away uncertainty. *Bless me.*

It lay heavy on his palm, yet familiar. An aspergillum. A container for Holy Water. He had used it at interments, sprinkling the Holy Water over the casket before it sank forever from sight.

It was an instrument of peace, not war.

Yet it had been thrust, hard, into his undefended back on a crowded escalator.

And thrown underfoot when the dirty work was done.

It was a sacred object. He hated to think of it in profane hands. He hated to think what profane hands might have pressed its warning hard into his back.

He put the aspergillum down, softly, on the gentler surface of the red suede sofa that Temple had insisted he buy at the Good Will. It looked rich as some Tiffany christening present against the crimson background.

Matt came out of WCOO at one-twenty that night. No fans were waiting for him, an exception to the rule.

The Elvismobile was waiting, though, a smooth silver cartoon car of a Millennium Volkswagen Bug sitting in a puddle of street-light like a grinning glob of mercury in a spotlight.

The car's optimistic, almost animated lines always made him smile, despite its purported origin from Elvis. Matt wasn't surprised religions were springing up around Elvis. People always needed to believe, and Elvis had a shamanistic way of encouraging faith even as so few around him had managed to have faith in his talent.

He was about to unlock the door when he glanced up and saw a familiar figure in a distant streetlight. Helmeted, jumpsuited, standing next to a motorcycle leaning into its kickstand.

No one was around.

Matt remembered the haunting motorcyclist who had pursued him during his Elvis-interview days, the traffic cop who had sentenced him to speed.

He moved toward the enigmatic silhouette, observing the bell-bottom pants, the pinched waist, the androgynous shape.

About twenty feet away, he knew.

Mariah had been right. Out of the mouth of babes. Or babes-in-training.

"You wanted something?" he asked. Loudly.

He needn't have worried. The empty night carried his voice like a microphone.

408 • Carole Nelson Douglas

"Hmmm," the figure said. "I don't like that car."

"I don't think you would. A car is an island of safety. Lockable."

"Do you believe in Elvis?"

"More than I believe in you."

"Believe in me."

He said nothing.

The figure separated from the tilting motorcyle. A Harley, he thought. Powerful. Not elegant like the Hesketh Vampire.

It came closer. "You got my message."

He nodded. "You picked out the earring."

She paused in advancing on him.

"You pushed Sheila, twice."

"Sheila? Is that her name? How . . . too appropriate."

"You pushed people into danger at the martial arts demonstration."

" 'People'? Not 'people.' Those close to you."

"Not that close."

"Not that much danger."

"You pushed me in the back with the aspergillum."

She laughed then, Kitty O'Connor, and stepped into the full light of the sodium iodide pouring down in shades of merthiolate rose-orange from above like a pink-grapefruit moon. Like a Dreamsicle he had used to savor in hot summers as a kid, ice cream on a stick.

She looked like a rock star in her black leather motorcycle jumpsuit. Or like Evel Kneivel before a new death-defying stunt.

"What do you want?" he asked.

"You."

"Hard to come by. People are not for sale on the open market."

"No, but souls are."

"Most people don't believe in them nowadays."

"I do."

He wanted to answer, *you and Satan*, but he wouldn't give her the satisfaction.

She was the most dangerous human being he had ever encountered, and that made her a kind of devil in an age that didn't believe in devils. He still did.

She came closer.

He stepped back without meaning to.

"I'm unarmed," she said.

"Fool me once."

"That was fun! You were so surprised. It's hard to find people who surprise anymore."

"Yes." He recalled the soundless slice of a razor blade on his skin. He had been surprised. "But once you surprise someone, it's over."

"Don't worry. I won't hurt you." Her voice was laced with irony.

"What do you want?"

"Nothing much."

He couldn't see her face behind the dark Plexiglas mask of the helmet. "But something."

"Your soul."

"A fairly intangible item."

"But it exists. We know that, don't we? You and I. We have that in common."

"Probably more."

"No. Don't presume. Nobody has anything significant in common with me."

He nodded, carefully. Like all narcissists she saw herself as unique.

She came closer, the leather squeaking, perhaps squeaking the protests of the creatures whose hides had been sacrificed to attire the shaman, the media figure of loathing and death.

He couldn't help moving, ready to defend.

"Don't worry! I don't want your sorry hide. We both know souls don't reside there."

"What do you want?"

"Your soul, priest."

"And where does it reside?"

"In your pride."

He did a rapid examination of conscience, a scan of what a distorted mind, heart, and soul like this would regard as pride. In anything he had done, anything he had said to her, in front of her, anywhere she might have eavesdropped.

He came back to their first—no, second—confrontation. In the alley behind ConTact. At night, like this. The sudden stabbing from the dark. The wound like the spear in the Savior's side. Mocking, blasphemous, bitter.

He carried the scar still, but not like stigmata. Like warning.

He remembered her anger against religion, against his religion. He remembered how he had stood up for the right—not like Peter, denying thrice before the cock crew—no, he had crowed like the cock, said he had been a good and faithful priest, which he had been and for which . . . prideful . . . assertion of truth, she had cut him.

And for which honest confession he had given her a weapon now.

"You want—?"

He could hear, rather than see, her smile. "It's not your poverty and obedience, is it?"

He took a deep breath. "You can't do this."

"Can't I?"

"—force me."

"Can't I?"

"I won't."

"You want to see them hurt?"

"Who?"

"*Who-ev-er.* No one you know is safe. Haven't you noticed?"

"Why?"

"Did God tell Job?"

"You are not . . . that."

"No. But I know how to extract my obedience."

"Why are you revealing yourself now?"

"Revealing myself. I like that. It sounds like the deity. Am I your burning bush? Forgive the play on words. Elvis knew that evil is an anagram. Live. I am only offering you the chance to live. Live! Live that others may live, not die. It's not so high a price to pay, is it?"

"You're crazy." He knew better than to say it, but he heard himself saying it anyway. "Why should I believe you. Even if I—"

"You wouldn't know. That's true. But you wouldn't know what would have happened had you not."

"I am not without allies."

"They are not invulnerable. Besides, should you go running for help, I might take it badly. This is between you and me. I'm not so ugly, am I?"

She had come closer than he had resolved to let her. Within two feet.

"Not . . . visibly."

"But you hate me! You loathe me!" She sounded exultant. "True temptation. Only I tempt you against everything you believe in. It will be interesting to see which way you'll go."

"I won't go."

"We'll see." She backed away, like a mocking vision retreating.

She had given him no deadline, demanded no specifics. They could have been discussing an exchange of money.

But he understood. She wanted nothing less than a soul, which was so very hard to come by nowadays. He supposed he should be flattered that she thought he had one to lose.

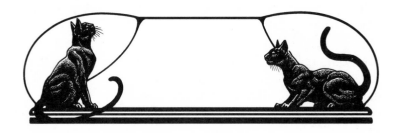

Tailpiece:

Midnight Louie Muses on Past and Future

It is with a sad heart that I bid adieu to the feisty little kiwi bird and all the exotic inhabitants of TitaniCon, especially that Siamese supervixen Hyacinth.

I will not really bid adieu to the Sinister Hyacinth as I am certain that our paths, and shivs, will cross again.

But I do happily bid adieu to the interloper in my kingdom, Miss Mariah Molina, who is a persipacious and eager child but not a welcome addition to my domicile.

As for who has been sleeping in my bed, I fear I know the answer to that mystery all too well. I can only hope that my feline loyalty and consistency will win the night as well as the day.

Naturally, I do not get credit for my role in unmasking the Khatlord killer (even though the victim was not a real Khatlord). I suppose he got what he always wanted: to be mistaken for the real made-up thing, a fictional Khatlord. That he had to die in the attempt is a sad commentary on how deeply some people ache to escape reality.

I do not understand the human propensity to hide behind false personas, whether they be an emotional false front or a physical one. (Although I must admit it was a hoot to witness Lieutenant C. R. Molina in the unlikely guise of a warrior princess. I would assume the "princess" part of that would really stick in her craw, had she been anatomically blessed with such a convenience.)

My Miss Temple certainly did blend into the crowd as a blond. And as for the Mystifying Max, he has been exceptionally true to form of late. I sniffed a lot of Khatlord boots before I found a recognizable scent. I must say his excursion to the Andromeda Amphitheater was most intriguing, even though it did take place in daylight. The stage itself was shrouded, as were many of the players in this episode, some of whom have not been unveiled yet.

Nor was I privileged this round to glimpse the Sinister Hyacinth's erstwhile mistress, Shangri-la, the magician.

Somehow I do not think she was absent from the preceding proceedings.

Call me Karma. But just this once.

Very best fishes,

Midnight Louie, Esq.

For information about Midnight Louie's newsletter and/or T-shirt contact him at *Midnight Louie's Scratching Post–Intelligencer*, PO Box 331555, Fort Worth, TX 76163, by e-mail at *cdouglas@catwriter.com.* or visit the Web page <*http: //www.catwriter.com/cdouglas*>.

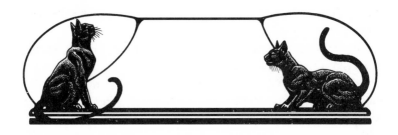

Carole Nelson Douglas
Muses on Masks

Actor William Shatner is famous for more than creating the pro-totypical space-captain role of the past thirty-five years, James T. Kirk of the starship *Enterprise*.

He is also credited with coining a contemporary catch phrase: "Get a life."

Reportedly, he was on a talk show when he yelled this now-common phrase at a devoted fan in the audience.

Certainly Shatner and all the *Star Trek* crew have seen fan fever running at its highest temperature. And certainly he has enjoyed what most actors hope for—playing a role that unexpectedly roots itself in the cultural continuum and supports him for the rest of his life. He has also faced what actors find hardest of all—relin-quishing a signature role in the face of age. First, Clayton Moore, the fifties's Lone Ranger, was legally forced to doff his mask and give up personal appearances. Then the *Star Trek* franchise wrote finis to Captain Kirk so it could continue the saga with other lead actors.

Life goes on, though, alien or not, even and perhaps especially on screen. Shatner has evolved other roles since starring in *Star Trek* on sixties television and in a series of feature films that bridged the seventies and eighties, including that of ghost-written celebrity author.

Still, it must have been a bitter assignment to participate in James T. Kirk's on-screen demise so that an imported Englishman and a set of younger actors could continue *Star Trek* into the next generation.

And that leads to the question of whether it is better to have no fantasy life at all, than one that is too all-consuming.

Realists have no patience with fans who dress in past or future costumes to honor favorite books, movies, and television shows. That doesn't stop countless annual weekend conventions in the science fiction/fantasy field, and occasional ones in the romance and mystery-novel world that allow fans to don special-occasion personas and even win awards for the elaboration of their recreated costumes and personas.

Sometimes the fan personas go from merely dressing a part to playing one, which is where role-playing games come in. And sometimes, especially with impressionable teenagers, the games become too serious, the fantasy never quite recedes, and then you can have suicide or even homicide.

Or would the extremes have happened anyway, without the costumes and props?

I once wrote a newspaper editorial, after a couple of Dungeons and Dragons enthusiasts had gotten into serious trouble, suggesting that role-playing games might be too dangerous to developing personalities. The editorial director of another paper wrote a fierce rebuttal, but I had just been playing devil's advocate.

I believe that exercising our imaginations is a peculiarly human privilege and responsibility, that costume and ritual are inborn manifestations of human creativity and spiritual longing, and that it is as harmless for as much of the time as other human pursuits are, such as the hunt for life, liberty, and happiness. Fantasy and empathy is where artists, dancers, actors, musicians, writers, magicians, and shamans come from.

No doubt a few personalities hide so long behind the admired persona that they can't step out from behind the mask. But most of us do, with many of us the better for it.